The New Frontiers Series, Book One:

The Ship

by Jack L Knapp

The Wizards Series

Combat Wizard

Wizard at Work

Talent

The Wizards Series Boxed Set (Combat Wizard, Wizard at Work, and Talent)

Veil of Time

Siberian Wizard

Magic

Angel (A Wizards Short Story)

The Darwin's World Series

Darwin's World

The Trek

Home

Boxed Set, the Darwin's World Series (Darwin's World, The Trek, and Home)

The Return

Defending Eden

The New Frontiers Series

The Ship

NFI: New Frontiers, Inc

NEO: Near Earth Objects

The New Frontiers Series Boxed Set (The Ship, NFI, and NEO)

BEMs: Bug Eyed Monsters

MARS: The Martian Autonomous Republic of Sol

Pirates

Western

The Territory

Short Novel

Hands

Want a free book? Drop a note listing typos or similar errors to jlknapp505@msn.com. Identify the error by copy-pasting the sentence it occurs in and suggest an improvement. I'll be happy to gift you a free ebook, your choice of any I've published. I'll also notify you of new releases.

COPYRIGHT

The New Frontier Series, Book One: The Ship

Cover by Mia Darien

ISBN: 9781720012108

Table of Contents

Prologue

"Good morning, Mr. Jindae."

Panit Jindae glanced approvingly at his secretary. Always efficient, always cheerful, always well turned out, she was an asset to any company.

"And good morning to you, Mrs. Stendall. Any phone calls or faxes from our friend this morning?"

"He's certainly no friend, Mr. Jindae! A right pain he is; I've tried to get rid of him, but he doesn't want to take no for an answer. Maybe he finally got the message, no faxes, no phone calls this morning. So far." Mrs. Stendall was English, and from time to time her speech reflected that.

"We can hope, Mrs. Stendall. Did the division reports arrive yet?"

"No, sir. I'll check with communications right after I get your coffee. If they've arrived, I'll bring them in. The Jamaican this morning?"

"Why don't we try the Kenya AA for a change?" Panit sounded hopeful; the Kenyan coffee was his favorite.

"I'm sorry sir, the shipment hasn't arrived yet. We have the Kona and a new shipment from Costa Rica, if you'd prefer that to the Jamaican."

"The Costa Rican, then. Newspapers?"

"On your desk, sir. I'll have the coffee ready shortly."

Panit nodded and entered his office. Hanging up his hat and coat, he sat down at his desk to begin his day.

He scanned through the headlines, then went to the business section. He read several of the articles, concentrating, occasionally making notes on a legal pad. The notes would be filed with others about recent developments in the transportation industry.

Not all had to do with auto manufacturing. Panit knew that occasionally things that appeared unrelated would impact the company's divisions. Attention to such details had brought him from engineering to sales, and from there to his current job.

Half an hour later, savoring his coffee while reading through the newspaper's financial section, he became aware of an annoying buzz.

Ridiculous! Considering how much the company paid to lease his fourteenth-floor office, surely *someone* could keep the climate system functioning? Pressing the intercom, he asked Mrs. Stendall to notify maintenance, then tried to concentrate on the article. The comments regarding recent automotive design and its effect on marketing were unfortunate, but perhaps the upturn in the economy might revive sagging sales?

The buzzing was louder. Intolerable!

"Mrs. Stendall, did maintenance ever respond?"

"Sir, they say it's not the air conditioner. It's coming from outside."

"We're fourteen floors above the street! We shouldn't be hearing this! Are they using *jackhammers* down there?" Fuming, Panit walked to the window. The lake view always calmed him, allowed him to concentrate on managing the different manufacturing sections. But the view this morning was different.

A clumsy-looking thing floated outside his window. He looked at it wide-eyed, and the graybearded fellow sitting in the device's middle actually *waved* at him! The nerve...

"Mrs. Stendall!"

Chapter One

Chuck Sneyd had never understood just how precarious his existence was.

Not wealthy, not poor; compared with other residents of Lubbock, the family was unremarkably middle class. The furnished apartment was small, but not excessively so, and both parents lived at home. His mother Pam worked in an office; his father Sylvester was a mechanic for a large ranch north of the city, where he took care of the farm machinery and helped out during haying season.

And then, one Sunday afternoon during his senior year of high school, a drunk going the wrong way on Interstate 27 drove head-on into his mother's Toyota. Silvester had been driving, Pam was in the passenger seat. The bodies had been identifiable, barely, from driver's license photos.

His family had not been 'loving' in the traditional sense. Chuck was not close to either parent. Even so, losing them was a shock.

It was the first of many.

The court-appointed probate attorney handled the details. There was insurance, enough to pay off their credit cards and almost enough to cover the loan on his father's three-year-old Chevrolet 1500. The credit union had accepted the attorney's settlement offer, rather than repossess the truck.

The apartment manager had pointed out that the rent had not yet been paid, so Chuck agreed to vacate as soon as he could dispose of the family's few possessions. Their clothes he donated to charity, a few personal things he simply dumped.

***

Chuck faced an uncertain future. He was essentially without family. There was an aunt and uncle, supposedly; his father had mentioned the names, but no more than that. Chuck had no idea where they could be found or even if they were still alive. His maternal grandparents had divorced. His grandmother had remarried, but had not kept in touch with Pam. His maternal grandfather had died soon after of pancreatic cancer.

He considered going to live with his paternal grandfather, but rejected the idea almost immediately. The old ranch where Chuck had spent his summers was a happy place no longer. His grandmother Mary Ellen had died late during the previous summer.

Her death had shaken Chuck, but Grandfather Morty had been devastated. His depression was such that he could barely talk to Chuck.

An uncertain future indeed; he would have to leave school and find a job. But then, just when things looked bleakest, a friend's parents offered to take him in for the final three months of school.

Chuck graduated with the rest of his class, but the experience taught him a lesson. He would pay his own way, or do without.

He had expected to attend college. If attendance at a university didn't work out, he could always live at home while he took vocational courses at the community college. But even that was no longer possible.

Maybe college was in his future, maybe not; in the meantime, he needed a job. Chuck didn't anticipate a problem finding work. This was West Texas, after all, and while work in the oil patch was hard, it paid well.

But there *was* no work. Drill rigs were being idled, experienced hands laid off; no one was hiring. One of the periodic downturns in the oil business had, for all practical purposes, shut down the oil exploration business.

Disappointed and depressed, Chuck walked along the sidewalk after the latest job interview, which had resulted in another refusal. By chance, he passed an Armed Forces recruiting station.

He looked at the men inside, all uniformed, all purposeful. Not for *them* the challenge of finding a job fresh out of high school! They *had* jobs, work that would keep them employed for years to come.

Chuck walked inside, hesitant, but curious. Perhaps they had written material he could look at before he decided?

The first man he saw when he went inside was a marine, a Staff Sergeant. He explained that yes, they did have handouts, but since his job was explaining what was in the pamphlets, why not have a doughnut and a cup of coffee?

And listen as he explained what the Marines were *really* all about.

***

Boot Camp had not been the challenge the recruiter promised.

True, a lot of boys who had grown up in cities had trouble adapting to the physical requirements and the strict discipline. Chuck had been cleaning up after himself most of his young life and he'd been hiking from the time he was old enough to follow Grandfather Morty around the old ranch.

Morty *explained* things, which kept Chuck interested despite the effort of keeping up with him, and as he grew old enough to explore on his own, only one portion of the ranch was off limits.

A huge sinkhole existed near the western fence line, and the walls were steep. Morty forbade Chuck to approach it, although the two sometimes watched the bats fly at dusk.

"See those crystals, Son? Notice how they have straight sides and a parallelogram shape?"

"Grandpa, what's a parallelogram?"

"You'll learn in a year or two, son. Those are calcite crystals, and they make the sinkhole's rim too slippery to approach unless you have something to hold on to. I thought about bringing a rope and going down inside to have a look, but never found the time."

"Maybe I could use a rope too, Grandpa?"

"No, Chuck. It's dangerous, and curiosity kills more than cats."

Chuck had often carried a light pack on his later hikes, and occasionally a rifle as well. Morty loved to hunt, and he'd enjoyed introducing his grandson to the practice. The low, rolling hills held deer and antelope, more than might be expected considering how dry they were. The challenge of outwitting one of the big bucks was part of it, but the meat was also welcome because money was always tight.

Chuck had quickly learned to shoot, including the advanced art of accurate snap shooting. Release the safety as he brought the pump-action Remington to his shoulder, find the front sight, align it with the rear notch, and gently squeeze the trigger. The recoil was light, easy for a teenager to handle, and the 6mm cartridge was lethal for the mid-sized game they hunted.

***

Marines were expected to carry much heavier packs, and for that matter the recruits would shoot the Marine Corps way. Even so, Chuck had no problem adapting. The dry, rolling hills along the Pacific were not that different from the hills near the Texas-New Mexico border.

He graduated from boot camp with a PFC stripe on his arm, thanks to his shooting ability, then headed off to Camp Pendleton's School of Infantry.

Joining the Combat Training Battalion was his first clue that the Marines had something different in mind for him. But first, he had to get through an abbreviated version of Marine infantry training. Only then would he be sent to the school that the Corps, in its wisdom, had decided he was suited to attend.

The Marine Corps boasts that every marine is a rifleman, and by the time they finish the School of Infantry, they are. The training for those who would be *professional* infantrymen was more intense, but at the conclusion of the course, whether cooks or bakers or communicators, they could be grabbed if needed and sent to fill in gaps as infantry marines. It was expected that they would function almost as well as professional infantrymen, should their services as riflemen be needed.

After graduation, Marine PFC Charles Sneyd reported to the Communication-Electronics School at Twenty-Nine Palms Marine Corps Base to undergo training as a radioman. But even in the Marines, there are often unintended consequences. Chuck was exposed to computer programming as a part of his training, and took to it like the proverbial duck to water.

He acquired a laptop computer from a fellow marine who intended to trash it. The battery would no longer hold a charge and anyway, he intended to upgrade as soon as he had the money. Video games require lots of memory and fast processors.

Chuck had spent considerable time in Grandfather Morty's workshop during the summers on the ranch, so replacing the laptop's battery was simple. No question, the machine was slow, compared to current models, but maybe something could be done about that? The Exchange had books, so did the camp library. And parts could be ordered online, couldn't they?

Chapter Two

Morton Sneyd, by most accounts, was a failure. His neighbors and acquaintances often wondered why his wife remained with him.

It had not always been that way.

Thanks to a ROTC scholarship and part-time work assigned by the university, Morty graduated from Texas A&M with an MS in Mechanical Engineering. The part-time work helped Morty support himself while in school. He had enough math credits for a minor, and briefly considered majoring in that subject; but employment opportunities for mathematicians were limited, while mechanical engineers could pick and choose from a list of several companies they wanted to work for.

But that would have to wait; ROTC had paid for his tuition and books, now the Army expected him to live up to his part of the bargain.

If Morty refused the commission, he understood that he'd almost certainly be drafted. He would also have to repay the government for what they'd paid out while he attended Texas A&M University. Not to mention that being an officer was better than being a private. So he'd gone along with his adviser's suggestion and accepted a reserve commission in the US Army, branch Artillery, with concurrent call to active duty.

The Korean 'police action' was finished for all practical purposes. There was no peace, only an armistice, but the North Koreans had lost most of their military assets. Their Chinese and Soviet allies were not enthusiastic about investing more in the failed effort. For the time being, there was no enemy to fight and the Army had more officers than it needed. It was also once again short of funds, a chronic condition between wars; transfers were rare and it didn't make sense to ship junior officers oversees with no immediate need for their services.

Morty soon found himself at Fort Sill, Oklahoma, taking the prescribed entry course for artillery officers. From there, he'd gone to Fort Chaffee, Arkansas, for duty with the Field Artillery Training Center. It was 'duty with troops', a goal for newly-commissioned officers.

Sort of.

Lieutenant Sneyd was soon involved in the minutiae of recruit basic training. Occasionally he would conduct an inspection, always while accompanied by one of the NCOs responsible for actually training the men, and occasionally he would be called on to resolve problems associated with turning civilians into soldiers. But most of his day was occupied with paperwork.

A loner with few friends, he spent most of his off-duty hours studying physics. In this way he became interested in the work of Newton, Einstein, and a relative unknown named Nikola Tesla.

Four years later, he finished his obligatory tour of active duty. Morty was glad to see the last of the Army, and likely the officers who knew him felt much the same about Morty.

Not everyone is suited for military service, and the tour of duty with the Training Center had forever changed his thinking. It left Morty with an abiding distrust, even resentment, of authority.

He tried to restart his interrupted career after leaving the Army. He sent out résumés and soon had job offers.

He worked for a year at Ford, designing parts for brake systems, but did not find the work challenging or interesting. Junior engineers produced technical drawings, while senior engineers decided which of several options would find their way into the final design. Morty's engineering skills had also grown rusty while he was in the Army, which didn't endear him to his supervisors. At the end of a year, he quit Ford.

A pattern was set: Morty drifted from job to job, doing competent work, but never really excelling. Between jobs, he began offering his services as a consultant.

Morty had found his niche.

Consulting was different; no two jobs were alike. He accepted the jobs he found interesting, and the companies he worked for had no grounds for complaint. The contract work wasn't steady, but it paid enough to support him and the new wife he married shortly after leaving his last full-time job.

Morty's work paid well, but there were often months between contracts. Fortunately, Mary Ellen's job as a clerical assistant in an accounting department brought in a regular paycheck. Morty would never be a wealthy man, never become a pillar of the community, but he was a good father to their children and a devoted husband to Mary Ellen.

One of his consulting jobs had paid well enough to indulge Mary Ellen in a lifelong interest in riding. Morty bought a small ranch, rundown at the time, but with grazing and water enough for the horses she loved. Between jobs, Morty helped Mary Ellen care for her small herd of horses and worked on upgrading the ranch.

And always, he tinkered. Occasionally he patented a device, which added to their income.

The small family was happy during the 1960s as the children, two boys and a girl, grew up. But eventually they left home and moved away, never quite happy in the small west Texas town where Morty and Mary Ellen had settled.

In time there had been a grandson, Charles, called Chuck by most.

His parents were, charitably, not good with children. The relationship was more dutiful than loving.

So it was that Chuck began spending his summers from the age of six at the ranch with his grandparents.

Morty spent time with him, teaching him about nature and showing him around the ranch and the town, while Mary Ellen taught him to ride.

The pattern was established. He lived with his parents while school was in session, then left for the ranch as soon as school ended. His parents never seemed to mind and Morty and Mary Ellen loved having him.

Chuck finished his junior year and headed for the ranch, not understanding that his grandparents, usually so content, faced a crisis. Mary Ellen had just been diagnosed with brain cancer.

She'd gone to the optometrist to complain that her new glasses weren't working well. The optometrist, puzzled by the failure, had examined her eyes again and spotted something. He referred her to a specialist, who had given them the bad news.

The neurosurgeon had been straightforward with them.

"There's not a whole lot we can do. The tumor is deep inside the brain, where we can't get at it. None of the drugs we use for chemotherapy can cross the blood-brain barrier, so they can't get at the tumor either. I'm sorry."

"Doctor, how long?" Morty asked, voice hoarse with strain.

"I'm sorry. The best I can do is give you a guess. Not long."

"How long, doctor?" Morty pressed.

"Perhaps six months. One day, there will be other therapies, but for now? There's really nothing we can do except provide palliative care. Again, I'm sorry."

"What about one of the cancer centers? Maybe there's some sort of experimental procedure?"

"Morty, you don't have insurance," the doctor said gently. "M.D. Anderson is probably the best cancer hospital in Texas, but it's my understanding that they don't even accept Medicare. So far as I know, they're not working on this type of cancer anyway."

"Thank you for being honest, doctor."

Morty took Mary Ellen home and cared for her as best he could. Chuck arrived soon after, but was largely left to his own devices.

A month later the cancer took Mary Ellen's sight, and three months later it took her life.

Morty, crushed, immersed himself in his work, seeking the only solace he'd ever known. Neither he nor Chuck knew how to deal with the tragedy. Chuck soon left the ranch, heading back to school; Morty barely noticed.

Chuck tried to understand; perhaps Grandmother Mary Ellen had provided the framework for their relationship? But whatever the cause, things had changed between the two of them.

***

It was during this period, when his grief was still raw, that Morty started reading the old notebooks Mary Ellen had given him. And discovered the notebooks, journals really, had been written by Nikola Tesla.

The notes fascinated Morty, and immersed in the old notebooks, he slowly recovered from losing his beloved wife. While reading, he discovered a passing reference to an unusual result Tesla had documented, but never pursued. Morty thought about it, then realized it might lead to something at least as revolutionary as Tesla's other discoveries.

There was no one to share his thoughts with, but also no distractions. Mary Ellen was gone now, Chuck was back in school and would be looking for a job after he graduated.

Left to himself, Morty spent long days working, trying different approaches to the puzzle. His first efforts didn't produce much in the way of results, but from time to time there was promise. When he needed money for a new precision tool or measuring device, he accepted one of several offers to consult, usually away from the ranch and west Texas.

In the evenings he thought, and like Tesla before him, filled notebooks with drawings and notes in the margins. As soon as the jobs were finished, he rushed back to the ranch, anxious to try out the new ideas he'd come up with.

Frequently, in the evening when he was too tired to work but not yet exhausted enough to sleep, Morty would walk up the hill behind his house and visit Mary Ellen's grave. From there, he could look out across the ranch she'd loved and explain his thoughts.

A lonely, obsessed old man, visiting his wife's grave of an evening? Some might have thought it strange, or a little pathetic.

Morty didn't. It gave his life balance.

Chapter Three

Chuck limped down the stairs and headed for the parking lot. Graduation exercises were scheduled to take place in two weeks and he had not decided whether he'd attend or not. For the moment, he was thinking 'not'.

He had no doubt that he'd find a job in a short time. His MS in Business Administration, coupled with a BS in Computer Science, meant that instead of taking the first offer of a job, he could wait for a better one. Then, finally, he could put poverty behind him.

The hitch he'd done in the Marines might also confer other advantages; Chuck was not only older, he'd held responsible positions and made decisions that held real meaning, characteristics that a future employer would value.

He had found few friends at UTEP. Compared with the marines he'd known, Chuck's fellow students had no real concept of life outside of school. Video games, drinking, chasing the opposite sex?

Was he supposed to hang out with them because they were fellow students? The idea was meaningless, even repugnant, after Fallujah. He'd been close to the men he served with, closer than brothers. Some were gone now, and the losses still burned.

Chuck had found the idea distasteful. The men were shallow, in reality no more than overaged boys. His fellow vets understood Chuck, but like him, they preferred their own company, their own private demons. He'd dated occasionally, but it made him uncomfortable. He had few conversational skills and as for dancing, that was out too. So he had reverted to his old habit, pre-service, of avoiding the company of others. The cause, lack of interest more than a conscious act of rejection.

Occasionally, he wondered; was he suffering from some mild form of PTSD? He had no way of telling and no interest in contacting an 'expert' who might find the condition, whether or not it really existed.

No one would be there to watch him cross the stage, not even his grandfather.

Chuck had no other close relatives, only an uncle he hadn't seen in years and an aunt he preferred not to see. As for grandfather Morty, he was busy with his latest scheme. He had no time to watch an empty ceremony, but he *had* invited Chuck to come to the ranch after graduation.

Well, why not? They'd been close once, before Grandmother Mary Ellen's death. Morty had seemed cold at the time, but in hindsight Chuck realized he'd not yet come to terms with his wife's loss.

He didn't have a job yet, but the job hunt could wait; the small pension from his disability rating was enough for his few needs, and thanks to his part-time computer work for fellow students and faculty, he had an adequate cash reserve.

Should he go? Chuck had always enjoyed the old ranch; he had but two regrets, the death of his grandmother, and never exploring the cavern where the bats lived. But Morty had been adamant at the time, so Chuck had obeyed him.

Even so, the cavern had fascinated him. He'd often ridden his favorite quarter horse to the hilltop overlooking the entrance and waited for the bats to fly. The mysterious feature and its population of bats, had wakened Chuck's curiosity and given him a lifetime interest in science, even though he'd chosen other fields to work in. Science majors, after all, didn't command the starting salaries offered to MBAs.

Did Morty really *need* him, or was this just another attempt to bring Chuck into one of his many schemes? Granted, some of them had paid off, but always in the past Morty had lost interest and sold his patent to someone who would market it.

Well.

They had been close, Chuck and his grandfather, so maybe the thing to do was spend time with Morty. That closeness, his only real human relationship, might still be there.

And who could say? Maybe *this* time he would finally explore that mysterious cavern.

***

Morty hung up the phone and smiled. He hadn't told Chuck exactly *what* he was doing, but he had mentioned that the new device was working and promised to be a financial success. If, that is, they could work out the bugs. Chuck hadn't commented, but Morty knew he'd gotten the message. Maybe Morty's comment had been enough to convince him to visit the ranch.

"Working" was an exaggeration. Morty had gotten *results*, but they were not consistent and the device was not reliable. In fact, it was prone to self-destruct under stress, which had so far prevented even a full-power trial.

He glared at the collection of motors, generators, and machines. How to *balance* the mess, how to ensure that *this* one wouldn't do what the last one did, fly apart under the gee forces? He'd avoided injury, but controlling the collection was a headache.

How had Tesla intended to do it? Had he even *gotten* to that point, or had he been satisfied to make notes and move on to something else?

From his writings, Tesla had decided to work on his broadcast power system. He might have intended to investigate the impeller later. There was no way to tell. As for Tesla, he had been more than an inventor. He'd also been a gifted machinist, at least for his time.

Modern lathes and milling machines were computer controlled now, although Morty supposed you could still buy the kinds that Tesla had used, machines controlled only by the skilled hands of a human. But Morty's hands were not that skilled, he'd known that from the beginning, so he'd bought computer-controlled machines. Now all he had to do was learn how to tell them what to do!

For the moment he was stymied. Hopefully, Chuck could help when he finally got here. So much promise from the new device...but only if he could solve the engineering problems.

***

The first impeller had been more than promising, showing that he was on the right track. Powering up the machine produced an impressive amount of thrust, but it came at the cost of vibration that shook the device to pieces.

Morty's first solution had been to reduce power, thereby slowing the machine's revolutions. That reduced the shaking, but at the cost of most of the thrust.

Which brought him back to the machines in his workshop. Clearly, he would need more-precise machining if the device was to be usable. There was also the problem of the coils to consider. They were added to the rotors after manufacture, complicating the problem. They would have to be balanced precisely as well as mounted in such a fashion that they would interact with the stationary primary coil. Tesla believed the resulting electromagnetic field was important.

The device also generated considerable torque, so Morty had come up with a simple solution. He gang-mounted an impeller with another that produced opposite torque. The two impellers produced double the thrust of a single-impeller model, but unfortunately, they also produced twice as much vibration.

It was discouraging; it seemed like every time Morty solved one problem, two more cropped up.

None of the paired impeller units had lasted more than five minutes before something failed. Either a circuit shorted, or more commonly a mechanical part had broken.

Had Tesla experienced similar problems? Had he foreseen what would happen, causing him to put this device aside while he worked on his broadcast-power system?

According to the notebook, Tesla had discovered the underlying principle, but after that the idea was never mentioned again. Possibly he had abandoned the effort as unsolvable. There simply were no materials available back then that combined light weight with the strength he needed.

But a century of progress had produced things Tesla could only have dreamed of; cheap, plentiful aluminum for one, high tensile strength corrosion-resistant steels for another. Even titanium was available nowadays. And then there were the carbon nanotubes and carbon-fiber sheets, just becoming available, and never envisioned during Tesla's lifetime.

There were also plastics that rivaled steel in strength but at less than half the weight. Who could say what Tesla's inventive genius might have produced if he'd had access to modern materials?

Morty had access to those things, and more. He'd come up first with a working Tesla turbine, then a Tesla transformer that generated impressive lightning bolts as well as ultra-high voltages and short-wavelength AC frequencies. That was when he decided to build one of Tesla's impellers.

The effort had helped Morty get through his grief after Mary Ellen's death and had then become an obsession.

But failure followed failure, each redesigned device solving one problem even as it revealed another. Maybe, with Chuck's help, that would change. After all, modern fighter aircraft were so unstable as to be essentially unflyable without computer controls. Could a similar control system solve Morty's problems?

Morty cranked the old pickup truck and headed for the town of Andrews. There was a tire company there that used machines to balance tires, so maybe someone could tell him how it worked. Maybe he could get his hands on a used one, cheap, and rebuild it? And convert it to do what he needed?

***

Chuck packed his bags and tossed them into the pickup, then swept and mopped the floor. He made a quick pass through the bathroom before calling the landlord to inspect the property. Chuck would not be there for graduation, and he would not be returning in the fall.

The truck's tank was full and a check of the oil and radiator levels showed nothing that needed correcting. An hour later, Chuck was on the road, a bag of sandwiches on the seat beside him and a case of bottled water on the passenger-side floorboard. He headed east on US 180 toward Carlsbad, New Mexico.

He refueled in Carlsbad, then continued east, soon crossing back into Texas.

The town of Andrews was straight ahead, although he wouldn't be going that far. Some twenty miles short of the town, he turned north and took the farm-to-market road that passed Morty's ranch.

Chapter Four

The device did not impress Chuck.

"Grandpa, *that's* the thing you're so excited about? Rube Goldberg would love it!"

"You're old enough to call me Morty, grandson, and yes, that's it. It doesn't look like much, does it?"

"Nope. Where did you get all that stuff?" Chuck looked at the odd collection of machined parts and pulleys.

"I salvaged a lot of the parts from other machines, the rest I made myself. Eventually, I'll be making all new parts from scratch. I admit it looks crude, but the proof is what happens when I fire it up. Give me a second, and you should also probably stand clear. You should be safe if you're behind me."

Chuck nodded and moved back as Morty flipped switches on a control panel. *Had Morty shrunk, or he grown*? It was much easier to look down at the old man and notice the wispiness of the white hair.

Despite his age, Morty was active, moving around with an agility that would have been remarkable in someone much younger. Chuck realized he was himself hampered as much as Morty, in part because of the wound. But he also understood that part of his mobility issue had to do with the hours he'd spent sitting behind a keyboard.

Maybe, now that he was no longer spending so much time working at the computer, he could work on his own physical ability? Even regain some of what he'd lost?

But now it was time to pay attention. Morty was describing each action, each flip of a switch.

"The important thing is not to bring everything online at once; the machine draws so much current starting up that it will trip the circuit breakers and then you've got to start again from the beginning.

"This switch powers up the front rotors." Morty pointed to the left side of the panel. "You have to let them get up to operating speed before you go any further. You also want to watch for vibration, and as soon as you spot the first sign of it, flip the switch off and let the rotors run completely down to a stop before you restart.

"The second switch brings up the rear ones, and they have to be counter-rotating at the same RPM before I do anything else." He pointed to flickering spots of white that soon stabilized, appearing to be stationary.

"That's what the painted dots are for, to let me synchronize speeds. If I turn on the main motor before that happens, things fly apart," He nodded at the wall. "You can see what happened when those earlier models failed."

Chuck glanced around. The damage wasn't obvious, but now that Morty had mentioned it, he could see dents in the pegboard lining the shop's walls. *Lots* of dents, some of them deep enough to crack the pegboard.

"You're lucky you didn't get hurt, Morty."

"I was careful. I knew as soon as I applied full power that I was getting into new territory. I shut it down the first couple of times without ever giving it a full-power trial, I was that nervous. There's a bunch of stored energy in those rotors alone, not to mention in the electromagnetic fields they generate.

"It's not obvious, but each one is part of a Tesla turbine. The rotors have coils near the edge that spin through electrical couplers, generating extreme voltages and strong fields. The fields are the important part, but keeping in place long enough, not to mention variable enough that I can control the output…"

Morty's voice trailed off as he concentrated for a moment, then resumed. "I've improved the rotors since then. I needed an adjustable dynamic balancer, and that's what those three slots I machined in the outer ring are for. They've got adjustable weights on a threaded shaft, you just turn the knurled knob to change the balance. It's precise, even if it is slow and fiddly. Anyway, it works.

So far."

"Those coils on the edge of the wheels; you called them rotors?"

"Right, the wheels are the rotors, and they have a kind of flywheel effect. As soon as the rotors spin up to full speed, they're essentially gyros as well as flywheels. Otherwise, the coils will cause enough drag to stop them from spinning when they start picking up the charge from the primary. The drag happens as the coils pass through the base coil's field. The base coil is that thick copper spiral underneath. I epoxied it to the base and so far, it's working. It carries a lot of current all by itself and if it fails, there can be a strong magnetic surge. But it only lasts a half-second or so.

"As for the coils, I copied the design from Tesla's notebook. They're a variation on his high-frequency coil, the one Marconi used without permission in his first radios, and he claimed they were essential.

"As the rotor spins, the coils charge from the primary in the base of the machine. That creates a revolving electromagnetic field. According to Tesla, rotating the coils around a central axis--that's what this main shaft is for—then rotates the entire field, causing it to interact with the fabric of space.

"I'm not sure I understand it, but I can't dismiss it either. Tesla was a genius; you know about his broadcast power machine, right?"

"I read about it. He never got it working, right?"

"He ran out of money, so we'll never know if it would have worked or not. His investors balked at how much it was costing. His original concept was *really* expensive, but he scaled it down by half. The one in New York only had one trial.

"He built a different tower in Colorado, smaller than the one in New York, but even so it worked well enough that Tesla thought his theory was confirmed. Anyway, he built the larger tower on Long Island. One difference, he dug a deep basement beneath the tower and put in metal grounding rods. His tower was essentially a huge Tesla Coil that was intended to turn the ionosphere and the Earth itself into electrical poles. A user could hook up an antenna and a ground and that was all he needed to tap into the field. Crystal radio sets work like that, no battery or power cable needed."

"Really? So what happened?"

"Earthquakes was the biggest issue, because residents complained. Plates fell off shelves, things like that. There were also lightning bolts as the coil's secondary built up to full charge and people were scared that they would set their houses on fire. Tesla was the only one that was really disappointed when the investors pulled the plug.

"Anyway, he was onto something, and when he wrote that the impeller could interact with space, I believed him. So I started thinking about it. I also had Einstein's ideas about gravity distorting space-time. Tesla likely never heard of the theories of relativity."

"So how do the coils charge? You said they're part of a transformer?"

"Right, the primary coil is built into the base that the machine is mounted on and the rotating coils are the secondaries. The coils spin up with the rotors at first, not really doing anything, but when I power up the main motor, the central axle revolves and the spinning rotors pass the coils through the primary field." Morty pointed to a heavy steel shaft running the length of each impeller. A pulley connected a powerful electric motor to the shaft by means of a thick rubber belt.

"That's a five-horsepower three-phase motor I salvaged from an industrial lathe. The two pulleys are different sizes, stepping down the speed of revolution; if I try to get the main shaft up to the same speed as the motor, that's when it starts flying apart. The gee forces are just too strong. Stepping down the speed keeps it from breaking."

"So what should I be looking at, Morty? You've got small motors driving rotors with secondary coils, and a big motor that's going to revolve this whole mess. What's with the rails the frame is mounted on? They look like railroad tracks."

"The frame has hooked flanges that hold it to the rails. They keep the frame from turning in the same way that the hooks on a roller coaster holds it on the track. There's a *lot* of counter-torque when I turn on the main motor. I mounted two of the smaller units so the torque canceled, but that one broke. This is the only one that's working now."

"I'll take your word for it. So I stand behind you, you bring up the power, and what's supposed to happen?"

"See that dial behind the frame? That's a strain gauge. I'll watch the machine, and with luck I can shut it down before it flies apart. But watch the gauge and you'll see what I saw."

Morty watched the spinning rotors, judging when they were at the same speed. The white blur stabilized, becoming stationary dots.

Satisfied, Morty flipped the final control, three switches ganged together to apply power to the big motor.

The high-pitched whine from the rotors changed and a new sound was added to the mix, a kind of rattling whirr. Chuck glanced at the strain gauge. The needle quivered, already halfway up the dial. Slowly it moved higher and the machine's frame crept forward on the rails. Chuck realized that if not for the strain gauge attaching the machine to a large steel girder, it would have flown across the shop.

A loud pop announced a tripped circuit breaker. The whining died away and the main motor slowed to a stop. Moments later, only the spinning rotors showed that anything unusual had happened.

"I'm ready for a cup of coffee, Chuck. Come on into the kitchen and we can talk about what you've just seen."

***

"I agree, you can't just dismiss the man, but I never heard about this being in any of Tesla's papers."

"He did a lot more than that, Chuck. Without Tesla's coil, there would have been no radio, and later on he built a radio-controlled model boat. There's no telling *what* he'd have accomplished if he'd had the financing he needed, but he never really had a sense of how to hang onto what he earned. He made money, no question about that, but he spent it or gave it away. The next time he needed something financed, he had to go to friends or businessmen.

"Some of the businesspeople cheated him. There's no other word for it. He got a pittance, people like Westinghouse made millions."

"You didn't say where you got the papers."

"Not exactly papers, it was actually a series of journals that contained notes about his daily work. Your grandmother is the one that bought them, there were in an old trunk she found at a rummage sale. It was locked, no key, so no one really knew what was inside. She paid $5 for it because it was heavy and she was curious.

"Except for Tesla's journals and a letter in his handwriting," Morty continued, "everything else was junk. He owed money to a man in Colorado Springs and he gave him the journals to pay off the debt; that's what the letter was about. He'd done that before, according to what I read, and later on he made a habit of running up bills and giving people some of his devices to settle the debt."

"Interesting. So grandma bought this, and you finally found something that's kept your interest?"

"Yes. At first, I started reading them because Mary Ellen gave them to me. I wanted to show that I was interested in her gift. I almost quit a few times, because Tesla's not the easiest guy to read! But after she died, I just kept going because I didn't have anything else to do.

"I really miss her, Chuck; I just wish I could have told her how I felt while she was alive. But I've never been able to show emotion, and now that it's too late I really regret that. Something for you to remember, Grandson. When you find your own life mate, don't be afraid to let her know how you feel."

"I won't, Grandpa. But I think grandma knew how you felt. She had to, considering how long you were together. You bought her the horses and the ranch, so I'm sure she knew."

"I hope so. But I should have *told* her." Morty's expression, so alert while he was describing what he'd found in the trunk, had turned sad.

Chuck changed the subject. "So what does your machine *do*, Morty? I can't deny that demonstration was interesting, but what would you do with it if you got the vibration and control problems solved?"

"Tesla said that it provide impulse, so I call it an impeller. You apply electricity, you get motion; it's just that simple. You don't need propellers or jets or rockets and you don't need to couple it to wheels. This one's still pretty crude, but even so it's an improvement over my first efforts.

"I'm using AC to drive the motors because that's what Tesla worked with, but DC might work better. Easier to control, I think. You could reverse the polarity of the electricity and cause the impeller to push backwards."

"Where did you get the coils on the rotors? Those aren't off the shelf components, something you can just buy anywhere."

"No, I made them. I've got a small lathe I use just for winding coils. I bought it used from a shop that does custom motor rewinding. I had to do some repairs to get it working, but I managed.

"I've had to do a lot of that, rebuilding, because I didn't have the money for new machines. The lathe was old and the bed was out of true, but after I rebuilt it, it worked fine. That was the last machine I needed so my shop is complete, for the time being anyway. My major expense these days is buying copper wire.

"I intend to make all the impeller parts from scratch when I'm ready for the final version. I'm not there yet, but the next version will use motors that I'll build myself. The rotors will have the moving coils built into the hub, and the stator coils will be part of the fixed shaft.

"I'll use thicker rods for the main shaft too. Heavier parts seem to make everything more stable, maybe because of the flywheel effect. Anyway, I can already do all that, so what I was hoping was that you could come up with electronic control systems to automatically do what I'm doing by hand."

"I can do that," said Chuck thoughtfully. "The hard part is designing and installing the instrument package. You need information, usable values, or the control units can't work. They also have to be in the right location if you expect good results.

"Instead of the DC motors you mentioned, why not use frequency-controlled AC? I'll need to measure the RPM of each rotor, but that's just standard stuff, easy to do. I'll set up feedback loops, based on the rotor speed, and run them through a small processor chip. I'll mount it on the frame, probably near where the pillow blocks are.

"Anyway, the processors will balance the rotor speeds

automatically so you won't have to worry about those. I'll use a central computer to control what the main motor does. A joystick will make it easy to vary the power to the main motor, so that's your speed control. If I add a switch on the joystick panel, I should be able to reverse the input so you can put it in reverse.

"I can also install instruments to detect vibration and automatically vary rotor speed to damp it out before it causes a problem. It'll take some thought, but I doubt I'll have any real problems. I should be able to have a working system by the time you finish your next version of the impeller. How many did you plan on using on whatever you want to build?"

"I hadn't gone that far. I figured to build a cart with maybe two, one on each side. That way, one could run counterclockwise and the other clockwise. That would get rid of the torque problem if the cart was stiff enough not to flex in the middle."

"Suppose you had four impellers, one at each corner, pointing up? Would it lift off the ground?"

"I don't see why not, but it would depend on the weight and how much power you had available. We'd have to be careful that all four impellers put out the same impulse, too. Control might be a problem."

"That's what computers are for, Morty. Why don't we try it?"

"Why would we want to do that, Chuck?"

"Morty, you've been thinking that this impeller might power cars or trucks, right?"

"Well, no. It seems to me that it might work all right for long-haul heavy trucks, but it's not really responsive enough to operate in traffic. Diesel and gasoline automotive systems work fine already, and for that matter there are several hybrid or all-electric vehicles already operating. No advantage, in other words.

"What I had in mind was using an impeller, maybe two, to power a ship. You could totally seal the hull, no openings at all below the waterline. Mount the impellers inside the hull. Advantage, fewer leaks, and also you could get rid of the rudder and the machinery to move it.

"An impeller-powered hydrofoil ship would be a *major*

improvement. Angle the impellers upward at twenty degrees or so and the lift would help the boat get up on the hydrofoils at slower speeds, meaning it could be maneuvered easier. Hydrofoils can't turn as tight as regular ships, but if the impeller system could keep the hull from leaning too far, you could make tight turns even at full speed.

"Anyway, that was my first idea. I thought about railroads too. It might be possible to do away with the locomotive entirely. They're already diesel-electric; the diesel drives a generator, and that powers a huge electric traction motor.

"It would be easy enough to adapt the electric output to drive an impeller, maybe several, so you wouldn't spin the wheels while the locomotive was getting the train up to speed.

"Suppose each railcar had its own impeller, maybe two? The engineer wouldn't deal with that diesel-electric system, he'd just control the power going to the impellers in each car.

"Edison built a system like that early on, powering each car separately, but it never caught on. Using impellers to counter the lean in a turn would also mean that accidents, where someone was going too fast to stay on the tracks, couldn't happen."

"That's not bad. Is this as far as you've gone?"

"Well, yes. But first, I needed to get it working and I don't know much about computers. I was hoping you could help."

"I can, but I can do a lot more than that," said Chuck. "You've got the basic idea, but we might want to think bigger. How about airplanes? Wouldn't your impeller work on those?"

"Well, sure. I don't see why not. You'd need a source of electricity and batteries wouldn't work, they don't have enough power. Generators, such as that diesel-electric system I mentioned, are too heavy to use in an airplane. Maybe we could use fuel cells."

"I doubt that electricity would be a problem. We'll have to think about it, but right offhand, I can't see any reason we couldn't adapt a turboprop engine by using the gearing to drive a generator instead of a propeller.

"We need to talk about the science behind this too. You say Tesla understood it?"

"I don't know. But I now understand a lot more about it than he did, I think."

"Really? You understand what Einstein meant when he came up with general and special relativity?"

"Well, yes and no. I understand some of it, but to be honest I think Einstein was wrong in a couple of ways.

"Anyway, we can talk about that tomorrow. I'm sure you're tired, and I've made up the bed in your old room. I've got some repairs to do before I can run that system again, so I'll work on the impeller while you get some rest."

Chapter Five

Morty found Chuck at the dining table, eating a breakfast of raisin bran.

"Sleep OK, Chuck?"

"I dropped off about 8:30 and didn't wake up until 7:30 this morning. I put on coffee if you want some."

"No, it would just keep me up. I'm going to have breakfast and then sleep for a while."

"You didn't sleep last night?"

"No, I stayed up and worked. I often work through the night. I sleep when I'm tired."

"This ends *now*, Morty. You get some sleep, and when you wake up we'll start getting you on a regular sleep schedule."

"It won't work, Chuck. I lay there and toss and turn, and finally I just get up. I figure I might as well work if I have trouble falling asleep."

"Not good enough, Morty. I just found you again and I don't want to lose you. Do you realize that we're each other's only close relative now, except for my aunt? And you never talk about her."

"I don't think I ever thought of it like that, and there's a reason I don't talk about your aunt. I just don't want to get into it. Nothing anyone can do, anyway."

An estranged relative? Chuck decided to let the issue drop.

"You get some sleep. I'm going to look around the property, and when you wake up, we'll have dinner and you can tell me how the impeller works. Or, at least, how you think it works."

Morty nodded and fixed himself a bowl of cereal. Chuck drank another cup of coffee and watched his grandfather.

Morty finished his cereal and went to bed. As soon as the old man started snoring, Chuck eased out of the house and headed for the workshop. He had a lot of thinking and planning to do, instruments he'd need, processors for each rotor axle to control RPM, a control system run by a computer, some sort of input device to tell the computer what to do. As soon as he got that working, he could decide what other software he'd need; the more he thought about it, getting the system under control was going to take a considerable amount of time and it was going to cost money.

Where was it to come from?

***

Chuck was at the dining table, working at his laptop, when Morty woke up. A loose-leaf notebook lay on the table by the computer and a mechanical pencil lay on the notebook.

"Afternoon, Chuck. I reckon I needed the sleep; any coffee left?"

"No, but I'll make a new pot. I could use another cup too. I've been running some estimates of what we'll need to automate the impellers. I'm thinking of using a simple processor with just enough RAM to run a control program for the rotors. I think I can use a Raspberry Pi processor and mount the RPM sensors onto the same plywood base where you're putting the transformer primary. I can probably use my laptop to control the main motor for now, the one that spins the primary axle, at least for this first test bed.

"I'll come up with an input system for steering as well as figuring out a way to control the output power. If we can dial the thrust up or down, that'll allow us to steer by using the impellers the same way boat captains do with twin propellers. We can start out with a steering wheel for surface craft, but later on we'll have to come up with something better.

"I'm going to be writing a lot of code over the next few days, but I'll take time to have meals with you, so plan on it. No more eating on the fly and sleeping when you fall down."

"OK, grandson. Reckon it won't be so bad, long as I've got somebody to talk to."

Chuck busied himself at the coffeepot and poured Morty a strong cup as soon as enough water had run through the grounds.

"You were going to tell me how the impellers work."

"Chuck, the important thing is that they *do* work, the strain gauge shows that. As soon as we get one we can run at full speed, we can calculate how efficient it is. I can do that by comparing the current draw with how much thrust output we get.

"That's a starting point. As soon as we've got two usable impellers, we can have some fun. I've got a stack of 3/4 inch plywood sheets we can use to mount things on and I was thinking of a boondock buggy. Bicycle wheels for the running gear, two in the back that just roll, plus one in the front that's steerable. How long has it been since you went chasing jackrabbits?"

"You're serious?"

"Sure, why not? Lots of room out back, plenty of jackrabbits too. Plus it will give us a way to test the system before anybody else sees it. Gotta have a working prototype if we're going to make people pay attention."

"You said you intend to make all the components yourself this time?"

"Well, most of them. No need to make that main drive motor; it's cheaper to just buy one."

"How much money do you have, Morty?"

"Not all that much. Maybe seven or eight thousand dollars in the bank is all, but I finished a couple of consulting jobs that I haven't been paid for. I figure they'll pay me when they get around to it."

"I'll need to look into that, then. Tell you what, machining the rotors and their dynamic balance adjustments, plus winding the coils, that's your job. We'll need four sets of those, and if you're going to make the coils for the motors to spin the rotors, wind those too. What I want is two complete impellers that are as nearly matched physically and electrically as possible. When you start shopping, buy matching main power motors too, and they should be single-phase. We'll be using batteries at first, and a two-phase inverter is likely to be larger than we need and probably a lot more expensive.

"I'll see about building a battery supply and hooking up an

inverter to generate single-phase AC. I'll also be designing the sensors and the automatic controls to keep everything balanced. I'll match those up with your rotors as soon as you get them built.

"Meantime, I'll also be contacting the people that owe you money. I'll shake loose as much as I can; letting them decide when to pay you is no way to run a business. I'll need to know what bank you're using and your account number."

"I'll get you a deposit slip, Chuck."

"You plan on putting in no more than eight hours a day, Morty, and if you feel tired at any point you take a break. But eight hours is your limit, okay?"

"If you say so, Chuck."

"Evenings are for you and me, grandpa. You're going to explain how that impeller works and I've got a few ideas I intend to bounce off you to see what you think."

***

Chuck spent most of his working time during the next two weeks contacting the firms that owed Morty money. Occasionally, he found it necessary to offer a small discount for immediate payment; most had paid up as soon as he telephoned.

Morty's bank account doubled, then doubled again.

Chuck finished working his way through the list, then printed out a balance sheet. Morty looked astonished at the numbers, then smiled. "I should have hired you a long time ago, grandson!"

Three weeks later, the first components that Chuck had ordered began arriving. As soon as Morty finished an impeller, Chuck installed and tested the control. The two then mounted the completed device on what both now called the Boondocker.

They finished the job late one afternoon, then wearily headed for the house.

Chuck had put ingredients into a crock pot before starting work that morning. The two silently enjoyed bowls of green chile stew, then Chuck washed up while Morty went out to the patio and found a chair.

The two were soon enjoying the cool West Texas evening.

Chuck had slipped a dollop of brandy into Morty's tea, hoping it might help him sleep.

"You know, I never liked walking in other people's footsteps, Chuck. That's why I went into consulting. If somebody in a big shop comes up with an idea, most of the other people working there won't disagree. Even if they think it's dumb, they don't want to be noticed so they don't say anything.

"That's not for me. I like to examine an idea from all sides, look at it and see how well the parts fit together.

"I did the same thing with physics. I don't think anyone yet has matched Newton, and for that matter I don't think Maxwell gets the respect he deserves. It's all Einstein nowadays."

"Einstein's reputation is well deserved, Morty. You can't ignore that he predicted gravity's effect on light waves, or for that matter his insight into the relationship between heat and particle motion. As for gravity waves, well, I suspect that sooner or later someone will detect those too."

"No question about what he did, Chuck, especially that part about heat. But I think he evaded the question when he claimed that gravity distorts space-time around a large mass. He did the same thing Newton did, he talked about *what,* but didn't explain *how* it happened. He just said it did.

"Anyway, I began looking at Einstein's ideas, and some of them didn't quite ring true to me. It's like that part about the dual nature of light, that it's a particle and a wave at the same time? It just didn't make sense to me."

"I knew about that, Morty. But Einstein didn't have anything to do with that model, and I don't see..."

"It's like the people who came up with that idea never looked at Einstein's equation, the one about mass-energy conversion. Did you ever try to work that one out?"

"I can't say I did. It came up in physics and the professor was damned near in ecstasy about it, but no one ever bothered to explain it. It was all about how beautiful it was, but I never could see that. It's just an equation."

"Well, I worked my way through it and it's not all that difficult.

In one sense, I think Einstein cut a couple of corners. Think about C-squared, for example. You've had basic math courses, and all you need is algebra to work that one out. You remember your algebra classes, don't you?"

"I think so, Morty."

"One of the basic concepts is that if you square something, you square *everything* that's part of the concept. For example, if you square two meters, you get four *square* meters, not just four meters. That's important; it's not just the numbers that get squared, it's everything, including units. It's also worth noticing that whenever you do that, you change dimensions, in the case of meters from linear to area. You're changing from simple concepts to complex ones, from first order units to second order ones."

"Okay, I can see that. But you're referring to squaring the speed of light, aren't you?"

"That's it. If you square the number, you must also square the units. Those are distance and time, usually kilometers and seconds. I can grasp what a square meter looks like, but what about a square second? Any idea of what that is?"

"Uh, I don't know. But it's just a way of including both terms, isn't it, going from first order to that second order you mentioned?"

"It is, in one sense. Mathematically, such an operation is perfectly allowable according to our rules. But if you consider that as a *dimension*, the square of the speed of light, it doesn't exist. Other than mathematically, of course.

"So Einstein included an imaginary unit in his formula, a dimension we don't have a definition for. But if you think of the formula itself as a single entity, not as separate units to be solved, then conceptually it works. Everything in that formula other than numbers, units of energy, mass, and time, just cancels themselves out.

"Anyway, if you expand all those terms to their defined values and work the formula, you'll find that all the units go away, leaving only a pure number. That's the conversion factor for mass to energy and vice versa.

"And that's what I think is wrong with the idea that light is a wave, which is to say energy, and simultaneously it's also matter. The conversion factor works out to something like 900 to 1 or maybe it's a multiple of that. I don't remember exactly, it's been a long time since I worked through the formula, but take it from me, it's a big number. So given that, how can light be both energy and matter? Electrons have some of that same duality also."

"So do you have an answer to this?"

"Nope. I'm perfectly content to say I don't know. But to say it has a 'dual nature', when the parts of that duality are not equal and more than that, unequal by perhaps 900,000 to one, it just doesn't seem to fit. It's a puzzle, and I don't know that we can resolve it with our current state of knowledge.

"Anyway, back to Einstein and something I think I do have a better idea about."

"What's that, grandpa?"

"Back to grandpa, are we?"

"It seemed right, somehow. It's like when we used to talk about things during the summer when I visited."

"Okay, if it makes you feel better. Anyway, I thought about Einstein's concept of distorting or warping space-time around a mass. I wondered about that. If you extend Einstein's argument, then space-time, or at least space, has to have a structure. You can't distort something that isn't there."

Chuck thought about it. "Okay, I can see that. So what is the structure of space, Morty?"

"That held me up for a while, but then I understood that there really *is* a structure, something that extends throughout the universe as we know it, something we're aware of, and also something that can readily be distorted."

"So what is this mysterious something?"

"Well, it's not ether, not quite. That theory was tossed out about a century ago, maybe too soon. But anyway, I figure the structure of space is made up of interlocking fields, gravitational and electro-magnetic for sure, and maybe even some we don't know about.

"Does that dark energy stuff have fields, and are they different than the other fields we know about? Light is electro-magnetic, part of the electromagnetic spectrum, so it's not surprising that it would interact with charged particles like electrons or protons.

"Then Einstein added gravity to the mix, and sure enough, observers saw light bend around a planet during an eclipse. Since then we've spotted gravitational lenses, so that's even more proof. Conceptually, we know that somehow, we should be able to use this information to unite everything in that grand unified theory that Einstein looked for. No one has managed to do it so far, but maybe the answer is in those interlocked fields."

"You're serious, aren't you? You think that space is full of fields that interact with each other?"

"Sure do. Small fields for the most part, around every ion, every bit of matter there is. Ions carry electrical charges, matter has its own little gravitational field. Bigger bits, like rocks and chunks, would have less of an electrical charge per unit of mass, but more gravitational effect. Don't forget that electrical charges are strong compared with mass, but short-ranged. Gravity isn't strong, at least not from small bits of matter, but the effect goes on forever, declining but never disappearing. So the gravitational effect is additive. Dynamic, too, all those small fields adjusting whenever they're disturbed.

"I call it the matrix theory, not that I get a chance to call it anything very often. Most professional physicists are tied to Einstein's concepts and they're not willing to listen to an alternative explanation.

"Einstein said that light would be affected by a gravitational mass, but why only a *large* mass? The way I see it, *any* mass must have an effect, even if the mass was very small and the effect difficult to detect? Is there some kind of threshold effect?

"Anyway, that concept of fields gave me another idea. Einstein pointed out that gravity affects light, but nobody extended that idea."

"Extended it how, Morty?"

"You know about Newton, right? The laws of motion? The one about every action having an equal and opposite reaction?"

"Sure, I learned about that in middle school. Eighth grade, I think."

"Right, so if the gravitational field affects light, doesn't it also mean that light affects the gravitational field? Go back to what I mentioned before and think of light as a wave, so that the energy of the light waves would set up a kind of disturbance or wave effect in the gravitational field?"

"I don't think I've ever heard anyone mention that, but it seems logical. It wouldn't be a very large effect, though."

"It doesn't need to be. Physics works with very large or very small numbers all the time. Now extend it again, Chuck. If I'm right, that the structure of space is fields interacting with each other, then the fields become the medium for transmitting waves. Like sound in water, you get compression and extension within the medium, so that the wave propagates through it.

"But extend *that* idea too. That means that light is really a variable, based on the density of the fields, and Einstein's value--he used an accepted value derived from Michelson-Morley, if I recall--is correct in theory, but not necessarily in practice.

"That, in turn, means that just maybe everything we know about the cosmos is more guesswork than science. Our entire body of knowledge about what's out there depends on our interpretation of intercepted electromagnetic radiation. But if our knowledge of how radiation behaves is faulty, then so is every bit of knowledge we've derived from it."

"Morty, are you sure of this?"

"Nope. I could be right, or the people who think that Einstein is all that they need could be right. It doesn't matter. It's just a way of looking at the data, interpreting it. Some do it with mathematics, some with tea leaves, and I do it mostly with logic. The math is probably correct, but logic comes in when we start to interpret what the math implies.

"Anyway, it doesn't matter what any of us think. Space is what it is. Someday, when we get out there, we'll know for sure.

"But for now, I got to thinking that maybe the impeller secondary coils are creating a field to interact with the *other* fields that are in space and also here on Earth. *They're* the secondary coils for a Tesla transformer, a high-voltage highly-magnetic transformer.

Two secondary coils in each rotor, four in the pair, charging from one primary coil in the base. Every time a coil charges and discharges, it creates a large, if brief, magnetic field.

"And since the charging and discharging happens while the rotor pair is moving, that means the field is also moving. So what I think we're doing is rotating a field in three dimensions, which is why the impeller pulls forward or pushes backward.

"But it doesn't matter what I think as long as it works. Put electricity in, you get motion out. No exhaust. No fuel, other than what's needed to generate the electricity. That means you can stack one impeller behind another or side by side if you want."

"What about that formula, F=ma? What's being accelerated?"

"I think the fields are attempting to accelerate the entire matrix, but what happens is that the impeller itself moves."

"So it doesn't interact with the atmosphere or anything like that?"

"I don't see how it could, Chuck."

"So we could build impellers and put them on, say, an airplane? We could put one in front of another as well as mount them alongside each other?"

"Sure, I mentioned that the last time we talked."

"So is there any reason this airplane couldn't just keep flying higher and higher, Morty? As far as the moon?"

"You think we should build our own spaceship, Chuck?"

"I think we should consider it, Morty."

"Where would we get the money? It would take *millions* to do that, maybe billions. I know that *NASA* spent billions on their capsules and the shuttle, for that matter so does everyone else who's building spaceships."

"Morty, if we had a working model, I'll bet we could find someone who would be willing to invest money. What about someone who already has factory space that could be converted? They might be able to retool to build what we need relatively cheap.

"That's one approach, but it's not the only one. We could even do it ourselves if we took it step by step. What if we built impellers for cargo ships or airplanes first and used the profits to finance a spacecraft? We could just add our propulsion system to completed bodies.

"We'd have to keep the impellers secret as long as possible, I think. It's not all that difficult to build an impeller, if you can do precision machining. For that matter, I didn't have much trouble writing code for the computers. Someone else could do it."

"Suppose we build that jackrabbit chaser first and see how that goes, Chuck. We can talk about spaceships later. Anyway, I'm tired. Whatever you put in my tea made me plumb sleepy."

"Sounds like a plan, Morty. Good night."

Chapter Six

The agenda had been full, meaning that the meeting ran overtime (again!) so Panit got back to his office later than expected. But the graybeard was there, waiting in the reception area, beaming.

And so he should; he was finishing a cup of Panit's excellent (and expensive) coffee. Panit unobtrusively signaled Mrs. Stendall, then walked into his office. She came in moments later. Panit raised his eyebrows questioningly.

"It's him," she confirmed. "His name is Morton Sneyd, and he confessed that he's the one that's been phoning and sending us all those faxes.

"He says he's invented something revolutionary. The device is mounted on that platform he was flying. I pointed out that he didn't have an appointment and that you were very busy, but he said he'd wait. Do you want to speak to him, Mr. Jindae?"

"I suppose I'll have to. You say his invention was attached to that craft, whatever it was?"

"Yes, sir. He claims his device flies, so I suppose that much is confirmed. He also said it doesn't use jets or propellers. I asked about the noise and he said it's not from his invention, it's from the generator that powers it.

"One of the maintenance people had come up to see what the noise was and he got a closer look at the thing from the lounge windows. He said in addition to the generator, there was a fuel tank strapped in front and a bank of batteries mounted behind the seat, big heavy-duty ones according to him, but no jet exhaust or propeller. I'm not sure what a bank of batteries is, but he seemed to know what he was talking about."

"Well, then. Why don't you show our visitor in? If he wants another coffee or a doughnut, give him one. I'll have a cup too, please."

"I'll see to it, sir. He's already on his second cup. He said it was 'right tasty'."

Panit snorted derisively and sat behind his desk, waiting. Mrs. Stendall held the door and Morton Sneyd walked in. "You're a hard man to see, Mr. Jindae!"

"There's a reason for that, Mister…Sneyd?"

"Right, Morton Sneyd. Call me Morty."

"All right, Morty. Why don't you tell me what's on your mind?"

***

Morton Sneyd strolled out of Panit's office an hour after he'd entered. He nodded at Mrs. Stendall, poured himself another cup of coffee and snagged the last doughnut on his way out the door. She raised her eyebrows at this bit of effrontery, undecided whether to be amused or irritated. The soft chime of the intercom caught her attention.

"Yes, sir?"

"Contact the chairman's secretary, please. I need to see him as soon as possible, and a telephone call won't do. This needs to be kept strictly confidential."

"Sir, we've had calls from a reporter. He heard about that flying platform. What should I tell him?"

"Laugh it off, Mrs. Stendall. A flying bedstead? Ridiculous!"

***

Sol Goldman hated high-stakes gambling.

Other companies might spend millions developing concept vehicles, but not Sol. Where was the profit in making something that couldn't be sold? He'd firmly quashed the idea, preferring his designers to work on incremental improvements which were almost guaranteed to pay off. His engineers avoided flashy, heavily chromed, high-powered models; that was for others. Sol's company made solid cars that sold readily and held their value. True, the luxury division pushed this to an extent, but since their profit margin was high, Sol considered that acceptable. It wasn't really a gamble as he saw it.

As for small stakes gambling, especially when there was an element of skill involved, that was different. Today he would play golf, and with luck, manage to take home a few dollars.

***

The other three players were impatient. Two, like Sol, headed manufacturing concerns. The third wasn't even a real businessman but only a financier. Sol had invited him because of his investment in the company. Besides, he might be another pigeon Sol could pluck on the course.

That hadn't gone well during the previous few weeks. Sol frowned in distaste, remembering, and wondering why he'd ever invited the man. But he had, and unlike Sol, who played a safe game, the investor often took the riskier shot. As a result, the pigeon had managed to extract a few feathers from *Sol's* tail, forcing him to become…creative.

And last week, the man had attached himself to Sol, watching every shot; you'd think he believed Sol was cheating! Goddamned jumped up...investor! Nothing behind him but inherited money, yet somehow, he'd managed to force himself onto the board of directors!

Worst of all, Sol had to handle him carefully. If he decided to cash in his investment without signaling his intent, move his money before Sol could do something to counter it, that would almost certainly depress share prices.

Even so, it might be worth it just to get rid of the man!

He headed something called "Fuqua Enterprises", which was in reality no more than a cover for his own investments. Foolish man, to think that he was on a par with Sol or others who managed *real* businesses!

Sol was upset.

He'd have been even more concerned had he known what T. French Fuqua had in mind.

***

Frenchy had his own sources within the company, and most of the time their tidbits of information kept him well informed, at least as well informed about how well the company was doing as the senior executives.

He'd found attitudes among rank-and-file employees to be an excellent indicator of company health. A rise in unhappiness among wage-earners had, more than once, signaled Frenchy that it was time to cash out his investment while it was still profitable.

The maintenance man who'd described the flying thing to Panit was one of his contacts. He'd called Frenchy a few minutes later, meaning that Frenchy understood what had happened before Sol himself was notified.

***

"Shall we get started? I had a meeting I couldn't skip, but we should still have time for a full eighteen holes. I'll probably have to leave after that, another meeting I'm afraid."

"Sol, you're the chairman. Can't you delegate some of that to the CEO?"

"He's the one I'm meeting. Him and Benjamin."

"Sounds serious, Sol. Nothing that will affect the business, I trust," said Lemuel.

"No, no. Possibly an opportunity, but no more than that."

"Anything I'd be interested in, Sol?" asked Frenchy.

Sol looked at him with barely-concealed distaste.

How could a man who didn't deal with boards, with deadlines, with meeting the payroll for thousands of employees consider himself their business equal?

But Sol was outwardly polite; Frenchy's investments in the company were sufficient that, should he decide to sell off his holdings, the company's stock prices would take a serious hit.

This, in turn, affected Sol; his annual bonus depended on how the company's stock was doing. So he was very careful never to show his true feelings about the man.

"I wouldn't think so, Frenchy," said Sol dismissively. "It's an issue I'll need to bring to the board, so you'll find out then."

"I see," said Frenchy. And smiled to himself.

He had more reason to smile later. He'd taken the three for a nice bit of change, again. Ability to manipulate stock prices did not necessarily extend to manipulating a golf ball around the course.

His phone rang as Sol and the others went to the clubhouse. He excused himself, walking far enough away not to be overheard. Glancing at the screen, he smiled yet again.

"Thanks for returning my call, Ben. What have you got for me?"

"Maybe nothing, Frenchy. Maybe a whole lot of something."

"You've made me curious, Ben. Does it have anything to do with what happened this morning?"

"Oh, yes. We've been contacted by a man. Strange fellow, by all reports; he's either a cross between Einstein and Edison or a crackpot."

"Really? Can't you tell?"

"Not yet; he *sounds* cracked, but then there was that flying bedstead thing. That's what Panit called it. One of my people in maintenance saw it, and he said the thing was flying, but it didn't use jets or propellers."

"So how does it work?"

"We don't know, that's the problem. He won't say. He just said it runs on electricity, and my man in maintenance confirmed that. He said the device had a battery pack and a small diesel-powered generator, of all things."

"Interesting. So when does Sol plan to bring this to the board?"

"Maybe as early as tomorrow. He's meeting with me this afternoon and we'll look at how much development would cost. The man wants an astonishing amount of money, too much really."

"You don't say! Does this fractured container have a name?"

"We've got a card. It says 'Morton Sneyd, Inventor'."

"Ridiculous name," said T. French Fuqua.

Chapter Seven

Panit had been invited to attend the emergency board meeting, but not as a principal; he sat with others in the back of the boardroom. Only members of the board had seats at the long table.

Old business had been dispensed with, then had come the announcement that a new business proposal had been presented to the company. Sol stood as soon as the secretary finished the routine preliminary announcements and sat down.

"Thank you for attending, gentlemen.

"I'll get right to the point. We've been approached by a man who claims to have invented a new, and different, propulsion system. I emphasize that it's a revolutionary discovery, not an improvement on the kind of thing we already do.

"I see this as risky. We need to decide whether to invest in this device, and if we do, how much money we're prepared to put into developing it.

"As I see it, we have two options. Should we decide to go ahead, we can approve a budget to explore the proposal. Or we can send him away, but if we do someone else might decide to back him. I can perhaps stall him for a time, but he's impatient. We need to decide quickly, yes or no."

"What sort of development costs, Sol?" Frenchy asked.

"Part of it involves an up-front payment to the inventor. He's got a price in mind that we can't meet, so if he's not open to negotiation, then there's nothing we can do. But even if he's willing to come down on what he's asking, I don't know that we want to get involved. As I see it, he's got an untried system. That's why it seems like such a risk to me.

"I suspect he came to us because he thought we had the manufacturing capability to produce the item he's invented. What he doesn't know is that we're currently using all our facilities. Our employees are tied up on other projects, meaning that we'd have to hire a lot more people to work on his concept. Which, by the way, is nowhere near perfected. He himself admitted that a lot of developmental work would need to be done.

"Add to that, we're looking at years before his device is ready to be marketed. I estimate at least five years, but because it's so new and untried, it may take longer. There will undoubtedly be licensing issues and patent searches, just for starters. He says it's revolutionary, but is it really?

"And we'll need reliability data before we could take the device to market. As a comparison, just look at how long it's taken Tesla to begin selling their electric cars."

"Will we have to take on more debt, Sol?" asked Frenchy. "If bringing this device to market takes as long as you anticipate, the debt will have to be serviced. Adding substantially to our current debt load will cause stock prices to fall, at least in the short term."

"So they will, Frenchy. You're interested in stock appreciation, as we all are, but I should mention that the possible payoff is very large. That's why I thought the board should consider the issue."

"How large is large, Sol? I'm sure I speak for all of us," French glanced around at the other members. "We expect gains commensurate with the risks we're taking. The longer we have to wait, the larger the potential gains have to be if the investment is worthwhile. We're already making money and stock prices are reflecting that, so that's an issue too.

"Why should we take on something so risky? Our foreign sales of heavy equipment are particularly healthy, even if domestic sales haven't fully recovered yet. We also have development costs for our new models to consider, they've been somewhat higher than expected, and we've got to absorb those. The recalls--well, we're all familiar with that. The lawsuits haven't helped either. Can we really afford to take on something expensive that might pay off slowly, if ever?"

"I brought Mr. Jindae here to explain that, Frenchy. Panit?"

Panit stood up and swallowed nervously.

"The proposal before us is to develop and market this new propulsion system. I doubt it will ever be useful for passenger vehicles, but it might work for long-haul tractors, the ones that pull those huge trailers. It might better be suited for railroad applications. It would be a significant improvement over current marine propulsion systems; submarines might be one of the early adoptees, because they wouldn't need propellers."

"Panit, we don't build submarines. We don't build ships either," grumbled Jerome Stokes.

"No, Mr. Stokes, and that's not what the proposal is about. Mr. Sneyd suggests that we build the power plants and lease them to shipbuilders. Trains would use different versions, but the idea is the same, to manufacture and lease the power units. Airplanes would be the natural market, possibly our *largest* market in the long term. Each application would require a different version of the device."

"And you think there are advantages to leasing rather than selling?" Stokes asked. "Will the government even *consider* that? Offhand, I don't believe they lease anything, and certainly not warships. They buy them outright and only accept completed units. For that matter, airlines buy aircraft.

"The advantage to us is security, Mr. Stokes. According to Sneyd, we might not be even be able to patent the devices. He suggested we'd withhold the core knowledge in order to maintain secrecy.

"But leasing would be only a means to an end; we'd be in on the ground floor for the big prize."

"And what big prize is that, Panit?"

"Potentially, the entire solar system, Mr. Stokes. And possibly more than that."

The buzz around the table created by this announcement took a long time to die away.

Frenchy took no part in it. He simply leaned back and waited. For the moment, that was his only option; the proposal had been presented to this company.

Risky, to be sure; but as Panit had said, enormously profitable if the gamble paid off. But if the board decided it was *too* risky…

He'd done what he could to discourage the others. Sol was convinced, but the board might overrule him. It had happened before.

But this board? They were as conservative as Sol.

***

"Come in, Mr. Sneyd. Coffee?"

"I already had two cups this morning, Mr. Panit. Can we get on with the horse trading?"

"Very well. I attended a meeting of the board of directors, Mr. Sneyd. Your invention is interesting, I can't deny that. The idea of flying a demonstrator up and waving in my window definitely got my attention! Anyway, I presented your ideas to the board just as you provided them to me.

"The fact is, Mr. Sneyd, the company can't afford to develop your invention. We have contracts we can't cancel, projects in development, patents we own...what you're asking us to do is abandon the business we've spent years developing. In some cases, we would be competing with our own divisions! You say you aren't interested in selling your discovery--is that still your position?"

"Yep. I don't intend to have this stuffed into a file and ignored. Humanity needs this! What if one of them dinosaur-killin' meteors is sighted? Then what? I want money, I told you that, but my main concern is developing the impeller propulsion system. Humanity needs the impeller drive!"

"Yes, of course. But do you have any concept of how much money you're asking us to commit? At a minimum, it would require an entire new division, new workshops, new design departments, experiments to find the best materials, teams of scientists and engineers, and even if we committed the millions needed we couldn't count on seeing a profit anytime soon, maybe for as much as twenty years!

"You may have built your flyer in your garage as you said, but you can't build an interplanetary craft that way! Even the other uses, railways, aircraft, those won't pay off for years, if ever.

"And what if your device can't be scaled up? What would

happen then? We'd be facing bankruptcy or begging the government for another bailout! No, no, even if you gave up the ridiculous idea of half the company's stock in exchange for your device, we can't take the risk and I don't think you'll find anyone *else* who's willing to take the chance. It's just too revolutionary.

"I suggest instead that you explore the idea of forming your own company. Perhaps you can attract venture capital. You do have some concept of how much you'll need, don't you?"

Morty looked back sourly. "I do, some of it anyway. I spent most of what I got from my other inventions and my consulting business just building this one, and now I'm almost broke. I asked for as much up-front money as I did just so you'd really have to try to develop the impeller.

"You're sure you won't give it a try, maybe in partnership with somebody else? That Space-X company, maybe? A shipyard or a railroad or something?"

"I regret to tell you that we considered all those options.

"It's simply too risky. We have stockholders we're responsible to, and our investors would lose millions just in writing down the debt load! Stocks would plummet, people would lose confidence--no, we simply can't do it. We'd be risking bankruptcy. I'm very sorry. I do wish you luck, however."

"Well, thanks for telling me the truth. I was hopin'..." Morty's voice trailed off.

"I understand, Mr. Sneyd. Really, I do. You're not the first person I've had to deliver bad news to. The fact remains that our core business is in manufacturing cars, light trucks, heavy machinery, and over-the-road tractors. The company invests in other ventures on occasion, but never to the extent of jeopardizing our main business."

"I reckon I understand, Mr. Panit. Thanks for your time. I'll let myself out."

Head bowed, Morty left the office.

He took the elevator and as it descended, thought about what he might do.

Should he fly the experimental model somewhere and see if he could interest someone else? Someone like Dean Kamen or maybe even Warren Buffett?

But Buffett didn't do startups, he invested in established companies. As for Kamen, he had his own inventions to develop, and probably he didn't have enough free cash to develop the impeller system anyway.

Should he simply give up on the idea of making money, put the plans on the internet and let every garage-inventor give it a try? What if the Chinese or Germans or someone like that put the money into development? What if it was the Russians?

He was still thinking, mumbling to himself, as he left the building. On the sidewalk, a man waited.

"Mr. Sneyd? If you have a few moments, I'd like to talk to you. Call me Frenchy."

***

Will Crane punched the call button on his cell phone after glancing at the caller's name.

"What say, Frenchy? Long time no see."

"It's been a while. I was wondering if we might get together; I've come across an opportunity that promises a very handsome payout if things go as I expect."

"How handsome, Frenchy?"

"Remember that Wilson deal? This is *much* bigger. There are risks, but the payoff is immense."

"Who else is involved, Frenchy? Besides you, I mean."

"You'll get a chance to see for yourself if you're interested. If you're free this evening, why don't we have dinner and talk about it? I don't want to say more on the phone.
Right now, I'm calling around to see who else might want a part of this, so I can give you a better idea who's involved when I see you."

"I'll be there. You've really got a nose for these things, haven't you?" Will asked admiringly.

Frenchy chuckled and ended the call, then punched in another number.

***

"Hi, Daddy! I didn't expect to hear from you!"

"I didn't expect to call, but I found myself thinking of you. How's school going?"

"Final semester, and I'll be glad when it's over! I'm not ready to go for the PhD right now, not that doing that would be harder, but it's been a long slog and I need a break. Going to come up for my graduation?"

"Sure, I wouldn't miss it for the world. What are you going to do after that?"

"Peddle my degree around, I suppose. Someone will need an architect."

"Is that the degree, MA in architecture?"

"Sure. Doesn't say much, does it?"

"No, not really. What do you want to do?"

"I'm thinking interior design for now. I like the artistic aspect that an architectural designer can bring to designing living spaces."

"Sounds like fun. What else is happening?"

"I'm at loose ends again. Jerry didn't work out. Too bad, I thought he might be The One."

"Sounds like you're taking it OK. I guess you had clues before the breakup happened?"

"You could say that." Frenchy waited, but Lina didn't explain.

"I'll try to make it for graduation. I'm working on something now, but I'll make the time."

The conversation went on for another five minutes, then Lina mentioned that she had an assignment.

Frenchy broke the connection and felt a momentary sense of sorrow. Somehow, the little girl who'd once been so important in his life had gone away. The young woman who'd taken her place...

Frenchy hardly knew her at all.

***

Will was the first of those Frenchy had invited to arrive.

He spotted Frenchy almost immediately, already seated at a

table in a nook where their conversation was unlikely to be overheard.

Conversational snippets from members and guests of members of the Union League were unlikely to become public knowledge. The staff was as discreet as any in the city. That said, conversations always became muted or stopped completely when waiters delivered drinks or dinner. Members understood that there was always a first time for everything.

"Howdy, Frenchy. You're looking well. All that squash playing, I suppose."

"I manage a few rounds of golf too, Will. How about you? That new girlfriend providing plenty of exercise?"

"What girlfriend, Frenchy?" Will's face was bland.

"The one that newsman snapped a picture of. She's definitely a looker."

"She's not exactly a girlfriend, just someone I met at an arts auction. Picked up a nice addition for my collection there."

"That's another way of looking at it, I suppose," chuckled Frenchy. "Artistic, is she?"

"Very." Will's voice was smooth; not even a hint of a smile crossed his face.

Frenchy wasn't fooled. Will preferred not to settle down and he changed girlfriends as often as necessary to avoid commitment.

No one had ever succeeded in reading Will Crane's expression. Some had tried, and lost money in the process.

Will had flirted with professional gambling for a time. Rumor said he still played poker, adding to what his investments brought in.

"How's your piggy bank, Will?"

"Well, it's not empty. What's on your mind, Frenchy?"

"I've found something very interesting. It might be risky."

"How big is the payoff?"

"If it works, enormous."

"Really? Tell me more."

"I'll wait, Will. The others are here now."

Will looked at the group that entered the door, and blinked. Even among Chicago's wealthiest, these men stood out. Combined net worth, probably north of a billion.

Yes indeed, Frenchy had sniffed something out. Not that all of them would invest, of course, but if they decided to take part, Frenchy's venture would capitalize at $200 million or more. That was serious money, and if the payoff was as big as he had hinted...

Will unconsciously rubbed his hands together.

Chapter Eight

Sol fretted on his way back to his office.

What to do? The potential payoff was so huge as to be incomprehensible, but at the same time, the risks were enormous. If he used his considerable private fortune to bankroll this Morty person, he might end up broke, even lose his position as head of the company.

There was no question of using company funds; thanks to the board's decision, that option was no longer available.

But transportation and the independent businesses that supported it made up the largest manufacturing segment of the national economy. If Sneyd's invention proved to be all he claimed, then a revolution in transportation would almost certainly happen. And when revolutions take place, new companies take over the top spots.

That flying device Panit saw would kill surface transport, no question about it. For one, Sneyd had made the device himself, which meant that it could be manufactured cheap and sold for less, far less, than cars were selling for now.

As for air transport, why would anyone even need an airport or a pilot's license, since the device could fly slow and low enough not to be dangerous? It could even hover, and unlike helicopters, required no special skill to operate.

Sneyd was a serious threat. Not only to the economy, but to the company and Sol himself.

The prospect was frightening. He would have to be stopped, but how?

The board had refused to support Sneyd, but that wouldn't stop the man. Where would he turn next? Railroads? Shipping? Aircraft? Would someone like Boeing be interested? They were certainly big enough, but like Sol's own company, they had long term contracts to consider. Would they be willing to take the risks?

Smaller companies might, Sol concluded, but probably not one of the majors. They stayed in business because they had the huge industrial plant needed to manufacture something as big as a jumbo jet. Even so, Boeing faced stiff competition from Airbus.

But maybe one of the smaller companies would be willing to take the risk? What then?

Well. The thing to do was to keep his, Sol's, nose in the wind.

There were a number of small manufacturers who had cut back on production recently, and if one began hiring people and reopening plants, then that was enough of a clue to look into whether Sneyd was involved. He, Sol, might need to directly intervene if that happened.

But for now, Sneyd needed money and Sol knew a thing or two about finance. Best of all, he could work behind the scenes, avoid direct involvement, and by so doing avoid risk-taking. After all, investors were by nature nervous. It wouldn't take much, no more than a word in the right place, to convince them that Sneyd's venture was too risky.

***

"So you claim to have all this money available, Frenchy?" asked Morty.

"The money will come from several sources," revealed Frenchy, "but there's more than enough pledged to get started. Some will be available immediately, the rest after the investment consortium I'm putting together liquidates investments."

"Who would run this plant you're offering to build?" asked Morty.

"I'll be the chief executive officer, but I'll answer to a board of directors. The other investors will be represented on the board, as will you.

"We're prepared to offer you a substantial initial payment for access to your invention, but the rest of what you're asking for will be in the form of common stock in the company. We'll work out the details later, after we form the company, but you'll own thirty percent of the stock, the investors will own sixty percent among us. I intend to reserve ten percent of the stock for employees as incentive payments.

"I know how much you asked for, but you'll not get that, nowhere near that much. You won't be poor, even in the beginning, but if your invention is as promising as you say you'll wind up insanely rich. You'll not only own stock in the company, you'll serve as a consultant, and we'll negotiate a reasonable salary for your work. How does that sound?" asked Frenchy.

"I mainly figured to set the askin' price high so they'd take me serious," Morty confessed. "They'd been ignoring me for weeks. I tried telephoning, sending faxes...I even sent 'em pictures of me flying the prototype! But nothin' worked."

"Where is the prototype, Mr. Sneyd?"

"Call me Morty, Frenchy. I ain't saying any more until I see the color of your money."

"How about I immediately deposit a million dollars into your bank account for access to your prototype? Within a day or two, I'll have a small engineering staff ready to examine the drive units--you did say they're relatively simple?"

"They are," said Morty. "I'm surprised nobody came up with it before now. But yeah, it's simple in concept and the important thing for your people to keep in mind is that it works.

"Development will require quite a bit of money," he went on. "A small engineering staff won't cut it. You're going to need people who can do precision machining, mechanical engineers to design layouts, engineers to design power systems, and materials science people just for starters. You plan to go right for the spaceship, or you want to develop one of the other ideas first?"

"We're interested in the aircraft propulsion system as the first major effort," said Frenchy. "We may build prototypes of your railway car, but I don't think there's enough short-term profit there to make investment worthwhile. You intend to equip each railcar with propulsion units and computerized controls, is that correct?"

"Right. No need for a big old engine up front. It should be

possible to use half a dozen units like the four on my flying prototype, just attach them directly to the frame of a flatcar. I figure that people who own cars, motorhomes too, might be interested in parking on a flatcar and just kick back while the flatcar takes them to wherever they're going. Just leave the drivin' to us. They'd drive on, snooze until they get there, drive off. No need to rent a car, no need to worry about traffic or bad weather, just relax and read a book."

"How would you control the flatcars?" asked Frenchy.

"My grandson Chuck says it could be done using computerized controls. A central computer would do the scheduling, command the car when it's time to pull onto the main track--you'll need two sets of tracks at least, you know, one east and one west, or one going south and the other north--so when you've got a car loaded, it powers up, then slides onto the main track. When the car gets to where a passenger is going, the car gets sidetracked just long enough to let him drive off."

"An interesting concept," acknowledged Frenchy. "But a second set of tracks for each railroad would cost billions."

"You invest money to make money, Frenchy."

"So you do, but you're asking us to spend money a lot faster than your proposed railway system would earn it back! No, that's probably for the future, if ever. The maritime system shows more short-term promise; some of our investors have extensive interests in shipyards and shipping, so they're in a position to profit from such a system. We'll see how the other ideas look before making a final decision, but a ship, that's doable now. A diesel-electric generator and multiple propulsion units, you said? No propellers needed?"

"That's it, Frenchy. Mount the impellers inside the hull on gimbals, so the ship can go forward, backward, sideways...you might even be able to lift it off a sandbar if it got stuck! That would probably take a lot more impellers than you'd need just to haul freight, though.

"You would also need backup batteries. Design a generator to power the batteries and the impellers at the same time; that way, if the generator fails, you've still got an immediate backup system. Maybe use two or three smaller generators for reliability."

"What if an *impeller* fails, Morty?"

"If you're using, say, thirty of them, you can afford to have failures. Just pull a defective unit offline, fix whatever went wrong. If you've got a spare on board, just bolt it in place when you pull the busted one. Power it back up and keep on goin'. Even if you had to shut down long enough to replace something, you'd be down for maybe an hour, tops.

"That's the beauty of electric drive, you can gang impellers together, as many as you want. Instead of huge, expensive, maybe even failure-prone units, just use smaller ones and hook on as many as you need."

"What about efficiency, Morty? Wouldn't larger units be more efficient?"

"Maybe, but that's something we'll find out by experimenting. In the meantime, use lots of smaller units for safety and reliability."

"And you wouldn't need external motors or propellers at all, would you?" Frenchy pressed.

"Nope," said Morty. "As for an airplane, you can put the impellers inside the wings so there'd be no more problems with a bird gettin' sucked into the jet intake."

"But wouldn't you need to use something like a turbojet engine, the kind they use for turboprops, to spin the generator? There's no battery pack right now that's light enough and that also has the storage capacity to power long-range flight."

"No, you're right. That interplanetary spacecraft I mentioned, that's going to need nuclear power. I figure maybe three of them small reactors Los Alamos is developin' would do it."

"Three? Why three?"

"Safety, Frenchy. One would provide plenty of power, but I'm a believer in safety. If you're out in the asteroids, you don't want to try hitchhiking home!"

***

Two months went by. Manufacturers, including Sol, began seeing changes.

"Send him in, Miss Porter. Then hold my calls."

"Yes sir, Mr. Goldman."

"Ben, you're resigning? Why? I thought you were happy with us. Is it that last raise? You know why we had to limit that, of course. You're the comptroller, you know how limited our funds are! Really, you've done well with us, so why are you resigning now?"

"I've decided to move on, Mr. Goldman. The salary isn't the whole issue, of course, but after that last negotiation, I decided I should keep my options open. I've already got a job offer, working for a venture capital firm."

"So it is the salary! But I explained why we couldn't afford..."

"So you did, Mr. Goldman. But I noticed that you and the board members were rewarded with a considerably better package than the one you offered me."

"I see." Sol's tone was frosty. "Well, you understand that our corporate interests aren't yours to reveal? Are you going to work for one of our competitors?"

"No. As I said, I'll be working for a venture-capital startup. This serves as my two-week notice."

Sol abruptly ended the discussion. "Thank you for coming to see me, Mr. Counter."

Well. There was no shortage of people like him. Sol would nose around. He could hire someone from another company, couldn't he? Maybe at a lesser salary?

***

Panit Jindae sent Mr. Goldman an email that same week.

Two of his senior design engineers had resigned. Hiring new ones would take time, and inevitably there would be slowdowns until their replacements could be brought up to speed.

Sol mentioned it later to his golf buddies. Frenchy had canceled; something had come up, he said. But the others were there, and Sol broached the subject as they approached the third tee.

"Something strange is going on. I've had an unusual number of resignations. Granted, the last raises weren't great, but..."

"Other companies are hiring too, Sol. I haven't heard anything definite, but according to one of the trade papers, Boeing's having to offer bonuses to engineers to keep them on.

"Someone has to be hiring, but no one's reporting new sales, certainly not enough to justify opening another plant or even put on another shift. So what's going on?"

"No idea. Something else, did you check the stock indexes this morning?"

"No, I didn't have time. I intended to, but the V.P. in charge of the design offices had a crisis. I think it's time for new blood there."

"You're talking about Jindae? I thought you were happy with him?"

"I was, but he's talking about pushing completion dates back, and that will slow the launch of the new vehicles. Some of the resignations were in his department. You'd think some insider was poaching our best people!"

"Ridiculous, Sol!"

"So how about other companies? You're on their boards, are they reporting problems?"

"No, Sol, we're not having problems. Maybe *you* should consider offering bonuses or higher salaries to keep your key people happy. Who's up first?"

Things were not exactly as Charles described. Still, no need to tell Sol. He'd figure it out, soon enough. Meanwhile, if Sol's employees *were* looking for better offers, perhaps a few discreet approaches would provide replacements for Charles' companies? Senior engineers, people with managerial experience, those didn't grow on trees. Perhaps it was time to have a quiet word with personnel?

Sol would understand. It was just business.

***

"Come on in, Morty. I've saved you a spot at the end of the table. Would you introduce your companion to the board?"

"Sure. This is my grandson Chuck, Frenchy. He's watching out for my business interests."

"Welcome, Chuck. But no one here is trying to take advantage of your grandfather. We're trying to come to an agreement that protects all our interests."

"That's good to know, Frenchy. I wouldn't want to invoke our fail-safe position."

"And what position is that, Chuck? Like I said, no one is planning to cheat Morty."

"For our part, Frenchy, the company gets exclusive rights to grandfather's impeller. We're willing to negotiate how much of the company Morty will own in terms of stock and his salary as a consultant, but he is interested in seeing that humanity benefits from his discovery.

"He considers the money secondary, an incentive to make sure than his invention isn't held back. If he ever feels he's being treated unfairly, he retains the option to release his invention to the world. He'll put the key portions of the technology on the internet where anyone who wants to can start tinkering in a garage workshop. That's how my grandfather started, working on an idea that Nikola Tesla had."

"That's right, Chuck, but don't forget that Tesla never developed it," Morty said. "I did that. Lots of people have thought about antigravity, but nobody has managed to fly a ship using it!" said Morty.

"Right, Grandpa. Anyway, if it goes out to anyone who has a computer, the secret is out. You would lose your lead time, which is what you're really paying for. China, India, Vietnam, Russia, they would soon be heading to space in a ship driven by direct impulse, where the only fuel needed is electricity. Eventually, they'll figure out how the impeller drive works, but the company should have maybe twenty years to exploit the drive before the secret leaks."

"We're paying a lot for not much, Chuck," Frenchy said.

"Twenty years; but suppose it's only ten years, Frenchy? Ten years of flying the only electrically-propelled spaceships in existence? Ten years of engineering development to work out the bugs in the system? Ten years to plant a colony on the moon and possibly even one on Mars?

"Ten years to start mining the asteroids? How much income will you gain just from doing that?

"What about claiming major moons, asteroids, even planets? What about actually putting settlements in place? Earth's nations may argue that space belongs to nations or the UN, but claiming is not possession.

"That ten year lead allows the company to tie up counterclaims in court while we keep exploiting what we find, and profiting. And you think you're paying too much for that?"

"I understand what you're saying, but we're bearing all of the development costs, doing the engineering, building the propulsion units...I wanted to talk to you about the name, too. We don't think Sneyd Impellers will sell. Eventually, we'll be mass-producing and either leasing or selling impellers, and our people with experience in marketing believe that we'd do better if we named it the Tesla Impeller."

"They do, do they? Grandpa, what do you think?"

"Don't matter to me as long as I get my share of the credit. How about the Sneyd-Tesla Impeller?"

"Frenchy?" Chuck waited for the answer.

"We'll go with that. Next on the agenda, I'd like to introduce the other prospective members of the board and the department heads."

"Sure, go ahead. Grandpa will be doing most of our talking from here on out. I'll just listen in. I'll need a chair, please."

Morty sat down at the foot of the table. A chair was brought and Chuck took his place at Morty's side.

"We'll make sure you have a seat at the table next time, Chuck. Meantime, I've got an agenda to follow. Help yourself to coffee or water.

"Next item to discuss, the company will have a board of directors. It will be organized similar to any other corporation. The board will consist as follows: Myself, chairman and CEO. Will Crane will represent the investment group and until they provide the pledged funds, the two of us will put up initial financing.

"This will take us through the startup phase. Ben Counter is CFO. He'll report directly to me in that role, and he also has a seat on the board.

"Mr. Jindae is a non-voting member of the board and head of engineering development, but that might change later on. We'll see how things work out. The rest of the people with us today will be working in his division.

"Mr. Sikkit is head of electronic engineering, Mr. Ruelle is head of design, and we'll be hiring a chief mechanical engineer in the next few weeks. We'll also hire manufacturing management as needed and sales staff when we have something to market.

"Morty, you are a board member, based on your stock in the company, but you're also chief scientist and consultant to the other divisions. We'll hold board meetings as necessary to discuss progress and resolve any problems that have cropped up. Is this satisfactory?"

"Sounds fine, Frenchy. You have any idea of how long it's going to take before we get a test craft ready to fly?"

"Not at this time, Morty. We've already spent a considerable amount of money hiring the department heads and doing initial research, so funds aren't unlimited.

"I've got brokers looking into land acquisition, but if that fails we've got a fallback position. I own property in New Mexico that extends across the Texas line, and we can build the main factory there if we can't find a better location."

"Why don't we just build it there to start with, Frenchy?"

"Couple of reasons. We're going to need access to electrical power, lots of it and preferably cheap. We'll need a work force.

"You can't find the kind of people we'll need on the farms and ranches. We'd have to bring people in, which would mean building roads. Eventually, I expect we'll need thousands of people when we begin production. Starting a plant from scratch involves a lot more up-front expense. We hope to attract additional investors, maybe even go public later on, but we'll need something more than a concept before that happens. We'll need a fully-operational prototype at the very least."

"I didn't expect all this, Frenchy. Instead of hiring all these department heads, why not just hire people to do the engineering and build the prototypes?"

"Prototypes don't bring sales, Morty. Will and I are planning to invest about ten million each in startup capital, and as our other investors buy in, the total commitment is expected to rise to at least 200 million. We can't let that money just sit, it's got to be earning income as soon as possible."

"I won't be cuttin' corners, Frenchy. Income, sure, but safety and reliability come first in my book. I ain't sending anybody out into space until we've got a system that will not only take us out there but bring us home."

"I agree, Morty. But before we build a spacecraft, we'll use Sneyd-Tesla Impellers to drive ships and airplanes. Both of those require licensing by government inspectors, so we'll need to be very careful about what we tell them. We'll show them that the drive works, then customers will sell themselves when they see what our ships and airplanes can do.

"As for a spaceship, full development will happen after we have the other systems operating. I don't see why we can't begin working on a prototype as time permits, a smaller one that will carry maybe ten people. I agree with your concerns about safety. The other systems I mentioned will generate usage data, and we'll need that before we design the propulsion system for the full-size space ship."

"So what do we do until we get an assembly plant? We'll need a shop so we can keep improving the impellers. The current version works okay, but right off hand, I know we can shrink the overall diameter and improve the mounting system. Chuck thinks he can upgrade the control system too."

"Actually, I'm glad you brought that up. One of our other investors owns a warehouse that's not being used and he's suggested that it be part of his investment. I think it would serve nicely as a place to put our shop while we work on those improvements."

***

Bennett Downing was penciling in notes on a pad. He closed the pad and covered it with a cardboard marked Secret.

"What's this, Fowler?"

"I'm not sure, sir. It appears to be a scan of a business card. We intercepted it, part of a routine system we use, but for some reason the computer highlighted it. I hoped you might know what's going on. None of the techs know why it popped up. We checked the name and there's a file on the guy, but he's no terrorist. He's just a harmless old crank."

"So why is there a file on him?"

"The file dates back to the Clinton administration. He made a number of statements back then that sounded vaguely anti-American, or at least anti-government. He was pretty quiet during the Bush administration, then became more active after Obama's election. He never advocated violence, and anyway he's getting pretty old. The last entry before this had to do with a medical procedure he underwent, an angioplasty. It appears that his heart isn't all that healthy. Anyway, he's just a person of interest, lowest classification."

"So who did you pick up the scan from, Fowler?"

Fowler pointed wordlessly to the cover page.

"Why would a self-proclaimed inventor...does he have any patents? Peer reviewed articles in journals? Anyway, why would he approach an automotive manufacturer?"

"To answer your first question, he holds no major patents. He has a few small ones for improved farming attachments, things that attach to a tractor. As for peer reviews, he submitted an article ten years ago that was rejected. Supposedly, he was looking at Nikola Tesla's inventions, and the article dealt with one of those.

"Tesla mentioned a way of converting electricity to motion, but he never patented it. He also never built a prototype, and his usual practice was to build a prototype and submit that for patent protection. This leads me to believe the item he mentioned was only an idea. Tesla had a lot of those that never panned out.

"Anyway, the article Sneyd wrote said he was working on something similar, and the documentation for his proposed article had to do with his early results. The problem was that he wouldn't say how he got the results, so no one would have been able to replicate his findings. There's a note attached to the review that suggests Sneyd is suffering from paranoia. Since the reviewer is a physicist and mathematician, not a psychiatrist, that was never added to Sneyd's profile.

"Tesla never developed his invention beyond the concept stage, as far as anyone knows. It was an offshoot of his bladeless turbine work and Tesla never got to the prototype stage with that either, so it went nowhere. He was never able to get the bladeless turbine to work reliably.

"Maybe that's why the computer kicked this out. There's an active program that's reexamining Tesla's work to see if we can find other things worth developing. He suggested that lasers could be made to work, and he used a form of semi-active control to operate a boat remotely. It's similar to what's being done with drones. DARPA thinks there may be other ideas in Tesla's notes that they'd be interested in."

"I wasn't aware of that. So what do you want to do about this intercept?"

Downing drummed his fingers on the desk for a moment.

"Update Sneyd's file to include this. Take a look at the classification of that file too. Maybe it's time to raise his classification a notch or two to show that we're following what he's doing. Let's keep an eye on the situation. If it's only a development similar to what he did with those farm implements, we can ignore it. Meantime, if he's got something that a major manufacturer is interested in, that has economic implications. Keep an eye on them too."

The file was updated and the classification duly changed.

The clerk who did the work was named S. Peter Tenno, and he had an unusual memory. He added this scrap of information to other tidbits he'd collected during the day.

That night, he carefully wrote down things he thought might be of interest to his shadow employer on a sheet of copy paper. He used an ordinary ball-point pen to do this, printing the information carefully in block letters. The sheet of paper lay on a granite slab, a scrap he'd bought cheap from a company that made countertops. The highly polished offcut had been sliced out, creating an opening for a kitchen sink, before the countertop was delivered to the contractor.

The offcut made an excellent writing surface and the pen left no impression on the granite.

A digital photo of the note was encoded and the code became a snippet included in an innocuous email. As soon as it went out, the paper original was shredded, the shreds mixed in with others from gas, credit card, and electric statements.

Mr. Tenno was a careful man. He lived within his salary, rarely even using a credit card. Most purchases were in cash. His Cayman Islands account grew year by year, and at some point, Peter would resign from his agency job and visit the Cayman Islands. Eventually he planned to settle in Central America, where the Cayman account would permit him to live a much better lifestyle.

He would have been offended to know that his report went not only to his Israeli employer but to another nation.

The Israeli also expected to retire at some point, to a place where *his* illicit earnings would allow him to live in luxury.

Chapter Nine

The warehouse had not been used in some time.

"More room than I expected, Morty."

"Yeah, it takes up at least half of the block. I wonder what they stored in all this space?"

"No idea. Maybe they just drove the trucks in and parked them until they were ready to deliver whatever they were storing. The roof is good; I haven't seen any sign of leaks."

"The place could use some paint, but I suppose that doesn't matter. We'll be moving out at some point anyway, as soon as Frenchy finds us a permanent home."

Morty and Chuck spent the first hour walking around the dusty building's interior, making sure the heaters and the air conditioners worked, the water system was in good shape, and the toilets flushed. Morty found that the electrical system would need extensive modification. Each major piece of shop equipment would require a separate circuit breaker, just for starters. While he was doing his evaluation, Chuck explored the second floor. Offices would go there, above the noise and dust generated by the shop equipment. Finished, the two locked the building and drove to a restaurant for lunch.

"This place will do until we get our own factory. I figure we lay out the ground floor in three areas, a large one for manufacturing, a smaller one for assembly, and the rear section by the loading docks for storage. We won't need much assembly space in the beginning, not until we start mass-producing parts. What did you find upstairs?"

"Plenty of room for offices, and a larger room we can use for meetings and a break room. No coffee or munchies in the shop area; too much chance of spilling something. I'll reserve one of the offices as my workspace. I'll need to set up a mini computer. The people that'll be working on automation will need satellite stations, so the computer will need the capacity to handle those. You wanted to redesign the rotors too. If you're going to shrink the mechanical parts like you mentioned, you're going to have to increase the speed of rotation, maybe use full motor RPM to get the same amount of impulse. That means a redesign of the control system."

"I'd like to kick the speed even higher if we can, Chuck. The only reason for keeping rotation speed down in the first place was because the g-forces built up as soon as the main motor kicked in. The high-speed rotors will have to use thrust bearings to hold them in place, so that counts as a redesign too. Spinning faster increases the g-force, and the bearings we've been using won't stand up to the increased stress. Not a serious problem, because high speed, permanently lubed and sealed bearings are available, but they're also heavier. It's just something to consider in the redesign. The ultimate limit to how fast we can rotate the main impeller shaft is the mechanical limits of the material we're using. Electrically, the coils will probably work at least as well when the rotors spin faster, maybe even better."

"What shop machines are you going to want, Morty? Keep in mind that your shop area seems large, but when you begin putting in industrial machine tools they take up a lot of space. You've got to leave space for the workers to move around, too. That's a safety consideration."

"I'll have the same kind of shop I've got at home, and there's plenty of room there."

"I wouldn't say plenty, Morty. I thought it was pretty cramped."

"Oh, there's room enough," said Morty, "but I understand what you're driving at. I've also got to leave room in the rear of the shop for a different kind of machine, 3-D printers. They make parts by adding material, not taking it away. One of the slowest parts of building the impeller is machining the rotors from blanks. I figure I can print the blanks, then refine the shape through machining. Some of the blanks may not have to be machined at all. While it seems slower at first, we'll eventually get more production in less time. I can put at least a dozen printers in the back part of the shop and leave the front for the bigger machines, the lathes and mills and precision grinders. I won't need as many, using the printers to produce blanks."

"If you say so," Chuck replied. "How many computers will you need to drive those printers?"

"I guess we'll see when they start arriving. The machines might have their own built-in computer anyway, just input a program and let the printer go to work. We might not need a separate computer."

"What kind of supplies do you need for the printers? You'll need whatever kind of feedstock they use, maybe several kinds. You might also need different nozzles."

"Yep, I mentioned a part of the warehouse where we could store supplies, and we can keep the printer supplies and different nozzles there. Anyway, I'll talk to Frenchy later on, and as soon as he gives me the go-ahead I'll start shopping. If I can find used machines, setting up the shop will go faster and we'll save money. I might even be able to buy machines immediately. If I have to buy new equipment, I'll probably have to order it, then wait until it's built. Hardly anyone stocks the kind of big industrial machines I want, hoping to find a buyer. They cost too much and sales are too slow to justify having them stockpiled. A lot of what I want is build-to-order, and that can take weeks. Still, if the choice is wait around or try to work with something I can get immediately, I reckon I can work with what's available."

"What about electric circuits? Does this place have three-phase capability?"

"It does, although the power company might have to increase the capacity of what's already installed. But that's their problem, and anyway it's the kind of thing they handle routinely. I'll look at the manuals when machines start arriving, but I don't think there'll be a problem. It's just straight industrial circuitry. We'll have to add separate circuits for each machine, but from what I saw there's plenty of capacity coming into the building. I'll get electricians to do an in-depth inspection to make sure I didn't miss anything, though, and they'll set up the wiring."

"Morty, you're looking forward to this, aren't you?"

"I am. About the people Frenchy's hiring, the best way to get new people up to speed is to show them a working model. As soon as I've got the equipment ordered, you bring the Bedstead here. We'll disassemble the impellers after showing the engineers what they can do, then let them start working on improvements. We'll use the Bedstead to test new impellers, although the frame will need to be redesigned."

"We've both got stuff to do, then. What about operating funds?"

"I'll give Frenchy a call. I'll start placing orders as soon as he puts money in the account."

"Don't forget the upstairs. The offices will need a good cleaning and a coat of paint, plus furniture."

***

The old warehouse went through a number of upgrades during the following weeks. Electricians spent a day inspecting the wiring, then wrote up preliminary work orders. They'd be back to run conduit and connect the machines when the shop equipment started arriving.

Frenchy, deciding he wanted to be part of the operation, took charge of redesigning the upstairs. A large meeting room was set up near the head of the stairs, and the break area was across the hall from the meeting room. The rest of the space was divided into offices and two bathrooms, located adjacent to the break area.

New people began arriving within the week. Morty decided where each engineer would best fit in, while Panit and Frenchy assigned people to the offices. Accounting was one of the first departments established; Morty and Chuck would henceforward place orders through purchasing, part of the accounting department. This in turn was headed up by a comptroller who worked with Frenchy, keeping him updated. Payroll was another necessary part of accounting, as was a section devoted to keeping track of taxes.

Frenchy hired a pilot to fly Chuck to Andrews County Airport. Chuck rented a medium-duty truck with an enclosed cargo bay and drove it to the ranch, backing it in place at the front of Morty's shop. The Bedstead had been partially disassembled after the earlier flight, in part so that the impellers could be inspected but also from an abundance of caution. Chuck would put it back together before loading it.

Reassembling the craft took most of the following day. Chuck finally opened the workshop doors at dusk and slowly flew the Bedstead into the truck's cargo bay. He strapped it in place, then locked the shop and the truck's cargo door. He got a good night's sleep in the ranch house, ate a bowl of cereal when he woke up, and was on the road at daybreak.

The trip back took longer than expected, but Chuck catnapped in roadside parks and drove on as soon as he woke up, sustained by truck-stop coffee and sandwiches he bought when he stopped for fuel.

***

"You made good time, Chuck."

"It was a grind, Frenchy, no question about it, but I've dealt with worse."

"That's right, your grandfather mentioned you'd been a soldier."

"Marine, Frenchy, Marine. We Marines are very picky about that." The two chuckled.

"That's a rented truck, right?"

"Right, we didn't have the money to buy one, Frenchy. Why?"

"We're going to need our own, either one like that or a larger one. Why don't you just park the truck inside the warehouse for now? Keep the Bedstead locked in the cargo bay. We're still running background checks on some of the new men, and there's no need to reveal what we're working on until later. Eventually, we'll offer them stock in the company. I think that's the best way to ensure their loyalty. Once we tell them what we have in mind, I don't think they'll be running to someone else with the story. They'll have too much to lose."

"Sure, Frenchy. Security is important. If the secret gets out, even what's involved in this first primitive device, we're out of business. Oh, we could keep going, but as for exclusive rights to asteroids or maybe even claim a moon, forget it. Everybody and his brother would be out there, roosting on some piece of desirable real estate. Probably getting themselves killed in the process too. But developing the impellers is only the first step. We're going to need a reliable source of electrical power for the spacecraft and we're going to need better spacesuits than the kind NASA is using if we're going to work in space. NASA's suit is pretty primitive, you know. I think we can do better."

"That's where I come in, Chuck. I'm invested in a small company that can build the suits. If you've got enough money, problems like suits and electrical power generation can be solved."

"Sounds good, Frenchy. I've never had that kind of money and neither has Morty. But I guess the thing for me to do now is go buy a truck."

"You pick the truck, let purchasing know what you want. Benjamin's people will take care of the negotiations."

***

Tractor-trailers began arriving at the former warehouse during the ensuing weeks. The early deliveries included a large forklift and two pallet jacks to move the equipment around when it began arriving.

The increased activity kept people busy, so no one paid attention to the man who drove by and took photos of the building.

He came back at other times, occasionally parking his van down the street where he could watch the building's entrance. He made notes of the time when people began arriving in the morning and when the last ones locked the building's doors and gate at night.

The process was the same in each case; a spry older man and a gimpy younger one arrived, opened the gate, then unlocked the personnel door into the main building. External lights were switched off and the building's main lights turned on. Other people began arriving around seven, and this influx tapered off by eight o'clock. Early arrivals wore ordinary workman's clothing and hard hats, while the last few wore office attire.

***

A sharp-eyed observer noticed that the younger man who

accompanied the oldster had a stiff knee. On two occasions, the young man remained in the building overnight. The lights were extinguished in the usual fashion and the gate locked, but a light remained on upstairs. The watcher concluded that the younger man had chosen to work late. He made it a point to arrive early the next morning, taking up a position where he could watch the gate. This time, only the elderly man arrived to open the building. He carried a paper bag that had the logo of a fast-food restaurant, located a few blocks from the building. That evening, the younger man left with the older one, locking the doors and the gate while the old man waited. Clearly, he'd stayed overnight in the building, probably upstairs in an office; this information was important to the man who watched.

Two months later, having observed the activities sporadically, the watcher was ready to act. The usual pair of men locked up and drove away together. The watcher remained in the back of his van, waiting for the traffic to decrease. He leaned back in his chair and catnapped.

The vibration from his cell phone woke him at 10:30 pm. The coffee in his thermos was still warm, no longer hot, but the man drank two cups anyway while he watched the building.

Finally deciding that there was no need to wait longer, the man opened the truck and pulled on a pair of surgeon's thin rubber gloves. He then picked up a battered toolbox and left the van.

Displaying no sign of anxiety or haste, he walked directly to the gate. There was enough light from a distant street light to clearly reveal the lock. It was a common design and the man had seen dozens like it before. He set the toolbox on the ground and reached into his pocket, but instead of a key, he took out a selection of thin lock picks. Opening the lock was the work of a few seconds. The man removed the lock and placed it, still open, inside the toolbox. Having someone come along and spot the open lock might cause a problem.

He carefully closed the gate behind him and walked up to the building's personnel door. This lock too presented no difficulties and it also went into the toolbox, the only difference being that he stuck a strip of tape to the building's lock so that he would know which one went on the door and which should be put back on the gate.

The lights inside were dim, but sufficient for his purpose. He looked around but saw nothing noteworthy. From appearances, it might be any machine shop and much of the space was empty. Pausing at the top of the stairs, he used his cell phone to take photos. They were blurry and dark, but they would have to do. Pocketing the phone, he entered the offices.

Forty-five minutes later, the man left the building and locked the door, making sure that he used the lock with the strip of tape. He removed and pocketed the tape, then walked to the gate. He locked this behind him and was soon back at his van. He started the engine and waited a moment to let the engine warm while he kept watch on the building. Fifteen minutes later he drove away. No security vehicle had arrived, so there was no alarm on the building.

The people running this place were amateurs, clearly. But in his business, amateurs were just the sort of people he preferred. More savvy people would have used better locks and probably equipped the building with internal alarms.

Other people in his profession had discovered such things to their sorrow. He himself had learned to be cautious, very cautious, the hard way. It was far better to spend time watching a potential target than to spend a greater amount of time locked in a barred room.

But the job wasn't finished, so caution was still his watchword.

He would return within a day or two to install a receiver/transmitter that would pick up the faint signals from the devices he'd left in the upstairs offices. He would then tie the R/T unit in with the recorder waiting in his apartment. But the hard part was done; from now on, he'd be getting all the information he needed with no need to reenter the building.

Chapter Ten

Morty was busy, working on one of the new machines. Frenchy watched him for a moment, then realized there was a problem. The old man looked positively gray, not only his hair but his face as well. How many hours was he working?

Frenchy realized it didn't really matter. They needed Morty alive, and healthy. Someone else might do as well, but again, they might not. He made a phone call, then called Morty off to the side.

"Morty, I'm going to take some of the load off your shoulders. You'll continue with the design and overall supervision, but I want Jim Sperry to take over production."

"Production, Frenchy?"

"Right, seeing to setup of the machines for now, but eventually overseeing production. You're trying to do too much, it's bad for your health and it's slowing things down. Jim can do the task-scheduling of people and machines and keep the work flowing. I'll also assign a clerk to make sure that supplies are available. You tell him what you want, he'll see you get it on time.

"Jim will do the same job when we begin assembly. You'll remain head of design, making sure it fits your vision, but he'll handle the management part. Think you can work with him?"

"I don't see why not," said Morty. "He's a good man. So sure, let him deal with scheduling. I've got all I can handle working with the engineering team. You want to talk to him, or do you want me to tell him what you have in mind?"

"I'll take care of it, Morty. You give us a design we can put into production, other people can take it from there."

***

During the following months, the improved system produced

several new models of impeller. Some went on the old Bedstead, but there were also three larger models, similar in design but with more robust components. Four of the intermediate-duty version were set aside; the engineers had decided the old platform had served its purpose. A newer, much upgraded platform would be built when there was time. And if the only time available was after normal working hours, so be it.

Neither Chuck nor Morty knew of what they had in mind, not uncommon. Engineers, given time, always have an idea how things could be done better. Some of the time, the ideas actually work.

Chuck now spent roughly half of his time working with a small team of programmers, rewriting the codes needed to operate the impellers. The new team had decided the instrumentation needed upgrading as well, especially instrumentation for the more-powerful impellers. In the afternoon, Chuck, and occasionally Morty, overhauled the basic Bedstead. The original parts of that relatively-crude device were soon replaced by redesigned and purpose-built components.

The latest iteration consisted of a stainless steel box frame, double-decked. Between the decks and taking up the rear half of the space were mounting slots for rechargeable batteries. The forward space housed two flight-control computers.

A pilot's seat was mounted near the front to balance the weight of the battery packs, and a panel-mounted joystick to the pilot's front controlled the computers.

While they worked in tandem for the most part, having two computers provided enough redundancy to make flying safer.

The original Bedstead's diesel generator had been removed; each new battery pack provided enough power for an hour-long test flight and the generator could be reinstalled later on if it was needed.

A perk of working in the production department was getting to fly the Bedstead.

The Bedstead, simply put, was fun to fly, and the people who discovered something that needed improving could immediately pass the information on to the people responsible for designing the fix. A signup sheet in the break room listed which engineer would fly next and which flight profile he was to follow. Flights had become so common that workers on the machines barely noticed when the nearly-silent Bedstead drifted overhead, flying a course around the warehouse.

Adventurous engineers sometimes flew the course backwards.

***

"Good morning, Richard. I don't understand why you want a personal meeting. I've done business with you folks for years and Gene has always handled my account before, so what has changed?"

"I know, Will, but to be honest, the government has tightened up on the kinds of loans we can issue. It's a question of collateral, you see. Gene didn't have enough information when your proposal came before the committee."

"I don't understand. I'm putting up some of my other investments as security for the loan. You're surely familiar with them, they're traded on the Big Board. Most of them, anyway. And the shares in foreign companies are also doing well. So what's the problem?"

Richard steepled his fingers and leaned back, chair squeaking.

"We're interested in knowing why you need the money, Will. You're asking us to underwrite a letter of credit that's considerably larger than anything you've needed before.

"It's possible that we might also want to invest in the same venture, which might reduce your exposure. While you have a knack of finding investments, they don't always pay off. I won't call you a plunger, Will, but some of your investments haven't been prudent."

"I've always paid off every dime I borrowed from you people!"

"You're not asking for dimes, Will. You're asking for millions of dollars, and you're not giving us much information."

"And I'm not going to. You stand to make money from interest on the loans, and that's as far as I'm willing to go."

"I… see." Richard leaned back and crossed his hands in his lap. "I rather thought that would be your answer, Will, but I confess I'm disappointed. You've been a good customer and I'm sorry to see you go.

"I'm sorry to inform you that we don't consider this proposal to be an acceptable risk, especially considering the volatility of stock markets worldwide. We believe that a correction is overdue, and when it happens, the stock you're putting up for collateral won't be enough to cover potential losses. The last correction was quite severe, as you'll remember."

Will nodded. He'd lost millions in the decline.

"The committee authorized me to approach you as I have, but since our meeting has not been productive I have no choice but to refuse the loan. The bank will not be funding your investment."

"Then I'll go somewhere else, and I'll be taking my accounts with me!"

"As I said, we're sorry to see you go, Will, but this is business. I doubt you'll find anyone else who'll be willing to underwrite your venture, whatever it is.

"Have you checked your credit rating recently?"

"No, I've had no need to. I have excellent credit, plenty of assets, no bankruptcies or foreclosures. Why would my credit rating be less than it was before?"

"I can't answer that, Will. Perhaps the rating companies can. But your credit rating is such that we'll need a lot more collateral than what you're offering before we provide you with the letter of credit you're seeking."

Will was seething when he left the bank.

During the course of the day he approached two other banks, and both refused to extend credit. He was much more thoughtful late that evening when he telephoned Frenchy.

***

Frenchy called for a ten o'clock meeting of the Board on Monday.

"Will?"

"Move we dispense reading of the minutes and approve the minutes of the previous meeting."

"All in favor? Passed, then. On to new business. Will?"

"It's about finance, people. Something is going on, something none of us counted on. I'm having trouble getting a loan! I counted on that to provide the funds I agreed to put in immediately.

"So far, the only finance offers I've gotten are from people I'm suspicious of."

"I've had problems too, Will. Who are you getting those offers from?"

"They're not from banks, I can tell you that. And I won't accept them because of the interest rate they offered."

"Too high, Will?"

"Too high, and for too short a time, Frenchy. I'm pretty sure organized crime is behind it. I refused, of course. I wonder how they knew I needed money?"

"Will, they almost certainly have someone at the banks where you applied for loans. They're crooks, but they're not stupid. They need banks too, and that means they pay off someone working at the bank. They may even control some of the bank executives, and I wouldn't be surprised to find they are part owners of the banks."

"I've never had this kind of trouble, Frenchy! I have to say, I didn't expect this."

"None of us did. I'm having trouble too, Will. Not so much from raising money, I had funds immediately available from sales of some of my stocks, but I haven't been able to find an acceptable site for the factory.

"The current shop, the one downstairs, is sufficient for design work and light production, but it's not big enough to modify aircraft or build a space-capable ship. Located where we are, we also can't keep snoopers away. All they'll need to do is park on the street and watch who comes and goes.

"That may be what's going on now, or maybe there's something more sophisticated involved, but in any case, security is a concern we've got to address.

"I expected to buy or lease a site, but every time I found one, someone else had been there before me. Whoever they were, they had taken out an option on the building. Which convinces me that someone is working against us. There's not that much demand for factory space in Amarillo or Lubbock, or wasn't. The other thing that bothers me is that they aren't buying, they're only taking out options.

"I'm thinking now that we need to consider building our own plant, probably on the New Mexico side of that land I own. The property extends across the state line, but since I've been getting opposition in Texas, anything we do there is likely to tip off whoever's working against us.

"Maybe the thing for me to do is act like I've given up looking for a site, so if there is some sort of organized effort against us in Texas whoever's doing it will back off. If there *is* someone in Texas trying to put a spoke in our wheel, he might not be paying attention to what happens in New Mexico. It's worth a try, I think.

"Anyway, that old ranch of mine barely makes enough to pay the taxes, so using it as a site for our factory makes sense. It's not much good for ranching, but that's been the only use for it up to now.

"We don't get a lot of rainfall up there, so the only water comes from wells and that source is going to play out eventually. There's water, but the fresh water is underlain by salt. We pump out the fresh water, the salt water migrates in. I talked to a hydrologist and he predicted that within twenty years, even cattle ranching would be gone. Whatever water that's left will be brackish at best. Meaning that the best use of that land is for our factory. There will be problems, but I don't see we have a choice.

"I'll work on getting a manufacturing and assembly building up as soon as possible, before any opposition can get organized on the New Mexico side. I'm not sure how long construction will take, but I'll start looking for a contractor tomorrow."

"What about the finance problems, Frenchy?" asked Morty.

"They're still there. I don't know what I'll be doing about those just yet. One idea that Jim and I have talked about is to start a marine operation using those heavier impellers. I'm still thinking it over, but if we had a working unit to show people, we might be able to generate some cash flow. That would certainly help.

"One possibility, I might have to spin the marine operation off and make it a separate company. This company would then begin operating as a holding company with the marine operation a separate company under the corporate umbrella."

"Table the discussion for now, Frenchy?"

"All in favor? So moved. Will, I'd like you and Chuck to remain behind. The rest of you, thanks for attending."

"Vote to adjourn?"

"All in favor? So moved." French rapped on the table with his knuckles. The other board members filed out.

"Let's walk down to the machine shop. I've got something to show you."

Chuck looked at him quizzically, but Frenchy's expression was bland.

***

The machine shop was noisy, and most of the men wore earmuff-style sound suppressors. Frenchy pulled Will and Chuck in close and spoke where no one else could hear what was said.

"We've either got a spy, maybe one of the employees, or someone is listening to what we discuss. That's the only explanation that makes sense.

"I don't think any of the engineers are doing it, but I'm having Panit's staff and your programmers checked out again, Chuck. We didn't do a real in-depth investigation before; we figured that if they'd been working for Panit, that was good enough. But maybe it wasn't."

"Most of the employees are people hired since we got the warehouse, Frenchy," said Chuck. "You think it might be one of the guys on the cleanup crew? We could change cleaning contractors if you think that would help."

"Maybe, but I doubt it. We're already shredding documents before we toss them; it's why I don't think the cleanup crew is involved.

"But what if someone has bugged this place? They could be listening to everything we say.

"Make no mistake, we're going to be stepping on a lot of toes when the impellers hit the market, so there's motive for any number of people to hamper our efforts. We're talking millions, maybe billions of dollars eventually.

"Factories that make jet engines or rockets will go the way of the people that made Conestoga wagons. If their factories don't close, they'll have to do a lot of expensive retooling and just maybe pay license fees to us.

"When that much money's at stake, people will stop at nothing. We probably made a mistake, not thinking about how much pressure our work would put on conventional systems, but it's not too late. We haven't done anything yet to really threaten them, and the only ones who know our eventual plans are part of management. We've all got far too much to lose to be selling the company out.

"Here's what I think we should do. We keep on working here in the shop, but we don't discuss anything upstairs about future plans.

"No more board meetings in the building. We don't really need to hold meetings anyway, and if something comes up that requires a full meeting of the board, I'll rent office space. If you need to talk to your people about anything sensitive, write it down, show it to whoever needs to know, then shred the paper.

"Get with your supervisory people and tell them why we're making the change, but do it quietly. Will, you let the other investors know what's going on," said Frenchy. "And stick around for a moment. I've got something else for you."

Chuck nodded and left. Will remained behind, still thinking about what Frenchy had said and wondering what else was going on.

"Will, we've got to scale back. Morty won't be happy, but he'll just have to live with it. We've got maybe two months of operating funds remaining, and if we don't get more financing between now and then, we're bankrupt.

"That gives us a deadline. We've got to come up with more money within that time frame, a lot more, or we're going to have to lay off some of our people.

The marine option will help if it works out, but we need money now. You get with the other investors, see how much they can raise within the next two months. I was going to handle that, but you can do it just as well as I can and I'm going to be busy arranging for the new building. I'll also start assembling a team to set up the marine demonstrator.

"As for me, I've got that Gulfstream II I can do without. I doubt I'll be doing a lot of traveling for a while and I can rent or borrow a plane if I have to. I'll be putting my boat up for sale too, maybe the house in Florida. All in all, that should bring in at least twenty million."

"You're putting up the boat? Frenchy, you love that oversized tub!"

"I can always get another yacht. If this works the way we expect it to, I can buy the *Queen Mary*.

"Anyway, I won't be doing any cruising for the foreseeable future. I should be able to raise at least twenty million by selling stuff, everything but the art collection. If I put *that* up for sale, the sharks will start circling. They'd know I'm desperate for money."

Will was silent for a moment. "I've got that Picasso. I bought it as an investment and people know I'm not fond of the thing. I can put that one up for auction without it raising eyebrows. With luck, it'll bring upwards of fifty million."

Frenchy nodded. "Get with the other investors and see how much they can raise. Explain what's going on and why we need a sudden infusion of cash. That building, the roads to service it, putting in parking, a reliable water and sewage plant... Let's keep things as quiet as possible for as long as we can, and rein in Morty and Chuck to keep expenses down.

"Anyway, we're going to have to spend a lot more up-front than I intended and we're not going to get the money from the finance industry.

"I'll dig out that survey from when I bought the ranch and have someone look at it. I've got an idea where I'd like to put the new plant if the land is suitable, and this time, we can design adequate security in from the beginning. As for roads, there's already a farm road going past my property and maybe the county will improve it. We'll also need our own railway spur eventually, but that can wait.

"I'm going to look for a contractor and show him what I've got in mind. I'll probably need an architect, too. Maybe Lina can recommend someone; she's in her final year, one more semester to get her MS in architecture at UNM. I haven't seen her for a couple of months, so I'll take her out to dinner and pick her brain."

"She might be able to design the building herself, Frenchy."

"She's not ready to take the professional licensing exam and I don't think we can take a chance, even with something simple, but she might know someone she'd be willing to work with. And just maybe, that someone who's got a license will allow her to help with the design. It would be good professional experience for her."

"Your daughter is smart as well as good looking, Frenchy. You should be proud of her."

"I am, Will. She's got good judgment too, better than I had when I was her age."

"Wasn't that when you met your..."

Will was cut off in mid-sentence.

"Let's let that particular dog keep sleeping, Will," said Frenchy.

***

Frenchy made an appointment with a lawyer he'd used before and began his search for a contractor in an unusual place.

"I'm starting up a new venture in eastern New Mexico, Bud. I expect to start fairly small and grow as needed. What can you tell me?"

"What kind of venture, Frenchy?" asked Bud.

"It's confidential, of course, but I can tell you we'll be involved in manufacturing."

"That might work out," Bud said. "The state's already got a mix of industries, agriculture of course, but mining and petroleum too. Lots of that in eastern New Mexico.

"There's the movie industry too, and then there's Intel to provide a high-tech base. I think there was a light airplane manufacturer in Albuquerque, but as I recall, that operation didn't work out. He was making business jets, good model reportedly, but he didn't have the necessary funding. Last I heard, he sold out to someone with deeper pockets. There's also a company out east of Albuquerque that's working on experimental aircraft, maybe drones.

And of course, there's UNM and Eastern New Mexico University. That one's over near where you mentioned. If you're doing research, there are the two national labs, Sandia and Los Alamos. Got a specific location in mind?"

"I own several sections of land north of Clovis," said Frenchy. "They're not profitable at the moment, barely covering expenses and taxes, so I thought of building the plant there."

"No other industry involved on your property?"

Frenchy shook his head. "Cattle raising. I've got a foreman that runs the place. He raises calves and holds them until they're breeding age. From there they go to dairies. As I said, it's not really profitable. At most, after expenses are taken out, there's just enough left to pay the taxes, and meantime the freshwater table is being depleted faster than it can recharge. What with the drought, groundwater is not seeping in fast enough to replace what's being pumped out.

"The cattle feeding operation will play out as soon as expenses increase. I won't mind shutting it down, but I hope I can find jobs for the foreman and my other employees. They've been with me since I bought the place and I hate the idea of just laying them off."

"I see. You're talking about the cheese industry, aren't you?"

"Right. He's raising Holsteins, milk cows. We supply the dairy farmers, they supply milk to the cheese factory."

"I'll need to research matters and find a local lawyer to work with, someone familiar with local provisions. He'll know the people to contact. Right off hand I can think of a few issues."

"Go to it, then. You mentioned that someone was building airplanes?"

"Right, it's not a big industry, but in addition to that light plane manufacturer, there's a boneyard operation. There's an old Air Force base near the town that has the necessary runway capacity, which made it cheap locate there. It's the end of the line for a lot of Boeing's jumbos; when a 747 reaches the end of its service life, it's flown in for salvage. The airframes have too many miles on them, but engines, seats, landing gear, and things like that can still be used.

"Anyway, the plane flies in, parts get stripped off by certified airframe mechanics, and the usable ones are shipped out to whoever needs them. The body is then crushed and the aluminum recycled."

"Interesting. Certified airframe and aviation mechanics do the disassembly, you say?"

"Right, there's also an aviation program at Eastern NM University. I don't know the details. There might be other schools too, but the important thing is that there's a ready supply of trained people available. You plan on manufacturing airplanes, Frenchy?"

"It's an option, but keep it quiet for now. We'll go public in due time."

"You sure you don't want to put your assembly plant near Roswell? It might be cheaper in the long run."

"Maybe, but I already own the land, so that cuts down on my initial investment. It also turns something that's not profitable into a productive asset."

"Even so, it won't be cheap. I knew you had money, Frenchy, but not this much. Aviation manufacturing costs a bundle."

"I've got enough to start small and grow, Bud. I expect civil aviation is due for a major increase over the next few years."

"You did hear what I said about that fellow that was underfunded, didn't you? He ended up selling out."

"I heard you. A lot of business is about timing. He might have misjudged his market. Maybe I can do a little better than he did."

"I'll get started, then. You know this is going to take time, don't you?"

"How much time?"

"That depends on how much money you've got and how many corners you're willing to cut."

"You know this is going to boost the state economy, don't you? Won't people be excited about that?"

"I expect the state government will be. No secret, the governor thinks she'd make a good vice president, maybe even president, so I doubt we'll have problems at the state level. As for local politicians, they're probably more interested in how many of their relatives you're hiring. And they might want more than that."

"You're talking bribes?"

"That's a dirty word in politics, Frenchy, but it's not unheard of. At the least, they'll want in on subcontracts, services, any number of things."

"Clean graft, in other words."

Bud looked at Frenchy and said nothing.

"I don't want this coming back to bite my ass later on, Bud."

"I understand, Frenchy. I'll get started this afternoon. There's a guy in Clovis named Roger. I'll give him a call and if he's too busy, he'll know someone else I can work with."

***

The sun was sinking beyond the clubhouse as the two men walked away from the 18th hole.

"Thanks for the invitation, Mister Gold. I don't often get the chance to play this course."

"I wasn't aware that you were a member, Walter."

"I'm not."

"But you've been here before? That means you were a guest. How often, Walter?

"Time or two." Walter smiled at his companion.

"I had you checked out, Walter."

"I'm not surprised. My reputation is my stock in trade."

"It's curious that your reputation only goes back about ten years. Before that, I couldn't confirm anything about you." The man known as 'Mister Gold' looked inquiringly at Walter, who remained silent. The slight crinkling of the skin by his eyes might have shown amusement, but if so it didn't reach his lips. They remained as they'd been, no smile, no frown. Walter rarely showed emotion.

"You'll have figured out by now that I have a problem. I'm hoping you can help me with it."

"People don't call me to get together for a round of golf, Mister Gold. I figured you'd get around to telling me about your problem, and if you didn't, well, I enjoyed taking your money on the course."

"That you did. Anyway, there's a man. His activities appear likely to affect my business interests. You were recommended to me as a man who could make difficult people see reason."

"I've done that, yes. You understand I'm choosy about which jobs I take, and I don't work cheap."

"I didn't expect you would. I've got a photo I'd like to show you. It's in the locker room."

"I'll look at it. You want me to influence that man, I'll decide how to go about it and let you know my price. Non-negotiable, of course."

"Of course."

"You understand that I'm the one who decides what is likely to make your problem go away, don't you?"

"I wouldn't have it any other way, Walter. I hire experts in any number of fields and I expect them to produce results without close supervision."

"Good. I think we understand each other."

***

Albuquerque's weather was pleasant, warmer than usual. A week had passed since the meeting on the golf course.

The street light changed and two young women joined a dozen people crossing Central Street. Some turned right, away from the crowd, while others joined the line of people waiting to place their orders in the Frontier Restaurant.

The Frontier had been around for a long time. Parking was limited, but this wasn't a problem; the lunch crowd consisted mostly of students from the University of New Mexico, and they walked to the restaurant. The sprawling campus occupied several blocks across Central from the Frontier, meaning that students often ate there.

The women chatted while they waited in line.

Neither paid attention to the Jeep that was parked half a block west of the Frontier on Central.

Walter added coins to the parking meter. He expected to be here for some time, and there was no reason to risk a parking ticket.

Chapter Eleven

Four days later, Frenchy's lawyer faxed him a list of people. John, the general contractor, had his office in Clovis, but his activities were widespread.

"Glad to meet you, Frenchy. What did you have in mind?"

"I'm building a factory on my property. I expect to grow as the business develops, so I'll want room to expand. I've also got some special design requirements, so keep that in mind when you come up with a proposal. I'll tell you about that when we visit the site."

"What facilities do you already have? Are you repurposing a previously used location, or starting from scratch?"

"It's a new site. The only thing that's there right now is a road. It was blacktopped sometime in the past, but it's going to need repair."

John made a note on a pad of yellow paper. "I don't do roads. I'll hire a sub with a professional crew to do that. You understand, road crews use different equipment and their people have different skills? My crew will put up your building, but I'll be hiring subs for any other jobs that are required. I'll include their bids with mine and give you an overall price. I'll serve as the general contractor, so you'll deal with me and I'll work with the subs."

"I expected that. My property runs alongside a state highway but I don't want to put the plant there, so we're talking half a mile to a mile from the highway to reach my site."

"Understood. What condition is the ground in? Is it level, what kind of drainage are we looking at, and have you looked into permits yet?"

"I was hoping you could take care of the details."

"I can, and actually it's better if I do. When can I get access to the site?"

"Why don't we schedule a time and go out together?"

"Not today. I've got other meetings that I can't skip, but how about tomorrow at 10 o'clock?"

"Works for me. I'll be here."

***

John brought along an assistant, who brought a digital camera and surveyor's instruments. They walked the property, John listening to Frenchy's ideas, the assistant taking photos, measuring slope and distances, and noting down information about the soil type. Two hours later, the small party headed back to Clovis.

"I'll need some time to work on this. How about I keep you advised of my progress and what we're looking at in terms of a completion date? As soon as I've got firm data to work with, I'll draw up a contract and we can discuss pricing. When the contract's signed, I'll need an initial payment. Since you own the property, I'm willing to wait for earnest money until we settle on what work is to be done."

"Sounds fair. You know what I've got in mind. As for the septic system and wells you mentioned, my ranch foreman has someone who'll do that. It's a man he's used before."

"That won't work, not for the kind of commercial setup you want. A ranch, maybe, but not a factory. You'll need a treatment plant for the well water and a sewage treatment plant for discharged water. The well water is probably good, most of the wells out this way are, but in New Mexico it pays to not take chances. Even if there's no arsenic, radon, or sulfur, the water will almost certainly contain calcium and iron. Hard water will eventually damage your plumbing, so it's actually more cost-effective to put in a treatment plant and get that stuff out before the water reaches the building. The facilities won't need to be big, but they'll have to treat all the water supplied to and discharged from your building. If you intend to landscape your factory, you can use untreated well water or treated sewage for watering plants. You mentioned expanding later on, so the system will have to be designed with that in mind. It will need to be capable of expansion, in other words."

"I hoped I wouldn't have to go that far. Funds are limited right now. I expect additional financing later on, but that's then, not now."

"The county people won't approve your plans unless they meet code, and that includes electrical, water, and sewage service. I'll put it into an appendix and you can approve that separately, but you'll need to come up with a solution before I begin construction. Depending on how many workers you intend to hire, you might get away with using portable toilets as a temporary solution. But that can get expensive in a hurry, so the sooner you get permanent systems on-line, the better.

"I didn't see any sign of a power line. The nearest source is probably twenty miles from your site, so we need to talk about that too. My workers will need power on site when we begin putting up the building, so if you don't have commercial power I'll need to rent generators."

"Put that on the back burner too. I hope to have my own generators available by the time you begin working. One of my associates says they're available cheap."

"Cheap can be a problem. You mentioned you were short on money, so let's clear that up right now. You can have the project done fast or you can have it cheap, but you can't have both. Your building, probably more than one based on what you're telling me, is not just four walls and a roof. The foundation comes first, and it has to reflect the work load you anticipate. Plumbing and electrical service have to be designed in from the beginning. Plumbing is more than toilets and drinking water, you've also got to have automatic fire extinguishers and fire hose outlets. There's a lot of other stuff too, stuff professionals keep up with so customers don't have to. I work with an architect; he has a library of standard plans that we modify, based on customer needs. It's faster than designing everything from scratch.

"I would normally schedule a crew, say the road crew, to work until the job is finished, then move another crew in. But if you can come up with the money, I can run multiple crews. A crew can build roads while another crew puts up the perimeter fence, and my people can be building footings while all that is going on. As soon as the footings are ready, I'll order concrete. There are companies in Clovis and Roswell, so I'll shop around.

"The good news is that the land is level and firm enough to support heavy equipment, so as soon as you approve the plans I'll get bids from the subcontractors.

"The up-front issue is money, since you're self-financing the project. In order for me to run multiple crews, the initial payment has to be enough for me to pay my subs. Think of it this way, you're essentially hiring more than one company, my company, the architect's, the subcontractors, and all of us need to be paid. We need up-front money to buy supplies and hire people, and I have to provide that from what you pay me. There will be additional draws as completion points are met, and I'll need money at each stage before I can move on. Even if there are hold-backs to ensure quality, the money will have to be available to put in escrow. The contract will include payment schedules, and meeting those is your responsibility. So long as the money's there when it's due, the rest is my responsibility. Fair enough?"

"Fair enough. We've got a deal."

***

Frenchy's home sold within a month and Will auctioned off his Picasso. Other investors put in additional money. The total was more than Frenchy expected, so he called John and approved using multiple crews. The first crews showed up the following Monday.

The need for immediate electrical power caused the first contract modification. Frenchy approved adding a power house. Under the modified plan, the power house would be completed first, then generators and the main electrical distribution box would be installed as soon as they were available. John rented portable generators for the building crews as an interim measure. Three large fuel tanks were installed on concrete pads near the power building. This area had its own branch road for fuel deliveries.

The second building added was a hangar, located several hundred yards away from the rest of the complex. Frenchy realized that locking their only impeller-equipped craft in the truck's cargo box was not secure enough. The Bedstead would go in the hangar as soon as it was ready. In the meantime, someone would stay in the warehouse each night. Instead of relying on the building's external locks, the watchman secured the doors from the inside. Most often, the watchman was Chuck or his assistant Mel; the other employees had families who expected them home at night. Chuck had not yet met anyone he wanted to settle down with, and Mel was divorced. An upstairs room was converted to a temporary bedroom by adding a bunk, a refrigerator, microwave, and a small television.

***

The factory site was transformed during the next three months. The road was repaired, concrete foundations poured, parking areas graded flat, and fences built. The water treatment plants were finished, then work on the first three buildings began.

The ranch's feeder operation had begun shutting down. As calves were sold to the dairies, no new ones were bought. This freed up employees, but they weren't laid off. The foreman assigned excess people to ride the range near the factory site. It was simple enough; load two horses in the trailer, add a bale of hay and a bag of grain in the front compartment, then send a rider to a line shack that was located five miles from the new plant. A relief rider went out every three days to replace the man at the line shack. The horsemen soon became a familiar site around the construction zone. The construction workers saw them, and gossiped. In the way of things, the rumors spread and the idly curious stayed away.

Wells were drilled and pumps installed early in the preparation phase. The tanker trucks would need water to sprinkle around the site as well as for wetting the poured concrete to prevent cracking. Sprinkling reduced the amount of dust in the air. Water was furnished to tanker trucks by an overhead pipe; a truck pulled in, the driver opened the tank's top hatch, filled the tank, then drove away.

The remaining output from the pumps was sent to the treatment plant, outside the fence in its own small building. From there it was piped to the rest of the complex. Waste water drained away to the sewage plant, then the treated water was injected via wells back into the ground. This minimized the factory's impact on scarce ground water. Other businesses had pioneered the approach, so county officials soon approved the system for Frenchy's factory. Treated and dried sludge from the sewage plant would eventually be distributed around the ranch, enriching the poor soil. Unlike city sludge, this would contain no contaminating heavy metals.

The power house soon held five large diesel generators. FEMA had bought them new, used them to power the trailer parks housing victims of Hurricane Katrina, then warehoused the units. The generators were eventually declared surplus and listed for disposal. Frenchy's purchasing agent bid on the lot, and soon the generators were on their way to New Mexico.

Morty found they required little more than inspecting the engines for leaks, changing filters, oil, and topping off the radiator coolant, then function-testing the generators. Each was connected to a load bank consisting of huge resistor coils and cooling fans, then run for an hour at their rated 150kw capacity. Inspections finished, the generators were emplaced in the power building.

Fuel was supplied to the power building via an underground pipe from the elevated fuel tanks that led to a distribution manifold. From there, it went directly to the generators. The arrangement was flexible; a generator could be shut down for maintenance while others continued providing power to the factory campus. The system prevented electrical power interruptions, important because the buildings were all-electric, including the heating system.

***

The hangar had a rear personnel door facing the other buildings and a second one alongside the garage-style rollup door. The latter pair faced the open prairie, meaning that no one working on the factory building ever got a look inside the hangar. A single-lane dirt road led from the main complex. Dust had drifted over the tracks left by the construction equipment.

The apparently-unused building attracted no attention, and the separate chain-link fence isolating it from the main campus discouraged snooping. A single locked gate, on the side of the fence facing the main complex, boasted a large No Admittance sign.

Inside the hangar, most of the space consisted of a large open bay. The Bedstead and the larger unit planned as its replacement could easily fit inside the bay. Separate rooms off the main bay contained a small workshop, a break room with such creature comforts as were available, and a bathroom. The break room had a tiny kitchen, a pair of tables with four chairs each, and two convertible couches. The bathroom contained a toilet, lavatory, and shower.

Frenchy telephoned Chuck as soon as he'd inspected the hangar building and accepted it. That night, Chuck and Mel remained at the warehouse when the others went home. Just before midnight, Chuck drove the truck outside and waited while Mel locked the rear door and the gate. A few minutes later, they left on their way to the new factory.

Chuck drove into Tucumcari that afternoon, fueled the truck, then parked. He wanted to arrive on-site after the construction people had gone. Mel snoozed on the front seat and Chuck slept in the back, stretched out on the rear deck of the Bedstead. Four hours later they got coffee and sandwiches at the truck stop, then headed for the factory site.

They arrived shortly after midnight. After parking the truck on the county road, Chuck powered up the Bedstead. Mel, seated on the rear deck, held on to the pilot's seat during the short trip to the hangar. Chuck kept the craft at a hover while Mel unlocked the personnel entry and opened the rollup door. He climbed back on and Chuck flew him back to the truck. Mel drove the truck away as Chuck eased the Bedstead into the hangar, its new home. He closed and locked the rollup door, then bedded down on one of the convertible couches.

Mel refueled the truck after reaching Tucumcari, then slept the rest of the night. Next morning he drove to the warehouse, parked the truck inside, then caught a ride back to the factory with Morty.

***

Chuck and Mel flew the Bedstead at night, after the construction people had gone. During the day, they worked in the hangar, building a much larger frame. This second unit would be a supplement to the Bedstead. A heavier duty machine, it would have space for four of the big battery packs, although the number installed would depend on how much power was needed for a flight. This unit, Bedstead II officially, 'California King' unofficially, would be large enough to test the aviation impellers when they became available.

The aviation model impellers would at some point be added to an airplane as an auxiliary propulsion system. After testing and certification, this would become the first aircraft licensed to use S-T Impellers for propulsion. Impeller-only aircraft systems would have to wait; the FAA would want a considerable amount of usage data before they'd approve such a radical idea.

Meanwhile, Morty intended to have a space-capable craft ready even while aircraft testing was underway. He wanted enough of a head start before the secret leaked that it would take competitors years to catch up, even if they figured out how the impellers worked.

***

Standard construction lights illuminated the main complex each night after sunset, although the crews had gone by that time. The lights were for the benefit of the on-site security force. Two operators also remained on site, taking turns to run the power plant. One generator was always kept running to supply power to the security lighting and the hangar building, while others could be added to the grid as necessary. The operators lived comfortably in one of two large trailers that had been brought to the site. Chuck and Mel remained in the hangar building during the week, and one occupied the second trailer on weekends while the other took some time off. More-permanent housing would become available after the complex was finished.

***

The factory building was finally ready for use, although work continued.

Chuck went back to the old warehouse building to take charge of moving the equipment to the new location. The operation took place after dark, in the hope that any watcher wouldn't realize it was happening until the convoy had gone.

Security was tighter than usual. Cars sat silent and unmoving at each end of the street that fronted the property, while another waited in the alley behind the warehouse fence.

Inside the building the electric forklift whirred, loading equipment. The first truck pulled away from the old warehouse building after midnight and waited in the street. Another truck was waiting; it moved into position as soon as the first had gone, backing up until the trailer's rear hatch was nestled within inches of the factory's rollup door. The building was lighted, though not as brightly as when the shop equipment had been in use.

The big forklift spun around and trundled to the first piece of equipment, already strapped on dunnage to make handling easier. The forklift driver slipped the forks into gaps and lifted, then transported the big lathe to the truck's open rear door.

As soon as the forklift had lowered the machine and backed away, two men used pallet jacks to lift it and move it to the front of the semitrailer. By the time they finished strapping the lathe in place, the forklift was back, this time with a milling machine.

The work continued until the trailer was loaded, then its rollup door was lowered and secured. A lead seal went into place beside the locks used to secure the two sides of the door and a crimping tool locked the seal in place. It wouldn't secure the door, but it would show whether any attempt had been made to access the cargo before the tractor-trailer rig reached its destination in northeastern New Mexico.

Grinders, 3-D printer/fabricators, and the rest of the equipment went into trailers. The leased forklift was left behind for the time being. Chuck supervised locking the building, leaving on the low lighting that was normal when the crew left for the day. The security vehicles joined the waiting convoy, one car in front, the other vehicles following behind.

Chuck took a last look around the deserted warehouse, then

climbed into the right front seat of the lead vehicle. The small convoy pulled away shortly before sunrise.

***

Two men were looking at the factory complex that now occupied what had been scrubby rangeland only a few short months before. "It's big, I'll say that. Somehow, Frenchy, after all the talking you did, I expected it would take longer."

"It cost me more than I wanted to spend, Morty, but you'd be surprised how greasing a few palms can speed things up. Even so, the water system still isn't quite right. The contractor thinks sand has moved in and plugged the holes in the lower well casing. I've got crews drilling additional wells, but getting the permits for those was expensive. I ended up hiring a guy who's the brother in law of a county commissioner. The man who put in the water reclamation system is related to another commissioner and also to one of the bigwigs in the county road department. I figure at least ten percent of the money went into the pockets of county officials."

"Frenchy, you didn't do that yourself, did you?"

"Oh, hell, no, Morty. I hired a lawyer, and his law firm knew someone who knew the right palms to grease. I even had to pay for a publicity company to come up with reasons why the county commission should fast-track everything. Maybe it was worth it. I expect we could have gotten everything done without the bribes...make that campaign contributions...but it would have taken at least a year longer, probably twice that long. But the buildings are finished, most of them. We can add other space by extending the factory building as needed. The new power lines from the grid won't be in place for six months, so we'll make do with generators until we get commercial power. I'm also thinking about putting in our own green-power plant. There's plenty of room on the ranch, so I checked out the costs. I could start with a photovoltaic system and maybe one or two wind turbines, plenty for powering the factory site, and later on I could expand and sell excess power to the grid using that line the power company is putting in.

"The PV plant won't come on line for about a year and a half and getting wind turbines up and running will likely take even longer. We'll start by operating on our own diesel power, switch to commercial power when it's available, then go to our own green system later on. We'll use commercial power as first backup and the generators as emergency backup, or maybe use them to power one of the marine systems when it's built."

"Sounds like you've thought of everything, Frenchy."

"Not me. The contractor did most of it, after I told him what we needed. I thought the increased security we'd gain from moving faster was important enough to spend the money. Speaking of spending money, it's important that we begin manufacturing impellers just as soon as possible. Time is not on our side."

"About security, Frenchy; the more people we hire, the greater the chance there will be a leak."

"I learned my lesson at the old factory, Morty. You've seen the fence around the campus, and that's only part of the story. Most of the employees won't have any idea of what we're doing. Later on, when we begin modifying aircraft with impeller systems, they'll know, but they still won't know *how* the impellers work. Only the engineers on your crew will know that, and they have stock in the company as an incentive to keep their mouths shut. As for snoopers, I've got ranch people on horseback patrolling outside the fence, the security company has people making irregular foot patrols on that dirt road around the site, and the gate house is manned. The guards can add barriers on the road if needed to keep people from entering the site. They work rotating shifts, with two constantly on duty. Others can be called in when needed."

"Where did you find all these people, Frenchy?"

"I didn't, I hired a security company. They usually work for the government, but that's on hold for now. They're happy to work for private companies. Some of the men working here were in the Middle East before they got this assignment. The guards secure the factory campus, the company runs the overall operation, and I check often enough to make sure they do."

"Sounds good, Frenchy. When does the convoy get here?"

"Probably about four this afternoon, Morty. Chuck will get them here as soon as possible. Bolting down the equipment, hooking up power, leveling and making sure everything is ready, that's going to take a few more days. I expect we'll be in limited operation by next Monday."

"Frenchy, you've done wonders. I didn't really believe we'd start turning out impellers this quick."

"You too, Morty. You've done wonders yourself, working with the engineering staff. Most of them are in awe of you, you know."

"Huh. Well, I'm in awe of Nikola Tesla. Now *there* was a smart man!"

***

A police cruiser arrived at the scene within five minutes of the call to 9-1-1. The driver reported their location at the scene, then followed his partner. An ambulance pulled up less than a minute later and was directed to where the victim lay. Other patrol vehicles followed, including an Albuquerque Fire Department ambulance with one of the city's on-duty paramedic teams.

Officers strung crime scene tape around the area while others took charge of traffic control and waited for the detective team to arrive. A sheriff's department vehicle and a state police car also joined the force, followed ten minutes later by a campus police car. The area was lit by the blue and red flashing lights from the emergency vehicles. Finally, one of the paramedics sought out the Albuquerque PD lieutenant who'd arrived to take charge of the crime scene.

"Another one, lieutenant. Another student, but this one's different. I don't think it happened here."

"Wait one." The lieutenant called to a sergeant, who came over and joined the conversation. "Doc thinks this one was a drop-off.

"Take a couple of officers and see if you can find tracks. Forensics will be here soon, so if you find tire tracks or anything else of interest have their investigators make a cast. Get me lots of photos and keep in mind that I've had a hard day already. Find me something nice, maybe the perp's driver's license."

"Lieutenant, you've been out in the sun too long. But I'll find anything there is to find. What do we do about that TV crew?"

"Usual drill. No comment, investigation is proceeding, results are expected. Pass that on to the public affairs officer, let him brief the press. He's done it before, he knows what to say."

"Yeah, the talking heads always ask the same questions, he gives them the same answers, and the civilians never seem to notice."

"I guess they don't think too much about it. What's the vic's status, doc?"

"Alive. Not badly injured, a little disoriented. Maybe some kind of drug. I'll pass it on to the hospital and they can do a blood test as well as do a rape kit collection for body fluids or hair, anything like that."

"Status of the vic's fingernails?"

"We'll find out. I asked permission and bagged her hands, so if there's anything there we'll find it when we get to the hospital. One broken fingernail, right hand, so maybe we'll get lucky."

"Get lucky for me, Doc. The public is gonna be on the mayor's case, he's gonna ream the chief, and I'll catch what rolls downhill. How many student rapes does this make?"

"Jeez, lieutenant, I don't remember for sure. I worked two others, one in March and the other one last... October, I think it was. But I know there have been several. Maybe ten in the last year?

"Did you hear what that NRA guy said? That every female student on campus should be automatically licensed to carry concealed?"

"Shit. That's all we need, Dodge fucking city.

"Doc, get the vic out of here before I break down and start weeping."

Chapter Twelve

The line of dust-covered trucks rolled through the gate. The drivers were tired, and it showed.

Chuck dismounted and walked ahead to where Frenchy waited.

"I think we should wait until morning to offload. These guys are beat and they need to be fed. They can bunk down in their cabs for the night. Let's just park the trucks inside and turn everything over to security until tomorrow."

"Works for me, Chuck. You know we don't really have a kitchen crew, don't you? The only thing we've got is microwave ovens and MRE's."

"I remembered. I didn't want to stop for dinner, so I had the trailing security Suburban load up on pizza as we passed through Roswell. They got a few cases of beer too. These guys have earned it."

"Sounds good. Warm the pizzas and pass out the beer, we'll unload tomorrow."

Chuck turned and signaled down the line. Miming chugging a drink, he waited for acknowledgement.

"They'll pass the word on by radio. We've been operating under radio silence to keep the chatter down. I didn't want to take a chance that a spy would realize I was gone."

"Smart, Chuck. Wait one..." Frenchy glanced at his ringing cell phone and looked surprised. "Frenchy here. What can I do for you?"

The distant voice talked for at least a minute before Frenchy said, "Oh, shit. Is she badly injured?" Another pause followed. "I'll get there as soon as I can. Let her know, please." The conversation continued, then Frenchy responded with "Thank you," and terminated the conversation. The pain on his face was obvious.

"Frenchy, what's wrong?"

"It's Lina. Chuck, I've got to get to Albuquerque. I'll call for a helicopter to pick me up here..."

Chuck interrupted. "Don't do that. I'll fly you to Clovis and you can catch a plane there for Albuquerque. You don't want a pilot to see all these trucks and wonder what's going on."

"You're right, but how...you mean the Bedstead? I've only flown it a couple of times, and never at night."

"I'll fly it. Get your jacket and meet me at the hangar building. Don't say anything to any of the drivers. Call that lawyer in Clovis and have him lay on a plane for you. I think they have jets there, but even if they don't it won't take you long to reach Albuquerque. He can also arrange for a car to meet you, and you'll be there in three or four hours. This is an emergency, right?"

Frenchy nodded and said, "Can we chance using the Bedstead, Chuck?"

"It'll be tight, getting there and back, but I can do it. I'll be ready when you get to the hangar building." Chuck turned and walked away as Frenchy began punching numbers into his phone.

Chuck tapped the combination into the lock and headed inside the hangar. Mel was drinking a cup of coffee in the break room when Chuck walked in.

"Status on the Bedstead's batteries, Mel?"

"Two fully charged batteries installed, Chuck. I swapped the depleted ones out last night after my last flight. Why?"

"I'll be taking the Bedstead out as soon as my passenger gets here. We'll need straps and a couple of blankets from the break room. He'll sit on the blankets and the straps are to make sure he doesn't fall off. He'll need a helmet too, so can I borrow your bucket?"

"Sure, Chuck. Who's going?"

"Frenchy. As soon as he gets here, you strap him in and I'll roll up the door."

"Where are you going?"

"Clovis, it's the closest airport. I need to look at a map."

"Use the computer, it's got an app. You going to print out a map?"

"I guess so. I'll use the GPS to lay out the course, but as long as I steer south-southeast, that will get me close enough to see the town's lights. I'll use Ned Houk Park, it's a big dark area that's just off the highway, as my final checkpoint when I reach Clovis. The Airport is almost a straight line from here if I cross over Ned Houk."

"Got it. You know you're stretching the range, don't you?"

"I figure I'll have maybe a ten percent charge remaining after I get back here, enough to land in the hangar. If I don't pick up headwinds, I should be OK. You stay close to the radio and if it looks like I'm not going to make it, I'll give you a call and you can meet me with the van."

"You've been on the road all day, Chuck; you've got to be tired. You going to be all right?"

"Yeah, this is not the first all-nighter I've pulled. I'd let you fly, but I've had more stick time using the night vision glasses."

"I suppose you're right, but if you need me, I'm only a couple of hours away in the truck. Too bad the King isn't ready."

"Yeah. We'll have to remember to add mounts for rear seats in case we have to haul passengers."

"Shouldn't be a problem. For that matter, I'll bet we could mount a seat and separate windscreen on the Bedstead."

***

Morty walked up to the gate entrance and spoke to the senior guard. "How long have the trucks been here?"

"Let me check the visitor log." The man clicked the mouse, waking the computer from sleep mode. He glanced at the entry and did a quick calculation in his head. "About four hours. Chuck and Frenchy talked about it, and Chuck told the crew to bag out after they ate. They're sleeping in their trucks."

"Where can I find Chuck and Frenchy?"

"No idea. I haven't seen them since the trucks pulled in. Maybe they're in the main building."

"I just came from there and there's no sign of them. I also checked the power building and the duty operator hadn't seen them."

"Want me to try the radios?" At Morty's nod, the man thumbed the transmit button.

"All units: anyone seen the director or Chuck?" He released the button and waited for a reply. He listened to the earbud for a minute, then looked up at Morty. "No one's seen them recently, but they didn't go out the gate. They have to be here somewhere."

Morty mulled that over. Maybe they were in the hangar. The security team wouldn't know what went on in there, and if they were asleep they might not be answering the radio.

"I want to get the trucks unloaded before daylight if possible. I don't want someone to fly over and see all those trucks parked in a place that's not officially being used yet. Find Chuck's deputy, the guy who helped control the convoy, and ask him to roust the drivers; I'll authorize a bonus if they can get the trucks unloaded and out of here before daylight."

"I'll send one of the guys. If you're paying, they'll be willing to lose some sleep. Four hours is long enough anyway."

"I appreciate the help. The locations inside the main building are chalked in place, so if the crews can drop off the equipment where it's supposed to go, that will be helpful."

"I'll see to it, Morty. Where do I find you if I need to ask something?"

"I'll be around. I'll also have my radio on." Morty patted the holstered low-powered radio he used for local communication within the site. The guard nodded and beckoned to one of the off-duty gate guards.

Morty left the building and walked a circuitous route to the hangar. Glancing around, he saw no one who might be interested in his activities. He punched in the code and opened the hangar building's gate, then locked it behind him before walking around the hangar building. The personnel door was locked and the rollup door secured in place. Morty unlocked the door and walked inside.

"Mel?" Morty called out, then spotted the man working on the frame of the next-generation Bedstead, the King. He walked over as Mel stood up.

"Seen any sign of Chuck or Frenchy?"

"Yeah, we strapped Frenchy on the Bedstead and Chuck flew

him to Clovis. I expect him back in an hour or so. Frenchy had some kind of emergency, neither one said what it was, but Frenchy was in an all-fired hurry to get to Albuquerque. Chuck's supposed to drop him off at the airport and Frenchy will catch a plane from there."

Morty scratched his head. "You think the Bedstead can make it there and back?"

"Chuck thought so. He's got the most experience flying it and the batteries were fully charged, so I'd say he's got a good chance. If he gets low on electrons, he'll call and I'll pick him up in the van. The Bedstead fits in the back, and no one will be able to see what I'm hauling."

Morty nodded. "Got any coffee made?"

"New pot. I could use a cup too." Mel laid his drill down and the two men walked to the break room.

"What are you doing to Bedstead II, Mel?"

"Punching holes to mount a pair of passenger seats behind the pilot's seat. I got the dimensions from the last mount we put on, the one for the pilot's seat. That damned stainless steel alloy does a number on drill bits, though. Even by resharpening them, I've gone through half a dozen tonight. Not your ordinary bits either, these are the carbide industrial ones."

"Yeah, I had that problem too. You have to keep the drill bit cool. I kept the tip cool with cutting oil and that helped, but it was still slow. What are you using for coolant?"

"Light machine oil. It works, even if it does smoke a lot, but you have to go slow and keep a lot of pressure on the drill."

The conversation was interrupted by a call over the radio. The tone control opened the channel, then Chuck's voice came through. "Mel, I need you to open the big access door. I'm down to maybe 5% charge and it's dropping fast. I'm only a mile out, so hustle it."

"Copy, Chuck. Be open when you get here. Do you need lights?"

"Negative, I'm using the night vision optics. Just get the rollup door open."

"Roger. Standing by." Mel trotted over to the control panel and punched the button, raising the big door. Five minutes later, the

Bedstead drifted slowly over the fence and eased inside. By the time Mel finished securing the door, Chuck had flipped off the circuit breakers and climbed wearily down from the pilot's seat."

"Cut it pretty close, didn't you, son?"

"Hi, Grandpa. Yeah, it was touchy there toward the end. I had to slow way down, just barely keep flying and milk as many miles as possible out of the batteries. I doubt I could have made another five miles."

"Any idea of what was bugging Frenchy?"

"Something to do with his daughter Lina. He didn't say what it was, but it was important that he get to Albuquerque fast."

"I hope she's not sick."

"Yeah, he dotes on her. If there's something wrong, I expect it will hit him hard.

"I guess he's probably there by now, and whatever the problem is, he'll tell us if he wants us to know. I'm going to bed, I've been about as low on energy as the Bedstead's batteries during the last couple of hours. No offense, grandpa, but I'm dead on my feet. I'll talk to you after I wake up."

"Get some sleep, Son. I just wanted you to know I've got the drivers unloading the trucks. I want them out of here before daylight. We can talk tomorrow."

Chuck stretched out on the couch as Morty nodded to Mel and walked out. Mel turned off the overhead light and headed for the Bedstead. He would change out the depleted batteries, then continue drilling the mounting holes for the passenger seats. Mel muttered to himself as he headed for the overhead crane's controls. Swapping out the heavy battery packs was routine by now.

The seat mounts should be removable, easy to change, but at the same time sturdy enough to lock the seats firmly in place. So how should he do that?

***

Chuck had been asleep almost eight hours when his cell phone rang. Sleepily, he fumbled, then pressed the button to accept the call. There was only a slight hesitation; few people had his number.

"Hello?"

"Chuck, this is Frenchy. Did I wake you?"

"I need to get up anyway. What's up?"

"I've got a problem. I need your help."

"You've got it. What can I do?"

"I'll be here in Albuquerque for a while, dealing with the police, but I need to get Lina out of here. I don't want her to be left alone in Clovis either. I was wondering if you could meet her and take her to the site?"

"Sure, no problem. What time will she arrive?"

"It'll take me a while to arrange for a plane, probably fly her out this afternoon, so she'll arrive in Clovis sometime about dark. I'll call you as soon as I put her on the plane. You'll have to land in the fields this time and hike to the airport.

"Chuck, you might as well know. There's been trouble, and we've been threatened."

"I... see. Okay, I'll deal with it at this end. Do you expect someone to be waiting for her when she gets to the Clovis Airport?"

"I doubt it. I don't see how anyone could know what we have in mind. I haven't even contacted the pilot yet. You're the only one who knows, and we don't yet have a timetable."

"What about you, Frenchy? Will you be all right?"

"I'm with the police now. I'll ask for an escort to the Sunport, and the officer can stay with me until I board the plane. Anyway, I'll be on a private plane and I'll have a pistol. One of my friends is friends with the chief. Best not to say more about it, except that I'll have a pistol and two extra magazines."

"You know how to shoot, Frenchy?"

"I know how to shoot." The grimness was there, audible even through the phone. "I spent some time on an indoor range when I wasn't playing golf or handball. I won't hesitate if I have to shoot someone, not after what's happened."

"Enough said, then. Give me a heads-up before the plane takes off.

"I'll take it slow this time, getting to the airport, and that will give me more battery cushion. I'll also need time to hike the rest of the way after I park the Bedstead. But don't worry, I'll be there when she arrives. Tell her how to recognize me, all right?"

"Will do. Thanks, Chuck. I owe you one."

"No sweat, we owe each other a few by now. I'll have my phone on and I'll let grandpa know where I'm going before I leave, but I'll be waiting when she gets there."

"You'll recognize her?"

"Sure. I've seen that picture on your desk, Frenchy."

***

Chuck brought the Bedstead to a hover and landed it in an alfalfa field, a mile northwest of the airport. The low silhouette was hidden among the plants; only the pilot's windscreen and the upper part of the seat back were visible. *Safe enough*, he thought. There was no reason anyone should be in the field during darkness, and he'd be gone long before daylight.

Crossing the field's barbed-wire fence presented few problems and he soon found the road he'd spotted before landing.

The hike to the airport helped him stretch out the kinks in his legs. His limp was barely noticeable, more stiff than painful.

Few people were around; Clovis' airport was not a hotbed of activity after dark. He bought a can of soda from a vending machine, found a bench to sit on, and sipped his soda while he waited.

An hour later, a small twin-engine plane landed and taxied to the terminal building. The propellers stopped and the pilot got out, then helped his passenger deplane. Folding up the steps as she walked away toward the terminal, he climbed back in the plane. Chuck went to meet her as the engines started and the plane taxied toward the self-service fueling point.

Lina was slender and tall, around 5'9" by Chuck's estimate. She wore dark slacks and a lightweight jacket. Her dark hair was already windblown by the light breeze across the open landscape.

"I'm Chuck. If you're Lina, I'm your welcome wagon. Sort of."

"My dad sent you?"

Chuck nodded. "He told me when to expect you. No luggage?"

"No. He said he'd bring my stuff later on by car. You have a helicopter?"

"Not exactly, and we've got about a mile to walk." Chuck looked at the flat-heeled open-toed shoes she was wearing. "I didn't see any cactus on the way in, but as soon as we're off the road you follow in my footsteps, okay?"

She nodded and fell in beside Chuck as he walked down the road, leaving the airport behind.

"It's...kind of dark out here. You said my father sent you?"

"Right, I recognized you from the picture Frenchy keeps on his desk. We're working together on the project. Has he told you anything about what we're doing?"

"Not really. I know that what he's doing has upset someone, but that's not unusual. He's pissed off people before. You don't make the kind of money he's made without also making enemies."

"Yeah. Anyway, we've had problems.

"Frenchy wanted to build the plant close to a city, but had a hard time finding a property. He figured someone was blocking him, maybe spying on us, so that's why we moved out here. He took care of all that stuff, hiring a contractor and building the site.

"I work on... a different part of the company. I flew him into Clovis, that's how he got back to see you as fast as he did."

"So you're the one. Dad didn't tell me much, just said it was an interesting flight."

"That's one way of looking at it. Anyway, he called and told me to pick you up and fly you out to the plant. He didn't say why."

"I had to leave school; I couldn't stay there, especially after what happened. And what that man said."

"I don't want to pry, but if there's something I should know about what happened..."

"I was raped, Chuck. That bastard told me to give my father a message. He said, 'This one was fun, at least for me. The next time it won't be fun for anyone. Tell your father to stop what he's doing.'"

"Shit! I'm sorry, Lina. But now I know where I'll put you when we get back. There are armed guards on the property, I'll tell them to keep a sharp eye out, but the hangar is locked all the time and Mel is there when I'm not.

"Before, all we had to deal with was suspected espionage. I guess it's better to know we have the kind of enemies that will stop at nothing. This time...I'll just let the guards know. They'll detain any trespassers that don't have a damned good reason for being on the property, and shoot if they have to."

***

"Roswell Daily Record. How can I help you?"

"You report on stuff, right? I mean, if I seen something, I can tell you about it and you'll put it in the paper?"

"No guarantees, but I'll make a note of what you tell me. The editor will decide whether it goes in the paper. First, what's your name?"

"You need to know that? You don't have to write it in the article, do you?"

"Maybe not, but if you've got news, why wouldn't you want people to know who you are?"

"I was waiting for...never mind. I was over north of Clovis, you know?"

"Big area. How far north, and is that due north, northwest, northeast, what?"

"Just north, okay? I don't want people knowing my business."

"I understand." The reporter doodled on his pad. Drugs? Poaching? Rustling? Visiting someone else's wife? He finished the list with an exclamation point. It would be worth looking into what might be happening north of Clovis!

Some of the farms had stopped production when the peanut packing plant went bankrupt, so there was a lot of nearly-deserted land out that way. Drug smugglers looked for open areas with few people to bring in their loads.

"Okay, what did you see?"

"I seen one of them flying saucer things. I figured you folks in Roswell would know more about it than this bunch in Clovis, so I called you."

The reporter almost laughed, then decided to play along. Even if this guy was nuts, there might be a humorous piece in it. Filling the local news section was always something of a challenge.

"We do know a lot about the saucers, as it happens. What was this one doing?"

"Going like a bat out of hell, that's what. It was one of them long kinds, what they call the cigar shape, you know?"

"Did it have the same pattern of flashing lights that other ones have had? And you never did tell me your name."

"It's Willie. Willie Guz... uh, just Willie G, okay? That should be enough."

Indeed, thought the reporter. *Especially since I've got your phone number*. "Go ahead, Willie."

"It didn't have no lights. I couldn't hear it making a noise either, so I knowed it was a long way off. That section of road has street lights and I spotted this thing because it blocked the lights. It was taking off from the Clovis Airport, had to be; it was coming from that direction, and it went right over Ned Houk Park, couldn't have been more than ten or fifteen feet up. Then it jumped straight up in the air like people say them things can do, and the next thing I knew it was gone. I figured it was likely headed for Roswell.

"People say there are lots of those flying things hid out in the caves down that way. You know that new cave near Carlsbad has never been explored, don't you? I'll bet that's where they're hiding. You watch, this one probably kidnapped someone from that airport."

"I'll look into it, Willie. I need to ask you something, it's just routine but it's on my list of questions I have to ask. Had you been drinking, Willie?"

"Not this time. I was smoking a cigarette, you know? And there that thing went, flying between me and the lights."

"I see. Okay, was there anything else?"

"Ain't that enough? A flying saucer kidnaps someone from the Clovis airport and that ain't enough?"

"I'll make a few phone calls, Willie, see if anyone's gone missing. I'll call you back if I need anything else. What's your phone number?" The reporter waited, then smiled. 'Willie' had hung up.

Two weeks later, a short paragraph appeared in the Sunday edition titled "Flying saucer spotted near Clovis Airport?"

No one paid attention. Roswell, sometimes called the 'UFO Capitol of the World', sees several such reports in the course of a year.

***

Frenchy drove in late the following day. He called Chuck, using the security agent's radio.

"How's Lina doing, Chuck?"

"She's settled in, Frenchy. Right now she's helping Mel install seats on the Bedstead and the King."

"She's working already?"

"Yeah. As soon as we landed, she wanted to know everything there was to know. She was pretty quiet at first, but she opened up a bit on the way to the hangar. Mel and I changed the batteries and plugged the ones we took out into the charger. She was all over that too, asking questions while we worked.

"I mentioned we were building a bigger craft and she started asking what kind of computers we were using and what programs we had installed. I suspect we've got another spy in our midst even if this one is friendly.

"By the way, we're going to need more food. We had enough for Mel and me, but feeding three is going to tax our supplies."

"I'll see to it, Chuck. I owe you another one, buddy. Tell Lina I'll be heading over to the hangar as soon as the workers are gone for the day."

"I'll put the coffee on, Frenchy."

Chuck was thoughtful after he hung up.

How would Lina fit in? More importantly, how should he treat her? Was she the general manager's daughter, or just one of the workers? And what of her recent trauma, the rape? She seemed interested in the Bedstead and the King, so maybe that would take her mind off what had happened. But would depression set in later?

I'm no psychologist, but I think work is just the thing for her, Chuck thought. *Even if she loses interest in what we're doing, modifying the Bedstead and working on the King, I'll bet she'd like to learn how to fly them.*

***

Frenchy's latest acquisition, a John Deere Gator, had been delivered a week earlier. The small hybrid, half truck and half all-terrain vehicle, came with a diesel engine. Frenchy kept it fueled from the tanks that supplied the generators.

He'd already made it a practice to drive the small vehicle around the property, looking at whatever work was going on and generally making something of a nuisance of himself. As a result, no one would wonder now where the Gator's tracks were going, even if they bothered to pay attention to them.

After the work crews left for the day, Frenchy finished loading the Gator's cargo box with supplies, including several painter's drop cloths that he'd picked up at a Lowe's in Albuquerque. There was already a large, heavy box strapped down in the front of the small truck's bed.

Frenchy parked the Gator by the hangar's rear gate and the three men carried the supplies inside. Lina swept away their tracks as soon as the last trip was finished. While no one would wonder about the Gator's tracks, footprints were another story; the building supposedly wasn't being used.

The four were soon seated in the break room, sipping cups of hot coffee.

"The food in the box is mostly dried or canned stuff that doesn't need refrigeration. There are a few frozen dinners you can have as soon as they thaw, and I've ordered a small upright refrigerator-freezer for here. That will make it a bit cramped in the break room, but it can't be helped.

"I've also got another convertible couch on order. It'll be here in a couple of days. What I had in mind was curtaining off an area for Lina. There are drop cloths and you've got wire and tools. Think you'll have any problem dealing with that?"

Mel let Chuck do the talking. "No problem, but I think maybe we need to tell the guards that someone will be living and working here in this building. There's no way we can work without someone noticing.

"Tell 'em to keep their mouths shut and keep unauthorized people away. Unauthorized people includes everyone except the four of us and Morty. The three of us will be spending more time over in the main plant anyway, now that the workshop is almost ready. No one except us knows that Lina is here, and I think we need to keep it that way."

"Agreed. Sorry, honey, you're going to have to stay hidden, at least for now. It's for your own protection. You okay with that?"

"I'm happy to hide. As long as I can pilot the Bedstead. That should be all right, shouldn't it?"

Frenchy looked inquiringly at Chuck. "What do you think?"

"I've let her fly it inside the hangar, moving really slow. I'd like to have her practice a few more days, staying inside the fence, then she can fly that test course I laid out. I've also told her to stay low and slow on that, at least for the time being."

Chuck looked meaningfully at Frenchy. "She's really jumped into working, and she's been a great help to us. I think she wants you to get her a bigger computer and a couple of design programs."

"I know," Frenchy sighed. "I'll get them on order.

"One thing, though. When she flies that course, I want someone riding along with her. The Bedstead will carry two, we know that, so I want one of you two riding shotgun. Armed. You think you can handle a gun well enough to protect her if it comes to that?"

"Yeah, I've got my .40 caliber Ruger," said Chuck. "Not a lot of range, but it's a good pistol within about 25 yards. Can't see much farther than that at night anyway."

"Take a look at that other box I brought in. It's not tools."

"Ah, you're a man after my own heart, Frenchy. Let's take a look."

The crate held four Colt rifles and an equal number of Glock pistols. Ammunition boxes filled two smaller compartments at each end of the crate, 9mm hollow points at one end, .223 caliber at the other.

"The rifles are the carbine version of the AR-15, with extension stocks. The ammo is the type intended for hunting, not military ball, meaning that the bullets expand when they hit something. The rifles are semi-auto only, but I can't see you facing a charging horde of soldiers. If you need help, call the guards. Most of them, maybe all of them, have combat experience."

"Works for me. I saw some of that too," said Chuck. "I'll keep my Ruger pistol, though, I like it better than the 9mm Glocks. Next time you come by, I'd appreciate a few boxes of .40 caliber hollow-points. If you can't get those, get the semi-wadcutter jacketed rounds. They work pretty good too."

"I'll see to it, Chuck. Hopefully, you won't need any of this. but after what that son of a bitch said to Lina, I want as much protection for her as I can get."

"I don't think he really knew what we're doing out here, Frenchy. He may not even know exactly where we are."

Chuck directed his next comment to Mel and Lina. "I want rifle racks on the Bedstead, the upright kind like police use in their cruisers, and before we fly it outside, I'm going to want racks on the King." Lina looked surprised for a moment, but Mel simply nodded.

"I'll go with Lina when she flies the course I've laid out, Frenchy," said Chuck. "Bottom line, if we're ever attacked, she flies out in the Bedstead while Mel and I hold off the attacker until the guards and the cops get here.

"I'll need more tools and supplies. Two exits were fine so long as we weren't facing an overt threat, but that's one too many if this is to be a defense bunker. Easy fix when you get me the tools; I'll reinforce the rear door and secure it from the inside. We can use the other personnel door, the one by the rollup doors, for entry and exit."

"Get me a list of what you need, Chuck. I'll see to it. Will you need help?"

"I'll borrow a couple of guys from the engineering crew, the ones that built this version of the Bedstead. They'll be working in the shop starting next week and they already know all there is to know about the Bedstead, so I won't have any problem getting help. A couple of them are just waiting for their chance to fly the King as soon as it's ready. You do know they're hoping to pilot the first spaceship, don't you?"

***

The major had an appointment. He paused for a moment, checking his watch. As soon as the minute hand touched 0900, he knocked sharply at the door frame, then entered as soon as he heard the gruff response.

The colonel was a busy man. It didn't do one's career any good to arrive early or late for an appointment.

The major marched to the desk and reported, voice flat. It was also not good to show too much emotion; someone might wonder.

"You sent for me, Sir?" The major's voice had just the right inflection. It should; he'd practiced it earlier that morning. His voice conveyed just the right mix of statement and question.

"This operation you propose. Have you carefully considered the possibilities?"

"I believe so, sir, but I'm always grateful for your wise counsel."

A touch of the toady, not too much, was also useful. The colonel would doubtless be astonished at how well his subordinates knew him, his moods, and his preferences.

"Suppose I approve your operation, Major. What do we gain if we penetrate this warehouse you're so interested in?"

The major's answer was prompt; the question was expected.

"If there's anything to this American company's machine, we get the information as soon as they have it themselves. Cost to us, not great. We have the assets, we only need to retask two or perhaps four men."

"And the operation they were working on, the one you're taking them from? What of that?"

"We do not believe it will be greatly delayed, Colonel. If you think it best, I could even hire outsiders. I have an agent in place who could do that and there would be no link to us."

"Suppose your assets are discovered. What would we lose if our interest is revealed?"

"That's a bit harder to answer, General. If our adversaries realize that we're interested, they might become more interested themselves. They'll almost certainly be more cautious."

"It's colonel, you should know that, André. You seem to forget, especially when you want something."

"Very sorry, sir. It won't happen again." *Not until the next time anyway*, Major André thought.

"Write up your thoughts in a memo, Major. Include your analyses of the questions I've asked. Have it for me by Friday afternoon.

"I'll decide after I've had a chance to study the proposal, probably by Monday, but I'll want to approve any operation before it's launched. We can't afford to have our people compromised. We have other operations underway, and unlike the embassy staff, we don't have diplomatic immunity."

"Yes, sir. I'll keep that in mind."

"See that you do. You're dismissed, Major."

Chapter Thirteen

Chuck ate a microwaved TV dinner and left the hangar, carefully locking the door behind him. Mel was still asleep and presumably Lina was too.

The curtains allowed as much privacy as possible, considering that three people unavoidably lived in close quarters during the week. There had been no friction so far; Mel and Chuck were careful not to say anything that would remind her of the assault, but otherwise treated her as a fellow worker. As for Lina, she enthusiastically joined the project. Whether in the technical work of maintenance and prepping the King for flight or the mundane work of cleaning the break room, she took a full part.

More importantly, she now smiled occasionally, a distinct change from when she'd first arrived.

Chuck entered the guard shack and asked to speak to the shift supervisor. She was briefing the guards who'd just come on duty, so Chuck waited politely until she finished, then signaled that he wanted to talk to her. She nodded and found him in her office as soon as she finished assigning the guards to their posts.

"How much do you know about what I do here, Maddy?"

"I know you have something to do with what goes on in the big building. I also know we're not supposed to ask questions."

"Close enough. I'm involved primarily with plant operations, but I also represent my grandfather's interests on the corporation's board of directors. I'm not exactly sure where that puts me in the hierarchy, but it would be fair to say I'm one of your bosses. Your company has its own director, but he works for us. Any problems with taking instructions from me?"

"None. I'll keep my contract administrator informed, of course, but unless your orders conflict with what he tells me, I see no reason why I shouldn't cooperate with you."

"Fair enough," Chuck said. "It's time to bring you into some of what we're doing. We'll be manufacturing devices and later on we'll be putting them on aircraft. We anticipate buying airframes for now, although we may eventually manufacture our own.

"I can't tell you more than that. For now, we're keeping everything low profile to maintain secrecy, because there are reasons why we can't go public yet. This has been an easy job for your security people up to now, but you should know that we've had a physical threat and an assault on one of our female employees. Corporate maneuverings are just business, we understand that, but when our people are threatened we take that very seriously."

"I can understand that. What you're saying is that a higher state of security alert is justified by events. Did this happen here at the factory?"

"No, it happened elsewhere and a police report was filed. If your supervisors feel it necessary, I can request a copy of the report.

"But the threat I mention was specific enough that I'm concerned the next attack could happen here. I'm not asking you to break the law, but we've had both a direct threat about company activities and criminal assault of an employee. In my judgment, stronger defensive measures are necessary. Based on that, and acting on my authority, you are authorized to employ whatever force is necessary to neutralize any threat to people or property."

"You understand that what you've just told me allows us to employ deadly force if we feel the situation requires it, don't you?"

"I do. This is not just about preventing industrial espionage, it's about protecting our people. We expected people to try to snoop around the plant, that's why we hired armed security agents. But we *didn't* expect the degree of physical threat we've become aware of and we certainly didn't expect an assault. The opposition has shown that they'll stop at nothing."

"I'll pass this on to my contract supervisor, and I'll also let the crew here know what they're facing.

"Should we consider increasing the number of guards on site? We also provide a security escort for Mr. Fuqua on occasion, not always, but when he asks for an escort we provide someone. If you're willing to authorize it, we can add protection for essential personnel to the contract. We have the assets to do that."

"If you think you need more people on site, clear it with Mr. Fuqua. For that matter, you might ask him whether he wants to authorize personal protection for others.

"For now, I think you've got enough people. You know that Mr. Fuqua has other employees outside the fence who keep their eyes open, don't you?"

"Right, and we've got a set of passwords we use when we talk to them, depending on the day of the week. We rarely see the cowboys, though. As long as they stay away from the graded area around the outer fence, there's no reason for us to contact them. They have radios to alert us if they discover a problem, and we keep one of our radios tuned to their frequency. If they call in a contact, we'll talk about it. So far, that hasn't happened."

"Sounds good. How many people are on your shift?"

"I've got six, two assigned to the gate, the rest circulating around the campus. When the plant goes into full operation, that number will likely double. We'll need more people to deal with the projected number of employees. Right now, I'm running three shifts of two. Each shift works four on, eight off, and this repeats once during the duty day. They man the gate in pairs for four hours, then they're off for four hours except for routine foot patrols every two hours unless there's an emergency. They can play cards, video games, watch a movie if they want. If they choose to sleep, that's okay too, but they're required to respond within thirty seconds if called. Breaking their shift into four hours, then giving them a break, minimizes the fatigue factor."

"Sounds very professional."

"It is, Chuck. We hire mostly military veterans and ex-cops. The vets also know when not to shoot, that's important when you're dealing with civilians. You don't want the adverse publicity and neither do we."

"Good. Anyway, that's all I've got for you. You might see a few more people inside the fence. They'll be moving in and around the various buildings, so don't get alarmed."

"I won't. We'll be going to a badge ID system as soon as your other employees start working, but we can begin using that now if you think it's necessary."

"I don't. The factory employees recognize each other by sight and we're not likely to interact with your people. As for the later badge system, how will you handle that?" Chuck asked.

"I've been told that your people will commute from Roswell and Clovis by bus. Before they board the bus, they'll sign in, get their ID's checked, and be issued their badges. When they arrive, no one gets off the bus without a badge. We'll have an agent waiting with a scanner when the bus pulls in, to check the badges and compare numbers. Once they're inside the fence, the badge color will tell security who's allowed to go where.

"Limiting access to sensitive areas is standard security doctrine. I imagine you'll be getting one of the blue all-access-anytime badges, but your company decides who gets what color badge; we just administer those decisions."

"Makes sense. Did Mr. Fuqua come up with this plan?"

"No. That came from a Mr. Jindae. According to our list, he's the plant's personnel director."

"That sounds about right, although titles keep changing. Okay, I'll leave you to your job. It's time for me to go earn my keep." Chuck smiled and left the office.

Maddy opened a laptop computer and began composing an email, then stopped. It would be better to update the guards first. The email to her directors could wait.

***

Frenchy left the site Monday morning and remained away during the rest of the week. He drove in late Sunday, just after dark, and parked outside the main building. The site appeared deserted, except for the guards manning the gate. He telephoned Lina to tell her he'd arrived, then walked through the moonlight toward the hangar. Moments later, a whirring noise announced that he was being met. The faint glow of a chemlight guided him to the rear seat of the Bedstead.

"Climb aboard, Dad. I'll have you inside the hangar in a moment."

Frenchy eased into the seat and wondered if he needed a safety belt to hold himself in place. He decided that the seat was enough and settled in. Prudently, he gripped the seat with both hands as Lina smoothly brought the Bedstead up, stopping as soon as it was high enough to clear the fence. She flew ahead, slowing as she approached the building, then eased the craft inside the darkened hangar. The door rolled down behind the machine and moments later, the lights were switched on.

"Welcome, Frenchy. Sorry about sending our rookie pilot to pick you up, but she insisted."

"Well, the flight was a bit rough, but they say any landing you can walk away from is a good one, right?"

"You two can just kiss my ass! I'm already as good a pilot as you are, Chuck. Mel said so!"

"He only said that because he was feeling miffed that I asked him to change the batteries after my last flight. Still, it's fair to say you're as good as me, since neither one of us has crashed yet."

"Setting a low standard, Chuck?" teased Frenchy.

"I wouldn't say that. She's taken over the Bedstead test flights, running that course I laid out. That gave us time to work on the replacement. It's a good thing Mel and I are almost done modifying the King; otherwise, I doubt she'd ever let us fly again!"

"How's that going, Chuck?"

"All we need now is the impellers, and they should be ready within a week or so. The computers are in, but I can't do a final calibration until the impellers are installed. The extra batteries came in last Wednesday, so we charged them up and installed them in the King. We've got cargo tie-downs on the rear deck and mounts for two seats, side by side. The windshields are part of the seat assemblies now, so all we have to do is put one in place and turn the cam-locks to hold it. It takes less than five minutes to install or remove a seat."

"Sounds good. Something else has also been going well. You

know I detached a crew to work on the marine systems, right?"

"I'd forgotten about that. You say it's going well?"

"That's why I'm here. We've got a unit ready for testing, and I thought Morty should get to do it. You can come too, if you want. We can leave as soon as you and Morty are ready. We'll be running the test out in Lake Michigan, a few miles from Chicago. We've got two working service boats, but since there's only one impeller for each boat and they run on battery power the crews have already given them a good workout. They're even simpler than the Bedstead and they work fine.

"But the big craft has multiple heavy impellers, a large generator, and more sophisticated controls than the boats. That's why I thought of Morty; we're getting close to what he had in mind for that other kind of ship."

"So what kind of hull did they mount this system in, Frenchy? One of those small freighters? I don't know that we're ready to put impellers on a passenger craft yet. People would wonder if they noticed there was no propeller."

"It's not a freighter. Actually, we leased a..."

***

"A *barge*? You mounted the system in one of those big flat-bottomed cargo haulers?" Morty looked doubtful.

"Yep. Why not? You can add an impeller to anything you need to move. Leasing this one was cheap. I think it might have been on its way to be scrapped, but it floats, so it will work for us. We didn't even have to do a lot of modification. There was no propulsion system to be removed and no steering gear to deal with. All our crew needed to do was weld brackets on the sidewalls for the impellers and add a bottom support for the generator. That's mounted midway between the bow and stern to keep the barge trimmed level. We're using the generator's frame-mounted tank, so we only have about two hours of fuel if we're running the generator at full power.

"The impeller brackets have swivel mounts that can be tilted up or down electrically, so they can be controlled locally using their own panel or remotely from the bridge. That's what we're calling the pilot's station, although it doesn't look much like a bridge. It's on the deck, a bit forward of amidships, but everything else is below in what we've been calling the engine room. It's really just a big open space. The generator's in the middle, the battery packs are behind it, and there are walkways along the sides where the engineer can access the impellers if he needs to. But it's still mostly open space.

"We had to cut two holes in the upper deck, though. We mounted the fan in one, the other is the exhaust opening. There's only a lattice of expanded-steel over that to keep people from falling through. We found out quick that when the generator is running, it's hot down there, and you also get fumes. I guess the exhaust pipe isn't sealed as tight as it should be, but the fan clears all that stuff out. We've run tests on everything, we just haven't taken her out yet."

"What about lights? We'll need running lights."

"We thought of that. They're there, and we also installed a small radar. The antenna's on a mast behind the pilot's chair and the display is located by the control panel. It doesn't have much range, but it should be enough."

"I guess I'll see what it looks like when we get there. But a barge? You're testing the heavy-duty impellers on a *barge*? What were you thinking?"

"I was thinking it was available. It's beat up already, so we can cut out the brackets, patch the holes in the deck, and return it to the owners after the test. But mainly, we chose it because it was available and cheap."

***

They arrived late on Monday, tired, but there was no time to rest; Morty wanted to inspect the barge before he took it out into the lake. He spent the rest of the afternoon checking out the controls and talking to the men who'd installed the system.

"We've only got about two hours of fuel, Sven," Morty worried. "That might be a problem."

"We've got twenty gallons more in plastic fuel containers, plus we've got the battery pack. We've also scheduled a towboat to take us out into the lake and that'll save fuel. There was already more curiosity around the dock than we wanted, and moving a barge under its own power would have attracted way too much attention.

"And don't forget, we've got the two service boats on the barge if they're needed. They're mounted in blocks on the forward deck.

"I hope we don't run into a nosy Coast Guard boat, but we should be okay if we do. They may think we're crazy, out in the lake on a barge, but we're legal. Mostly."

"I wonder what the towboat crew will think?"

"They think we're hauling drugs. One of the crewmen asked me if I could fix him up with something. I gave him the fish-eyed stare and told him he didn't want to mess with the people who chartered the barge. He didn't get curious after that."

"That looks like the towboat heading toward us," said Morty. "Get everyone on board and we'll get this show on the road. Or on the water, anyway."

***

"Cast off the tow!"

The towboat backed water as Sven moved up to the bow. The barge slowed, inertia moving it closer to the tow vessel. Using the slack produced by the maneuver, Sven knocked loose the ratchet holding the towline. The two wing wires had already been taken in, so with the ratchet released, the barge was no longer under the boat's control. Sven took in the line and began flaking it down as the towboat drifted ahead.

"You sure, Morty?"

"We won't need the tow," Morty said confidently. "I've run quick tests on each impeller, the computers are on-line, and as far as I can tell, everything is ready. We've got all the power we need, at least for a couple of hours, and if something happens to the generator we've got enough battery reserve to make it back to port. Jim and Sven can operate the individual impellers using local control if something goes wrong with the computer, but this test is mostly about using just the joystick and the control panel.

"The only thing different from what we did with the Bedstead is that this is our first centralized-control full-power test using multiple heavy-duty impellers. I don't expect trouble, but if we find a problem, we've still got the two service boats. They use the smaller impellers, and we know those work just fine."

Sven finished securing the line and went down the ladder into the engine room. Jim, the power plant engineer, thumbed the intercom.

"We're ready. The generator is at idle but it will throttle up automatically under load and the impellers are ready to answer the helm. Or the joystick. Whatever."

"We can call it the helm, Jim. We'll save joystick for the Bedstead and the airplane, when we get one. Release control to the bridge."

"Control to the bridge, aye. You have control."

A bank of green lights lit in front of Morty's seat. He buckled his seat belt, then swiveled the display until it was beside the small radar screen, leaving him with an unobstructed view forward. The radar sweep painted the shoreline north of Chicago, which showed up as a blur eight miles aft and to port. There were no vessel contacts nearby.

"Check your seat belts. Life jackets on?" A glance confirmed that the passengers were ready. "Impeller swivels are set to five degrees rise, switch is for forward impulse, I'm engaging the impellers--now."

For a moment, nothing happened. The whining noise from the 'engine room' rose in pitch, noticeable despite the diesel generator's muffled roar. A sloshing noise replaced the slap of Lake Michigan chop against the barge's sides.

"We're moving, Morty!"

"Don't sound so surprised, Frenchy. You had a ride in the service boat and you've flown on the Bedstead. The only thing different is that this time we're using ten heavy-duty impellers. I've got a *lot* more thrust available."

"I can't help it, Morty. This thing is huge! And there's no propeller, no jet exhaust, nothing but green lights on a monitor and a guy with a video-game joystick!"

"You'll get used to it, Frenchy. You're still intending to pull this power plant after we finish today's test, right? You also mentioned during the flight that you've bought a small ship. How much longer to pull the original power plant and fair over the holes in the hull?"

"Should be finished in another week. I hired workers at the port to gut the hull, except for the decks, bulkheads, and the ballast tank. The rudder and control mechanisms are gone, the prop shafts and bearing supports too. Getting that big diesel engine out is the only thing left.

"Jim ran the calculations regarding weight distribution and the brackets for the main components of the impeller drive system are ready, so maybe a month from now we'll be ready for our first sea trials.

"We might have to rebalance the hull when everything is installed, but I doubt there'll be a problem. We might not even need to ballast the ship. The accelerometers and inclinometers are sensitive enough, but it remains to be seen whether the autopilot program can adjust the impeller gimbals fast enough to counter wind and wave.

"But if it works as expected, we can increase the hull's load factor by at least ten percent. She won't flex as much either, because the impellers distribute the load more evenly. Which is probably just as well; she's an old ship, ready to be sold for salvage when I bought her."

"Frenchy, you don't plan on going public after the sea trials, do you?"

"Not unless the secret leaks out. As for using it to haul cargo, I won't turn the ship over to the new master until he's familiar with the power system. Plus we've got to certify engineers and mechanics and at some point, we'll need to talk to the Coast Guard."

"Put it off as long as you can, Frenchy. We're a long way from letting people know what we're doing."

"OK, we'll register MV *Tesla* in Liberia. No more inspection problems!"

"You're in charge of that, Frenchy. Just be careful."

"Don't worry about it, Morty. You just make sure the system

works!"

"Speaking of which, in case you haven't noticed we're up to five knots. I'm going to increase power now."

Morty eased the joystick forward, then adjusted another control that was mounted on the control panel at his side. For a moment, nothing happened. The readouts on the screen changed from five degrees up-angle, forward orientation, to eight degrees up. Pushing the joystick forward caused the diesel clatter to increase as the generator responded to the additional load. The swishing noise from the barge's bluff bow grew louder, then quieted.

"Impellers coming up to eighty percent forward impulse," Morty said, then paused.

"We're showing six degrees up-angle on the deck, Frenchy. I think we're on plane."

"Morty, I think you just made history. For the first time in history, you've managed to bring a raked barge, all one hundred and ninety five feet of it, up on plane! And without a jet exhaust or a propeller of any sort!"

"Told you it would work. It's on plane because the impellers are lifting the bow. But this thing is not very maneuverable, not like a regular hull. I'm going to bring her back down to five knots now, then level the deck. I want it as stable as possible when I try doing a few turns. Still nothing showing on the radar scope, so I think we're safe."

"Make it so, Captain Morty."

"Aye, aye, Admiral Frenchy!" Both chuckled, then laughed aloud at the exchange.

Easing back on the joystick, Morty watched the readouts as the barge's bow settled slowly into the water. Gently he moved the thumbwheel until the swivel readouts moved back to their earlier orientation.

"Stand by for maneuvering. We'll do a turn to port, followed by a turn to starboard, then we'll try to spin in place."

Selecting the starboard impellers only, he gently eased the joystick forward. Obediently the big barge swung to port. A moment's pause while he pressed buttons, and Morty again moved the joystick forward. The barge's hull turned to starboard. Behind them, the wake described a shallow 'S' shape.

"We'll try a speed turn now, then an emergency braking maneuver. Make sure your belts are secure."

Punching the buttons, Morty switched the port impellers to aft. The starboard impellers were still set to forward. Pushing the joystick forward, he increased power. The barge skated on the surface, spinning counterclockwise within its own length.

"Brace for emergency stop."

Morty switched the port impellers to forward, watching the readouts change. The barge resumed moving slowly forward. Punching buttons on the panel, Morty switched all the impellers to ten degrees up, direction aft. Increasing power, he carefully watched the screen.

The barge slowed, shuddering as the following wave slapped against the stern, but because of the up-angle on the impellers there was no tendency for the hull to bog down. Reducing power, Morty eased the setting to zero as the barge stopped dead in the water.

"Still think we'll need that towboat to get back to the berth, Frenchy?"

"I'm convinced, Morty. You want to try anything else?"

"You decide, Frenchy. Why don't you swap places with me and give it a try? Then we'll let the others have a turn. It's actually fun if you don't get carried away. As long as you keep some up-angle on the swivels, you won't sink her."

"What would happen if you went full power with the impellers pointed straight up, Morty?"

"I don't want to try that, at least not yet. She might start flying, but then again, she might not. The programming might not be able to keep her balanced. We'd use a lot of fuel in a hurry, too.

"It's just a self-propelled barge as long as we're floating and nobody would believe the things we just did with it anyway. But a flying barge, that's different. We'll eventually have that other hull ready, the one we don't talk about. You can try maneuvering *that* one any way you want."

"Maybe I will, Morty. Maybe I will."

***

Will took the controls after Frenchy. He brought the barge slowly into the slip. Backing at the last moment, he powered down the impellers.

"I think we're done, Morty. Are you finished with engines?"

"We will be, as soon as Sven secures the lines to the dock. He could probably use a hand with that. I'm ready to return control to engineering, so Jim can run any final checks he needs to make, but as soon as we're snubbed up to the bumpers I'm done.

"The crane crew and the mechanics won't be here until tomorrow morning, so I'm going to bag out on that foam pad and sleeping bag. If the rest of you decide to sleep, make sure someone's on watch."

"I'll stay up, Morty, it won't be the first all-nighter I've pulled. Well done! You've given us everything you promised, and more. What are the mechanics going to do when they get here?"

"They'll disconnect the batteries and unclamp the impellers first, then pull the computers. The only thing remaining aboard after the impellers and computers are gone is the battery packs and the generator, and there's nothing secret about them.

"The impellers are going back for teardown. We put this set under a lot of stress and we'll need to see if there's any signs of wear. Good night, Frenchy. I'll talk to you tomorrow."

Chapter Fourteen

"Morty, wake up. Don't make any noise, we've got company."

"Company, Mitch? What are you talking about?"

"Security just called. There are four men heading for the dock and they're armed, according to the guy in charge of security. He's notified the police and called his office for backup, but they don't have an armed response team available. He advises there's nothing the two of them can do at the moment except to observe and record."

"We don't have weapons aboard. I never expected... all right," said Morty. "Wake up everyone and notify Frenchy, Sven, and Jim that I intend to get underway. Have Sven cast off the lines, then report to Jim in the engine room.

"We'll move away from the dock using only the batteries, so tell them not to fire up the generator until we're well out into the harbor. I'll want all impellers on line, control transferred to the helm. Don't use the intercom, I'll see the lights when Jim switches over to bridge control. If we keep the noise down, those men may not realize we're gone.

"Mitch, you and Frenchy use those push poles I saw when I inspected the barge yesterday. They're racked along the sides on the upper deck, under each of the rails. When you're ready, push as hard as you can. It won't be easy, but the farther away from the dock, the better. The impellers whine and the intruders will hear the noise if they're close enough."

"Got it, Morty. You'll be at the helm? Where are we going?" asked Mitch.

"East until we clear the entrance, then south. We did our testing north of here, so whoever those people are, they may expect us to head for an area we're familiar with. Gary, Indiana, is down that way, and there may be other harbors between here and there.

cautious approach, he might not have time to get the barge out of gunshot range.

Faint scraping sounds from the port side, followed by a pair of splashes, indicated that the mooring lines had been released. Sven was a bright fellow; instead of bringing in the lines, he'd simply dropped them over the side. Moments later, the lights on the console came on. Jim had brought the impellers on line and transferred control to the bridge.

"Yes!" Morty muttered. He flipped switches on the panel. Moments later, whining noises indicated that the swivel motors were re-directing the impellers.

Morty added power and the barge began moving, curving away from the dock to starboard. The space between the gunwale and the dock widened.

Morty powered up the port impellers and the barge's course straightened, taking it out farther into the harbor. The gunmen now had no chance of boarding the barge, and probably little chance of hitting anyone on board should they open fire.

The first sweep lit the scope as the radar came to life.

"Damn!" Two blips showed, positioned between the ground returns from the jetties at the harbor's entrance.

"Jim, on intercom."

Moments later the engineer replied. "You've got steerage way, right?"

"It won't do us much good, I'm afraid. There are two boats waiting at the harbor entrance. They're just sitting there, so I suspect they're working with the intruders. I can see flashing lights back on shore so the police are on the way, but they won't get here in time. I don't think we can afford to take a chance.

"Here's what I want you to do. I'm powering down the impellers, so as soon as they're at idle, unclamp the swivel locks. Just unclamp the locks, leave the impellers in place. As soon as you've done that, come topside. We'll need the two service boats, so get them in the water but don't leave without me. Got it?"

"Can do. What about the people on deck?"

"Load them in the boats. I'll join you after I do what I can to was nothing more he could do; without waiting to see what happened, he stood up and walked to where the boat waited.

Below decks, the unclamped impellers shot forward, flying free of the swivels. Control and power cables popped loose and moments later, the impellers smashed into the barge's steel bow.

The barge shuddered. Loud crashes from below were followed moments later by heavy splashes ahead. Some of the impellers, at least, had punched through the hull. Water poured in through the gaping holes and the barge began sinking, bow first.

Morty stepped into the boat and made his way to a seat.

"I think it worked. With luck, the impellers went through the bow and what's left of them is scattered on the bottom. But even if they didn't, they're wrecked. The barge is sinking, which will make recovery difficult, especially now that the police will be watching. *We* should be able to find the wreckage, but it would be dangerous for anyone else to attempt it.

"Jim, take us to shore. Frenchy, telephone the harbor police and tell them that we've been the victim of attempted piracy."

***

Morty and Frenchy met the others in a waterfront restaurant after the harbor police had finished questioning them.

"I'm hungry, Morty. It's been a long night."

"I could eat, Frenchy. Who *are* those people? And how did they know we were working here?"

"No way to tell, Morty. Someone could have been tracking you since you flew the original Bedstead outside Panit's window. It wasn't just Panit either, other people saw you.

"But whoever they are, they had people on shore and boats out at the harbor entrance. That shows they've got resources and a high level of organization. I wonder if they're the same ones who were spying on the warehouse?"

"Maybe, but they could also be watching *you*, Frenchy.

"Considering all that's happened, I wonder if the government is involved. For that matter, it might not even be *ours*. Governments would have the people to mount something like this on short notice, but I can't think of anyone else who could.

"But look at everything that's happened. We're reasonably sure someone was spying on us while we were working in the warehouse. You and Will experienced financial pressure, which takes a considerable amount of influence. Add to that those people, whoever they were, that shut down your search for a factory site.

"So far, everything sounds government to me, but there's that attack on Lina and the warning from that crook. That doesn't sound like government.

"But whoever the opposition is, they've got assets they can bring in on short notice and money they're not afraid to spend."

"It could be a criminal gang, Morty. Crooks don't mind giving their people weapons either."

"Yeah, but why would crooks be interested in what we're doing? We don't really have anything yet, nothing they could use I mean.

"Governments or large corporations, now, they'd find a lot of use for what was on that barge. Sol's company backed off, but considering the potential profit, I can see other companies taking the chance. Especially if they got the secret without paying for it.

"As for governments, the first nation in possession of a workable electric-drive spaceship has a strategic advantage. Our government or any number of others, we can't rule any of them out.

"I don't know how they found out we were working on something special, but it doesn't matter. What's important is that they're well-financed and will stop at nothing."

"You're right," said Frenchy. "A lot of people would want a working impeller, so this puts a lot more pressure on us. We're almost ready to launch our first marine system, but we've got to shift into high gear with the other models. We really need an aviation version."

"You know, it could be *more* than one enemy," suggested Morty. "Think about it for a minute. There was no overt attack at first. The warehouse and the financial stuff all happened in the background, before we got the factory built.

"But then came the incident with the warning." Morty avoided mentioning the rape; Frenchy didn't need a reminder. "That was an overt criminal act. It's different enough to make me think there might be more than one group involved.

"The criminal part, the use of force, was close enough to last night's attempt that they might be related. I agree with what you said about needing an aviation model, but it also means we need to keep security tight. It means that we have to be suspicious of everyone and start cranking out more impellers. That's the only way we're going to stay ahead of what they might try next.

"I'll also take a look at how the factory handles things. Components aren't much of a problem, but the completed impellers have to be locked away. I already intended to set up a secure area to work on the spaceship, so adding a storeroom for impellers won't be much of a problem.

"By the way, the aviation impellers you mentioned? We've already got the design; we've been waiting until we have at least eight ready, and for all I know Chuck may have already installed them on the King.

"I expect it will take a month or two of flying the King to get the test results and for that matter, we can use Bedstead data. If anything, the bigger models should be more reliable because they use heavier structural components. But I don't see any reason to wait, so as soon as we can turn out enough impellers, you'll have your aircraft system.

"I'm going to need another engineer, maybe two, as soon as I'm ready to start on the ship. I need someone who's experienced at designing spacecraft and he or she won't come cheap. And you need to get cracking on the spacesuits too."

"I'll do that. Spend what you have to, Morty; I'll figure out a way to raise the money. I'll have to; our entire investment will be nearly worthless if someone starts producing impeller-powered craft before we do."

They called it a night soon after and headed for the hotel rooms Frenchy had rented.

***

The boats blocking the harbor entrance had vanished as mysteriously as they'd appeared. The impellers crashing through the barge's bow and the sinking of the craft, or possibly the arrival of police on shore, had interrupted whatever plan was underway.

Frenchy met Morty for breakfast and they resumed the discussion.

"I'll have salvage boats out as early as possible," said Frenchy. "I don't think whoever was out there expected you to do what you did."

"I don't see how they could, Frenchy; I just thought of it at the last minute!

"I couldn't allow the impellers to be taken, not complete and functional anyway. The control programs and computers either; it would be too easy for someone to reverse-engineer them. Speaking of salvage, you should also put one of our people on board the vessel to keep the crews from getting too curious. Maybe cut up that barge for scrap when it's picked up."

"Maybe I will, if it's completely wrecked. But if it's salvageable, I'll have the bow replaced and the generator and impeller mounts taken out, strip it down to the bare hull, then return it to the people I leased it from. That's better than having the insurance company ask questions we don't want to answer.

"I also can't afford to waste money, Morty. Bad enough that I've got to have the barge repaired, but I understand why you did what you did. And that ship you want to work on? It's going to be expensive."

"If I hadn't, Frenchy, we'd have lost everything. Even if we'd recovered the barge later, the secret would be out. The impellers might be gone too, stolen, but even if they didn't understand *how* we were doing it, they'd realize that we were converting electric power directly to motion.

"Someone already knows more than I like; they probably don't have exact knowledge, but they know we're doing something and they're interested. By now, they probably know about the new factory; we can't afford to assume they don't.

"I know you're not flush with money, but it's time to upgrade security. You're going to need more guards."

Frenchy nodded, tight lipped. "That's an added cost I'd hoped to avoid, at least until later. But I understand. I'll see to it, somehow.

"Maybe you or Chuck can go out with the salvage boats tomorrow?"

"No, we're both swamped with work at the lab. Getting both models of the impellers redesigned to make manufacturing easier is taking longer than either of us expected. Quality control, too, it has to be built into the manufacturing system from the beginning. But no half steps; the system has to work from day one."

"Agreed. I'll start looking for an airplane, you get me the impellers to power it."

"How big an airplane, Frenchy? I'd just as soon start small, maybe use as few as two impellers. What about a twin engine craft, say something equipped to haul five or six passengers? I'll need that much lift for the batteries and two to four impellers, depending on room inside the fuselage."

"You're talking about an airworthy plane, not a junker like the ship we bought," said Frenchy.

"You want to get out and walk if something breaks during that first flight?"

"Well, no. But what about a military trainer? Something on the order of a two-place dual-control instruction job? The government sells those from time to time, and I might be able to get one cheap."

"That might work. Look into gross lift capacity and see if it's enough for at least one battery pack and two impellers. I think we need to install them in pairs, for balance as well as reliability. As for interior space, mount the battery pack in the fuselage and if there's no room for the impellers, hang them under the wings in pods. Until we know how it's going to handle with impeller power, I won't remove the other engines."

"Won't be very aerodynamic, Frenchy. I'll talk to Will about it, he's the expert. But if it can fly with them mounted under the wings, I'm okay with that.

"How about we leave the engine shut down after we get things rigged up, run some taxi tests using only the impellers? They don't care whether you're rolling along the ground or flying at ten thousand feet. I'm sure Will's going to insist on a good checkout before the plane flies."

"You'll get it, Morty. Will's got a pilot's certificate, so he should be the guy in charge of ground testing at least and if he's willing, flight testing too. I'm sure he'll want to handle it, considering how much money he's invested. He spends too much time chasing women and gambling, work will do him good. I'll talk to him."

"You do that. I need to get back to the lab, so…"

"Have a good flight, Morty."

Chapter Fifteen

Weeks went by and the factory campus continued to change.

As soon as buildings were accepted, crews prepped spaces for travel trailers to house the people who would live on site. This temporary arrangement would work until permanent dwellings could be built.

The construction people had finished their latest project, grading, leveling, and compacting an airstrip and adjacent parking area. They finished Friday afternoon and moved their heavy equipment to the next work site, the factory's parking area.

Will landed a leased Piper Super-Cub on the new airstrip early the following Monday morning. After taxiing to the parking area, he and Frenchy deplaned and tied the plane down to the stakes that the construction crews had installed before moving to the parking area. The plant would eventually need extra hangars, larger ones, to house airplanes as they came off the assembly line, but for now the tiedown points would do. The two finished closing the plane's doors and cargo hatch just as Morty drove up in the Gator.

"Didn't expect you fellows this early. Something wrong?"

"Not exactly. Is Chuck available?"

"He's probably asleep by now. They work nights in the hangar, but if you need him I'll wake him up."

"Why don't we just head for the hangar? We can meet there, because this mostly concerns the two of you."

"Okay, if you're done with tying down that plane, hop in. It's likely to be a little crowded, but we're not going far."

The Gator bumped its way along the dirt road to the hangar. Morty popped out, still spry despite his advancing years. Frenchy looked at him appraisingly. The old man had to be in his late seventies, maybe in his eighties, but you'd never know it considering how alert his mind was and the way he moved.

Morty punched in the gate combination and they went inside. He locked it behind them as the trio headed for the hangar door. This too had a lock and Frenchy noticed that it required a different combination. The door locked automatically as soon as it was closed.

The lights in the hangar bay were on, but no one was working.

"Maybe they're in the break room, having breakfast. If not, I'll wake up Chuck. We don't need Lina or Mel for this." Morty headed for the break room. Frenchy and Will slowed and looked around as they crossed the hangar. The Bedstead and Bedstead II, the 'King', occupied the open space, the smaller Bedstead parked nearest to the rollup door.

"They've been busy. That big lifter looks almost ready to fly. Why don't we take a look at it while Morty finds Chuck?"

Will nodded and the two walked over to the King, which now mounted four of the large aviation-model impellers, one at each corner. When they became available, eight would be installed, but four were sufficient for the first round of tests.

The impeller housings were similar in external appearance to the ones on the improved Bedstead. The mechanism and the gimbaled mount were inside sealed, opaque fiberglass globes, the only external difference being that the ones on the King were larger.

A rolling metal table stood near the forward end and several tools lay about on the table's surface. Cables snaked through holes in the deck, waiting to be connected to the pilot's control panel.

"If that's all they have left to do, this thing will be flying by the end of the week." Frenchy pointed to the cables. "Those connect to the computers inside the chassis, located forward between the upper and lower decks. They've been in place for a couple of weeks now, waiting for the shop to deliver the impellers. The computer is linked through other cables to plugs at each impeller station.

"At a guess, they've been running checks to make sure nothing has been cross-connected. As soon as they mount the control panel, they'll hook up the remaining cables, calibrate the computer system, and run a quick test. It looks like everything else is ready."

Will glanced up as Morty joined the two. "They'll be along in a minute," he said. Will noticed that Morty looked tense, an expression he'd worn since he came from the break room. Glancing behind Morty, Will saw Chuck. His face was red and he looked somewhat disheveled. Well, maybe he'd been asleep.

But why would that upset Morty?

Moments later, Lina approached from the break area. Her face was pink.

Oh, ho, thought Will. *I wonder if Frenchy noticed?* But a glance showed the same bland expression Frenchy usually wore. His poker face was intact.

Will smothered a grin and turned to look at the King. Picking up one of the cables, he examined the plug carefully until he had his mirth under control. *Their business*, he thought.

Morty cleared his throat. "What did you want to talk about, Frenchy?"

Frenchy looked directly at Morty, never sparing a glance at the others. "We're going to have to change directions slightly. I had hoped to be hiring a manufacturing crew by now, but we're going to an automated production system instead. It will take a bit longer at first, but we'll turn out more units faster when it's running. We've got time, because I just got the notice that we wouldn't be getting as many battery packs as we wanted."

"Really?" asked Morty. "I didn't have a problem."

"That's because you were only ordering them a few at a time, or so they said. We'll eventually be ordering thousands of the larger units, and producing those is an order of magnitude more difficult. The battery cells are essentially the same, they're just packaged differently. Voltages and current availability are different too, because of the number of cells and how they're connected to each other. But the models we're ordering put us in direct competition with people who want them for cars and home power systems."

Morty nodded. "So what do we do now?"

"We continue with small scale manufacturing and work out any production bugs that crop up. The King, Bedstead II, will be ready for testing soon and we can fly it with only two packs instead of the four it's supposed to have. We've got enough battery packs for that, they're identical to the ones on the Bedstead, so we can swap the packs around.

"I've also found an airplane for testing the aviation system. We'll install the battery packs inside the cabin, two to start with, maybe more later on. The plane's a used de Havilland DHC-6 Twin Otter. Plenty of lift, in other words.

"It's configured for passenger use at the moment, so we'll need to pull the seats to make room for the batteries. Will wants to mount the impellers externally under the wings, probably inboard of the two turboprop engines. After we're satisfied the impeller system is reliable, we can swap out the turboprops for turbo-generators."

"That's disappointing, Frenchy. Not the plane, that sounds fine and your plan sounds good, but I hoped we'd be farther along by now," said Morty.

"The battery problem is out of our hands, but I'll keep pushing. We've still done a lot, Morty. *You're* the one who told me quality comes first and that takes time. Anyway, I consider this an opportunity, not a real setback; while we transition to automated manufacturing, we'll be building our own green power plant. I've been working on that, and most of the ground work is done."

"A power plant?" Morty looked dubious.

"We need the power, you know that, and we can sell the excess to the grid. That will help our cash flow and at the same time, it's a security measure.

"Speaking of security, I need to talk to the person in charge. The opposition will stop at nothing, and the guards need to know that."

"I already talked to one of the shift leaders, Frenchy. She said she'd pass the information on. I didn't authorize an increase in the number of guards, though. Do you think we need to do that?"

"I thought about what Morty said back in Chicago, Chuck, but alerting them to the changed situation is probably good enough for now. Anyway, I was thinking that if the opposition manages to interrupt getting commercial power out here, that would increase our expenses because we'd have to stay on generators for a lot longer than I intended. If they control our power, it also gives them the ability to shut us down or at least put us back on our own generator system, which is less-reliable than commercial power. That would also drive up expenses, and we can't afford to spend money if we don't have to. How much do you know about solar panels and wind turbines?"

"Well, as much as anyone, I suppose. Anyone who's not in the business, I mean."

"We're about to be in the business, Morty. We've filed an amended charter that changes the company's name. Our original documents were filed in Delaware, so we're staying with them. As soon as they approve the change, we'll be Eastern New Mexico Green Energy. How does that sound?"

"It sounds fine, but it won't get a spaceship off the ground."

"That's where you're wrong, Morty. I intend to sell excess power to the grid and the money will keep the company afloat. It's going to take time to build your ship. Just look at how long it took NASA to get the Shuttle off the pad.

"Another advantage, we can sell power without worrying about secrecy, which we can't do with the impellers. Another advantage, New Mexico will shortly require power companies to use more renewable energy. In part this is economic, because the costs to generate renewable energy are falling.

"The electric producers won't take advantage, because they've got investments in coal, gas, and nuclear generation. They'll hang on to those as long as possible rather than spend money on new equipment, but the new regulations will force them to begin closing some of the older, less-profitable plants. That's where we come in; I'm hoping we can take advantage of that. They can build their own green installations, but for the near future, it might be cheaper for them to buy from independents like us.

"PV panels have dropped to maybe half what they were a few years ago, and we expect that by the time we'll have to replace the first ones the costs will be as low as ten percent of our initial outlay.

"We'll tie the PV system in with twenty generating fans to start with, expand to fifty or more if the demand remains strong. Green power is coming, Morty. We might as well jump in while we can."

"Those things are expensive, aren't they?" asked Morty.

"We're projecting three and a half to four and a half million for each two-megawatt generator. That includes the ground anchors, the foundation, the tower, everything. It only takes about three weeks to install a unit, but there's also build time to consider. You don't buy those off the rack.

"Anyway, as financing becomes available, we'll contract for a generator and a company to install it. I think we can get financing for that, there's nothing controversial about a power plant. The contractor works out of Amarillo, but he'll be buying concrete from suppliers in Clovis and Roswell, maybe even Lubbock and Las Vegas. The foundations take a *lot* of concrete, which won't hurt our reputation with the locals. They'll be upset that we're not hiring as many assembly workers as we originally intended, but buying supplies locally will soften the blow.

"That's how I pushed through that earlier change, by reminding New Mexico's people how much money I'd be spending. The power company has agreed to tie in their new 345-kilovolt line, although they weren't happy that we'd stop buying from them at some point. I sweetened the deal by promising that we'd sell power through them as soon as we begin producing excess.

"Anyway, they'll upgrade their existing lines to provide immediate commercial power, so we'll be able to buy from the grid until the wind generators and PV plant are online. And after that, we'll stop buying and start selling."

"I guess if that's what we've got to do, that's what we'll do," said Morty. "I'm disappointed, but I suspect you know that already. Still, as long as we're moving ahead, something is better than nothing. Switching to automated manufacturing and diverting resources to the power plant really slows us down, though. Too bad about the battery packs."

"Dad, any reason we can't begin working up the *design* of a spacecraft?" Lina asked. "I'm about finished with what I was doing on the King. I've got the software I needed now, so I can work on the design while you deal with getting the power plant off the ground."

"Sure, you go ahead. Work with Morty, he's got ideas about

what he wants.

"Morty, I might be able to buy scrap aircraft aluminum from that company in Roswell. Maybe we can get enough of it for you to start building your spacecraft. One thing, though, that idea you had of using small nuclear reactors? That's on hold. I sounded out Los Alamos when I was checking on the green power system requirements, but they didn't want to talk to me.

"There's one other option I'm looking at, although it's going to piss off a lot of officials in this country. I started by asking the Chinese if they could allocate more of the rare earths we need for batteries, but they weren't interested. But as soon as I mentioned that we might be building marine systems and airplanes, that got their attention!

"Shipping is a major concern for them because their economy depends on trade. More ships are better as far as they're concerned. When I casually mentioned that we might be interested in nuclear power plants, you could see the light bulbs go on over their heads."

"You didn't mention what we were doing, did you?" asked Morty anxiously.

"No. I just said we were interested in maritime operations and that we were interested in using nuclear-electric power in cargo ships.

"The new models are safer as well as cheaper, and they really perked up their ears when I mentioned small reactors. They're doing something with those, no idea what. I told him that we would use a standard hull size and shape, meaning that we could carry more cargo than the *NS Savannah* did. That one was only a demonstrator anyway, and because of the hull design it could never haul enough to compete with diesel-powered freighters.

"Anyway, I explained that our ships could haul the same amount of cargo at reduced costs. As soon as I mentioned that, the Chinese representative did everything but kiss my hand!"

"Be careful, Frenchy. You don't want to let them know how we plan to use the reactors. My main aim was to get the impellers out where humanity could use them in an emergency and we're doing that, but we won't make much money unless we get a jump on everyone else."

"Trust me, Morty, I won't tell them anything. I'm well aware of the money issue too. Those things are expensive! That's another reason we want a reliable income stream. Anyway, that's all I've got for now, at least for you. Will, anything you want to add?"

"Not yet, Frenchy. I'll get checked out in that Twin Otter as soon as it's delivered. Shouldn't have any problem landing it on this strip, even without paving the runway. The Twin was designed for short-takeoffs and landings on unimproved runways. I'll meet the pilot in Clovis and he can check me out there before he catches a flight back to California.

"I'll get it here as soon as I can. We'll need our own refueling facilities, though; the turboprops use low-sulfur S10 diesel fuel that's not yet common in New Mexico, so we'll need our own supply."

"I'll see to it, Will. We don't want the fuels to get mixed up. Tell you what, I'll put a tank and refueling shed here on the side of the parking apron."

"Fine, Frenchy.

"We've got a plan and a management staff, so we're almost ready to transition to stage two. You handle the power plant negotiations and financing, Morty and the engineers produce the impellers and pass them to Chuck for testing, and I'll manage the aircraft division. Panit is managing the factory campus now, while Trent is in charge of marine operations. Jim is familiar with how the impellers work, so he'll captain the ship during the shakedown trials. He'll turn the ship over to Trent as soon as he's satisfied and return here to assist Morty. Trent will hire a captain and crew for the *Tesla*, which is what we're calling the ship, and as soon as it's operational his people will start hauling cargo. Which will also add to the revenue stream.

"It's a good plan, but I think it should be discussed the next time we hold a meeting of the board. There won't be a problem, but we need to keep things official. You know about it, and I know about it, but the other investors don't."

"You're right. I'm more used to financing things than running them. I'll call a board meeting for...not next week, we'll be working on getting the King flying and the *Tesla* launched for her shakedown cruise. How about two weeks from now?"

"Works for me, Frenchy," said Will. "If that's everything, then, maybe we should think about heading back for Clovis?"

"You get the plane ready, Will. Morty, I'll see you later. Chuck, why don't you and Lina stick around for a few minutes. I'd like to talk to you."

"I'll see you later, Frenchy. Will, if you've got a minute, there's something I'd like to discuss with you."

"Sure, Morty. What have you got in mind?"

"You're going to be in charge of aviation, so I wanted to ask a favor. Do you think you could…?"

Chapter Sixteen

A short, heavy-set balding man walked down the hallway. He wasn't smiling, because he'd been summoned to the office of his superior. He knocked on the door and waited. A male secretary answered and gestured across the outer office to the door into the colonel's office.

Major André Kotcheff took a deep breath, tugged at the hem of his coat, then went in and stood in front of the desk. He waited while the colonel studied the paper before him. This gave the major a few moments to study the colonel. *Too much good food, too much vodka, not enough exercise*, he thought. *I need to get out more, maybe work out or at least get in some running. I don't want to end up like this fat fool.*

"You failed, Major. This is *your* failure. All that money, wasted, because you got nothing. Nothing!"

"Sir, I wasn't there. I was here in New York the entire time. The people I hired were competent, but who could have expected..."

The colonel interrupted him. "I was here in New York too, but then I didn't spend scarce money for nothing! You're supposed to *anticipate* what people will do, Major! This report...it doesn't say enough, not *nearly* enough. I allowed you an operating budget, but you managed to blow all of it, *every last dollar*, and you have nothing to show for it! What were you thinking?"

"Sir, I saw an opportunity. As you know, we're observing what those others are doing, but we can't get inside the new plant where they make those devices. Our satellites pass over the factory four times a day, so we know nothing important has happened yet.

"They have a factory, but it's not in full production. They're not buying enough supplies, for one thing, and they're not shipping anything; we know that because we're watching the trucking companies. The only way they can get supplies in or move the devices out is by truck, and that's not happening.

"What they do have is a few workers, and maybe enough material on hand to make a few of the devices. We don't know, because we don't have nearly as much background information as I would like. For that matter, we only recently became aware of their new facility.

"I knew they had people working in Chicago, but they weren't involved with manufacturing. I have contacts among the dockworkers, so I'd have known if that was going on. All they were doing was working on a barge.

"They rented welders and air compressors, things like that, and on Wednesday they returned them, so I knew they were finished with whatever they were doing. But I repeat, all they'd done was do some welding and cutting on the barge, not manufacture some sort of secret device. That was the situation until last Tuesday. But then my people reported that they used a rented crane to emplace a large generator on Wednesday afternoon *after* they'd returned the tools they'd rented, so I judged they were moving into a new phase of whatever they were doing. I suspected that they were going to move the device across the lake to a new location. It had to be something very heavy, otherwise they wouldn't have needed the barge. I have the report from my agent in Chicago, Colonel. Would you like to see it?"

"No, Major. I have *your* report, and *you* were in charge. *You* made the decisions. *You* chose to spend money trying to capture this barge.

"A *barge*? What were you thinking? Or were you even thinking at all? Did the fact that I was out of my office somehow make you confident that you could go ahead without consulting me?"

"No, sir. I didn't have time to contact you, Colonel. I *had* to act, because I don't have assets in Michigan. So that's why I decided I had to hijack the barge before it left.

"The people in Chicago took delivery of a cargo Thursday. I don't know what it was, they did all the uncrating on the barge, and my agent couldn't get a look at it. Whatever was in the crates, they immediately moved it below the barge's upper deck.

"He got a look at the crating materials, but there was no label or anything to tell what was in the crates. I realized that for the first time, they'd probably moved a completed device away from their factory.

"We can't get in there, but if I could get my hands on the machine it wouldn't matter. We have very good scientists and I'm sure they can reverse-engineer this thing, whatever it is.

"So I told my agent what I wanted done, sent him the money, and he hired reliable people. He also put armed men on a pair of power launches in case the people on shore had problems, and paid a towboat operator to stand by to go in and bring the barge out.

"They were in a harbor with a dock behind them, land on both sides, and our boats between them and the entrance. There was nowhere they could go and no time to dismantle the device and carry it away.

"My agent had men on shore to board the barge, and as soon as they'd captured or eliminated everyone, the boats were to come in.

"I didn't even expect to need the launches; they were intended to guard the towboat while it moved the barge. We had a place to moor it, and once it was in our hands we would have as much time as we needed.

"It was a chance for us to find out exactly what this thing is and see how it works; all we had to do was take it away from them. Who could have guessed they'd blow holes in the barge and sink it out in middle of the harbor?"

"They *blew holes* in it? How could they have expected your people to be there? Explosions take preparation, Major, you don't just scuttle a barge without preparation!"

"I don't know, Colonel. But the men on shore heard loud bangs and the barge sank, so it had to be scuttling charges."

"Can we use divers to find the barge, Major?"

"We know where it is, colonel, but we can't get to it. There's a patrol boat cruising in the harbor and a salvage crew working."

"So you failed," the colonel said heavily. "Your agent, the man you entrusted this to; was this your plan, or his?"

"I came up with the idea, move in quick and take the device, but he decided how to accomplish the task. He was the man on the scene; I trusted him to see the job was done right."

"One more of your many failures, major! What led you to believe you could trust this man to do what you wanted, instead of taking our money and disappearing into this benighted country?"

"That was indeed an error, Colonel. I believed that he was trustworthy, because he was one of the men you've used before. I should have investigated further or even gone to Chicago to oversee the operation myself."

"That...will be all, Major. You are dismissed."

Well, that worked, thought the major, t*his time. But I'm going to have to do something about him before long.*

Chapter Seventeen

Frenchy's 'talk' lasted about fifteen minutes. A chastened Lina headed back for the break room while Chuck remained.

"I'll watch myself. I know Lina is likely to be changed in some way by what happened to her, but I can't simply reject her. I'll be careful."

"She's a grownup, so that's all I can ask."

"On a different topic, Frenchy, I've got a suggestion. We might be able to divert attention from what we're really doing if we made a production of shutting down the old warehouse and putting up a For Sale sign."

"Keep talking."

"How about this? We get a locksmith to change all the locks, then shut off all the lights except one. Put a guard on the warehouse at night, maybe only for a week or two, then just lock the doors and the gates. Leave everything locked down so that it looks like we've given up. If anyone is still watching the building, they're welcome to break in. The only thing we've got left there is the forklift, so we bring it with us and either return it to the company we leased it from or buy it. We already need a forklift to move stuff around."

"A red herring? I don't know whether the opposition will buy that, but I suppose it can't hurt. Okay, I'll see that it's done. Anything else?"

"We'll be flying the King by this weekend if you want to come out. This time, the ride will be more comfortable because we've got permanent seats in the back and a wider windscreen. It's not a complete canopy, but even so, it should be a comfortable ride. Want to give it a try? Maybe even learn to pilot it?"

"I like the idea, but I don't have the time. I'm really busy with negotiations; we're working out the details of property easements for the high-voltage line and how much I'm prepared to contribute, directly or indirectly, to political parties. I won't do it myself, but I'll see that it happens. I've got lawyers handling the low-level meetings, but the big guys want to talk directly to me. This is all word of mouth, no paperwork, so trust is important."

"Trust from crooks. That's what this really is, you know, paying bribes to crooks."

"Shhh. Don't use the B-word! Those are campaign contributions, given in good faith!"

"Yeah, right. Investments is what they are, and they're probably deductible too."

"Sure. I'll probably set up a foundation, Will and the others will too. None of us will turn down an opportunity to reduce our tax bite. In a sense, the government will be contributing about a third of what the politicians get." Frenchy shrugged. "It's just the way things are done now."

"I suppose. Anyway, I'm going to bed. I've been up about sixteen hours and I've got to get up again in about six. Mel can work on the wiring, but I will do the final checks of the King myself. I'll also be writing the manual for this one, working up altitude limits and power consumption times based on loads and weather. The batteries work better in warmer weather and wind is a major factor, so that has to be included too. The King isn't aerodynamic at all."

"I can see that. Will and I were talking and he mentioned an old saying among pilots. 'Given enough power, even a brick will fly.'"

"Makes sense. Anyway, I'll see you next time. I'm going to try to finish up work on the King so I can take a few days for the *Tesla's* shakedown cruise."

Frenchy nodded. "If I don't get back here before, I'll see you when we sail. You've done a good job with the improved Bedstead and the King."

"Thanks." Chuck reached out and the two shook hands, then Frenchy turned and left.

***

Three days later, Lina and Chuck finished the wiring and setup on the King, then installed two freshly-charged battery packs in the aft compartments. The King could accept up to four, necessary for heavy loads or longer flights, but for the initial tests two would be plenty.

The Bedstead had never been flown at high altitudes and the King would observe the same limit, meaning that even a single battery pack with 10% remaining charge provided enough power to land the craft.

The battery compartments were connected in parallel to a main power buss; regardless of the number of battery packs, voltage remained the same. Each battery pack added about half an hour's flight time if loaded to maximum gross weight, meaning that the King could haul passengers or cargo for about two hours before the batteries would need recharging.

The King was a truck; the re-designed Bedstead was more akin to a sports car.

Mel made himself scarce, flying the Bedstead and adding hours of use. Lina and Chuck appreciated the opportunity, but limited their contact to hugs and occasional kisses. But Mel, being considerate, called the hangar ten minutes before he brought the Bedstead home after each flight.

So went the remainder of the week. By Friday, the King was ready for its first test. Chuck intended to hover at low altitude, no more than a foot off the hangar floor, for the first half hour, then try a sequence of simple maneuvers. Moving forward, backing, turning, and drifting broadside to port and starboard would show that the control system was working as expected. The batteries would have enough residual charge remaining after the tests to park the King.

Mel had made an alteration to both craft. Thick straps now ran on each side of the pilot's station, terminating in a large canvas bundle behind the passenger seats.

"What's this, Mel? Is this something you came up with on your own?"

"Not exactly, Chuck. The Bedstead gets one cargo parachute, the King gets three. I talked to Morty about something that had been bothering me; we're going to be running new kinds of flight tests, and that's going to include high altitude and maneuvering tests. Anyway, he had the parachutes shipped in and I installed them."

Mel climbed up on the Bedstead and pointed out the features. "The chutes are attached to a four-point suspension system, two links in the front and two at the rear. They're adjusted so that the craft sinks rear first at a thirty-five-degree angle. This is something like what astronauts did, land backward. If the chutes are ever deployed, that gives the crew a chance to walk away from it since it will be descending rear first. The adapted pilot seats provide excellent back support.

"The ripcord runs under the seat and the handle is clipped here, between the pilot's legs. Don't pull that D-handle unless you intend to come down by chute."

"How high are you planning to go, Mel?"

"Eventually, three or four thousand feet, Chuck. That's high enough to do some roll tests and recover from them. I'll take it in stages and only roll about ten or fifteen degrees to start. I'll try it at low altitude first, see if the impellers will tumble, and if they do find out how long it takes the computer to reset. If I can't reset it in time, having the parachute may keep me alive. I hope.

"Anyway, the way I've got it planned out, if there's going to be a problem it should happen before I gain much altitude."

"Okay, I can understand that. But you be damned careful. We need old, not bold, pilots. These things are perfect illustrations of that old pilot's saying about enough power and flying rocks. We haven't needed to worry much, because up to now, we've remained low and relatively slow."

"I'll have to push the envelope during the tests, Chuck, but Morty and I both feel better about me having a means of survival.

"I don't see us ever needing ejection seats, but an individual parachute for the pilot might someday be part of his flight equipment. I'll also install a passive instrument package to measure the impact force, just in case I'm ever forced to deploy the chute."

"You're not going to test it before you need it?"

"Nope, it's a one-time thing. A parachute is a parachute. If it doesn't work, well, the pilot won't be any worse off. But we've got more than a thousand hours on the latest-model Bedstead, and so far, it's as reliable as any helicopter."

***

Mel waited with Lina as Chuck strapped himself into the pilot's seat. The King sat quietly, a huge beast that bore no relationship to anything intended for flight. For that matter, neither had the original Bedstead or the heavily-modified replacement.

Chuck glanced at the charge indicator, centered in the console to his front, then flipped the switch for the main power buss. Twisting the motorcycle-style throttle on the stick... the thumbwheel was gone, the twist throttle replacing it..., he listened to the faint whines as the impellers powered up. Pressing a button, he watched the dials as the computer made minute adjustments to each impeller.

Frowning, Chuck noticed that the portside forward impeller was drawing almost ten percent more power than the others. Odd, but since he was only going for a low-level hover...

It was something to look at later, he decided. He wasn't going anywhere, just bringing the craft to a hover and holding it a foot in the air. This test would last half an hour, then he'd try out the directional controls before landing.

But we need to replace that impeller before the next flight, he thought.

Nodding to the others, Chuck eased back on the floor-mounted joystick. The long joystick allowed very sensitive adjustments to the computer's input, something that had proved considerably more difficult when using the Bedstead's short game-style controller.

Impellers whined as he eased back on the stick. The King wasn't as responsive as the Bedstead, but he could feel the added power as the bigger unit trembled. He glanced to port and starboard, bringing the deck level with marks on a pair of vertical stands; the simple devices provided an instant reference for the hover test.

Chuck centered the control stick and watched the instruments. Satisfied, he took his eyes off the panel and glanced at Lina. "Look ma, no hands!" Chuck gleefully exclaimed.

Lina glanced at Mel and both shook their heads ruefully. "Kind of full of himself, isn't he?" said Mel.

"He's a showoff, that's for sure."

"Think I'll take the Bedstead out for a spin. You can watch him while he sits there and watches the lights blink."

"Okay, Mel. With Chuck flying one and you flying the other, I might just as well find a book to read."

"Absolutely. You've worked as hard as any of us, you deserve a break. I've been meaning to tell you, you really pitched in. It's been a pleasure working with you."

"I've loved it, Mel. It was just what I needed."

The high-pitched whine suddenly increased. They glanced around, wide eyed, and realized Chuck was frantically trying to control the craft.

But to no effect; the King pitched up and attempted to roll clockwise. The low altitude meant the bow could lift no more than a few degrees before the starboard aft corner struck the floor. The impeller snapped off, the frame twisted, and smoke gushed from beneath the deck as the main buss shorted out. The whining noises faded as the king slammed to the floor.

Chuck slumped unmoving over the control panel that had slammed into his body during the crash. Mel climbed onto the deck, reaching for the buckles, as Lina ran for the nearest fire extinguisher.

***

Will taxied the small business jet to the parking ramp and he and Frenchy exited, walking down the boarding stairs that had been rolled out as soon as the plane landed.

"Little bit fancier than that dirt strip by the plant, Frenchy."

"So is your plane, Will." Frenchy chuckled. "But we'll pave the airstrip in a month or so. That runway will eventually support an airliner, maybe even one of the jumbo jets."

"Going to take more than paving to do that, Frenchy."

"I know. That's in the works, laying the foundation first, then paving the runway, just not right away. Doesn't look like anyone is here to meet us. I guess we'll have to take a taxi."

"Wonder where Chuck is? He said he'd be here. He wants to go on the shakedown cruise, and I think he's earned it.

"Morty decided to skip this one. He's not all that interested in the marine system anyway, not now. Designing it, that was one thing, but using it doesn't really interest him. But I really expected Chuck to be waiting for us."

"We're running a little late. Maybe there was a welcoming committee that picked him up. Do you think we should call Trent?"

"Why don't we just go on out there?"

"Why don't we? No taxi, Will, I'll rent a helicopter. It's faster, and just in case they decided to start without us, we can board the *Tesla* at sea. Trent's message said they had a fairly small window of time to head out."

"Do it. I'll see to our bags." Frenchy nodded, then walked toward the terminal while glancing at his cell phone.

There had been no calls or texts from Chuck or Trent Stokes. *If there had been a change of plans regarding the upcoming shakedown, Trent would have called, wouldn't he?*

Shaking his head, an unconscious reaction, Frenchy walked into the terminal to see about finding a helicopter to fly them out to the *Tesla*.

The trip took just over an hour. The ship was still tied to its moorings, although a faint haze of diesel smoke drifted from the stack.

"Looks like they're getting ready, maybe running tests. Anyway, we're in time."

"We'll go back to shore; landing on the ship doesn't appeal to me if we don't have to. I'll give Jim a call, see if he can send someone to pick us up."

The pilot touched down on a hotel helipad long enough to drop off Frenchy and Will, then lifted off on its way back to the airport. The two men caught a taxi in front of the hotel. Sven was waiting when they arrived at the dock with one of the ship's boats, and he took them to the *Tesla*.

"Morning, Trent. Have you heard from Chuck?"

"He's not coming. There was some sort of mishap and he was shaken up. He said go ahead without him."

"I'm sure he's disappointed, but we're here now so you can get on with what you were doing."

"Jim's doing most of it, Frenchy. He's down in the engine room, doing a last check of the impellers."

"What's the ship's status?"

"The diesels are at idle, the batteries are fully charged. It only takes a few seconds to power up the impellers, so we're just about ready.

"Come on up to the bridge, you can watch from there. It'll be pretty empty, just me for now. We had the computer system available, so we automated everything we could. Later on Sven will come up to give me a hand.

"The wheel is still mounted, but it's only connected to springs to give a feeling of resistance. It's there in case someone gains access to the bridge or we need to make it appear that this is a conventionally-steered ship.

"Anyway, what I'm getting at is we don't need a helmsman. All maneuvering will be done with the impellers, and as soon as we're clear of the channel, we'll set the autopilot. That's controlled by the GPS unit, so the only time we expect to need a human at the stick is when we enter or leave harbor. The rest of the time, he'll stand a watch as lookout and be available in case there's some sort of emergency.

"We shouldn't have any problems in the channel, it's deep and wide enough. The big container ships come in here, so we won't have a problem. The channel is marked too, with buoys; we just stay in our lane and make sure we don't run into any of the small craft. There's very little large traffic right now, plus the sonar and the radar are on. We can be underway in less than a minute, according to Jim. Right now, we're just waiting for the tide to turn."

"Make it so, Captain Trent."

Trent grinned, then picked up the telephone. "Sven, bring in the anchor and stow it, then stand by the mooring line."

"Aye, aye, captain."

Moments later they heard the whirring of the electric winch. The ship drifted briefly, responding to the turning tide. Loud clanks, accompanied by splashing, sounded as the anchor came up. A strong smell, rich with the effluvium common to harbors everywhere, reached the bridge.

"They classify this as a lay berth," Trent commented. "Berthing at the dock would have been usual, but we're not loading cargo and the harbor master didn't want us taking up space that's needed for bulk offloading. He also considers us deadlined, waiting for repair parts. We filed the departure paperwork by mail, but it won't get there before midmorning, and by then I expect to be at sea."

"Irregular?"

"Very. But it's easier to get forgiveness than permission. We can't go through the usual departure routine, because we can't allow a pilot on board. He'd smell a rat right away as soon as he saw us controlling the ship with a joystick! You might eventually get hit with a fine, but it won't be much compared with what we've already spent getting the *Tesla* ready for sea trials."

"What about the Coast Guard?"

"They might check us out, although there's only one or two coastie boats and a lot of ships using this harbor. Shouldn't be a problem, in other words. Even if they do get curious, we've got standard equipment for navigating in American waters and that Liberian registry will stop a lot of questions. Wait one."

Trent phoned Sven, waiting on the forward deck, and told him to stand by to take in the bow line to the mooring buoy. His next call was to Jim. When he reported all systems ready, Trent ordered control shifted to the bridge. Standing in front of a panel, he watched the shifting lights.

When he was satisfied, Trent thumbed a wheel to increase power to the impellers. A small wheel, conveniently mounted for use by either hand, stood up from the panel. Trent pushed gently forward and the *Tesla* inched ahead. The mooring line sagged as the load came off.

"Take in the bow line." Trent's voice showed no sign of tension. This might have been an ordinary departure of a conventional ship.

Frenchy looked at the shoreline. No one appeared to be paying attention. A minute later Sven came up the ladder and joined them on the bridge.

"Ready for departure, Captain. Lines and anchor stowed, deck secure."

"Take the helm, Sven." Trent stepped back and took his seat in the leather-upholstered chair reserved for the captain. Sven sat down in an equally comfortable chair and swung the control panel into position.

Responding to Sven's input, the ship swung around and moved slowly down the channel.

"We'll keep the speed down. Most other ships need a minimum speed to maintain steerageway, but since we don't use a rudder that's not something we have to worry about. The only ship traffic is a fisherman going out, so we'll stay behind him. Seas are low, winds light, and we've got ballast in the tanks so the ship will be stable even if there's a problem with the instruments or the impellers.

"I'll engage the anti-roll system as soon as we hit the open sea, but it shouldn't be needed. There's coffee, so grab yourselves a cup and enjoy the ride."

"You only need three of you to control the ship? I was sure you'd have more."

"We'll need deckhands later on when we start shipping cargo and there's always maintenance work on a ship, so yes, we'll need a couple of seamen. We'll work out manning charts when we get back.

"This one's just out of drydock, the generators have less than a hundred hours on the clock, and while the batteries aren't new they've been through a complete discharge-recharge cycle. The impellers *are* new, they've been run for testing but that's all.

"Almost everything is automated, so Jim should be able to handle everything below-decks by himself. In a pinch, Sven will help him while I take over the helm.

"I've got my master's ticket and Sven is studying for his, any ocean, any tonnage. Eventually he'll captain his own ship. For now, there's not much on the ship that he can't do, and like I said, most of the system is automated. Jim's not interested; he's hoping to command a different kind of ship."

"This is a shakedown cruise, right? What if something goes

wrong?" asked Will.

"There are tugs available, but I don't see us needing them. We've got four diesel-powered generators feeding two banks of batteries, so even if the diesels fail we've got emergency power. Propulsion and steering are split into separate systems for safety, controllable remotely from the bridge, or in an emergency from local stations in the engine room. I'll exercise that system after we make sure the primary is working fine.

"We've run individual tests, everything is nominal, the only thing we haven't done is exercise all systems while under way. I'll go to full power after we're well off shore. Feel like a trip to Bermuda?"

"Wait a minute, isn't that where all those ships have disappeared?"

"You don't really believe all that stuff, do you Frenchy?"

Frenchy shrugged, but didn't look convinced. Trent glanced at Sven and both looked away, smiling.

Chapter Eighteen

Will and Frenchy arrived back at the plant the following Monday. They were met by Lina, who walked up as they finished tying down the Piper.

Frenchy hugged her, then asked, "What happened to Chuck?"

"He was doing the first hover test with the King. Something went wrong and it almost flipped over. He had a high current reading on one of the bow impellers, but said he thought it was okay. It was, for the first few minutes, but then it crashed.

"The frame is bent, one of the batteries caught on fire and the other will require a factory rebuild. Chuck hit the control panel. He has two cracked ribs, but the doctor said he should heal with no problems.

"The King is going to need rebuilding, probably from scratch. We sent both batteries to the factory. There won't be replacements right away, but maybe they can do something with the wrecked ones.

"Mel has already added a roll bar to the Bedstead, right behind the pilot's seat. The King will have one too when it's rebuilt. It extends above his head and it's wide enough to provide at least some protection to his arms.

"Chuck didn't *roll* the King, it was too close to the floor, but it could happen when they're out on the test course. It's better to have the protection before it's needed."

Will nodded thoughtfully. "Good idea. I'm glad that I'll have wings and controls if I have to shut down the impellers in flight. How much will the ribs affect Chuck's schedule?"

"He says he can keep going. He can't do heavy lifting, but he can do drilling and riveting. Mel and I can lift things and help do what has to be done, so it won't be all that bad. We've also got the overhead crane for lifting heavy things like the batteries."

"Don't let him overdo it, Lina."

"He's pretty stubborn, Dad. Reminds me a lot of you." She grinned as Frenchy winced.

"So how did the cruise go? You were out all day, weren't you?"

"Right, we came into port after dusk, tied back up to the same mooring buoy after Sven lowered the anchor. Almost everything worked as expected, but we had to shut down the anti-roll system. I sent Morty a message suggesting that we might install four of the smaller impeller units and use them as a dedicated anti-roll anti-pitch system. In a pinch, they could also help with maneuvering, but we didn't have a problem during the cruise. Everything else worked as expected. I was a bit disappointed that Morty passed up the chance to be part of the voyage."

"He has some sort of bug, or maybe it's allergies. That's probably why he didn't want to go. They've been rough this year."

"Welcome to New Mexico. Even the plants fight back out here. But he's a tough old coot."

"Remember that he *is* old, dad. I didn't like the way he looked, so Chuck and I talked him into taking a few days off and resting.

"He wanted to help with installing the impellers on the Twin Otter's wings, but Chuck nixed that and he finally left. Grumbling all the way, as you might expect."

"I'd like to see how that's going, Lina, and then I'd like to take a look at the King. Was anything else damaged?"

"Just Chuck's pride. He said the computer wasn't able to control one of the impellers and he was lucky. I'll tell you this, *I* was scared stiff for a moment!"

Frenchy looked at her questioningly. She nodded back. "Yes, dad. I was really scared."

He got the unspoken message. Whatever was developing between the two of them, Lina thought it was serious.

"Anything I should know about, honey?"

"Not yet, dad. We'll let you know if there is."

"We?"

"We."

***

Will's new airplane, the De Havilland Twin Otter, had finally arrived. He met the pilot in Clovis and underwent a day-long transition course, then flew the Twin to the plant. The engineers took out the passenger seats, then began modifying the plane.

Morty, insisting that he was feeling better, watched engineers install the second impeller under the port wing.

This one, unlike the models now being used on the Bedstead and the King, bore a much closer resemblance to the cylindrical housing used on the original Flying Bedstead.

Frenchy and Will walked over, Will to see how the installation was going and Frenchy to have a close look at the old man.

He did indeed look ill. His skin had a grayish cast and he was wearing a clip across his nose to hold his nostrils open. Only his eyes showed the same enthusiasm Frenchy was accustomed to seeing.

"Allergies that bad, Morty?"

"Worse than usual. You're supposed to use these when you sleep, but I figured they'd work just as well during the day."

"Lina said she and Chuck had talked you into taking some time off, Morty," said Frenchy.

"Aw, I just couldn't stay in bed with Chuck gimping around like he is. I'm just watching and doing a little supervising now and then; it's not as if I was *working* on anything."

"Don't overdo it, Morty. Anyway, these aren't the same impellers we're using on the other craft."

"They are, it's just that the housing is different. I mounted the first ones vertically on the Bedstead, but later on I mounted them in gimbals so they could point in any direction. That's why the casing for the later models is ball-shaped, so the impellers can be shifted around. But the plane has flight controls, so it's easier just to hang the impellers on a fixed mount that's always pointing forward.

"We can still get limited controllability by varying power settings, and I added trim tabs that can change the impeller heading up or down by five degrees. I doubt we'll need more than that.

"We'll do ground testing first, taxiing on the runway, and I reckon we can refine the orientation of the impellers a bit before the plane takes off. I was thinking that we might just hang the plane from that crane in the assembly plant. We could feed in just enough impulse to see what effect the impeller angle will have.

"I talked to the engineers already. Prin Sikkit's the head of electrical engineering, he'll work on the trim controls. Slip's the guy in charge of mounting the impellers. Come on over, I'll show you what he's doing. Will, you'll want to take a look at this too."

The three walked over and looked up at the wing mount. The impeller hung close to the fuselage, almost touching it, but far enough back to clear the propeller arc.

"We installed the mounts so the impellers would be as far back as possible. I didn't think it would be a good idea to interfere with airflow around the leading edge of the wing root or cause turbulence in the prop wash."

"Good thinking, Morty. At any rate, it's balanced. I'll have some idea of whether it will fly as I go through the ground tests. I would prefer wind tunnel testing, but I don't suppose that's possible."

"No, but Slip has a program for his computer that lets him model what's likely to happen. He ran virtual tests using different mounting locations.

"Putting the impellers outboard of the engine changed the wing loading characteristics too much. Slip also mailed off a question to the manufacturer, asking about moving the turboprops outboard. He just told them we were considering mounting a cargo pod inboard on the wing and wanted to know what they thought of the idea. Haven't heard back from them yet."

"I'll want to take a look at the airflow pattern too," said Will. "I'll taxi the bird, keeping the speed down at first, then run up the engines. But I'll keep it down to less than takeoff speed until I'm sure it's safe.

"Maybe we can use ribbons on the leading edges of the wings to see what's going on with the airflow. But I know what to expect from an unmodified Twin, so if this doesn't affect flight characteristics too much it should be okay. The Twin Otters were designed to take off and land on short airstrips, so there's quite a bit of safety built in when you're flying from an airstrip as long as ours is."

"You're not afraid to fly it, Will?"

"No, I'm just being cautious. But I'll fly it, because this is the first step in making me a few billion dollars. That's worth taking a few chances."

"Keep your calendar open, then. We'll be ready for ground tests next week and you'll want to be here for those."

"I'll do more than just be here, I'll be at the controls or at least watching closely!"

As they talked, Will noticed a group of men following a fork lift carrying a large pallet. Another followed immediately behind. Each pallet carried two of the globular impeller containers.

"What's going on, Morty?" He pointed to the forklifts and the gaggle of engineers following behind.

"I had the remaining impellers pulled from the King. We're doing a complete teardown on all of them to find out whether Chuck's problem was with the impeller or whether it was something in the software.

"The Bedstead and the King are flying test beds, but they aren't like the *Tesla* in a sense; we can't totally isolate any of the systems while we're airborne, and the way they're designed now, they've all got to respond to a single control input. We may find later on that it's better to have two systems for safety, each controlling four of the eight impellers.

"I looked over possible redesigns after the accident; we're mounting each of the Bedstead's impellers at the corner right now, but on the long sides. It wouldn't take much to add two to the front and two at each rear corner. That was what I had in mind all along, but up to now we haven't had the impellers available.

"Anyway, that would mean that each corner has two impellers, one at the front or rear, one to each side. We could then arrange dual controls so that one computer manages the front and rear impellers, while a different computer controls the four side-mounted ones.

"A central computer, responding to the joystick, would supply inputs to the subsystems. If one or even two impellers failed, the program could be set up to fail-safe, so that the computer shuts off whichever system isn't working as expected. In an emergency, the pilot could override the computer and shut off one of the subsystems manually. He'd lose power, but with proper design the other subsystem could fly the craft or at least bring it down gently."

"What if both impellers on one corner go out, Morty?"

"I think the craft could still be landed. It wouldn't be easy, but it could be done. The pilot would have his hands full, that's for sure. Use the two diagonal systems to provide lift, use the one corner that's still under control to keep the unit balanced as it lands.

"The controls are pretty responsive. Might be a hard landing, but I think it would be survivable. We can try something like that while we support the Bedstead on cables, then try cutting power to a corner. See whether the system really will balance it long enough to get on the ground."

"Hairy. I'm looking at this from the pilot's perspective," said Will.

"Hairy indeed. But survivable, I hope. Otherwise, the pilot and any passengers are screwed."

***

The Twin Otter had never been named. A fast paint job added a '- 1' to the numbers on the vertical stabilizer and that was deemed good enough. Maybe planes would get names later on. For now, to the company it was simply Airplane One.

Prepping and ground testing had taken almost three weeks. Will had conducted some of the tests himself; he'd pushed hard, taxiing slowly at first using the turboprops while looking for any crabbing or unusual feel from the controls, then increasing the speed. Satisfied, he switched to a combination of turboprop and impeller power.

Chuck, still favoring his sore ribs, had climbed in and strapped into the new flight engineer's station, located behind the copilot's seat. He'd followed Will's instructions faithfully, adding power to the impellers when ordered, then shutting them down one at a time to see how that affected the plane's handling characteristics.

During and immediately after each test, Will recorded his observations. He would translate his verbal notes later and compile a written log of all that had been done.

The final ground test used impeller only, starting on the apron of the runway.

Chuck kept a separate record of his own test results, compiling battery consumption rates in relation to power and also noting Will's impeller trim settings.

The final test had seen them rolling rapidly down the runway, approaching takeoff speed, before Will ordered Chuck to dial the impellers back to idle. He taxied back to the parking area, using only the turboprops, then shut down the engines.

Will helped steady Chuck as he climbed down from the plane.

"I don't know if you noticed, but I had enough speed to take off during that last test. I held her on the ground and then backed off, but I'm confident we won't have a problem. Ready for a flight test tomorrow?"

"I'm ready. Just don't bend the bird, I might have a tough time getting out if you rip the wings off."

"Don't worry about it. That almost never happens."

"Almost? Are you *serious*?"

"Sort of; it's been known to happen. Not to me, though. I'm one of those old and not very bold pilots you hear about. I want to live to spend some of the billions we'll make from owning our own asteroids."

"Me too; Grandpa would never forgive me if I got myself killed. I came closer three weeks ago than I like to think about!"

"And is your grandpa the only one who might miss you, Chuck?"

"Certainly not, Will. If you didn't have me, who would be crazy enough to fly with you while you tested this contraption?"

The two grinned at each other, both aware that Will's question had referred to Lina, who managed to be there at the end of every testing session. She often walked off with Chuck and the two had their arms comfortable around each other's waist.

But Chuck had adroitly deflected the question. The two men

understood each other and found no need to discuss Chuck and Lina's increasingly-affectionate relationship.

***

Sol Goldman was afraid. Not so much because of his unfamiliar surroundings, although he'd never been in a place like this, but because he sensed the precariousness of his position. The world he'd learned to live in was shaky, and many of the things Sol had taken for granted were no longer assured.

The bar was a dive, no question about it. Fortunately for Sol's peace of mind, only one old woman sat nursing a beer at the bar.

He took off his coat and tie, unbuttoned his collar, and rolled up his sleeves. He still didn't look like the sort who'd frequent this place, but on the other hand he didn't look like the successful business executive he was. Ordering a beer, Sol carried it and his rolled-up coat and tie to a booth near the back. With luck, he wouldn't have long to wait.

Slowly sipping at his beer, Sol watched the door, waiting. Ten minutes later Walter walked in. He stopped at the bar long enough to order a beer for himself, then joined Sol in the booth.

"I got held up. Business...it took longer than I expected. Anyway, the burgers here aren't bad. You want something to eat?"

"I'll pass, Walter. I may have more work for you."

"I've got time. That was what the holdup was about, my being paid. Guy owed me, and we discussed the matter. He saw things my way but it took a while. Anyway, what kind of work?"

"That message I had you send Frenchy, I don't know if he got it," said Sol carefully. "The only thing he's done is go low-key. It took a while to find him, but he's still going ahead with what he was doing.

"My friends are with me on this, and we think he's dangerous. Frenchy's not a bad guy, it's just that he doesn't understand business. He's also a loose cannon; he has no idea how dangerous he is. But he's a threat to the whole economy."

"And that's why you're after him, because he threatens the economy? Mister Gold, I know you're the guy with money and you're looking to hand me some of it, but I've got to say that sounds a little fishy."

"I'm not the only one, Walter," Sol repeated. "I'm here because I know you and because we've worked together before. That's the only reason."

"So this threat you're talking about; this guy Frenchy will cost you money, is that what it's about?"

"Well, it's more than that."

"Look, you need to open up a little. I can always go somewhere and off somebody, but that doesn't sound like what you want. The more information I have, the better chance I have to do what you *really* want, stop this guy from doing whatever the hell he's doing. What is that, anyway?"

"He's building a device. We don't really know if it's going to work the way he thinks it will, but the threat's real enough, and dangerous. There are too many jobs and too much money riding on this for us to ignore what he's doing. He's built a factory, so he's further along than I had hoped and now it won't be easy to shut down.

"He's spent a lot of money...chasing down how much took me a while…but I understand finance and spending. That's how I found him. People associated with him have also been spending money. Anyway, his factory's out in the middle of nowhere, meaning it won't be easy to get to, but I want it shut down."

"So where is this place?"

"Northeastern New Mexico. He owns the land, Frenchy does, so there was nothing I could do to stop him. I tried to close off his financing, but he still managed to get money from somewhere."

"So if this factory caught fire, that would work for you?"

"Probably, and if you can do it without loss of life, that would be an ideal solution. But like I said, it's surrounded by a whole lot of nothing. Not even a town, it's just out in the middle of a pasture or something. How would you burn it?"

"If it's out in the boonies, that makes it easy. All I have to do is get close and set the brush on fire. New Mexico's pretty dry, they have a lot of forest fires and brush fires. Grass fires too, now that I think about it."

"You're well informed, Walter."

"That's how I work, Mister Gold. I read a lot, watch the news, you never know when something will come in handy."

"So how would you get into position to set this fire? It's private land, so if anyone saw you they'd know you didn't belong there."

"I'll just do what I always do in a case like this, hire people who know what they're doing. I'd go along to make sure they do a good job, but there are plenty of people available who know about sneaking around in the woods and brush. Ex-soldiers mostly, but there are others too. Some are Russians and there are even a few who were mercenaries in Africa.

"Like I said, they're available. It's just a matter of picking people who have the skills and don't care what they do so long as they get paid for it. Speaking of pay, it won't be cheap."

Sol nodded, then took a pen from his shirt pocket. Picking up a napkin, he wrote a number on it.

"We have a budget in mind. Would this work?"

Walter glanced at the number and smiled.

Chapter Nineteen

Chuck and Mel were drinking coffee in the hangar.

"How long before you plan on doing flight tests on the Bedstead?"

"We're starting tonight, Chuck. I'll start with stability tests, then do maneuverability testing while the engineers look at the data. We're expecting a weather front to move in later this week, which will give me a chance to do some wind tests to see what effect they have on handling. I'll stay low while I'm doing it, though, probably under ten feet.

"I'm thinking I'll just run that course you set up," Mel went on, "the one that goes through the canyon before circling back here.

"We've got basic flight instruments on the panel now, so eventually I'll want to try an instrument flight and landing. But first, I'll want to know how responsive the system is, and I'll do it during daylight so I can take over if I have to. At some point we'll need to do high altitude testing.

"Even by combining tests, I figure a month, maybe six weeks, to get it all done."

"I've also got flight instruments on my panel in the Twin Otter," Chuck said. "Will wants me to try flying it from the backseat, using only the impeller controls. The turboprop controls are up front, but in theory I should be able to control the Twin using impellers alone. Maybe even land it, if the tests go okay."

"No stick or rudder controls?"

"No. I shouldn't need them, and if we're wrong, Will can take over. I'll control yaw, turn left or right that is, by advancing or retarding the impeller power settings, and I can control pitch with the trim controls.

"As for turns, I can trim one impeller to point up and the other down to set up a bank, then point both up to complete the turn. I'm playing with a difference of ten degrees at most, so an impeller turn won't be as quick as it would be if I was using the ailerons and the elevator. Precision maneuvers just aren't possible, but maybe the impellers could be used in an emergency. Will can take over if it looks like things aren't working. We'll be somewhere around ten thousand feet, giving him plenty of airspace to recover.

"But it's only an interim measure. Later on, the impellers will provide thrust, but the aerodynamic controls will be used to fly the plane.

"I'm more concerned about you, Mel. The Bedstead was never intended to operate at altitude. Grandpa flew it to about forty feet, the original model I mean, but it was really touchy. It was so unstable that he didn't stay up there long. The computer was in control, which probably helped, and he was careful not to try any sharp turns."

"We're going to have to go higher if we're going to take this system into space, Chuck," argued Mel. "We won't know if everything works until we try it in space. Maybe not go into orbit, but above the stratosphere at least."

"I understand the need, but I'm still concerned," Chuck insisted.

"Chuck, would *you* fly the tests?"

"Mel, I *intended* to. But right now, I'm stove up from crashing the King, plus the team handed us an aerial system earlier than I expected. I can't do both, but Will and I agreed that I was the best guy for the Twin Otter testing so I'm stuck.

"But I'm worried about you. Have you thought about a parachute for yourself? Maybe a sports chute?"

"Chuck, I wouldn't know a damned thing about jumping; that's why I put that cargo chute on the Bedstead. The way I see it, I'll be strapped into the seat if I have to deploy the chute, and that should keep me from being killed.

"I don't really expect to *need* it, it's just there as insurance and it's also protection for the Bedstead. We've got a lot of time and money tied up in that thing, and right now it's the only thing that's flyable."

"Test pilots wear a chute, Mel. You could take a class on sports jumping, that doesn't take long. Then you could wear an individual parachute. That's *real* insurance."

"Don't worry about it. I'll be all right; you just worry about you and Will. The Twin doesn't have any parachutes at all, and you'll be flying at ten or twelve thousand feet."

"I considered that, but with my busted ribs I couldn't get out fast enough anyway. No reason to worry. Will has thousands of hours of flight time, and anyway we've got two power systems to work with. Not to mention having plenty of runway if we ever need to land without power."

Mel left to check the battery installation on the Bedstead.

Chuck finished his coffee and walked over to the King. No question about it, the frame was bent, the deck had buckled, and the starboard aft impeller had sheared off; it would require a major rebuild.

He worked out ideas in his head as he walked around, studying the damage. He was engaged in this when Morty walked in.

"Hi, Grandpa. Come down to look at Chuck's Catastrophe?"

"No, I wanted you to know that we got the first truckload of aluminum from that salvage company. Some is trash, but some should be usable. The skin panels and struts might have to be heated to anneal them. That's fairly simple, but it will have to be done if we expect to use the aluminum on that ship we don't talk about."

"Still cheaper than buying new, I think. Any plans for that one?"

"Yep, I've got drawings and some of the specs in my computer. That's preliminary data only, I want to talk to the engineers and probably to Lina, but I think it's doable. I'm also planning to hire an aeronautical engineer to oversee the building project."

"Lina, grandpa?"

"Right, she's almost finished with her degree in architectural design. Might as well get her input."

"That makes sense. Grandpa, you still don't look so good. Why don't you take a couple of days off, get some rest? Maybe go into town, check into a motel, see a movie? Have a couple of good dinners and relax. You'll be ready for another 78 years when you get back!"

"It's 79, grandson, but I'll be okay. I've always worked hard, you know that. It's what I do."

"I know. Maybe it's what you *used* to do. Now it's time to sit back and let me pick up some of the load. More of the load, I mean."

"I'll think about it. Maybe after your ribs heal up. When are you taking the Twin up?"

"Probably just before dusk. Will should be waking up about now. We'll do a checkout of the plane and when it's dark enough, we'll go."

"Flying the tests in the dark? I'm not sure I like that idea and I don't think it's necessary. No one is likely to notice the impellers where we mounted them."

"They might notice when we shut down the engines and the props stop spinning."

"I suppose," Morty agreed. "Well, I'll leave you to it. I'll see you when the test is over."

***

Will and Chuck did a preflight inspection, walking around the Twin. The light needed for the inspection came from the dim glow of the shielded runway lights.

No longer a 'Twin Otter', it now had two Sneyd-Tesla impellers slung from mounts inboard from the engines. They fitted between the propeller arc and the fuselage, and there was less than six inches of clearance on each side.

Chuck watched as Will wrapped his hands around the smooth front of the impeller housing and gave it a hard yank, checking to make sure it was firmly mounted. Satisfied, he continued with his inspection, checking ailerons and elevators as well as the state of the tires. When he reached the other impeller he gave it the same treatment. Finished, he helped Chuck into the passenger compartment and stowed the small ladder.

"Ribs still hurting, Chuck?"

"Some. They're getting better, though."

"Good. I'm not expecting a rough ride, but when you're flight-testing you're never really sure. I plan to keep the speed in the middle of the envelope today, just take her up and fly.

"This bird isn't stressed for aerobatics anyway. Mostly it hauls cargo or passengers into remote areas that don't have airports, not the kind that can handle bigger planes. That's where the short takeoff and landing capability comes in. It's a good transport plane for parachutists, too.

"Anyway, you get settled in, I'll warm up the engines."

"Sounds like a plan," agreed Chuck.

Will settled into the cockpit and started the two turboprops. While they warmed up, he ran through a number of other checks, including establishing radio contact with Morty. Satisfied, he spoke to Chuck over the intercom.

"Ready?"

"Wind 'er up, Captain."

Will didn't respond verbally, but the fuselage quivered as the Twin began moving.

For the moment, Chuck had nothing to do. The computer screen showed a blinking green square in the upper left corner, indicating that the system was operating. The two virtual gauges that would register power usage by the impellers indicated zero. The impeller trim controls were set to neutral, the small joystick centered.

Chuck kept an eye on his panel of flight instruments. The altimeter hadn't changed, nor had the artificial horizon. As he watched, the airspeed indicator quivered, then began moving up the dial. He glanced at the window, but there was little to see. The moon wasn't up.

Suddenly the shaking stopped. The Twin was airborne. Will set the controls for a gentle climb straight ahead.

There was still nothing to see outside the windows, so Chuck watched his flight instruments. Not much was happening. The airspeed indicator soon stabilized at 140 knots, then slowly crept up to 150. The plane was now cruising at an altitude of 4500 feet.

The intercom clicked as Will pressed the talk button. "I'm ready to start the test now, Chuck. Set your impellers for two percent impulse."

"Copy, Will. Two percent it is." Chuck gently rotated the thumbwheel set into the panel.

Looking at the gauge, he reported to Will. "Two percent set. Two percent thrust indicated, amp draw minimal."

The airspeed indicator crept up to 153 knots. The power indicators for battery amps barely registered.

The plane slowed to 150 knots as Will reduced power. Satisfied, he clicked the intercom again. "Increase impellers to ten percent. Take it slow so I can watch what's happening."

Chuck responded, "Copy. Coming up on ten percent." Moments later, he reported, "Ten percent registering."

This time the airspeed indicator barely quivered as Will throttled the twin turboprops back. Over the next few minutes, the airspeed slowed, then stabilized at 120 knots.

"I want to judge the effectiveness of the impellers on the plane, but I intend to stay within the plane's performance envelope at all times. Add impeller power, bring up the speed to 150 knots, but do it slow. Don't exceed fifty percent impeller power without my okay. Copy, Chuck?"

"Copy 150 knots, don't exceed fifty percent power." Chuck gently rotated the thumbwheel while watching the airspeed indicator. Two minutes later he eased the last adjustment into place.

"Steady at 150 knots. Impeller power output is 37%. Current draw...best way to judge that is to tell you that at this power setting, we have about three hours remaining flight time on battery."

"Understood. I'm going to reduce power to the turboprops now. You add impeller power as I do. I want to see what our airspeed is at 50% impeller output."

"Copy, Will." Chuck eased the thumbwheel ahead, watching the airspeed. He reached half power on both impellers and watched the plane slow to 86 knots. "I'm at fifty percent power, Will."

"Roger. The turboprops are at idle. It's possible the props are creating a small amount of drag, but even so, we're still well above stall speed. Maybe next time I'll shut the engines off entirely. How much battery capacity is left?"

"At 87 knots...hang on a minute...you've got 135.6 minutes

estimated. If you want 90 knots, the impellers will draw more juice, so you'll have less flight time. Headwinds or tailwinds will also make a huge difference in battery reserve."

"Copy. Well, we've got plenty of airspace underneath and nothing but desert ahead. This time, you're going to attempt to control the plane from your station. Set up for a gentle bank and a turn to port. You know what to do, right?"

"Right, angle up on the starboard impeller and down on the port one, using the trim controls. Center them as soon as I've got enough bank angle. Increase power to the starboard impeller while I'm doing that.

"I don't think I want to reduce power to the port impeller at this point, though. The turn would go faster if I pulled off power, but we've got time."

"Right, you've got the idea. Okay, I'm hands off, you're flying the bird. Go ahead when you're ready."

Chuck concentrated on the instruments, carefully dialing in trim settings on the impellers. The right wing came up and the left wing eased down. As soon as the instruments indicated that the plane was banking, he set both trim controls to up and added power to the starboard impeller. Slowly, the directional heading indicator swung as the Twin banked smoothly left in a gentle turn to port. The altimeter indicated that the plane was sinking slowly, but it was nothing to worry about for now. As the plane completed the turn, he reduced power to the starboard impeller, leveled the plane, and reset the trim controls to neutral.

"I lost some altitude, but I'm ready to bring us back on course. What direction should I take?"

"Steady as you go, and try keeping your altitude above 4000 feet. Try using only the impeller trim controls to bring us back to 4500 feet, see how much battery charge that takes. Again, remember you're trading altitude for speed, so make sure you don't drop below stall speed.

"Increase impeller output to 75% if you need to. You could get to 4500 by increasing speed and using the elevator, but that wouldn't tell us what the impellers can do when they're set for gentle lift.

"Stall speed is listed at 58 knots, but it might be higher since we added the impellers on the wings. That's bound to disrupt airflow to some extent, so let's figure that it might stall as high as 65 knots.

"Let's go with 70 knots as our safe lower limit, so use that as your do-not-exceed lower speed. One more thing, we've got about thirty-five miles to the airstrip and I don't want to drop below ten percent battery charge.

"We'll be coming in from the west, so you should be able to spot the airstrip through your left window. As soon as you have the runway in sight, let me know. I'll take over at that point and land using the engines, with no impeller input. Can you do that?"

"Piece of cake, Will."

Will's voice was dry, even over the intercom. "Don't get overconfident and end up with crumbs. You just do what I said and we'll talk about it when we're on the ground. Maybe later in the week we'll practice dual landings, using the engines and the impellers. We'll start slow, give you time to get used to the idea, but maybe in a couple of weeks you'll be ready to land the plane on impeller power alone."

"You think I'm ready for that?"

"Not yet, Chuck, but you will be. What would you think about getting a pilot's license? Your grandfather mentioned that to me, said it would be a good idea for later on. I'm a certified instructor, but I don't do it because it takes too much of my time and I don't need the money.

"But I can teach you what you need to know to get started. We can conduct ground school classes here, do practice flights in the afternoon, take a break for supper, then do the impeller tests after dark. It will be a lot of work, but I think we can do it. The FAA exams can be taken online, last I heard, so you can do the prep work here. You're still hurting, so this will also give you a chance to do something productive while your ribs heal.

"Anyway, you'll need a medical exam to start the official process, so for that we'll have to wait until you're healthy.

"Plan on spending a few days in Clovis with an instructor later on, that's easier than renting a single engine plane. He can issue the student pilot certificate and sign off on it before you solo, but I can take it from there."

"I like the idea, don't get me wrong, but I may need to help Mel and Lina get the King flying."

"Delegate, Chuck, delegate. Don't try to do everything yourself. Spend time with Lina, but *not* with a wrench in your hand. We've got other people who can do that, the same ones that rebuilt the original Bedstead and built the King's impellers. They know what they're doing. Let Mel handle the King, okay?"

"Well. All right, I guess I can give one of the engineers a try, see if he can do things the way I want them done. But if this doesn't work, my first priority is getting the King flying, not getting a pilot license."

"It will work, Chuck. Your grandfather has had to stand back and let others carry the load, you can too. Remember what I said about Lina. Make *her* your first priority, that would be my advice. Frenchy's too, as soon as he finds out how things are going with the two of you.

"Trust me, both of us have made that mistake, taking on too many projects at once. Things might have been different if...

"Well, no need to go there. We learned the hard way that money can wait, relationships can't. As for that license, the hard part is developing a sense of situational awareness that's not limited to just two dimensions and you've already got that from flying the Bedstead. You've also learned to trust your instruments. You've spent a lot of time flying during darkness, more than in daylight. Don't worry about the license. It'll be a piece of cake. I remember hearing that somewhere."

Chapter Twenty

Will met Chuck later that afternoon and handed over the manuals Chuck would need to study for the FAA exam.

There was a what appeared to be a college-level textbook on meteorology, while an equally-hefty tome dealt with the theory of flight. Both showed signs of extensive use.\

There was also a paper listing online resources from the FAA that could be downloaded in PDF format. This list included two handbooks, *The Pilot's Handbook of Aeronautical Knowledge* and *The Airplane Flying Handbook*. So much to learn before he would be ready to take the written exam! There was also the pilot's manual for the Twin Otter. Will advised Chuck to set that one aside until he had his pilot's license.

The trailer he shared with Mel gave him a place to study.

Mel and Lina worked on the King during the week, and that meant they were in and out of the break room at odd times. They were also prone to interrupt Chuck to ask questions, which ruled out studying in the break room.

Chuck set up his computer on the trailer's fold-out table and tied it in to the new LAN that one of Prin's engineers had installed. He laid out a legal-sized tablet and a pair of pencils for taking notes, then added pens and a small sharpener for the pencils. While some notes could be recorded on his computer, there was no real replacement for paper and pencil to sketch out the ideas that would help him understand the concepts in the books.

He soon settled in to his new routine; study in the morning, fly in the afternoon, then catch a few hours of sleep. When time permitted, meet with Will and the engineers, the ones who were building the modifications that would eventually be installed on the Twin Otter.

He was chronically short on sleep, but made sure he set aside time for Lina. Opportunities for the two to be alone were limited. It was frustrating, but the heavy work load made the schedule necessary.

Occasionally Chuck thought about how nice it would be if he could just take Lina away for a while, but he knew that his grandfather would not understand. The old man worked a schedule that would have exhausted a much younger man. Chuck could not, would not, betray Morty's trust.

Three weeks later, Chuck and Will flew the Twin Otter to Clovis. Chuck spent the next few days getting a medical exam and the dental exam the doctor recommended. He also took the FAA written exam and passed it easily. By the time he finished, Will had found an instructor and booked time for Chuck to fly a Cessna 172.

"The instructor is new to the area, only been here about a month. He owns his plane, flies out to the ranches delivering stuff most of the time, but he also does instructing on the side. I talked to him for a few minutes and went up for a short hop. I like the guy, so we'll see how you do with him. Trust is important so if you don't think he's the one you want to learn from, let me know. I'll find someone else."

"If you like him, I'm sure I'll be okay with him too."

The instructor turned out to be a late-middle-aged man who had flown airplanes all over the world. A retired Marine Corps pilot, he'd taught flying in Florida, then worked as a crop duster in Texas before moving to Clovis.

He held current certificates all the way up to Air Transport Pilot, but had only worked as a transport pilot for a few months.

"Didn't like it. Too much like driving a bus. I had enough of that kind of thing when I was flying for the Corps. Nowadays I fly where I want to and if I don't want to fly, I don't."

Chuck, the former marine, found they had a lot in common.

***

Chuck soloed in the Cessna 172, then spent the next few days gaining experience, working to increase his skills, and adding flying hours to his logbook. With the instructor's endorsement, he took and passed the FAA Private Pilot Practical Test. The results were faxed to the FAA and Chuck received an interim private pilot's certificate.

While Chuck was busy gaining his certificate, Will was in Dallas updating his own license. While there, he contacted an FAA examiner and sounded him out about certifying an aircraft with non-standard propulsion.

The man was dubious, but interested. "Let me know when you're ready. I'd fly with you just to see what you've come up with! I'm going to want to see it work on the ground first, mind you." Will promised to send him an email as soon as he was satisfied the plane was airworthy.

Will rejoined Chuck in Clovis and they flew back to the plant, having been absent more than a month.

Much had been done while they were away.

The King was fully repaired and ready for further testing. The larger, heavier craft had more power than the Bedstead, but at the same time there was more inertia involved so that piloting required more anticipation. Mel had decided to do most of the impeller flight tests in the Bedstead, considering it the safer craft to fly.

Chuck managed to spend an occasional few minutes in the hangar during the following weeks, but he was no longer an integral part of the Bedstead-King team. He resented it briefly, but understood that he could no longer give his complete attention to what they were doing.

He did manage to be present for the King's first extended flight, but Mel was the pilot. The improved flight-control system worked flawlessly. Chuck was also there two days later, when Lina took the King out and flew the course Chuck had originally laid out for the Bedstead. He was waiting somewhat nervously when she returned an hour later, bubbling with excitement. Mel watched, smiling, as the two exchanged a very intense kiss.

Chuck finally managed to squeeze in a flight in the King two days later; his other duties made scheduling the time a challenge. The bigger craft required a different set of reflexes, but by the time he'd finished flying the test course, he was comfortable piloting it.

The Twin was also undergoing changes. Will had insisted on a number of improvements. When he wasn't teaching Chuck to fly, he worked with the engineers to make sure the changes were what he wanted.

Externally, the plane once again appeared to be a stock Twin Otter. The impellers were gone and the underwing attach points faired over.

Internally, the former 'flight engineer's station' was gone, replaced by panels beside the pilot and copilot's stations. These were smaller and simpler than the version Chuck had used.

Chuck ignored them while learning to pilot the Twin Otter. They served no purpose for the time being, but they would be necessary when the impellers and battery packs were reinstalled. The original two-battery capacity would be expanded to four, acceptable now that new batteries were beginning to trickle in.

The new, more powerful impellers would be internally mounted. They would also have considerably more freedom of motion, the swivel mounts no longer being limited to ten degrees. Final numbers were still being worked out. For the moment, only the flat aluminum plates they would attach to were present, riveted to several frame members.

Chuck soloed in the Twin Otter a week later.

"All you need now is flight hours. I got mine by flying cross-country solo."

Chuck agreed, and together he and Will worked out a flight plan.

"Stay well clear of military installations," Will advised. "You don't want to attract attention. Avoid high mountains too, the wind patterns can be tricky.

"It's late summer, so expect thunderstorms; watch the weather carefully. Some of those storms in the plains spawn wall clouds and tornadoes. It's no fun trying to fly a plane without wings."

"I understand. If in doubt, sit it out, and do it on the ground."

"You've got it. Go into town, have a good meal, pick up a souvenir for Lina. She'll miss you, you know."

"I know. I'll miss her too."

Six weeks later, Chuck was finally able to get away. Early one Friday morning, he took off from the factory's airstrip and headed for Albuquerque.

He refueled there, then headed west to California. The Twin Otter had range enough with a maximum fuel load to easily reach an attended airfield. While fuel for the turboprops wasn't yet common, the airfields he intended to land at had the S10 diesel on hand or could have it trucked out from a nearby city.

***

Chuck landed in Clovis eight days later; he'd discovered the plane was due for a maintenance check. He turned the plane over to the mechanics, rented a Super Cub, and got checked out on that. He landed the Cub late that afternoon at the factory's airstrip.

He had managed to grow a scruffy beard while he was gone. Lina took one look at it and told him to go shave.

Chuck was tired, but Lina had been insistent, so he headed for the trailer to shower and shave.

Things had been switched around in his absence. The bunk bed he'd used was folded out of the way and the queen-sized bed in the main bedroom had been made. The room even smelled different.

He briefly considered opening up the bunk bed, but decided that could wait. Dropping his dirty clothing by the shower, he stepped in and sighed blissfully as the hot water relaxed him. Lathering up after the shower, he shaved off the beard, wincing when the razor pulled at the hairs.

Well. Longer hairs take more softening before they can be shaved without discomfort, that was probably it.

Chuck finished shaving and tossed the razor in the trash. He picked out a comfortable set of khaki shorts and a T-shirt, then bagged up his dirty clothing to take to the hanger. Something else was different, but his tired mind wouldn't settle on it. But he stopped halfway to the hangar building and stood there, thinking.

Where were Mel's things? He hadn't kept much in the trailer, preferring to keep most of his clothing in the cabinet in the break room, but hadn't there been a couple of shirts and a pair of pants in the closet?

Had something happened to Mel? Chuck resumed walking.

But no; Mel was there when he entered the hangar, working on the King. He came over and shook Chuck's hand when he walked in.

"Congratulations! Will says you're a pretty good pilot and you'll be better when you've got a few hundred more hours in your logbook. How was the flight?"

"Long. Boring, mostly. I was wondering, aren't you using the trailer now?"

"Nah, I'm staying here in the hanger. Seemed better that way." Mel's eyes crinkled as if he had difficulty not laughing aloud.

"Let me get a cup of coffee and I'll take a look at what you've done with the King." Chuck walked into the break room and found a cup, mostly clean.

The break room seemed different too. Puzzled, he got his coffee and went back to where Mel had resumed work.

The new King was sleek and functional. It boasted eight impellers and the four between-deck slots each contained a battery. The brackets on the rear deck had been replaced by folding metal tiedown loops for cargo.

The King finally deserved its name. It was, despite the smooth, faired lines, a workhorse. Chuck nodded in approval; finally, it was what they'd intended all along, a heavy lifter that could be shown to prospective buyers.

"Looks good. I thought about flying it today, but I'm beat. I'm heading back for the trailer. If Will asks, tell him I'll talk to him tomorrow. And not to wake me up before noon!"

"Oh, we won't." Had there been a slight emphasis on 'we'? Weird. Chuck walked back to the trailer and climbed the steps. The other change became apparent when he closed the door behind him.

"About time you got here, Chuck. I thought you pilots were faster than that!"

Yes indeed, there had been changes.

Chuck smiled and walked to where Lina waited.

***

Four months had passed since Chuck's cross-country solo.

The Twin Otter now carried four battery packs in the cabin, arranged in two stacks of two. Four impeller units on swivel mounts had been installed at the plane's center of balance, on floor-to-ceiling aluminum racks. Instead of wing spars, the impellers now pushed against the fuselage.

Were the new impellers powerful enough to lift the plane straight up, perhaps with no need for a takeoff roll? Chuck wondered.

He decided to discuss the idea with Will when time permitted.

Two turbogenerators had been ordered and the manufacturer had promised delivery within thirty days. Will didn't anticipate problems; the turbogenerators were, after all, no more than an adaptation of a tried and true design that burned the same fuel as the turboprops.

The latest-model impellers had been manufactured using the improved, highly-automated assembly system. Engineers who'd built the improved Bedstead and King now supervised a system of computer-controlled welders and robots. Parts were taken directly from manufacturing lines, then assembled into a complete impeller that needed only testing and fitting within a protective housing.

While not yet at full production, the plant had already produced more impellers than could be used. But Morty had plans for them.

Chuck found that the cavernous plant had been walled off into two main areas, plus the secure storeroom. There was no door in the wall separating the large areas, so people working in the smaller manufacturing plant could not directly access the larger assembly section. Access to each area was gained solely thorough doors opening from the outside.

As an additional security measure, the doors were twenty feet apart and a pair of guards manned a control booth between them.

Assembly was Morty's area, and Chuck was the only person other than members of Morty's team that was allowed inside. Lina consulted with Morty, but had not yet been granted direct access; the two met in the hangar building's break room and Lina did most of her design work by computer anyway.

The assembly area workers had their own machines, rollers, sheet-metal brakes, and cutters for forming sheet metal.

Salvaged titanium and aluminum parts from the Roswell boneyard were trucked to a wide rear entrance, offloaded, inspected, and then the useful pieces were taken inside to be reformed.

Rejected aluminum or titanium pieces were stored outside the building until there were enough of them to make a shipment worthwhile, then trucked into Clovis. The metal joined other shipments bound for recycling plants, where they would be melted and shaped for reuse.

During this time, armed guards kept people away from the door and a canvas-like curtain prevented anyone from seeing what was being worked on inside.

Hidden behind the curtains, a skeletal framework filled most of the space in the assembly room. Oddly-shaped pieces of sheet metal lay here and there about the floor. Other pieces stood against the wall, placed according to plan.

Morty's empire was organized, not that an observer would realize it immediately.

The impeller storage room opened off the assembly area. Completed assemblies had been palletized and stacked inside, waiting to be installed on the machine taking shape in the center.

Chuck looked at the apparent chaos on the floor and glanced at Morty. "How long, you think?"

"Six weeks if we get the nuclear plants, but Frenchy is having trouble with Los Alamos. They're dragging their feet, which means someone is putting pressure on them. He thinks it might be the same bunch that caused him so many problems a year ago. Anyway, he's spoken to a Chinese group but he still hopes that the national lab will come through."

"Yeah, I can understand that. But at least he may have an alternate source. What about the space suits you ordered? You designed those, didn't you?"

"Not exactly. I worked with the designers but they did the actual work.

"These will be minimalist suits, they'll keep your body under pressure and there's enough air for an emergency, but that's all. Unless you've got the accessories, that suit is only good for about an hour. And if you need a potty break, you're out of luck."

"I'll remember that," muttered Chuck. "Go before there's an emergency, right?"

"You've got it, Chuck," grinned Morty. "It's a crappy job, but if you want to get rich from space travel, someone's got to go out there and do it."

***

Chuck took off in the modified Twin Otter late that afternoon. His course took him north, skirting the mesa to the west of the plant. He intended to chop power to the turboprops after circling the tiny hamlet of Broadview, bleed off airspeed, then turn south after passing Grady. He would conduct the remainder of the return flight on impeller power alone. If everything worked according to plan, he would be landing an hour after sunset.

He completed the southbound leg and turned east, the plane now silent except for faint wind noises. The sun cast long shadows across the high desert landscape.

Perhaps that was why he spotted the slight movement on the ground. Puzzled, he fed power to the impellers and banked around to have another look. Perhaps it was a bear; they often came down from the hills when their natural food crop failed, looking for scraps and an occasional unwary pet to substitute for what nature hadn't provided.

But this was no bear. *What would a guy in camouflage be doing hiking through the desert*? Chuck wondered. *There's nothing out there for the next ten miles except the airstrip. For that matter, where had he come from?*

Curious. He resumed course and landed ten minutes later, coming in well below stall speed with the impellers pitched up at a 45° angle. The only issue he experienced came from the reduced airflow, which caused the control surfaces to feel mushy.

The next planned modification wouldn't need them at all; two small impellers would be mounted forward of the cockpit to control pitch and yaw. The main impellers could then be pointed up, allowing the Twin to land vertically like a helicopter.

Chuck tied down the Twin and walked to the hangar.

"Mel, see if you can get Will on the radio. Ask him if he'll service the Twin, fuel it up and swap out the batteries. I'd appreciate you giving him a hand if you can take the time."

"Sure, Chuck. Is something wrong?"

"Maybe, maybe not. I spotted a man on foot a few miles west of here, and I can't think of a good reason why anyone would be walking out there. I don't understand how he got *this* far. I think I'll take the Bedstead out and have a look.

"Not much water anywhere out that way. I'll take along a case of bottled water. If he's lost, he's probably dehydrated. But I'm going to need access to Frenchy's locker too. I want the night vision goggles and I'll probably take a few other things as well. Just in case he's *not* lost."

"Sure, go ahead. You might consider taking Lina along as a second set of eyes?"

Chuck thought about it. "Good idea. Probably be just a cruise in the moonlight. I'm probably being overcautious, taking the night vision goggles and a rifle along, but better to be safe than sorry.

"When I get close to where I spotted him, I'll leave Lina with the Bedstead while I have a look. If he's lost, I don't see how but I suppose it's possible, I'll give him the water and point him back to where he came from."

"Chuck, you sure you saw someone out there? This isn't just a way to get some stick time in the Bedstead, is it?"

"Not a bad idea, but not this time. Something about the way that guy was walking looked funny. I don't know exactly what it was that bothered me, because I was looking down from a couple of thousand feet. Could be nothing. But I'll feel better if I check it out. Not sure how long I'll be, but if I'm not back by morning notify security."

Getting the Bedstead ready and strapping down the rifles and the case of water took almost an hour. It was already dark by the time he flew over the fence and headed out into the desert. The ghostly glow in the night-vision goggles was clear enough, and with the moonlight and sparse desert vegetation Chuck had no problem finding his way to the approximate location where he'd seen the man. Finding a clear area, he set the Bedstead down. A bottle of water went into one of his cargo pants pockets, a spare magazine in the other.

Lina wasn't happy when Chuck left her.

"You really think you'll need that?" she asked, pointing to the slung rifle.

"Nope, but there *are* wild animals around here. The riders that patrol this part of the ranch are always armed. Nobody on foot *ever* comes this way, which makes me curious why that guy is where he is.

"I'll offer him the water and send him on his way. If he doesn't want to go, the rifle might be needed. Lost or not, we don't want him snooping around the plant."

Lina nodded, still not convinced. Chuck vanished silently into the darkness, the goggles allowing him to avoid the brush.

An hour passed and part of another. Lina was nearly asleep when she heard the first loud noise. Moments later, others followed, a fast rattle. Now awake, she wondered; *Is that a machine gun? Surely not, not here!*

Almost a full minute later, there was a different kind of noise, sharper somehow. It was followed by four others, each separated by a second or two. Then silence resumed.

Nervous, she touched the controls several times. *Should she go find Chuck? What if he needed help?*

Chuck's appearance caught her by surprise.

"Don't ask questions, and I need you to do exactly what I say, okay?"

"Chuck, what…"

"No questions! Not now, I don't have time. I need the Bedstead. I want you to wait for me over there by that big rock. I doubt you'll need it now, but keep the rifle with you and keep your eyes peeled."

Lina seethed at the peremptory tone, but remained silent. Why did he need the bedstead? And why leave her here?

What had Chuck done?

She settled down on the sand and leaned back against the rock to wait. Worry for his safety had given way to a different emotion.

Chapter Twenty-one

The trip back was made in silence for the most part. Finally, just before reaching the factory campus, Lina asked what had happened out there in the desert.

Chuck was evasive and she soon became angry. He tried to explain his reasoning but without including details, and she wasn't willing to accept that.

The discussion went nowhere at first, and when he reluctantly told her in general terms what had happened, it went downhill.

Chuck parked the Bedstead and waited for Lina to say something. But she walked away, heading for Mel, who'd just walked out of the small break area with his first cup of coffee in hand. She spoke briefly to him, then left the building.

"Mel, what's going on?" Chuck asked.

"Said she'd explain when she got back. Wants me to help her do something."

Chuck was curious, but too exhausted to pursue the matter. He poured a cup of coffee for himself, then fell asleep before he could drink it. An hour later, he was awakened by voices.

"Mel, can you give me a hand?" Lina was carrying a basket.

Mel glanced at it; was that clothing?

"Sure, give me a minute to finish tightening this bolt." He laid the torque wrench aside and straightened up.

Spotting Chuck where he'd lifted his head from where it had been resting on his arms, he suggested quietly, "Why don't you head for the trailer? We'll talk after you get some rest."

Chuck nodded, still half asleep, and headed for the door.

Behind him, Lina led the way to the lounge. Mel was bursting with questions, Lina not disposed to explain.

She set the basket on a table, then began shoving the futon she'd used before into place as Mel brought out the curtains from a cabinet.

"I need you to help me rehang the curtains," Lina said. Mel could no longer hold his curiosity in check.

"You're moving back here?" Lina nodded, not trusting herself to speak.

"Okay, but if you want to talk about it, I'm a pretty good listener," Mel said.

"Not now, Mel. Maybe later."

***

Lina was sleeping when Chuck got back to the hangar. He nodded at Mel, then picked up a cup of coffee from the break room. The curtains were back in place and drawn to provide privacy.

Chuck noticed, but said nothing. What was there to say?

He took his coffee over to where the Bedstead was parked and began unstrapping the equipment locker he'd loaded the night before. Opening it, Chuck took out a rifle and began field-stripping it.

Mel watched, trying to avoid the appearance of snooping, but Chuck worked without comment so Mel decided to forego questioning him.

Chuck cleaned the rifle with practiced speed, then reassembled it. He replaced it in the locker and removed the short-handled shovel. He brushed off the blade carefully, then oiled the metal part before replacing it in the wooden brackets.

Half an hour later, the locker once again secured behind the locked door, Chuck came back into the hangar bay.

"I'm heading out, Mel. If you need to find me, I'll be working on the Twin Otter. You need any help with the King before I take off?"

"No, I'm almost finished. The batteries are charged, everything's in place and hooked up to the main bus, and the new computers checked out.

"I'll finish up what I'm doing on the Bedstead, do a quick preflight, then change out the batteries. I might take it out tonight for a quick test, but if not, it'll be available tomorrow night. You're not interested, Chuck?"

"I don't think I'll have time, Mel. I'll be busy with the Twin Otter. Will's got a guy coming in later this week to inspect the modified system, and if he gives us the okay, we'll paint 'Experimental' on it and start flying legally.

We need to put as many hours on the system as possible and I'll be doing half the flying. Too bad you don't have a pilot's certificate; it's a fun bird to fly."

"You sure about this, Chuck?"

"Not my choice, Mel."

"Okay. Well, I've got my hands full here, Chuck. I'll be running the tests on the King after I get the batteries installed, and more-extensive tests on the Bedstead. That's quite a bit, and keeping Lina busy may help. She'll also be working with Morty part of the time, helping with a design project. I'm not sure what it is, but they've been doing quite a bit of talking. I wasn't sure you'd heard about it, being busy with your flight training, so I thought I'd mention it.

"Anyway, I'm hoping I can start altitude testing later in the week, either the Bedstead or the King. Funny thing about that; if the computer is just a little off, you start to sideslip and it begins to go where you aren't pointing it.

"The instruments might be the problem. I'll look into it, but if the deck isn't level, the computer can't control the flight. That might be a bug, the computer thinks the deck is level when it sends commands to the impellers. It's the old problem, garbage in, garbage out."

"Yeah, we had that problem early on," agreed Chuck. "That's why we went with computerized control. The computers fly the craft, the pilot flies the computer, but you still need a pilot when things start to go wrong."

"Gives a whole new meaning to 'fly by wire', doesn't it?"

"It does. But it's the same as the new fighter jets, they're all computer controlled too. From the F-117 on, most fighters are too unstable for a human to fly. It's all computer control in the new ones."

***

Frenchy was not happy. He was discussing the holdup from Los Alamos regarding the mini-reactors.

"Here's the thing, Frenchy", Mark said. "You've got two strikes against you. One, you have to certify that the reactors won't be used in flight. That's a requirement, even if it's not in the law, because Congress won't allow it. Their constituents remember rockets blowing up and the talk since then is about whether a spacecraft with a reactor on board might blow up on its way to space."

Mark, Frenchy's chief legal officer, had been attempting to negotiate with officials from the Los Alamos National Laboratory to acquire the compact fission reactors Morty wanted.

"We're not using rockets, Mark. I explained that."

"It doesn't matter, Frenchy. It's too easy to convince people there's a danger, whether one exists or not. That's half the problem. The other half is worse."

"Go on, Mark."

"You've got political opposition, Frenchy. I won't call them enemies, but it's close to that and they're spending big money. They're buying opposition to whatever it is you're doing. Expect licensing issues, fees, taxes, you name it. You've only started to feel the itch. Politicians love money, they'll do whatever it takes to keep it coming."

"It's that bad, Mark? Do you know who's leading this opposition?"

"No idea. There are several players, including the company you once owned a part of. When you pulled out, that sent the stock prices down and people lost money. They haven't forgotten. Payback is what they live for."

"Has to be Sol, then. Bastard cheated at golf too."

"I've heard that name. I don't know how involved he is."

Frenchy thought for a moment. "Depends on whether he's feeling threatened. He's not a risk-taker. Different divisions of the company are involved in manufacturing engines, including engines for heavy equipment. I'm not sure if that includes marine systems, but I wouldn't be surprised to find it does.

"Sol's not above dirty tricks, although whether he'd involve himself in anything illegal...I don't know. I just don't know. Like I said, I watch his golf card when I play with him. And anyone who would cheat at golf...well, we're not talking big bucks. It's pocket change to Sol. But I saw it happen more than once, and to me that means it's not an accident. Sol will do whatever it takes to stay on top."

"Does your group have the money to put on a lobbying blitz? Hire several firms to grease the ways?"

"Not any more. We thought we did, but there have been holdups, glitches, things like the agreement with Los Alamos. We thought it was a done deal, but now it's unraveling."

"It's a national lab, Frenchy; that means politics is involved. They might lease the power plants as back-up to your wind and solar system, but count on it, that's all they'll be doing. Los Alamos will send their own engineers and they'll work with your people as far as siting and so forth is concerned, but they'll control how the equipment is used.

"Last I heard, the idea was to lease a power plant for ten years, then swap it out for a new one. They intend to take the old one back to Los Alamos for refurbishing. It's basically a nuclear plant in a box, which means it's easily replaced."

"That's why it appealed to us. I guess we'll have to look elsewhere to solve our power needs."

"Frenchy, why not just go with conventional systems? If you can't get nuclear plants, use diesel, turbogenerators, maybe even fuel cells. Those aren't under the thumb of politicians. Would they work for you?"

"They might. I'll look into it, Mark. Anyway, thanks for meeting with me today."

"It's what you pay me for, Frenchy. I just wish I could give you better news."

"You've given me an honest report, Mark. I can't ask for more than that."

***

Sol was puzzled, but not particularly alarmed.

He'd expected a report by this time, but had heard nothing. He looked at the cell phone again, but there had been no calls.

Getting up from his desk, he walked over and looked out his window. The plant spread out, much of it visible from Sol's office. He'd often found the view soothing, but not this time.

Why hadn't Walter called in? Had he run into trouble of some kind?

Well, Walter was reliable, even if a bit too independent for Sol's taste. He would call when he had something to report.

Sol dismissed it from his mind and went back to his desk. He was soon back studying the production report, the problem with Walter pushed to the back of his mind.

***

The Twin Otter was undergoing modification yet again, this time getting the craft ready for the inspector. A lightweight bulkhead, located immediately behind the front cabin, was being bolted into place. This isolated the crew cabin from the impellers and battery packs in the rear of what had formerly been the passenger cabin. The oversized rear door, made removable for dropping parachutists, made it easy to swap depleted batteries for freshly recharged ones.

Will hoped that the inspector would be satisfied with a flight test. If he insisted on inspecting the propulsion system, the craft might not get the certification they needed. If he was satisfied with the Twin's demonstrated ability to fly using the impellers, the system would remain secret.

Eventually someone would find out, maybe even figure out how Morty's invention worked, but every year, every *day* of delay was golden.

The bulkhead job was finished by midafternoon. Will inspected it, then took the Twin Otter up for a short test hop and pronounced himself satisfied. *Cutting it a little close*, he thought. *The FAA inspector will be here tomorrow morning.*

Will fueled up the wing tanks, then parked the Twin and tied it down. The plane was as ready as possible, but it would be up to the inspector to decide if that was good enough. Will had talked to him while Chuck was busy getting his license and the man had seemed friendly, but that might not make a difference.

Inspectors were highly professional and usually sticklers about rules, unwilling to sign off on the paperwork unless they were convinced a plane was airworthy.

***

Mel stifled his curiosity.

He'd left enough openings for Chuck or Lina to open up about the rift, but neither would confide in him.

Chuck had come closest. "I guess she discovered I wasn't the man she thought I was. I wish it had been otherwise, but I guess it's better to find out now than later.

"Anyway, good luck with your testing. I'll be tied up for the next two days. Will and I are going to be flying the Twin Otter. If the FAA inspector passes it as an experimental model, we'll be able to fly it legally. I figure within two years, certainly less than five, we can have light aircraft flying on impeller power alone."

"Good luck, Chuck. I'm sorry you and Lina couldn't make a go of it. She's been down since you two broke up, but maybe, with a little more time?"

"I've been down too, but there's nothing to be done. I did what I had to do..." Chuck's voice trailed off as Mel looked at him quizzically. "I've said too much already, Mel. Let's drop it, okay?"

"Okay, Chuck. Again, good luck tomorrow."

Chapter Twenty-two

"So where's the power plant? All I see is what's on the wings, and you just told me they're not jets."

The inspector sounded testy. It appeared that he'd come a long way for nothing and wasted time in the doing.

"The plane uses a proprietary device," explained Will. "How it operates is a company secret. We've logged thousands of hours of operation, so we know it's reliable. I can also tell you that we use two of the devices in this plane as a safety measure. At this point, I'm prepared to demonstrate that it works."

"Flight hours?" asked the inspector suspiciously.

"No. This is our first airplane. I'd like to start by taxiing, if you're ready."

"Wait a minute, Hoss; if the turbogenerators aren't somehow providing thrust, what do they do?"

"Short answer, they keep the batteries charged. There are battery packs in the aft compartment, plus the proprietary thrust units. Turbos charge the batteries, the batteries power the...well, we call them Sneyd-Tesla Impellers, for the inventor and the man who inspired him. I guess it won't hurt to tell you that the original concept was first proposed by Nikola Tesla. But the proof is in the flying. What say we give it a try?"

"Are those batteries you mentioned fully charged?"

"Sure, we start out with them charged and the turbogenerators recharge them in flight. Why?" asked Will.

"Suppose we don't turn on the turbochargers; will the batteries provide enough power to taxi?"

"Well, yes. We've done extensive testing on battery power alone. But I won't take off unless the turbos are operating."

"But you did mention ground testing, taxiing. So let's just get in and see how that goes."

"No problem. Strap yourself into the copilot's seat; I'll let you familiarize yourself with the controls before we take off, but you shouldn't try to fly until you've had a familiarization course using impellers. They're not magic, and if you don't know what you're doing, the system can be dangerous."

"*Everything* is dangerous if you don't know what you're doing. Show me what you've got, Hoss." The inspector had spent a lot of time in Texas, and it showed.

Will pointed out that the flight controls worked just as they had when the plane flew using the turboprops. "One thing, the turbogenerators are computer controlled. They throttle up under max load, throttle down during cruise."

"Another uncertified system?"

"I suppose you could call it that, but don't worry," said Will. "We've got at least an hour's reduced-power flight time on battery alone. That's plenty to get us back to the airstrip."

"But we're going to do taxi tests, so that will deplete the batteries, won't it?"

"I'll run the turbos long enough to top off the batteries before we take off."

"Any problem with me doing the taxi tests?"

"Nope, knock yourself out. The stick by your seat is the directional control for the impellers; just push straight ahead to accelerate, pull back to slow down. Throttle control is that wheel on the side, it controls how much power is sent to the impellers.

"Pay attention to that gauge at the top of the 'T', it shows remaining battery charge. It's based on percentage of full charge, so don't let it drop below halfway. The red strip on the left is less than ten percent, and if it gets into that area while we're airborne, expect me to start looking for a place to set down.

"Otherwise, the airstrip is yours and you can taxi to your heart's content. Just don't exceed takeoff speed, and for that matter you should probably stay at least ten knots per hour below that."

The inspector nodded, then cycled the ailerons, watching through the cabin windows. He wasn't able to see the elevators work, but could feel the vibration as they moved. Cycling the rudder produced the same sensation. "You need to put mirrors up where a pilot can see the tail assembly, Hoss."

"I'll make a note of that, inspector."

"About those impeller things, how many hours have you operated them?"

"Total, including all units, several thousand hours. We've never had a failure that was attributed to the impellers. There were problems early on, mostly in the instrumentation and control systems, but not the impellers."

"You've got a logbook, logbooks? You mentioned 'all units'. I take it that means you've got more than one of the impellers?"

"We've got several. Two of them are in the back."

"Takeoff speed?"

"She gets light on the wheels at 65 knots, higher than you might expect. Part of it has to do with the altitude here, but the batteries are heavy. So are the impellers, for that matter. Even so, we're 3250 pounds under max gross. So keep the taxi speed under 65, okay?"

"Understood. Alright, the turbos are off, we're on battery alone. Just push forward?"

Will nodded. "Take it slow until you have a feel for the controls."

"Roger. Do I need permission to taxi?"

"You've got it. This is our only airplane, so you won't run into traffic."

The inspector gingerly pushed forward on the control stick, but nothing happened. "What am I doing wrong? That throttle thing you mentioned?"

"Right, push the thumbwheel forward, watch the gauge until it indicates 25%. Bring your power up first, then push forward on the stick."

"Got it." The thumbwheel was answered by a low rumble that climbed to a whirring noise. "That noise, is that your impellers?"

"Correct, we haven't managed to engineer that out. Eventually, as we improve the system, we think it can be made to operate silently. Anyway, the turbos will hide the noise after they're powered up."

The Twin trundled down the runway, responding to the rudder after it picked up speed. "Seems like it steers just like any other plane. No torque effect at takeoff?"

"None. It flies like any other plane. Instead of jets or propellers, the impeller provides the thrust. As for torque, that's the main reason we use two impellers. One provides enough thrust for flight, but since we're still experimental we don't intend to take unnecessary chances. Takeoff power is 86% impulse...we consider 100% to be emergency power...and that's plenty, even loaded to max gross. Oh, and you won't need brakes to stop; just pull the stick back past neutral to reverse. The impellers work either way."

"Okay, I'll take it back to where we started. Start your turbos now. As soon as you're satisfied with the battery charge, take her up."

***

Chuck glanced at the new paint on the front cowling. The bold EXPERIMENTAL stood out against the white background. He performed a walkaround inspection, glanced at the windsock, then climbed in. Thumbing the impeller power wheel, he set it for 50% and listened to the whining noise build as he buckled in. A switch on the control panel was labeled START, and as soon as he pressed it the computer started the port turbo, and as it began to rev, the starboard turbo began spinning.

Satisfied, Chuck cycled the flight controls, watching through the newly installed rear-view mirrors, then moved the thumbwheel forward until impeller power registered 86%. Pressing gently on the control stick, he felt the plane accelerate. Locking the stick in its forward detent, he took off.

Climbing rapidly, he throttled back to 50% power as soon as he reached cruise speed. Trimming up the controls, he settled in for what he hoped would be another boring flight.

***

Mel finished stripping the computers and the battery compartments from the King's frame. The first test flight had revealed a problem; the four batteries blocked the airflow between the upper and lower decks, allowing heat to build up inside the frame. The engineers were working on a solution, but whatever they came up with would require stripping the interior components down to modify it.

He'd been working alone for the past month. Lina chatted with him briefly in the mornings, then left for the main building where she was doing something with Morty in the mysterious assembly section. Chuck was busy flying the Twin, building logbook hours, Mel supposed; he hadn't been back to the hangar since that last conversation.

Mel walked over to the trailer later that afternoon, taking a couple of beers. Maybe Chuck would open up if someone made the effort.

But the trip was wasted. Chuck wasn't there, and apparently hadn't been there in some time.

Now worried, Mel went back to the hangar. Where was Chuck living? Was he even staying on site?

Mel went over to the main building the next morning. A pair of guards controlled access to Morty's assembly area, and Mel's name wasn't on their list. They were willing to tell him that Morty and Lina were inside, as was Joe, the engineer Frenchy had hired. Whatever they were doing in there, it probably had to do with the new man's specialty, and they didn't want visitors. Mel figured it likely had something to do with Morty's spacecraft, because that was what Joe had worked on out in California. But no Chuck.

Disturbed, Mel walked down to the main guard shack, located where the road entered the campus.

"I've been looking for Chuck. You know who I'm talking about, right?"

"Sure, he's one of the pilots. He comes through the gate occasionally, but he spends most of his time around the airplane. I *think* that's what he does; we don't put things like that in the log." The guard checked his list. "Nope, he finishes flying late in the afternoon and only comes inside after that. He doesn't usually stay long, an hour at most, then he leaves again. Want me to try his radio?"

"No, don't bother. It's not that important."

Mel thought about the strange events, then called Frenchy. Someone had to know what was happening; suppose Chuck had developed some sort of delayed PTSD? Whatever had happened between Lina and him, maybe it had been more of a shock than Mel realized at the time.

Frenchy was out of town, but his secretary promised to mention the call when he returned.

Should he also call Morty? Mel thought about it briefly before deciding it wasn't important to interrupt whatever the old man was doing. As for Lina, she'd had plenty of chances to open up if she wanted to.

Finally deciding there was nothing more he could do, he headed back to the hangar. The work load was piling up.

***

Mel shut off the lights, then rolled up the large door.

It wasn't as easy as before; Chuck was still missing and while Lina was now in the hangar, she had gone to bed for the evening. Whatever she was working on with Morty, it left her tired at the end of the day, so Mel was reluctant to ask for her help.

He flipped the night-vision goggles into place, then powered up the Bedstead; the King was still waiting for a solution to the cooling problem. Moments later he cleared the fence and headed out, following the new, longer, course he'd laid out. Accumulating use data was still important.

An hour later he passed near a man sitting motionless atop a small rise. Not Chuck; this man had a horse tethered a few yards behind him, grazing while the man watched. This had to be one of the ranch's workers. The men no longer worked with cattle but there was still work to do, including watching the rangeland around the factory campus.

Mel slowed, responding to a sudden impulse. He parked the Bedstead on a flat area and hiked back toward where he'd seen the watcher.

"Hello up there! I'm friendly. My name's Mel and I work at the factory. Got a minute to talk?"

"Shore. Reckon I've heard the name. You sit tight, I'll be right down."

Mel heard a stirring from the hill and moments later, the man rode his horse down the slope to where Mel waited.

"How did you spot me in the dark?"

Mel hesitated, then replied. "Night vision goggles. How did you find *me*? It's even darker down here."

The rider chuckled. "I didn't. But Pard here, he sees pretty good at night. He either spotted you or smelled you. Anyway, what can I do for you?"

"I was wondering if you know a friend of mine, fellow named Chuck Sneyd."

"Shore do, I saw him earlier this evening. I stopped off to bring him a meal and a jug of water."

"He's living out here?"

"Yep, got himself a tent. He's got a burr under his saddle about people trying to sneak up on y'all. He mentioned it to us, so we watch the area close while he catches some sleep. He usually wakes up and takes over the watch after midnight. I'd be careful, was I you. He's packin'."

"Really? He's armed while he watches?"

"Got him a pistol. I allow they're handy, but I prefer my Winchester. That ol' 30-30 ain't let me down yet, and I'm plumb used to it by now. Want me to give him a message? I'll see him when he wakes up."

"You could tell him his friends are worried. I haven't seen him for a month, maybe a little more. Just tell him you talked to Mel. He'll know who I am."

"I'll do that, Mel. I'm Port, but you might see Mitt or Roy if you're out and around. We swap off. I'll be at the line shack one more day, then Mitt takes over for me."

"Thanks. I'll be going, but maybe I'll see you again."

"You be careful, now. Sometimes the critters out here in the brush ain't friendly."

"I'll do that. See you around." Mel turned and headed back to where he'd left the Bedstead.

What would the rider think if he heard the whine, or worse, saw the silhouette against the stars? Best to stay low until he was well away. It shouldn't be much of a challenge, using the goggles. *I wonder if Port has goggles? He didn't say, but if I was riding after dark, I'd have a pair. I wonder if he can see me, even in the dark?*

The mystery of where Chuck was staying was solved, but living in a tent and watching the area behind the factory? No question, it was strange behavior.

Was it simply that he didn't want to face Lina, or was it something else, maybe PTSD? Could this compulsion to keep watch have something to do with their breakup? Or had something else happened since then?

Mel finished flying his route, then returned to the hangar. He closed the door, turned on the lights, then changed out the batteries for fresh ones. After connecting the chargers to the depleted batteries, he recorded the trip in the vehicle's logbook and headed for bed.

***

Chuck's strange behavior was never far from Mel's mind during the next two weeks. At one point, he spotted Chuck; he had just left the gate and was headed around the south fence.

His limp was more pronounced now; whatever he was doing, it wasn't helping his knee. But Chuck had rebuffed his earlier efforts to talk and he was a grown man, able to make his own decisions. Mel sighed and headed back for the hangar; the engineers had finally come up with a system of ducts that should keep the interior of the King cooler. It should be ready for a flight tomorrow.

As it happened, Mel didn't get to test the new model.

Lina woke him later that afternoon. "Mel, I need your help. Do you know where Chuck is?"

"I think so. Why, is something wrong?"

"Chuck's not answering his radio. Mel, there's no easy way to say this. Morty died this afternoon and I need to let Chuck know."

"Shit! What happened?"

"He was working on the ship, helping install the rear hatch, and he just fell down. There was nothing we could do, when we got to him he wasn't breathing. We called the nurse practitioner, she stays here during the day now that we've got people working, and she thinks it was a heart attack. She tried to revive him, but he didn't respond.

"We've called for an ambulance. They'll pick up the body and take it into Clovis, but I need to let Chuck know."

"I think I can find him. Is Frenchy here?"

"No, he's still in Santa Fe. There was some sort of problem with the state and taxes. Will flew him up there."

"Give them a call. I'm sure they'll get here as soon as they can. I'll find Chuck."

Chapter Twenty-three

Chuck sat in the assembly room, head hanging. Morty's body was gone, been taken to a funeral home in Clovis.

He'd taken the news stoically at first, then suddenly broke down, unable to contain his emotions. He fought his tears unsuccessfully, then wept for a time before regaining control.

"I'm going to need some time off, Panit."

"I'll let Frenchy know, Chuck. Is there anything we can do?"

"I can't think of anything. I'll have his body shipped back to Andrews and take it to the ranch. There's a small cemetery behind the house, maybe half a mile back. He took me to see it when I started working with him. He planted wild flowers and kept the weeds cut before, but I don't think he's been back since we started the company. There's no telling what it looks like now, but my grandmother is buried there and I think Morty would have wanted to be with her."

"Are you sure you can find her grave, Chuck? It's probably overgrown by now, and you haven't been there in at least a year."

"I can find it. I got to know that area pretty well during the summers I lived with them. There's also a stone that stands out from the low weeds that are common around there.

"Damnit, I should have *been* with him. He worked too hard, I tried to get him to slow down but it was always a chore. Maybe if I had been here I could have done something."

"Chuck, Morty was an old man. No one can hold off death forever. He went fast, according to what I was told, and he worked on something he loved right up to the end. He probably never knew what happened. Death doesn't get any better than that.

"Unless you were standing right by him with a set of charged paddles, there was nothing you could have done. And maybe the paddles wouldn't have worked."

"I keep telling myself that, but I was wrapped up in my own concerns. I never even stopped to talk to him the last time I was here. I just flew the plane and... well, I was doing something else too, but the range people could have handled that. I wanted to get away, I just couldn't handle what happened with..."

"With Lina. I heard, Chuck. She's unhappy too, and she couldn't even find you when Morty died."

"Panit, I didn't have anything I could say to her. There was nothing more for either one of us to say. I tried to explain, but she wouldn't listen.

"Anyway, that's water down the river now. We're different people, I guess, and we just don't see some things the same way. She sees things the way a college student does, but I was a Marine before I was a student and Fallujah changed me. I guess there's no going back for either of us."

"I wouldn't give up on her just yet, Chuck. Anyway, Frenchy and Will are on the way back, estimated arrival time is about two hours. Do you have time to talk to them?"

"I guess so. I'm not sure how long it will take to get Morty home, to Andrews I mean, and there's nothing I can do until that's taken care of.

"I need to make a phone call, see if the funeral home in Clovis can handle it. If they can't, someone in Andrews can. One more thing, I want a military style headstone for Morty. There's a simple stone for my grandmother, but I want one that mentions Morty's service. He never went overseas, but he served and it shouldn't be forgotten. That's important to me."

"Charge the arrangements to the company, Chuck. You select the stone, have them contact us.

"I don't suppose you've thought about it, but you're Morty's heir. We've got the documents on file. I don't know about what arrangements he made for any other property, though."

"I talked to his lawyer, he's got an office in Andrews, when I was trying to collect what some of the businesses owed grandpa. I'll give him a call when I get there.

"The old ranch isn't worth much, but I don't want to see it sold off. It's got that cemetery, you see. As soon as Morty's laid to rest there, that's the two people who were more family to me than anyone else."

"I doubt you'll have a problem. His holdings in the company listed you as next of kin."

"I'm really the *only* kin, except for an uncle and aunt that grandpa refused to talk about. He never said why, but there was a rift. I don't know how to contact my uncle, and for that matter he might not even be alive now. Even if he is, I wouldn't know what to say to him."

Panit made a note on the tablet. "I suppose we should look into it, just to clear up any questions. I'll need the name of the lawyer. I'll give him a call, but even if he has a will on file, the papers Morty filed here will supersede that."

Chuck nodded. "I'll get you the name later. I'll stay here until Frenchy shows up, but I'll need to go into Clovis after that. The mortuary company will want to know how they're going to get paid."

"Like I said, charge it to us and I'll let Frenchy know. Where will you be?"

"I guess I'll go over to the hangar. Mel's probably there, but he's pretty good about leaving people alone when there's nothing to be said. I don't really want to talk to anybody right now, but I'll tell Frenchy what I've got in mind when he gets here."

***

Lina entered the hangar from the rear personnel door. Chuck was sitting in the small break room, nursing a cup of cooling coffee and looking at nothing.

"Chuck, I'm so sorry. I know how close you and Morty were."

"Hi, Lina. Yeah, he was more father than grandfather to me. I just don't know...I'm really going to miss him."

"You know how proud he was of you, don't you?"

"We never talked about things like that, Lina. We did before, when I was growing up, but that was when I was a kid. We talked about a lot of things during the summers when I stayed on the ranch.

Grandma, too; I rode with her almost every day and we talked about everything.

"It was never the same after she passed away. It hit grandpa hard too, but at the time we never mentioned our feelings. Neither one of us was ever very good at that."

"What are you going to do now?"

"Make the arrangements, and after that, I guess I'll see.

"I don't know, I've been flying the Twin, but that's so routine now that I'm not sure I'm still interested. This has been a shock, even though I should have thought about it happening. But grandpa had so much energy..."

"I know. I couldn't believe it either, not at first. He was such a part of the ship... do you know what we've been working on?"

"No, I've stayed busy flying the Twin. We needed as many hours in the logbook as possible, but that's pretty much over now that we've got the experimental certification. The inspector approved that, based on how many hours we've operated the impellers and how well the flight demonstration went.

"As for those logbook hours, each flight of the Bedstead counted four times because there were four impellers. The barge also counted, as did the marine system that's operating now. The Twin's flight hours counted twice. All told, we had almost five thousand hours of operation in the various logbooks.

"Anyway, he approved the system for experimental purposes and crew training. No passengers, but then we don't really have the room. The seats are out and the batteries and the impellers occupy almost all of the space in the passenger cabin. What it means is that any certified pilot can fly the Twin now, once he's familiar with the impeller system."

"We're almost finished with the first space-capable ship, Chuck. It's smaller than Morty wanted, but the hull is finished and the impellers are in place. We're working on fuel storage and running tests on the fuel cells. There are other things to do after that."

"You've got the cells in?" Chuck's surprise showed.

"Right, we haven't given them a full test, but they're in place. It's basically the same system you're using, a charging system that feeds the batteries. They serve as an accumulator, meaning power is instantly available without waiting for the fuel cells to increase output."

"Sounds like you've got it under control."

Chuck's voice was listless. He'd perked up for a moment, but now he seemed depressed again.

"Chuck, I'm sorry. I wish none of this had happened. We were happy for a while, you and me, but then..."

"Yeah, I know. I just...did what I had to do. We didn't talk much about what happened to you before you came here, but you mentioned that the man who raped you had a white stripe in his hair. That's pretty unusual, so I remembered what you said. Anyway, you don't have to worry about him now."

"Chuck, I don't know if that makes me feel better. I'll have to think about it. I've got to go back to work, so will you give me a hug before I leave?"

Chuck wordlessly stood up and opened his arms. The hug lasted longer than Lina had expected; it seemed as if neither wanted it to end.

***

The man drove the backhoe toward his flatbed trailer. Reversing up the ramp, he parked the machine, then began chaining it down. He would return later; he had promised to set Morty's headstone in place when it was ready.

Chuck had chosen white granite and kept the inscription simple; Morton Alleyne Sneyd, the dates of his birth and death, US Army below that, followed by the years when he'd served. Chuck had refused the offer of a cross incised above Morty's name; the old man hadn't been a believer. He wouldn't have wanted a lot of extra stuff.

The few people who'd come to the graveside service had offered a hug or a handshake and a few words of condolence, then left the small cemetery. Lina was the last to leave, and only departed after Chuck promised to call her as soon as he left the ranch.

Chuck stood by the raw mound, trying not to think, only remember. Errant tears dripped down his cheeks. He already missed Morty; it felt as if someone had removed some vital part of his character.

He slowly walked the half mile to the ranch house, planning to stay overnight. By the time he'd arrived at the house, he'd changed his mind. It was too soon, there were too many memories.

Chuck found his old backpack and dusted it off. He loaded the pack, a coil of rope on the bottom, a blanket atop that, then food and water enough for two days. He buckled the cover over the pack, shouldered it, and walked away from the house.

If he hurried, he might be in time to watch the bats fly.

***

Three days later he drove into the factory campus and parked. Lina had been expecting him. She came out and met him as he exited the pickup.

"I'm glad you're back, Chuck. We need to talk, but first Dad wants to see you. He's in the assembly building I think, or if he's not there he's down in the hangar with Mel. Let me give him a call. Don't go away, okay?"

"I'm too tired to go anywhere, Lina. I finally did something I've wanted to do for a long time. I'll talk to Frenchy, but then I'll be ready to crash. I guess I'll see about one of the bunks in the hangar."

"I made up the bed in the trailer, Chuck. I dusted it down and aired it out too."

"Lina, the trailer holds too many memories. It hurts too much, okay?"

"So we make more good memories, Chuck."

"Lina...does that mean you're moving back?"

"Yes. I won't pretend I'm happy about everything that happened. That incident...well, it shocked me.

"What shocked most was how ready you were to accept the violence. No attempt to notify the authorities, you just..."

"They didn't give me a choice, Lina," Chuck said tiredly. "I intended to take a case of water to the man I saw, it's pretty dry out there, but there were... I don't think I should say anything more. It's better if you don't know what happened. But you heard the gunshots. The first ones were when they opened up on me."

"They *shot* at you?"

"Yeah, they did, and they had full-auto rifles. Some kind of AK-47 knockoff, modified to fire full auto. They had no training, or not much; that first guy sprayed his whole magazine at me!"

"I thought that was *you*! You had that rifle from the storeroom, the one dad brought here."

"It's semi-auto only, you have to pull the trigger for each shot. I only had a narrow field of view with the night vision binoculars, and they washed out as soon as that first rifle fired. I was blind until I flipped those up, after that I shot at the flashes from their guns."

"What were those men doing on the ranch? I know dad never gave anyone permission to be out there!"

"I think I know. The one I saw had to be a scout, out ahead of the others. I'm guessing he stopped and let them catch up after it got dark. No idea how far behind they were, but if they had been together I would have seen them and called the sheriff. But one man, I thought he was lost.

"Anyway, the other three had an ATV with a cart hooked on behind. The cart contained several jugs of kerosene and a six-pack of empty bottles. There's only one reason they had those."

"You mean fire, right? They were planning to *set fire* to the factory?"

"Got it in one. They also had a lot of ammo for the rifles. Whether they'd have shot people trying to get out of the plant, I don't know. It could be they just liked having automatic rifles and lots of ammo, there are people like that. But yes, I think they planned to fire the buildings and slip away before morning. Two people riding the ATV, two in the trailer, which would have been empty then; so yeah, they'd most likely have gotten away."

Lina's phone rang and she answered it. The conversation was short.

"Dad's at the hangar building, looking over the King. We can meet him there."

"Okay. Want to walk with me?"

Lina nodded and Chuck took her hand. Together they walked to the hangar.

Frenchy was washing his hands when they came inside.

"The only oil or grease is in the bearings and they're sealed, but somehow, whenever I get close to machinery I get greasy.

"Chuck, we need to talk. You're Morty's heir, so you inherit his share of the company and his seat on the board, but I'd also like you to take over the job he was doing. You know more about the impellers than anyone else, more about the control systems too.

"I've already talked to Will; he'll hire a pilot to take your place, which will free you up to be in charge of the ship. It's almost finished; I only wish Morty had lived long enough to see it fly."

"It's that far along? How did you manage that?"

"The engineer we hired had assistants, people he was comfortable working with and who knew their way around a spacecraft, so we hired them too. I'm sure the guy they worked for is pretty unhappy; he lost his chief engineer and two dozen experienced people, everyone in fact except the people working on his rocket's propulsion system."

"We're copying their bird?"

"No. Ours looks a lot like the old space shuttle except bigger, and with thicker wings and wingtip vertical stabilizers. That part makes it look like the lifting bodies the Air Force used for reentry experiments. According to Jose...good man, by the way...the design could function in an emergency to get the ship down without burning up. He thinks."

"I'm definitely interested, but can we wait until tomorrow? I'm bushed. I hiked back to the ranch, fixed lunch, then started driving. I need a day to recover. But I've got something I want to discuss with you, so will tomorrow do?"

"Sounds good. Suppose we meet at nine tomorrow morning. That give you enough time?"

"Nine it is, Frenchy. The ship sounds interesting, but first I need sleep."

Chapter Twenty-four

“So how long have you been working on spacecraft?” Chuck asked.

Jose, ‘Call me Joe’, was showing Chuck around the craft he and Morty had been working on. “Seems like all my life. I started out working on Apollo 13, then switched to the Shuttle program after Apollo ended. After that, I started a consulting company. I was working on reusable civilian orbital vehicles and thinking about retirement when Lina’s father contacted me. When he mentioned you folks were developing an all-electric drive, I got interested. A lot of people have been working on that concept, but they’re not getting much thrust. When Frenchy told me you had a craft that was already flying, that hooked me.”

Joe pointed to the ship and continued. “What we’re doing here, as far as the frame and exterior hull is concerned, is basically what we did when we built the first shuttle. We don’t have to deal with rocket engines, fuel tanks, or the plumbing and pumps that go with them. This bird *looks* like the shuttle to some extent, or maybe more like one of the experimental lifting bodies we built for the Air Force, but it’s not nearly as complicated. We also don’t have to bother with tiles over the skin; Morty told me we wouldn’t need to re-enter the atmosphere the same way the shuttles did. Just as well, because we can’t; at the very least, we’d have to replace all the external photovoltaic panels after every reentry.

“The big challenge was figuring out where we’d store the hydrogen and extra oxygen. The fuel cells use both, so taking this ship beyond the atmosphere means we have to carry separate fuel and oxidizer systems. You also don’t want to run into a situation where you have to choose whether to breathe or use the oxy to power the fuel cells. That means extra oxygen and it's also where the solar panels come in."

Joe pointed to the fuselage. "Those are high-efficiency thin-film photovoltaic units, mounted over a rigid metal substrate. They're protected on top by thin glass panels, so everything is a lot more durable than you might expect.

"The units cover most of the body and the wings, top and bottom, so whichever way the ship is oriented some of the PV cells will be working. They can't provide takeoff power in Earth's gravity, but they'll work fine in space.

"Based on the efficiency figures Morty gave me, they'll generate enough power to provide constant acceleration at a tenth of a gee. We'll run the fuel cells at reduced output anyway, just to keep the ship warm, but in an emergency the PV cells can bring you home. Come on inside and let me show you what we've got."

"So you've designed a hybrid," said Chuck. "The ship uses batteries and fuel cells during takeoff, the fuel cells and PV panels to recharge the batteries and provide sustained power in space?"

"Well, it was Morty and me that designed it, but you've got the idea. Lina also did a lot of the work, the interior layout she did by herself, but she also helped design the interiors for the wings. It's not just hydro and oxy tanks, there's also the electrical and plumbing runs.

"Morty wanted to use nuclear reactors but we couldn't get those, you probably know about that. The hybrid is an interim step, because we can't carry enough fuel and oxy for extended trips.

"Bottom line, there's still a lot of work to be done before we try to build a real interplanetary ship. But we've got to take this one into space and make a few mistakes just to see what we're doing wrong. It will be far better than the shuttle ever was, but it's not a true interplanetary ship.

"Back to the interior design; the suits that Frenchy got us will work for extra-vehicular activity, but we want the interior to be a shirt-sleeve environment. People can't be expected to live in spacesuits for a week.

"Another issue, on longer trips the crew will need room to move around and more privacy than they get in the space station. If you're going to take ordinary people into space, the space around them has to be as much like their home environment as possible.

"But that's the future. The interplanetary ships will have to be bigger and that's when we'll need the nuke reactors. Given that much power, you can accelerate continuously at one gee, only going weightless during turnover.

"We may not even have to turn the ship, at least I don't think we will, just reverse the impellers so that instead of pushing forward to accelerate have them push backwards to slow the ship down. I'm still thinking about that. It might be cheaper to flip the ship and switch the cameras so they point backwards in the direction the ship is going. If you feed that view to the screens over the pilot's seat, it will look like that's the direction you're going."

"Seems strange."

"You'll get used to it, controlling a spacecraft using display screens. I did. Anyway, we just finished installing the hatch that Morty was working on, so the hull exterior is complete. I did a pressure test while we were waiting for you to get back and the ship's holding pressure, although there was a slight drop in the central section over twenty-four hours. That may have to do with the seals, not quite in their final position, or maybe it was because I used three atmospheres of pressure for the test.

"That gave me a differential between the ship and the outside of two atmospheres. In space, it will be only 70% of one atmosphere inside the ship, zero outside, so the seals may hold. Meaning that in space, we might not have any leaks at all.

"But we'll have extra oxygen anyway, just in case. There are scrubbers in the crew section that are designed to remove carbon dioxide before it can build up to dangerous levels. Taken all in all, I don't expect any problems with the ship's internal atmosphere.

"If I'm wrong, we'll just have to wear the suits and hook up to the ship's oxy and electrical systems until we're back on the ground. The front compartment didn't show any leaks, neither did the aft power section, but the cargo section amidships has that big loading hatch. If there really *are* seal problems, that's where they'll be.

"Easy solution, depressurize the central bay unless we're stowing and securing cargo. We could probably get contracts to launch satellites, so I can see us having to work in that section getting them ready to deploy. It's a lot easier if you don't have to wear the suits, though.

"The aft section is where the fuel cells are. The hydrogen is in tanks in the starboard wing, dissolved in ammonia. We extract the H2 and pipe it to the fuel cells. They pull their oxy out of the internal atmosphere, so we'll need to keep that section pressurized. I won't be using pure oxy back there, probably a mix of 50% nitrogen and oxy."

"Sounds good. Let's take a look at that aft section."

"This way. It's not quite finished yet. The cells are in and connected, but the radiator piping isn't. The system puts out a lot of heat and we're going to need some of it for cabin heating, so there's a divider with separate fans in the heat exchange system. One channel of the 'Y' fitting leads to the cabin radiators, the other goes to a system of external radiators. They're the things that look like fins, running the length of the fuselage on both sides. The solar cells will absorb or reflect solar heat, meaning that if we don't heat the cabins, we'll freeze our butts off. Can't have that.

"We went with molten carbonate fuel cells, MCFC, expensive in a sense because we've got to install the plumbing to dump the waste heat the cells generate. I hate that idea, wasting heat, so I intend to eventually pump it through a Stirling cycle engine/generator. It increases the efficiency of the MCFC units."

"So the cells generate too much heat? Is that why you put them in the aft section?"

"It's easier to deal with the heat problem that way, yes. The ship's frame is titanium and so is the skin in the engine section, so heat isn't a serious problem.

"I'll do what I can to test the complete system on the ground, first inside the building, then during local flights that don't go past the stratosphere. We might have to tweak the handling characteristics; the local trips will tell us how much we still have to do."

"Sounds good. Grandpa was always concerned with safety, so taking it one step at a time makes sense to me. How close are we to flying this bird?"

"A week, maybe ten days at most before first lift off the cradle. The pilot and copilot stations are in, but we still have to install cabinets for storage of crew equipment and we haven't built them yet. Passenger seats, too; based on Morty's figures, this ship is overpowered, so we need good seats for the rest of the crew. I doubt I'll accelerate this one past maybe four gees. Unless people are trained to deal with that much acceleration, four gees can cause blackouts, so I'd really prefer to never go beyond two gees."

"How much power will the fuel cells put out?"

"They're designed for a sustained maximum of a megawatt. You could draw more than that, maybe an additional quarter megawatt for a short time, but that consumes more hydrogen and generates a lot more heat that has to be dumped somehow. I won't go past the design maximum unless there's an emergency."

"I see what you mean about being overpowered! You have the mounts in place, but you haven't installed the impellers yet?"

"No, Morty wanted to wait on that. They're in that locked storeroom that's behind the back wall over there. We'll use eight units for main propulsion, they'll be mounted on the frames in the aft compartment. We'll put four up front, right behind the radar set. They're intended primarily for attitude control, but they're on gimbals, so they can also add forward impulse. We've put four batteries in the aft compartment and two up front here. In theory, you could unbolt the bow section and use it for an escape capsule. There's just about enough power from the two battery packs to bring you down through the upper atmosphere. From there, you use the flight controls in the wings to land dead-stick.

"The numbers say it would work, but it's strictly a last-ditch system. Still, I guess if the alternative is to use the escape capsule or burn up, it's a good thing we'll have power wrenches stored in the crew lockers. The ones that aren't made yet.

"Why don't you look around, get familiar with the layout, while I help the crew build those lockers? Lina designed the pilot and copilot's stations, so she can show you where everything is."

"Thanks, Joe. I'll do that."

***

"So this is the pilot's seat?"

"Morty called it the commander's seat. It has a full set of controls, but we anticipate that the copilot will control the computers that will do the actually flying. He's also responsible for everything that's happening inside the ship.

"The commander monitors what's going on outside, plus he also directs crew operations while loading or unloading cargo from the central bay. That's the tentative division of assignments, anyway. We've got two armored glass ports up front and two small side ports so the remaining crew and any passengers can see out, but the pilot and copilot won't need those except in an emergency.

"The primary system relies on the cameras. We've got a camera at the tip of each wing, steerable, two more fixed cameras that face front, and one steerable camera that faces aft. The controls are on the board between the commander's position and the copilot's, so that in an emergency either can choose what camera feed they want to display. All of them feed into that big display screen in front of the commander's and copilot's stations. Normally the commander decides on which display he wants, but we've provided for emergencies.

"The cameras are better for flying than using direct viewing, because the cameras can be zoomed to give telephoto or wide angle images. They're also shielded; the pilots won't ever be blinded by some kid with a laser pointer."

"That doesn't happen very often, Lina."

"Once is too often, Chuck. Morty and Joe were all about being prepared before it happens."

Chuck sat down in the commander's seat as Lina slid into the copilot's. He glanced around, immediately recognizing what most of the controls were for; they were essentially the same as the ones on the Bedstead, the King, and the Twin.

"Are those the only gauges?"

"They're backup only. The primary system displays are around the edges of the screen, easy for the copilot or spacecraft commander to see."

"Joe mentioned a radar. Where's the display for that?"

"You'll see it when we power up the screen. The radar display is in the center, the left side is for the port wing camera and the starboard wing camera is displayed on the right. It's switchable; you can use the nose cameras instead if you prefer, although they only show what's ahead, while the wing cameras are mounted far enough back that they also show the forward section of the ship. We've not settled on a protocol yet; we haven't had power connected to everything yet, and for that matter we don't want to put the radar into service while there are people in the building. That's one of the things Joe mentioned, the testing we can't do until we get into the air."

"Have you tested the building's ceiling hatch, or do you intend to fly out through the doors in the back?"

"Probably be best to use the side doors, don't you think? At least for the first flight. Morty didn't want to use the overhead hatch if he didn't have to. He was afraid it would cause it to leak next time we got a heavy rain."

"He was always a worrier, wasn't he?"

"He was. Even so, he was happy. I don't ever remember him being depressed or sad."

"You're right. The impellers, for that matter the ship, are his life's crowning work. That's his real monument, not that stone I ordered."

***

Chuck and Lina settled into an uneasy relationship, something that was better than being apart but no longer what they'd had in the beginning. Chuck occasionally caught Lina looking at him as if she wondered what kind of person lived inside. How could someone be so...ordinary, and yet be capable of violence?

He understood her concerns, but decided it was something she'd have to work through. He lost no sleep over the men he'd shot; they shot at him first, he'd only defended himself. For that matter, it seemed obvious that they had intended to burn the factory and one was likely the man who'd raped Lina. His only regret had nothing to do with killing the men, only the haste he'd had to employ to conceal the bodies.

Working in darkness and depending on what he could see in the night-vision goggles, he'd enlarged a cave in the side of an arroyo. He dug it out, dumping the dirt in the bottom, then put the bodies and their weapons inside before collapsing the ceiling. The collapse had extended to the top of the arroyo wall, leaving a fresh scar; but the area was deserted, so it should be safe enough; the ranch hands had no reason to ride down into the arroyo and there was no livestock on this part of the range.

It was not the best arrangement, but it was the best he could do. As it was, he'd barely gotten the Bedstead back inside the hangar before the sun came up.

***

Joe's estimate was optimistic. Finishing the ship, hooking up everything, storing equipment on board and fueling the tanks took four weeks. The first flight took place on Saturday, after the shop crew had gone home. Chuck served as copilot, Joe took over as commander. No other passengers were on board.

Chuck couldn't fault Joe's control. He brought the impellers on line, rotated them to vertical, then advanced power to 38%, the pre-calculated setting. Chuck, by prior agreement, kept his fingers on his controls in case the ship lifted too fast.

But the big craft smoothly lifted from its cradle and hovered in place, rock steady. Joe held it there while he tweaked flight settings.

Chuck, as copilot, monitored the fuel cell output and battery charge. Everything seemed to be working normally; there had been a small initial decrease in battery charge, but then the automatic controls cut in and the fuel cells increased their output. The battery packs crept back to 100%, fully charged.

"I'd like to test the system before we take her outside, switch off the batteries one at a time to make sure they're all working as expected. You ready, Joe?"

"Go ahead, Chuck. At worst we'd drop a few inches into the cradle, and this bird should handle that with no problems."

"Understood. Switching off the aft battery packs in sequence, starting now."

A few minutes went by as Chuck isolated systems. At one point, he pointed to a gauge indicating oxygen levels in the aft compartment. "Looks like the fuel cells are pulling more than expected."

"That's why we're doing this. Mount a tank in the cargo hold, hook it in to the aft compartment, and increase oxygen flow before we try a high-altitude flight. We can try increasing regulator pressure, but if that doesn't work we might have to change out the pipes from the wing tanks. Same pressure, but higher volume. Anything else you want to look at?"

"No, I'm done. You ready to land?"

"I am. But I think we're ready to try an outdoor flight tomorrow. Refuel tonight, install that extra tank and piping, look at the computer log readouts to make sure we didn't miss a gotcha moment, then take her out. You want to fly as commander or leave me in the hot seat?"

"I think it's time I got my feet wet, Joe."

Chapter Twenty-five

Sol was grumpy.

Months had passed with no word from Walter, and today he was meeting with politicians.

This left him feeling unclean, even though it needed to be done; all that money his company's PAC paid out, from time to time politicians needed to be told what they could do in return. He'd already met with a senator and two Representatives this morning, plus four staffers from other offices.

There was one final Representative to see. This one was probably the worst of the lot; how had he managed to get himself elected? It said something about the American voter, that was for sure.

But none of this showed on Sol's face. His expression was open, welcoming, when the short, bald-headed man walked in. Sol met him with a handshake and glanced meaningfully at the receptionist. By now, the woman knew the routine as well as Sol himself did; she would buzz his phone after fifteen minutes to see if he wanted to end the visit.

"Welcome, welcome, Mister Chambers! Can I get you a cup of coffee, or maybe something stronger?"

"It's been a long day, Sol. I don't need more coffee, but maybe if you've got some of that good Tennessee sour mash stuffed away somewhere...?"

Sol smiled and opened the cabinet. He poured a glass half full of Maker's Mark and added an ice cube; by now, he'd dealt often enough with the man to know his preferences.

"Just the thing to rev up your motor after a hard day on the Hill, Mister Chambers."

"Well, we're not in session, but that doesn't mean the work

stops. I've been meeting with constituents and visiting a few of our leading industrialists. They're people like you, Sol, the folks that keep our economy humming. I'm nearly talked out!" Chambers drank a healthy slug of the whiskey. "But I'm always interested in your problems, you know that."

You sure are, Sol thought. *Especially when you smell money.* But his voice was smooth, unhurried; none of the contempt showed.

"I wanted to talk to you about something I've discovered, something I consider to be a real threat to the American economy. Running a business is tough enough, what with having to compete against foreigners and all that cheap labor. It was bad enough when they were shipping in cars and trucks made with sweatshop labor, but now they're doing the designing in Japan and places like that. They're over here now, using honest American labor for the grunt work, but the high-paying jobs stay overseas."

Chambers grunted and sipped his whiskey.

"None of the jobs are in my district, either. You're right, it's a shame. But how is that a threat to the economy? Sounds to me like it's more of a threat to *your* business, Sol." Despite the stiff drink which Chambers had almost finished, his eyes were shrewd. A functioning alcoholic, he somehow managed to drink copious amounts and still show almost no effects until late in the evening. His personal staff knew to have his car ready and drive him home before he passed out. They were successful, most of the time.

"No, it's not about the Japanese carmakers. I know how to deal with them. It's about how we all do business, working with parts suppliers and contracts and financing. Businesses need to look ahead, sometimes far ahead, so that everything runs smoothly.

"There's this fellow, though, he doesn't understand that. He doesn't know a lot about business either, but I hear he's starting up a factory. I don't think he's going to succeed, but you see, the way he's going about it leaves all of us manufacturers in an uncompetitive position. Some companies have had to move their main offices overseas just to stay competitive.

"I know how much you value competition among private businesses, Mister Chambers, I've heard you mention it often during your speeches. But you see, if we're left behind by this new business model, we'll have to pay more for financing, American jobs will be threatened, investors will lose money. Some of those investors *are* in your state, Mister Chambers, and some are in your district. Your state pension funds are invested in my company as well as others like it, so I thought you would have a real interest in seeing that we're not threatened by unfair competition."

"Cut the horseshit, Sol. You're feeling threatened by these people, you want me to see what I can do.

"Best thing to do is send out some letters, get one of the regulatory agencies involved. They require lots of paperwork, it takes lots of time, you know how slow the government can be. Any particular one, maybe more than one, you'd like me to encourage? And where is this company located, anyway? What is it they're doing that's got your underwear in a knot?"

"Well, as to which agencies might have jurisdiction...."

The conversation continued for another ten minutes, a necessary part of the charade. Chambers now understood what Sol wanted and how he could help him get it. He also knew that Sol would 'continue to support him', that the campaign money from the political action committee would keep coming and might even be increased.

The exact amount wasn't specified, but there was no need; the PAC could be generous to its friends when campaign time came around.

Sol washed his hands as soon as the man left. Still not satisfied, he washed them again. It was just business, he understood that, but still...

His right hand felt slimy.

***

Chuck examined the page carefully. "I don't see anything wrong with it, Joe, but suppose I read through it and you tap the copilot's controls to see if I missed anything."

The page was part of the checklist for piloting the spacecraft, necessary for eventually training crewmembers and for eventual acceptance by government regulators. But that was in the future; for now, the checklist would help the spacecraft commander avoid the feeling of being *too* familiar, avoid missing a step in bringing the complicated machine from standby to ready.

"Check oxygen sensors, power compartment."

"Checked, nominal."

"Fuel pumps on standby, computer control selected."

"Standby, selected."

"Check batteries, charged."

"Checking batteries now. Forward batteries, port, 100%. Forward, starboard, 100%. Aft, portside outboard..."

Meticulously, the two continued the checklist. Chuck penciled in two corrections before reaching the final item on the checklist: power on, main buss.

"I'll type up the corrections and write the program for the computer."

"The three computers have to agree, or the errant one gets automatically kicked out of the system. The pilot also has the option of cutting its power. I suppose you could call the pilot secondary, not that I like the idea much. I still miss having a real stick that's cabled directly to the flight controls."

"Joe, you're not *that* old. That went out with radial engines. You're not strong enough or quick enough to control any of the jets flying today. It's all fly-by-wire, all digital, now."

"It might be obsolete, but my three-quarter Spitfire is more fun to fly than anything with a jet strapped on it!"

"I've heard the same from guys with replica Mustangs, Joe. Anyway, I'll get these into the computer and have a hard copy printed up for us by tomorrow."

***

Chuck was writing code when a buzz interrupted him. He checked his cell automatically, but the buzz wasn't coming from his belt holster. Finally, he picked up his grandfather's phone, still lying where Chuck had left it after he collected Morty's personal possessions.

A glance at the screen revealed that the charge was down to less than half and that the caller had an icon, a government eagle, by his number. Maybe they were calling to offer condolences, even though his grandfather had passed three months before. Chuck pressed the call button.

"Hello?"

"Mister Sneyd?"

"This is Charles Sneyd, yes."

"I'm sorry, I was calling a Mister Morton Sneyd. Is he there?"

"Who's calling?"

"I represent the Defense Advanced Research Projects Agency. Morton Sneyd sent us a proposal some time back, and I'd like to discuss it with him."

"That won't be possible, I'm afraid. My grandfather passed away. I don't recall him mentioning that he'd contacted DARPA."

"My condolences, sir. Charles, you said? The fact is, Charles, we didn't take his proposal seriously when he sent it to us. We get a lot of ideas and most of them are...well, impractical."

"So you trashed his proposal. What caused you to change your mind?"

"His name came up in connection with another matter, so we retrieved the file and took another look. While I'm not ready to go beyond this point on the telephone, we hoped to discuss the matter in person. Are you familiar with what he was working on?"

"I am. Intimately familiar, in fact; I wrote the control software for the first units."

"You have operational units, then, more than one of them? His letter didn't mention that." The man was quick, picking up information from Chuck's comment.

"I'm guessing he sent the letter before I began working with him, because he never mentioned it. We improved the early device and most of the bugs have since been worked out. That said, what do you have in mind?"

"We have a team of investigators we'd like to send out there to meet with you. Are you still in Texas? Would it be possible for you to meet with them?"

"No, we've moved to New Mexico. I don't see why we can't meet, but it won't be just me, others are involved now. I suspect Morty was interested in your agency financing development of his invention?"

"That's essentially correct. He also wanted us to help with problems he was having. We have staff who are experts in a number of fields."

"I'll have to confirm with Mister Fuqua, so how about I talk to him or better yet, have him contact you? You have a name and number he can call?"

"I'm the office contact, Oscar Norton, but others will be at the meeting. When should I expect a return call?"

Chuck wrote down the man's number, said goodbye, and ended the call. Thoughtfully he found the charger for Morty's phone and plugged it in. Who could say, there might be other calls.

He used his own cell to call Frenchy. Let him set up the meet, maybe decide whether he wanted one of the company's lawyers present.

In the meantime, Chuck had a test flight to prepare.

***

"No, you'll be pilot-in-command, Chuck. I certified Lina as copilot only. She needs to get her own pilot's ticket before I'd be comfortable with her in command, and besides we only have the one spacecraft so we don't need her certified yet. Got a name for the bird?"

"Just a number, Joe. We'd probably need approval from the front office to name this one. Frenchy's latest brainstorm has us reorganized as a division of New Frontiers, Incorporated, which is only a holding company but even so, the board would want to approve the name.

"Still, we need a second command pilot. We're not immortal, none of us. Have you thought about that? It's not what you were hired to do, but what about you?"

"Will needs more hours in the spacecraft...you really should have a name, you know… but as soon as Will can take time off from what he's doing with the Twin, I'll run him through a certification exercise. Command Pilots need ordinary FAA certificates first, we can add special certifications later on.

"One day, those records will be important, but for now, we'll just keep them confidential. Frenchy's team of lawyers insist we dot every T and cross every I."

"What about you, Joe? You're certifying the rest of us, which means you're de facto certified yourself."

"Can't pass a flight physical, Chuck; my ticker's only a little better than Morty's was. No, I'd love to fly this thing, maybe even all the way to the moon, but if I come along I'll be a supernumerary. Will or you will command, the other will be the copilot. Lina will probably want to come along, but I wouldn't want to list her as crew until she gets her pilot's certificate.

"The lawyers insist on that. It's a test flight, so something is likely to go wrong and real pilots will be needed. Murphy always flies the third seat, the one you can't see, but trust me, he's along on every flight."

"No flight physical? But what about that prop job you told me about? And you did some of the early tests on Number One too."

"I only did the hovers and low-level flights, following the King through that test course you laid out. As for the plane, I can't talk myself into selling her but I'll never fly her again. She's in a hangar in Bakersfield and once a month someone goes out and cranks the engine. She's flyable, but to be honest she's part of my past, not my present. That's why I don't sell her, I'd be selling my own past."

"That's too bad, Joe. I really expected you'd fly the first space mission."

"No, I knew when I came here this was likely to be my last hurrah. I enjoyed building this one, already got some ideas for the next one, but if I fly in it I'll be a passenger.

"I'm enjoying the engineering, though. We've got a good team. I wasn't sure about you at first, but you've also fitted in well."

"I had to, Joe. I couldn't leave Lina with you guys all the time. Some of the boys are unmarried, you know."

Joe chuckled. "I hadn't thought of it like that, but I can see your point. Anyway, Frenchy talked to me yesterday. He's getting anxious, wanted to know when the first flight above the atmosphere would take place. He also asked if the Bedstead and the King would fly off our wing. I had to tell him no."

"Why would he have wondered about that? They don't even have a *cabin*, just a windshield, and they've not been tested at altitude."

"He thought they could fly if the pilot wore one of the spacesuits, but I nixed that idea. I think he thought we'd use the others as chase craft because they've been flying alongside us during the preliminary tests. Mel and Lina did get in some flight time, because we needed someone to watch what the controls were doing and keep an eye on the externals, but we flew at *their* altitude, not them at ours.

"I'm just glad we didn't lose any of the solar cells. I wasn't sure how well that epoxy would hold; we couldn't use a heavy coat over the outside layer of the glass without degrading performance too much."

"You were right to tell Frenchy no. I guess there's no real reason Will and I can't take her up. As soon as we get Will certified, anyway. He's got the hours, so let him fly as command pilot. I'll be happy to copilot for him."

"I expected that, but I didn't want to decide. You're the company's biggest stockholder now, after Frenchy. Will's up there too, but he didn't invest as much as Frenchy to start with and Morty got some of his shares as part of the initial agreement. Anyway, that's business, not flying stuff. I'm glad you're okay with Will flying left seat."

Chapter Twenty-six

"You are to take the message that's attached to the email we just sent you. Hand it to the colonel. When you have done that, come back. I have further instructions for you."

"Uh...who am I speaking to?"

"I am General Stroganoff. Is enough. Follow your orders."

"Yes, General. Be right back, sir."

The major printed the attachment, glanced at it, and had time to think *Holy shit!* as he carried it down the hall.

The American phrase seemed particularly apt, considering what the attachment said. More than a simple email, this one had the supreme leadership's emblem across the top of the page.

Would the colonel follow the orders? He had to know what this meant, what was unstated but a virtual certainty. The colonel's family would at least get a pension for the service he'd rendered as a junior officer, before he began to rise through the system. Before he'd turned into a bureaucrat and forgotten what operations were about.

Reaching the colonel's door, the major knocked once, then opened the door. The colonel stood with his back to him, just turning around. The glass of vodka spilled, his face darkened toward purple, the colonel opened his mouth to roar at this insignificant CLERK who dared barge in...

"I have received a priority message, Colonel. You are to read it and follow the instructions. I am to respond, to say that I gave you the message. I have done so. Good day, Colonel."

There was just time enough to see the colonel's face turn white. The instructions were clear. He was to report to New York and catch the first flight home for 'debriefing'. The major didn't envy him; such debriefings were sometimes fatal, and always bad news for the debriefee.

Back in his office, he picked up the phone. "Sir...still there?"

"Of course I am! I've been waiting for you to respond!"

"Yes, General. Sir, I printed out the message and placed it in the colonel's hand myself. He was reading it as I left."

"Very good, Colonel. That's the good news. There is better news, you are in charge of the office for now.

"The promotion is permanent, the assignment is not. You will be joined soon by General Oleff. He will take over. If he cannot be released from his current assignment, I'll take the job myself."

"Sir, is there a problem?"

"Perhaps. We shall see; it appears that the Americans have something we urgently need."

"Sir, we don't know *what* they have. *They* think it's important, but there's no way we can be sure. We've made one attempt, but the Americans destroyed their device. We...that is, the colonel...decided to monitor the situation. We may try again."

"We have information you lack, Colonel. It appears the Americans may have a working antigravity device."

"General, my agent saw no evidence..."

"Speaking of that, how much does he know?"

"Not much. I gave the instructions myself, only that we wanted to capture their barge and tow it up the lake. He didn't know what we were looking for, just that we wanted the barge."

"Are you *certain* he knows nothing?"

"I don't see how he could know more, General. Unless the colonel, my predecessor I mean, told him."

"Do not use the man again. If further action is necessary, we will handle it from here.

"Your task is to gather as much information as possible. There is a list of names attached to the message, see what you can find out about them.

"General Oleff will take charge when he arrives, but at the moment he's unable to turn his own project over to his replacement. It may take time, but I expect you to have the information waiting.

"If you should somehow stumble over this antigravity device, we want it. Not that I expect this to happen."

"General, my agent said nothing about the barge floating. He said his men reported that it moved under its own power, but if they had antigravity, wouldn't the barge have been floating in the air?"

"Not necessarily, although your thinking is commendable. Suppose this device is not yet perfected, that it's not powerful enough to float the barge, but only make it lighter?"

"I... see, General. Yes, that could explain what our agent reported."

"Follow your orders, Colonel. There have been too many failures already."

"One question, General. You mentioned other evidence?"

"Yes. I suppose it can't do any harm; I'll send you the relevant satellite photos via the secure link. Are you able to interpret such photos?"

"I believe so, sir. If the photos are clear."

"They're clear enough. It appears that the Americans have refitted one of their shuttles with the device. They also have two other flying craft, smaller, that accompany the large craft when they fly it. They only fly at night, so the photos are unclear, but you can clearly make out the shuttle and the other two.

"They have no wings and fly slowly, so the only possible explanation is antigravity. We must have this, the chairman himself has commanded it, so you will assist General Oleff to see that it is done.

"One additional task; you will go to the airport to ensure your predecessor makes his flight. Do not allow him to remain in America; he must return home for the debriefing. Do you understand?"

"Yes, General. I'll see that it's done."

"You will do it *yourself*, Colonel," the general said. "Report to me when you have carried out your orders."

"Yes, General. I will not fail."

"See that you don't, Colonel." The dial tone indicted that the general had hung up.

***

Chuck said nothing, content to watch the new arrivals as they sorted themselves out after entering. He was at the meeting to provide technical expertise if needed and the lawyer was there to keep Frenchy from being impulsive.

That said, the meeting was Frenchy's.

"Come in, Gentlemen. My name is Fuqua; I'm the chief executive officer of the New Frontiers Corporation. You've already spoken to Mister Sneyd; the other gentleman is our lead corporate attorney, Mister Hazzard."

"Thank you, Mister Fuqua. I'm Brigadier General Fuller, US Air Force, and I'm chief of the delegation. Colonel Ponder, US Army, is my deputy. We're currently detached from our various services and assigned to DARPA. Colonel Warren represents the Air Force, Major Hooke is a Marine, Colonel Tindall is Army, and Rear Admiral Sessions represents the Navy and Coast Guard."

"You've got us outnumbered, General," chuckled Frenchy.

All were in civilian clothing, so there was no way to tell if any were pilots; they might have been staff weenies. The marine looked familiar, although Chuck couldn't recall ever serving with him. Maybe he'd shown up in Fallujah at some point. Things were confused most of the time and painful at the end.

"We have various interests, Mister Fuqua, and considering how promising the device appears, the services wanted to see how useful it would be."

"I understand, General. I wonder why Morty never mentioned contacting you?"

"I can't answer that, Mister Fuqua. His letter was too vague for us to take seriously. If he'd had a *working model*, that would have been different.

"We see any number of proposals, frequently several during the course of a month. Most of them range from impossible to impractical. So Mister Sneyd's letter was scanned and a file started, but that was as far as our interest went. Keeping records is routine, because you never know what might turn out to be useful.

"But that was then, and now things have changed."

"How so, General?"

"Are you aware that the Department of Transportation is interested in your company? Not to mention the Federal Aviation Administration and the Federal Communication Commission? I may have missed one or two, maybe the National Security Agency. They've got feelers into every aspect of America, and for that matter the rest of the world. I wish *we* had the level of computing power they take for granted!"

"Why are they interested in an obscure holding company? We've been chartered less than six months, although we had other companies before incorporating New Frontiers," said Frenchy.

"According to our sources, they're responding to Congressional interest. I got *my* information from a clerk in the Department of Transportation's Congressional Liaison Office, and he knew about it because he helped draft a letter, responding to a Congressman's inquiry.

"The Congressman himself didn't write the letter, of course, and for that matter he may not know anything about it. A lot of business is done by staffers using their elected official's name. But departments have to respond as if the Congressman himself wrote the letter. In this case, the response pointed out that they had no reason to get involved with your company at this point. Perhaps it would be better to say they had no justification, because they'd almost certainly try to keep any House member happy. That's where department budgets come from, after all."

"My, my," Frenchy's voice was soft. "I ran into opposition in Texas and I'm getting pushback from Santa Fe too. I wonder who has the clout to get the federal government involved?"

"Someone with deep pockets, Mister Fuqua. The government runs on money, and the first thing a newly-elected politician does is form a reelection committee to collect more of it. Even before they take the oath of office, they're raising money for their next campaign. Money talks in Washington, Mister Fuqua, and at the state level too. You've got enemies, whether you know about them or not."

"They're too late. They might be able to delay us, but they can't stop us.

"We, the corporation that is, own the rights to the device you're interested in. We got them from the inventor, Morton Sneyd, and his grandson Chuck now owns Morty's shares in the company. He's also deeply involved in product development. We're committed to bringing the device to its full potential."

"I understand. What you might not realize is that we also have considerable clout in Washington. Not to put too fine a point on it, we have our own political allies, people who want to see the devices we develop manufactured in *their* district if possible, but their state at the very least. We dispense considerable pork, Mister Fuqua. Pork talks too."

"I'm surprised. I expected you to offer development money, but at the moment we're adequately funded. We don't have a lot of surplus, but we're moving ahead, so it's not as if we were faced with a shutdown if we didn't join forces with you."

"We've got money, Mister Fuqua. In practical terms, we draw from several budgets, so the limit of what we can offer is quite high. Perhaps even better, some of our funds are difficult to trace. I mention this, because Mister Sneyd said you have an operational device to show us?"

"We do. We currently have two operating vehicles that use only the impeller drive system. We've flown the latest models for more than a hundred hours each, meaning that since the craft use multiple impellers we've got considerable experience with them. It's fair to say we have thousands of operational hours using the impellers. I expect you want to see them, so I can make them available for a demonstration if you wish."

"Is one of them the airplane you converted? The Air Force and the Navy are interested in that. We're also speaking for the Marines and Coast Guard, because they'll provide a share of the funding."

"I hadn't intended to mention the airplane. We intend to eventually manufacture our own planes, but we'll start out by modifying off-the-shelf airframes. I'm not sure how that would fit in with what you do."

"You're thinking business-class planes?"

"For now, but there's no reason we can't scale up. Passenger planes, cargo planes, it doesn't matter. The system will work on any of them."

"You might be surprised to learn how many Gulfstreams we buy every year," said General Fuller. "Would it be possible to take a look at the plane? A functioning airplane, using your system...I'm sure that would be of interest to the steering committee."

"We could probably take one or two of you up for a test flight," Frenchy said cautiously. "Are any of you rated aviators?"

"We all are. Colonel Ponder is rotary-wing only, Admiral Sessions is rated in tactical aircraft, but the rest of us have multi-engine experience. Is there some reason we can't all get an opportunity to fly in your plane?"

"Chuck?" Frenchy asked.

"We can do it if you've got the time. Here's the problem, the plane has been modified; we needed the cargo space, so we closed that off with a bulkhead. That means we only have space for a pilot and copilot up front. I suppose we could fit seats behind the crew space, but we've never had a reason to. We've got more than enough lift to accommodate passengers, just no place to put them."

"Perhaps later, then. But can you manage at least a takeoff and landing for each of us?"

"Chuck?"

"Not a problem, Frenchy. We can probably do a little better than that."

"Thank you," said General Fuller. "Is your system suitable for Navy use, aboard ships I mean?"

"Surface ships and submarines both. As a matter of fact, Morty proposed that we test a submarine vehicle, but we aren't in that business and none of us have the expertise needed."

"Not to jump the gun, but part of what we bring to the table is expertise. Are you willing to sell us the rights to your device?"

"No. We might consider licensing it for military use, but we would retain all rights to the system."

"You understand that if this system is all you say it is, it confers a strategic advantage to the nation that owns it?"

"For a short time, yes," said Frenchy. "But all discoveries

eventually become compromised. Just look at jet power; two countries independently developed jet engines, but soon everyone had them. Radar too, secret in the beginning, but as soon as others knew it was possible they started working on their own systems. It will be the same with the impeller drive.

"Our problem is this; if the government owned the system, they might share it with other favored nations or use it as a diplomatic bargaining chip. So no, we can discuss leasing, but we insist on retaining control."

"I understand Mister Sneyd is a veteran. Sir, you're a former Marine; are you willing to keep your country from gaining a strategic advantage? Is this the sort of patriotism they teach Marines nowadays?"

"I'm not sure *what* they teach at boot camp now, General, but they teach something different in government and business courses. Have you ever heard that patriotism is the last refuge of the scoundrel?"

"I think I might have heard that, Mister Sneyd, but my boss thought it was worth a try. About those demonstrations, do you suppose we could adjourn for lunch and do that afterwards?"

Chapter Twenty-seven

"The plane, we can fly it now; but the others, we don't fly them in daylight. Too much chance they'll be compromised."

"Well...I intended to mention this at some point," said General Fuller. "I'm afraid you're *already* compromised. DOD not only knows about your devices, they've even got photos. Satellites use infrared, you know, and one of your buggies gets really hot. Once they located that one and concentrated on it, the others showed up too.

"The thing is, if we have photos you can bet the Russians and Chinese have them, also the Israelis, the Japanese, the North Koreans, and everyone else with a half-decent intelligence net. They don't need satellites, they can just buy the scans."

"Shit! *All* of them?"

"Count on it. *We* watch for interesting stuff and we know the other teams do too."

"Frenchy, you might as well send the workers home. Pick a couple of the guys who've flown the Bedstead and ask them to stay, they can be relief pilots in case we need them. We might as well fly everything but the freighter. That's still undergoing development."

It isn't, Chuck thought, *but there is no way I'm letting a government spy, which is what these brass hats really are, anywhere close to the ship.*

Or even inside the building; by definition, they're bright, so they'd catch on that we have a spacecraft even if we haven't flown it higher than a dozen yards off the ground.

They have satellite photos, but that's not the same as looking at the ship close up. From ground level, it looks like a modified space shuttle with elements from the Air Force lifting bodies. We might even be able claim it's a cargo plane, but better not to have to try.

Lifting bodies were designed for aerodynamic efficiency, and with the engines mounted internally they might actually work as cargo haulers. Or even bombers.

The visitors trooped out to the small kitchen area. *Microwaving MRE's was probably good for them*, Chuck thought, *considering how long it had been since senior officers had to make do with Meals Rejected by Everyone.*

Chuck touched Frenchy's arm, holding him back for a moment.

"I'll fly the Twin, Lina flies the Bedstead, both of us with one passenger. Mel takes the other three on the King. We'll park on the runway and load our passengers from there. The only thing they'll see is what we want to show them.

"I won't get fancy. I'll demonstrate that the plane flies. Lina and Mel can fly and hover, but only at low altitude. If they take their passengers out on the test course, that should demonstrate how reliable the system is.

"I'll have them bring the passengers back to the runway before the batteries get low. We can send them on their way from there, then do battery swaps inside the hangar. Don't take chances, these guys are smart and we don't want them to see anything they shouldn't."

"Sounds good, Chuck. I'll watch what I tell them, you have a word with Lina and Mel."

***

Lunch finished and escorted by Frenchy, the DARPA delegation trooped out to the runway. The Bedstead and the King were parked behind the Twin. Lina and Mel stood nearby, anonymous behind tinted helmet faceshields.

Two guards stood between the DARPA group and the three craft, armed, but with pistol holstered and rifle slung. They were obviously prepared to respond if necessary.

Chuck walked over to the visitors.

"Gentlemen, first a short briefing, then we'll take you out to demonstrate that our systems do everything we've said. I have room for one passenger in the Twin. I intend to give whoever is flying with me a quick checkout on the controls. You might consider that when you decide who gets to fly with me.

"Lina is the pilot of the smaller craft, we call it the Bedstead, and Mel will pilot the King, the larger one. All three use our impeller system and have no other means of propulsion.

"The pilot's controls for each craft are simple; a proprietary computer system controls the impellers and the pilot flies the computer with a joystick. It takes care of everything else.

"I emphasize that the *pilot* is in charge. We are not authorized to do more than answer simple questions about where we're going and what altitude we'll be flying at, things like that. If you have questions, please save them for when you get back and I'll answer them so long as they don't involve trade secrets."

"I've got one quick question before we start, Chuck." The speaker was the Marine, Major Hooke. "Why in the world did you name that smaller craft 'The Bedstead'? If that's not a secret, I mean."

"Simple answer, because the first version had a flat deck and upright units at each corner. An observer mentioned that it looked like a flying bedstead and the name stuck. The other unit was originally named the California King because it was larger. We shortened it to King because it was more convenient."

"I take it the impellers are pointed up, for lift? Wouldn't it have been simpler to mount them on a plane so they pushed straight ahead? At least, do it that way at first."

"We didn't have a plane at the time. What we *did* have was enough material to build the original Bedstead. We, my grandfather and I, operated on a very skinny shoestring in the beginning."

"I see. But it doesn't look like a bedstead now, does it?"

"No. The round objects you see are external housings. The impellers are mounted inside, and no, you don't get to see them with the covers removed. But the name stuck. It's a bit kitschy, but we like it."

"Let's go over and take a look."

Chuck led the way to the King. "As you can see, this model has eight impellers, two on each of the deck's four sides. The Bedstead has an impeller at each corner, enough for flight, but it is rated to carry no more than a quarter ton of cargo or a single passenger, all we have seating for.

"The King can carry up to two tons, although we prefer less. The controls are more responsive that way, and we prefer not to run a premature crash test by overloading."

After waiting for the chuckles to die away, Chuck continued. "You'll notice that the impeller housings are totally sealed. There's no air inlet or exit, so no hidden propellers or jets."

The five nodded thoughtfully. "You mentioned control problems. Have you had such problems, or crashed one of your devices?"

"No crash. You're pilots, you all know what happens to an aircraft's controls when you approach max gross weight on takeoff. They get mushy and you have to baby the plane into the air. We get some of the same effect from the impellers.

"I should also point out that if we increased the load, we would be nudging the computers' limit of controllability. They operate within set parameters, and we believe it's safer not to push those limits.

"But it's not a problem today, so why don't you decide who will fly with whom? I'd like to get started, do the demonstration flights, and hold a short debrief when we're finished."

The five officers sorted themselves out and four of them found seats aboard the lifters. Lina and Mel checked to make sure that seat belts were fastened, then lifted off, Mel following Lina as she headed away from the factory campus.

"I'll fly left seat, Admiral. I won't be doing any of the air combat maneuvers you're accustomed to, the Twin isn't built for that."

"I didn't expect you to, Chuck. You fly, I'll watch."

Chuck flipped the switch as soon as they were buckled in, starting the turbos.

"Admiral, we use electrical power for the impellers. The engines on the wings are turbogenerators, turboprops converted to drive generators instead of propellers. Two turbogenerators gives us 100% redundancy. There's also a battery system and it's capable of powering the plane unaided, but only for a limited time."

"Impressive, Chuck. Speaking as a guy who often flies over blue water, I always like having power in reserve! I've made two water landings and that was two too many."

"No water landings today, Admiral. I've been watching the gauges while you were talking and we've got power from the turbogenerators.

"Next step in the takeoff checklist, bring up the impellers. As soon as they stabilize where I want them, I'll take off."

Chuck operated the thumbwheel, then gently nudged the stick forward until it reached its detent. He continued as the plane began rolling. "From this point, it's like flying any other airplane. I've selected takeoff power from the impellers, and as soon as I reach sixty-five knots she'll start to fly."

"Interesting. You started moving immediately. What would happen if you locked the brakes and waited until you had full power?"

"I'd probably get a lot more acceleration and quicker liftoff. No need to do that with this bird, we've got plenty of runway. You're thinking of carrier takeoffs?"

"Carriers or short-field. My first comment is, no afterburner. Perhaps no chance of aerial refueling either. Do you have any idea whether your impellers can take the gees that a fighter pilot loads onto his plane?"

"I doubt it, Admiral. We had problems early on with material failures because they couldn't stand up to the loads we put on them. I'm guessing that impellers wouldn't be suitable for fighters, at least not Navy fighters.

"Still, they wouldn't need to crash onto the carrier deck like you do with your other fighters. It would be more like landing a helicopter."

"Well, maybe. But you do have heavy-lift capability?"

"Lift we've got. You're thinking of a standoff fighter platform that controls the surrounding airspace with missiles?"

"It's an idea. We tried that with the F4, it didn't even have a gun at first. The new fighters all have guns, but they depend on missiles to do most of the killing."

"Then you'd need a new kind of fighter, not just modify something you already use. The impellers are controllable within limits, we can rotate them up or down a few degrees. You could use that capability to operate at higher altitudes than conventional fighters, fire your missiles downward and let them home on their targets from above. They'd gain a lot of speed that way, so you'd need to factor that into the missile design. You'd pick up longer range as well as higher closing speeds from the gravity assist."

"Hmmm..." the admiral was lost in thought, exploring the possibilities.

Chuck flew on, banking left, then left again, now heading back for the runway.

"You mind if I take the controls?"

"Go ahead. It's straight stick and rudder flying, maybe a little heavier on the controls than the jets you fly."

"I started in prop planes at Pensacola, so maybe I remember how it feels to fly using muscle instead of hydraulics."

"Runway's in sight, Admiral. Think you can land us?"

"Let me do a couple of turns first, get a better feel of the controls. If you don't mind?"

"No, go ahead. I'll follow through on the controls anyway, and if it looks like you're about to get in trouble I'll take over."

"I wouldn't have it any other way, Chuck. Thanks."

The landing was smooth, a greaser.

Chuck complimented his passenger. "Not bad, admiral. You'll doubtless do better with practice."

The admiral chuckled. "Son, I've used that line myself more than once. It was a good landing and you know it. This beats the *heck* out of trying to land on a deck that's moving around, and doing it in the dark to boot. I also didn't mind in the least that we stopped at rollout instead of an arresting wire stop. I've *done* it, but that doesn't mean I like it. Most pilots don't, the ones that will admit it. The others lie."

The Bedstead and King were still out flying when they taxied to the parking area. The admiral walked around, looking at the turbogenerators under the wings, examining the large hatch where the batteries were loaded.

"You haven't mentioned cost, Chuck."

"No, that's Frenchy's area of expertise. I suspect we can compete with people who manufacture jet engines."

"That's good to know. Budgets are tight, you might have heard that, and adopting your system would be expensive. We can't afford to scrap our other systems, especially fighters, not considering how much we've spent on them already.

"We might be able to modify the tankers and the airborne command and control birds. Loiter time, though, we'd have to look at that. We'd also have to work out fuel consumption tables. I'm sure you have your own figures, but Navy planes operate in a different environment."

"You'd know more about that than I would, Admiral. The turbogenerators use roughly the same amount of fuel that the turboprops did, maybe a little less because we can operate them at their most efficient speed. The batteries even out the demands on the power system."

"Interesting. Chuck, I probably shouldn't tell you this but I'll be recommending that we explore your system. How we use it, though, we'll have to work that part out. You seem to be insistent on secrecy, and to be truthful that's going to be a major stumbling block."

"That's not our problem, Admiral, it's yours. You'll simply have to find a way to deal with it."

***

Frenchy called them together after the DARPA group left for Washington.

"What did you think of them, folks? Let's start with Lina first. You flew with the Marine, right?"

"I flew with all of them except the admiral. We made a couple of stops and swapped people around, because the army officer and the marine were interested in both machines. The marine mentioned using the Bedstead as a possible scout vehicle and the King as a replacement for tactical trucks, especially where there's no road net.

"They have serious problems with IED's, and they immediately realized that if you aren't limited to roads the enemy can't plant bombs in your path. You could also fly supplies over walls, doing all your loading and unloading inside. You might even eliminate at least some of the pilots, fly the haulers by controlling them remotely."

"Smart people. I hadn't thought of that. But they were definitely interested, right?"

"Very much so, Dad. They have problems and they understood right away that we could help solve some of them. The Marine understood that our lifters, expanded to a larger size of course, could replace the hovercraft they use to land troops and supplies on an enemy-controlled beach. He mentioned that a hollow frame, big enough to mount the impellers and batteries but with a large opening in the center, could land an entire shipping container prepacked with supplies. It could also land a troop unit that would be ready to deploy immediately. Instead of a shipping box, think of two rows of seats, facing outboard. The troop carrier would have a solid spine down the middle for the batteries and seats for passengers on the sides. Think of a long, skinny H shape, with the crossbar representing the spine for the batteries. The troops would load aboard the ship, maybe from one of those Marine Corps assault ships with the hollow space in the hull?

"They would fly the troops directly to the shore, do evasive maneuvers if necessary to keep from being targeted by gunfire, then pick a spot and drop off the troops. He also mentioned the possibility of mounting supporting fire units on the landers, machine guns on the front alongside the pilot's compartment, mortars on the aft part of the H.

"He said he thought the Coast Guard would also be interested in that version. They do rescues, so they could take a passenger-model lifter out and load up refugees or take people off sinking ships"

"Bright people," said Frenchy admiringly. "They *think*, that's for sure. I mentioned to the chief of the group, General Fuller, that we had experienced delays. We would like access to nuclear power plants, but he didn't appear to think that would be a problem.

"I guess we have to wait now. Even DARPA is part of a bureaucracy, and we all know how fast those operate. Just look at how long it's taken them to answer Morty's letter!"

Chapter Twenty-eight

"Got a minute, Lina?"

"Hi, Dad. Sure, give me a sec to finish up." Lina closed the display, apparently the interior of a new spacecraft that she was designing. Frenchy wondered, but decided to ask about it later.

"Okay, what's up?"

"Maybe nothing. I got to thinking, though, and I wondered if you're happy here. You were planning a career in architecture and this is a long way from that. Does it bother you, wasting your education?"

"Who says it was wasted? I'm helping design the next generation of spaceships! It's not traditional architecture, but it's close enough; I'd be designing washrooms if I worked for a major firm.

"Even if I opened my own business, I'd be beating the bushes for customers. Without a reputation, people aren't willing to risk millions of dollars by hiring an unknown. That's why so many go to work for an established firm, just so they can work in the field. Santiago Calatrava gets to design billion dollar bridges and buildings, newbies don't get the chance to do that kind of work.

"I can, and in a sense, I already have. I *love* it here."

"You're also spending some of your time flying the lifters, the Bedstead and the King. I overheard Mel talking about a pilot's license. Are you thinking of doing that?"

"I have to. At some point, I want to captain my own spaceship. Joe says I can't do that unless I've got an ordinary pilot's license first. I need to know so many things, meteorology, navigation, things like that. Chuck has promised to help me if I get stuck."

"Speaking of Chuck, is he part of the reason why you love it here?"

"He's part of it," Lina confirmed. "I think maybe he's too quick to react, but it also could be that I'm too slow.

"I don't know. I just know I was terribly unhappy, even depressed when we were apart. Is that love, Dad?"

"It could be. I can't decide for you, but if you're happy, that's good enough for me.

"One of the reasons I brought this up is what happened to Morty. None of us live forever, and I wanted to discuss what will happen to you when I pass on."

Lina turned pale. "Dad, are you saying you're *sick*?"

"No, no, I feel fine. I had a checkup six months or so ago, blood pressure was up, but not enough to be alarmed about; I just thought we should talk.

"You'll inherit almost everything, you know. I made provisions for your mother, but she won't get my business interests. You will, and that includes the company. You'll own a significant amount of stock, not enough for an absolute majority, but assuming Chuck backs you with his shares, you'll have the votes to take over the chairmanship of the board.

"Someone else will likely be CEO, though; you don't have the education or experience for that. Anyway, that's a question for later, I just wanted you to know what arrangements I've made."

"Dad, you'll be around for a long time. I don't want to worry about that now, I've got too much else to do. Want to see my concept for the cargo transport Major Hooke talked about?"

"Sure, but there's another project that may actually make us more money in the end. I've been talking to a man named Dolph Petterson. I hired him to take charge of a new department, Plans and Projects."

"How big is this department, Dad? I thought that was what you and the board did."

"Right now, it's just him. Tell you what, why don't we get together? You, Will, Chuck, Dolph, and me? I think you'll understand why I hired him after you listen to his ideas."

***

Chuck pushed the control button, starting the motors that

opened the huge doors. As they slid aside, the soft light of pre-dawn banished the shadows inside the assembly area. He turned and gave Will a thumbs up, letting him know that the doors were fully open.

Impellers whined inside the assembly area and the dark gray spacecraft lifted gently from its cradle. Chuck watched carefully, then held his hands straight out to the side as soon as the ship was clear of the cradle. Using both hands in a come-here gesture, he backed away. The ship drifted sideways, following. When the far wing cleared the door, Chuck slowly swung his arms down. Will eased the big ship to the ground, allowing the skids under the wing roots to touch. Chuck trotted inside the assembly area and moments later, the doors began to close. Ducking underneath, he waited for the automated process to finish, watched to make sure the hatch sealed tight, then headed for the open hatch.

Before taking his seat, he picked up his new helmet and hung it by the copilot's station. Unlike his old motorcycle helmet, this one locked to the neck collar that was part of his pressure suit.

Will sat in the left seat, watching the computer display on the forward screen change as it completed its preflight checks. Chuck glanced reassuringly at Lina and Joe, seated against the aft bulkhead, as he buckled himself into the copilot's seat; they were the only passengers for this first flight to space.

"Any problems, Will?"

"Negative, everything's nominal. I haven't tried the radio, but I won't use it unless there's an emergency and it worked fine during the low-level test flights.

"The fuel cells are online, fuel and oxidizer flow nominal, batteries are fully charged, impellers are at idle, direction full up. Just waiting for you."

"Hey, being doorman is very important. I've been thinking about dressing up my pressure suit with a yellow stripe down the leg, maybe even wearing a tie!"

Will chuckled. "Run your own checks, Chuck. The sky is waiting."

Chuck watched carefully, scanning the checklist on his screen, switching his view between the printed list and the computer display.

His check ran longer than Will's, but ten minutes later he was ready.

"Checks complete, all systems nominal. Ready when you are, Will. Captain, I mean."

"Roger. Lifting now." The big craft drifted slowly upward, turning gently in response to Will's input. Moments later, forward impellers whining louder, the nose lifted and ship accelerated, climbing gently toward the sky.

Chuck watched the accelerometer readout drift toward the 1.25 gee line. Will eased back on the thrust from the four aft impellers, tweaked the directional impellers behind the radar, and the big ship's acceleration decreased to one gee.

Satisfied, he switched control over to the airfoils as the ship headed for space.

"This won't take long. We'll take her up to 120,000 feet today, stay at that altitude long enough to see how things look, then bring her down and head for the barn.

"Time to put your helmets on, folks. The air's pretty thin out there and there's no need to take unnecessary chances.

"As for your suits, don't be surprised if the tubes inflate. We're not flying a fighter and the cabin is pressurized to 8000 feet, so I don't expect the gee-tubes to inflate. But if they do, close and lock your helmet faceplates immediately.

"Interior heat is set to 70° F and the computer will automatically dump excess heat through the external radiators."

Will was silent for a few moments, then reported, "Losing aerodynamic control. The airfoils are getting mushy. Airfoils are centered and locked, switching to impeller steering at this time."

"Switching to impeller steering, copy. Noted." Chuck entered the time and altitude in his log. The ship had just passed through 80,000 feet, but the changeover from aerodynamic to impeller control had been seamless.

The ship kept rising and the sky continued to darken. Chuck monitored the lights and gauges on his board and occasionally wrote down the altitude. The computers would generate a more-precise record, but Chuck's handwritten notes were backup if for some reason the computer log couldn't be retrieved.

Joe and Lina were smiling as they looked out the two small glass ports. The curvature of the Earth was clearly visible. Far below, white clouds blocked much of their view of the surface.

"I'm not seeing any problems, and the flight is going as planned," Will reported. "I'm keeping us at a constant one gee acceleration for comfort. I'll go weightless as I get ready for turnover, then we'll head for home, same acceleration or less; no reason to stress Joe's ticker. What do you think?"

"It's beautiful, Will. The stars are like...well, it's like the holiday lights people put up. But there's no twinkling, just jewels on black velvet."

"I agree, Lina, it's beautiful. Maybe one day I'll get used to this view, but I'm like you, it's the kind of view that few people have ever seen. You doing okay, Joe?"

"I'm fine, Will. I didn't experience any stress at all. It's like flying in an airliner, except smoother and quieter."

"That was my intention, Joe. There's no need to pull high gees, I've got the kind of control the Apollo and Shuttle crews could only dream about. For that matter, I could reduce the acceleration, drop it to a half or a quarter gee. Some authorities think that a lower gee environment puts less stress on the circulatory system."

His voice became more businesslike.

"Radar is clear, no airborne returns, so either no one noticed us or they think we're a military flight. I'm ready for turnover. Prepare for zero gee. We'll complete turnover, then head for home. We should be in the barn forty minutes from now. Want to take us home, Chuck?"

"Absolutely."

"Your ship, Chuck. No flat tires, okay?"

"I'll watch out for nails, Will."

The control handoff was easily executed; Will simply lifted his hands from the commander's panel. Chuck put his fingers on his control board and the computer continued to fly the craft. He pushed a button on the panel, initiating the automated turnover.

"Powering down the impellers... rotating now… reversing... powering up the impellers, prepare for one half gee."

Moments later, he reported, "Slowing. I show altitude as decreasing. I'm bleeding off speed and controlling the rate of descent with the impellers. Skin temperature, warm but within acceptable limits."

The feeling of weightlessness changed to a sensation similar to what passengers feel when an elevator slows. Chuck watched his display, flying with impellers, but ready when the airfoils regained bite.

"Skin temperature nominal, no sign of heating," he reported. "I'm maintaining rate of descent with the impellers. Trim is eight degrees up. Rate of descent, one thousand feet per minute.

"I'm going to bleed off more speed and altitude. We'll overrun the factory and have to bring it back around if I don't. I'd rather do it up here where I've got altitude to burn."

"Copy, Chuck. You're doing fine."

"Switching to airfoil control at this time."

"Roger, airfoil control. Watch for loss of control. I'll monitor and bring up impeller steering if needed."

"Roger."

The ship continued to sink as Chuck reduced speed further. The factory came into sight far ahead, a green patch in the desert brown.

"Take her down, Chuck. Let Frenchy do doorman this time, I'll give him a call."

Chuck nodded, feeling there was no need to acknowledge Will's order.

"Frenchy, Will. Got a moment?"

"Absolutely, Will. What's up."

"Estimating home in less than zero five. Can you open the door?"

"Sure. Give me a moment. Maybe you need one of those pushbutton garage door openers."

Chuck switched off the radar as he approached the campus, then eased the ship to a hover just outside the assembly building. Following Frenchy's signal, he floated it slowly into the cradle. Glancing at Will and getting a nod in return, he shut down the impellers, then switched off the pump that controlled hydrogen flow to the fuel cells. Will watched closely, but said nothing. Chuck was doing what he was supposed to.

"We're on battery, Will. Ready to switch off main power?"

"Dump the log to a thumb drive first, then shut down the computers and pop the hatch. Switch off main power as soon as the hatch is open. What did you think, Joe?"

"Good flight, Will. Any problems with the controls?"

"No problems at all. I kept waiting for Murphy to stick his finger in, but I didn't see any problems. I'll want to look at the computer log, but as far as I'm concerned, that was a perfect flight."

"I agree. We didn't learn anything, because nothing went wrong. One day it will, so be ready," said Joe.

"I wasn't surprised. We've already got more than 200 hours in the log, low altitude with the Bedstead and King as chase, so the only thing different this time was the altitude we reached. I'd have been very surprised if anything unusual had popped up," said Chuck.

***

"How did it go, Chuck?"

"Good, Frenchy. Will has the computer log, we'll know more after we see what's on that, but if you've got a minute, I'd like to talk to you."

"Let me check in with Will first. Meet you in the hangar?"

"Sounds good. It's not private, you can have Lina and Will sit in if you want. It's just that I had a concern, based on that visit from DARPA."

"Your concerns are my concerns, Chuck. We'll meet you there in half an hour or so."

Chuck nodded to Mel, typing at a keyboard, when he entered the hangar.

Dumping out the stale coffee and rinsing the pot, he added grounds and fresh water, then pushed the start button. He changed out of his flight suit and hung it up to air out while the coffee brewed, then went out to see what Mel was doing.

"What's rattling, Mel?"

"Just summarizing the gripes in the maintenance log, Chuck. I'll be flying the Bedstead next week, and there's a couple of notes I wanted to put in the King's log before I forget."

"Anything major?"

"No, one of the bulbs in the panel burned out. The only concern is that this is the third bulb that's gone out in that circuit, so one of us needs to check it to make sure we're not getting a voltage spike. I'll deadline the King until I can find the problem."

"Maybe I'll have time to help, but if I don't I'll mention it to Lina. Frenchy's on his way down and I put fresh coffee on."

"I wouldn't mind a cup. I could use a break too.

"Next week, I'll finally get around to doing those altitude tests. I kept putting them off, then we had to deal with Morty's death and the visit from the DARPA people. I still had more flights to make using the King, so I just never got to it. I've got time now, so it shouldn't be a problem."

"Sit in if you want when I talk to Frenchy, Mel. Maybe you can tell me if I'm getting paranoid."

"Sure. Paranoia is a good thing, there's always someone after you if you look hard enough."

"I've heard that." Chuck's voice was dry.

"Heard what?" Frenchy walked into the break room.

"Just wondering if I'm being paranoid, Frenchy. Got a question for you, how's that green power plant coming along?"

"The contractor should be finished with the PV panels in a month, maybe six weeks. The inverter is already installed.

"We'll begin getting our first wind generators in six months, maybe a bit less. Their factory is overworked, but the rep said he'd try to hurry our order through. They'll use their own contractor for installation, it has to do with their insurance, but we should be fully operational in nine months to maybe a year. Why?"

"How much trouble would it be to add more solar panels to your order?"

"Not much. There's some lead time between order and delivery, but I could do it. Why? Do you think we need more capacity?"

"In a sense. I don't really feel good about those DARPA guys. I think they figured out more than we wanted them to know."

"Really? I don't see how. We never showed them an impeller,

not the inside. The outside is just fairing, either carbon fiber or fiberglass. There's nothing to see."

"You're right, but there's something to *hear*. That whine...I listened to it, and it sounds like an electric motor, spinning something."

"Um. You think that's enough of a clue?"

"I don't know. Probably not. But it occurred to me that we only have *one* factory, only *four* craft flying and *all of them* flying out of here.

"And *they* know where we are, where the factory is.

"Suppose someone from the government showed up and just *took* the ship, maybe the King and the Bedstead too? They're not licensed, not inspected or anything, so they could claim there were safety issues.

"It wouldn't be the first time something like that happened. Remember that Soviet jet, the Foxbat? It scared the hell out of people until that pilot defected. The Soviets eventually got it back, but by then it had been flown and the engines torn down to see what made them tick.

"Suppose DARPA did that to us? Or some other agency, maybe the Defense Department?"

"Keep talking."

"I've got a place on Morty's ranch we could use in an emergency. I went exploring after the memorial service; I always wanted to see what was down in that hole, ever since I first saw the place. But I was just a kid back then and Morty told me to stay away, so I did. There's a big sinkhole that opens into a cavern, a huge room that's been dissolved out by the carbonic acid in groundwater. Part of it collapsed a long time ago, so it's sort of like Carlsbad Caverns except without the big formations.

"I'm guessing, but I think the collapse only happened a couple of thousand years ago which is why there are almost no stalactites.

"Anyway, I roped down into the cave and took a look. It's big enough right now to hold all our stuff, including the Twin, and if we cleaned out the fallen rock, even the ship would fit inside."

"So what does this have to do with the PV panels, Chuck?

"I was thinking that I could set up a PV power station between the cavern and the ranch house, big enough to power the house and Morty's shop. They're the cover.

"Small towns gossip, so all I'd need to do was cancel the contract with the power company and explain that I was going off-grid, now that I'm not living there full time. Within a few days, everybody in town would know.

"Make the power station a little larger than needed for the ranch and I could easily divert enough power to make the cavern livable. It's dark as hell down there right now, chilly too. That's okay for storing equipment, but it would be pretty uncomfortable if we had to spend a long time down there.

"I was thinking of putting an insulated shelter in and doing everything by electricity. Heat, hot water even... there are pools back in the cave... lights, maybe even enough to power a workshop like Morty's. We'd also need some sort of electric lift. I roped down, but we'd need something better."

"What about security, Chuck?"

"You've seen the ranch. It's isolated, not much traffic on that farm-to-market road even.

"Near as I could tell, I'm the only one who's ever been down in that cavern, and for that matter I only explored part of the big room. I don't think it would be a problem."

"You're not planning to move anything yet, just run a power line?"

"That's it. I think we should store at least some of the impellers there, though. Computers too, for the manufacturing software and the control programs. Just so we don't lose everything. We could start over if we had to."

"I'll get you the panels, Chuck. For that matter, why don't you just drive the truck out to the site and load what you need? I'll order replacements, they should be here before the contractor is ready for them.

"Who's going to install them on the ranch?"

"I'm thinking I could borrow a few of the engineers, the ones who have a few shares in the company.

"It's not rocket science; pour footings, bolt down the racks, install the panels. They'll need to be wired in, but our guys can handle it.

"I'd need an inverter to convert it to household AC. Now that I think about it, it should be three-phase AC. I can justify that, because Morty used three-phase in the shop. Couple of buried Romex runs, one to the cavern, the other to the ranch, done.

"I doubt anyone will pay attention. Putting up a PV system is the sort of thing Morty would have done and they know we were working together."

"Go ahead, then. But don't move anything until I look at this cavern, okay? Running electricity to it, that's not a real problem. We could probably explain that. Other things might be more difficult.

"I see your point about needing a bolt-hole. It's a shame, but I have to say that I don't trust the government, not any more. The low-level employees are mostly all right, but they take their orders from politicians, and to be honest I don't think they work for us now. They hang on tight to budgets, especially if the money is being spent in their district."

"*Too* tight," agreed Chuck, "and you're right, the reasons are political. They don't like funding anything they don't approve of, even though a *previous* Congress did."

"Shame, really. It makes you wonder how much longer the republic can endure."

"Or whether it should," Chuck responded.

"Yeah. I don't know if things are really that bad, but sometimes I wonder," said Frenchy.

Chapter Twenty-nine

Chuck was away for most of the next month, working at his ranch during the week and returning to the factory each Friday afternoon.

A team of four had moved in full time.

In the afternoons, after they'd finished the day's work on the photovoltaic array, they rebuilt Morty's original rabbit-chaser. Then improved it.

They began by swapping the front steerable bicycle wheel for the steering gear and front axle from a junked Ford roadster, then switched out the rear axle with one from a front-wheel-drive Chevrolet. The original plywood frame had proved unable to handle the loads, so that too had vanished.

The new version had begun life as a Volkswagen microbus. Two impellers had been added inside the cabin's middle and the battery packs to run them now filled the rear of the bus, where the engine had been originally. The men now used the strange little vehicle to commute back and forth to Clovis and Roswell on weekends.

Chuck shook his head when he first saw the contraption. *Remind me never again to leave engineers with too much time on their hands*, he thought.

Chuck used the Twin to commute; Will flew with him as copilot Sunday evenings, then took the Twin back to the factory. He flew to the ranch on Friday afternoons to bring Chuck back to the plant.

Chuck's weekends were spent flying the big spacecraft and improving his relationship with Lina. Most of his flights now were in the left seat, with Lina as copilot. She was not yet licensed, but it no longer seemed to matter.

Three weeks after beginning this arduous schedule, Chuck and Lina flew the ship to orbit, remaining there for more than an hour. No new checks or experiments were conducted, at least not officially, and no log entry took place during that time. Lina answered a question by explaining they had practiced operating in zero-gee conditions.

This answer raised a couple of eyebrows, but since the flight went off without a hitch, no more was said. Chuck and Lina ignored the few grins and the rare, almost-quiet, comment about a '200-mile-high club'.

***

The photovoltaic system, finished, now powered the ranch and the cavern.

The microbus had been locked in the barn, the batteries and impellers removed and stored in the cavern. Chuck flew the engineers to Clovis, where they caught flights to other locations; they were on vacation, the first in a year for some. Chuck flew back to the plant and reported the job finished to Frenchy.

In celebration, Frenchy invited Chuck, Lina, Will, Mel, and the newly-hired Dolph Petterson out to dinner at the Cattle Baron Steak House in Roswell, where he'd reserved one of their smaller rooms. Chuck wondered what the new man did and why Frenchy had invited him along, but it was Frenchy's money so he didn't comment.

The steaks were excellent, perfectly cooked, and drinks were replenished quickly. The party soon relaxed and conversation flowed freely.

Chuck noticed that Dolph had little to say; perhaps it was because he was new, not yet part of the team who'd worked so hard for so long to get as far as they had. But Frenchy spotted the look, and understood.

"You're probably wondering about Dolph," said Frenchy. "He's the new head of the Plans and Projects division."

"I didn't know we had one," said Will. "What does this division do?"

"Pretty much what Dolph wants. So far, he's the only one assigned to it."

"Frenchy, I thought we were doing our own plans. Except for the opposition you and Will experienced, the only thing that slowed us down was lack of money. No offense, Dolph; I'm just trying to understand," said Chuck.

"Not an issue, Chuck. I wanted to call it the Department of Philosophy, but Frenchy wouldn't let me. He said that would sound weird, so we settled on Plans and Projects."

"So why do we need this, Frenchy?"

"Why don't we let Dolph tell us about it?"

"I'm not here to develop your device, Chuck," said Dolph. "I've got other ideas. 'Plans' has to do with the company's future, 'projects' is about earning money. The company needs a lot of it to finish the projects you're already working on.

"Let's start with your insistence on secrecy, then talk about how that affects your finances. I'll ask questions, you tell me what you think. Socrates invented this method, but it's the best system I know of for people to educate themselves."

"Okay," Chuck said. "About the secrecy; my grandfather understood that the way to make a lot of money is to get to space first, to actually start *working* out there.

"Not like the space station, they're like lab rats in a can, except that the can's in space. As for money, if DARPA ever gets their collective butts in gear, our money problems are over."

"Chuck, how much money has the company spent so far developing your invention?"

"Well, it's mostly grandpa's invention. I helped and I gave him a few ideas in the beginning, but it was always his. As to money, we've spent millions. I don't know how many, maybe Frenchy does."

"Ben has the exact figures," said Frenchy. "But you're right, we've spent millions, and so far, we've only earned back a few hundred thousand from our marine operations."

"Just so," said Dolph. "And now you're hoping a government agency will fund your future activities. You're handing *them* control over your product."

"No, we're keeping that in-house. We've only talked leasing with them."

"When you have *one* customer, you're at that customer's mercy. I've got a better idea, but I'll get to it in a minute.

"You mentioned leasing; why?"

"It gets the impeller system going and we keep control. Impeller driven planes, ships, submarines, maybe those landing craft too, we expect to earn millions leasing those."

"Frenchy has described what it takes to build a device in general terms, but control is at least as important. Who are you going to hire to operate the craft? Where are you going to find the mechanics and repairmen you'll need? And what about hackers? Can someone slip malware into your computers?"

"Not possible," said Chuck. "The computers aren't online."

"But where do the *computers* get their programming? Don't tell me you hand-program each of the computers that control your machines."

"No, we use...damn. The original computer is online, the one I used. I've got an anti-virus program, but that's only as good as the virus definitions."

"Right. You need to record a master file on a *separate* hard disk drive, make sure there are no surprises in the program, then lock it in a vault. Use it *only* to create other programs, record them on thumb drives or whatever, then use the copies to program the new computers as you install them. And you're correct, never connect those computers to any sort of remote system.

"Second, let's talk about government money, which also has to do with your security idea. I agree that you shouldn't give away information on how to create the drives, but if you lease them to *anyone*, especially the government, they'll soon know all there is to know. And someone will insist on a competitor getting the information, because governments *hate* monopolies unless they're getting paid not to."

"So how do we stop this, Dolph?"

"Don't lease anything, don't rent it, don't sell it. Keep everything in-house. That means you're going to have to shut down your New Mexico plant and move your operation offshore. Maybe the Cayman Islands, maybe find your own island or even build one."

"You don't think small, do you? Build our own island?" said Will.

"If you put yourself at the mercy of *any* nation, then *that nation* controls your future. Maybe not immediately, but the option is always available if they decide to go that route. Only if you own your own extra-national country are you really in charge of your own future."

"Dolph, you sound like some sort of anarchist," said Mel.

"No, I'm simply being a realist. You might be able to buy a national government, but the temptation is always there to stop taking your golden eggs and go directly to the goose. Governments change. The official that offers you sanctuary today may die or be deposed. As soon as the US government understands just how powerful this revolutionary system of yours is, they'll take control of it. If they can."

Silence fell while people thought about Dolph's comments.

"You mentioned money, Dolph," said Frenchy. "Most of our funds are tied up in what we're already doing, the factory, the generating station, and the test units. You're suggesting we abandon those things?"

"No, keep them, but *distribute* your manufacturing operation and control it from a place they cannot touch."

"Maybe the moon?"

"Eventually, Chuck. Meantime, while you're waiting for DARPA, there's a better way to make a lot of money. How much do you know about Japan's nuclear power system?"

"I know a lot of it got wiped out by an earthquake," answered Lina.

"Right, but not all and Japan is only one example. But it's a way to make a *lot* of money over the next few years while not being dependent on any one customer."

Frenchy listened to the exchanges taking place, and smiled. Chuck smiled back at him and nodded, a tiny movement; maybe Dolph wasn't as crazy as he sounded.

"Keep talking, Dolph."

"How much weight can your ship lift, Chuck?"

"With two people aboard? Two tons, maybe more. It's big, which makes it heavy. Not much extra lift for cargo, in other words."

"Could you increase the number of impeller units?"

"We'd have to attach them externally, but I suppose it could be done. We'd need more fuel cells too, and that means more on-board fuel."

"Is there any reason you can't put the fuel cells outside the fuselage? Attach them in the same way you attach the impellers?"

"We could do that, I think. The cells are in stainless steel housings, and for that matter we could put the pumps and most of the plumbing outside the hull. But why? That would leave the ship empty, nothing behind the pilot's cabin but the lifter arm for handling cargo."

"You'll need to keep that manipulator arm, but whether you mount it internally or externally doesn't matter. The idea I'm trying to get across is that you want to leave the cargo bay empty, except for reinforcing it longitudinally. Your cargoes are likely to be heavy."

"Keep talking, Dolph."

"The Japanese government has a problem. So do a lot of others, but for the Japanese it's critical. They've got a lot of spent fuel rods, still dangerous, just no longer powerful enough to operate a reactor at full efficiency. It's called high-level waste and developed nations are stuck with a *lot* of it.

"Right now, the rods are stored underwater in huge concrete tanks, waiting for someone to figure out how to dispose of them safely. Vitrification is a suggested first step, blending the spent fuel with glass, then enclosing it in a stainless steel tank.

"There may be other steps involved, but you get the idea. Expensive, and also a political problem; where do you put everything when you're done? The usual response is, not in my back yard; NIMBY. But suppose we offered to haul that spent fuel to space and dispose of it?"

"There's already too much junk in space, Dolph," said Chuck. "The Japanese might not care, but the Russians, Chinese, and American governments would throw major fits if you tried to put those tanks in orbit. And just because they're in orbit doesn't mean they'll stay there. There have been satellite crashes and at least one had nuclear material on board."

"That might be another source of income, disposing of old satellites before they can break up," said Dolph, "but as for the nuclear material, the obvious solution is to send it to the sun."

"I don't know; I just don't like the idea of something hitting the

Sun like that comet hitting Jupiter. That left pockmarks that were visible for a long time."

"Can't happen, Will. Fly the tank or used satellite past the first Lagrange point, accelerate it toward the sun, and release it. It doesn't even need to be very exact; gravity will take it the rest of the way, like a comet.

"*No* material can survive solar temperatures. It melts when it gets close enough, then turns into a plasma. That plasma, which consists of nothing but ionized protons and electrons, will differentiate according to the mass of the nucleus and most of it will be pushed away by the Solar wind. It's the ultimate dispersion method, scattering the nuclei throughout the solar system.

"How long will it take, to pick up a cargo in Japan and fly it past the Lagrange point? Or at least near there."

"A day, maybe as much as a week depending on how much acceleration the ship can achieve," said Chuck. "You're shooting for something like what a jet airliner does, take off and accelerate at less than a gee of acceleration? Instead of leveling off like the airliner does, just keep going up?

"But not go into orbit, since you're under constant acceleration until you reach the release point. You could direct the impellers to keep you on a straight line, but why bother? If you go faster, you just spiral around Earth, getting farther out each time you go around. You'd need to time the course so that you release the spent fuel when it was heading toward the Sun."

"But wouldn't it keep spiraling, Dolph?" asked Lina.

He sighed. "No. It wouldn't be *accelerating* after it was released; any future acceleration would come from the Sun's gravity. The resultant spiral might take months, even years, to reach the Sun, but regardless, it would be effectively disposed of. Your space truck then reverses course and begins to slow down, spiraling back toward the Earth."

"Dolph, each trip is going to take a lot of fuel. You would need a lot just accelerating to the Lagrange Point, even more to slow down and control your descent through the atmosphere."

"Right. You'd want to stop at a filling station."

"*What* filling station? There's nothing out there but empty space and satellites!"

"Just so. You'd need your own satellites, maybe a couple of dozen of them eventually. Perhaps a hundred, who knows? Simple, automated systems, a tank to hold the water, a photovoltaic array to generate the DC current to warm it enough to keep it liquid. More current to electrolyze it and power pumps and compressors. Tanks to hold the hydrogen and oxygen. You might need a fleet of service craft just to haul water to the stations and perhaps deliver hydrogen and oxygen to stranded spacecraft.

"Think spaceborne tankers; If a station is running low on fuel, call for a water tanker. But it might be better for an outbound ship to orbit long enough to top off the fuel tanks, then boost the cargo past the Lagrange point before turning for home."

"You're talking about a lot of ships. Who would operate these?"

"Your company, or a separate company that's part of your overall system but optimized for space operations. That will keep your system secret a lot longer than if you leased it or sold it to someone else.

"That brings up the next topic, education. You're eventually going to need a *lot* of people to operate your ships. They're not going to be easy to find, and you won't know whether you can trust them. That means you'll need your own school system, and it will have to be distributed to any nation that will allow you to set up a campus under your rules.

"Make *your* schools different, not like any other school system. Concentrate on education and avoid distractions. Students would live on campus during the week, perhaps go home to their parents on weekends, assuming they have parents that you consider trustworthy. Some of the students might live in the dorms the entire time.

"You should discourage contact with non-school society where possible. That's the only way to keep drugs and crime out, and you should also beware of intrusion by religious figures."

"How would you do that? They're everywhere!"

"Simple. The *students* keep it out, on pain of summary dismissal. One mistake, the student is publicly dismissed. Control bullying too; zero tolerance.

"Make education free, include classes in philosophy and arts as well as science and engineering. You want well-rounded students with the broadest knowledge base possible.

"Make the schools about education, about learning. Those who can't keep up with the science-based program, turn them to a different track, maybe hydroponic farming or whatever, or dismiss them if you must with no possibility of return."

"That seems harsh, Dolph." Lina frowned.

"It is, and yet it's not. Eventually, you want to send people on extended voyages to the outer planets. You don't want bullies as part of your crew, you don't want people who are controlled by their vices. Individual differences, absolutely allow those, but not differences that would keep anyone from functioning as part of a team.

"As for the cost, it will all be paid for by the company's profits. The space trucks will earn an enormous amount of money and never need to go into deep space at all.

"Holy cow, Frenchy! Where did you find this guy?"

Chapter Thirty

"Mister Goldman? Senator Byington would like to speak to you if you have a moment."

"Certainly, I've always got time for the Senator. Put him on."

Sol's first thought was that this was another effort to get him to increase his donations, either to the senator's campaign or to his party. He resolved to say no this time; after all, what had the senator done for him lately?

"Sol, how are you? I just wanted you to know I haven't forgotten about that request we talked about. I wanted to let you know that I've finally gotten a response, actually three of them. The agencies are willing to help, but at the moment their hands are tied. Legally, there doesn't seem to be anything they can do. That company you mentioned? It's now a holding company, all they're doing is spending money. It's legal too, they've crossed the T's and dotted the I's.

"They're not selling anything yet. I know the company contacted DARPA, but the Defense Department people dug in their heels when Transportation and the FAA sent them a request.

"I reckon it might be time to rein them in, the Defense people I mean, but they've got so many fingers in so many pies that it might be difficult. A lot of companies, some in my state, are manufacturing everything from trucks to MRE's, so I've got to be careful.

"Anyway, it looks like our best approach is to watch and jump in as soon as there's an opening. I'll know when they start selling whatever it is they're making and I'll be ready to call for hearings. The Marines want them to build assault craft, I've found out that much, and as soon as they sign the contract I'll have a reason subpoena the company officials. It'll slow them down, maybe even stop them.

"Transportation is looking into what they're doing, so are the aviation people, we're *bound* to find something. If we can throw enough obstacles in their way, they might just give up and quit. Maybe sell off whatever they've been doing if it looks like they won't be making any money.

"If that happens and you decide to invest, I might be interested too, so don't forget to let me know before you finalize any deals."

"Senator, you called me up to tell me that maybe sometime you could actually get results? But so far, you've accomplished nothing?"

"Well, it's not like that, Sol," the senator argued. "These things take time. If we move too fast, we'll get nowhere. There's an election next year you know, and if we call hearings about nothing, that will hurt the party. I don't have that much of a margin myself, not the way the polls are trending, so I have to be careful about how I do this. I just wanted you to know I haven't forgotten about that talk we had."

"I'd have been happier if you had actual results to report, senator."

"I expect to have that information in due time, Sol. Anyway, there was one more matter I wanted to mention..."

"Excuse me, senator; I'm at a board meeting, so I'll have to get back to you later."

There was a click in the headset, then a dial tone.

Senator Byington looked at the handset in amazement.

Sol Goldman had just hung up on a United States Senator.

***

"I think it's worth developing the orbital refueling station. The wind generator costs are coming in about as expected, but the PV system cost considerably less than what we budgeted.

"I've been running cost estimates, and I think we can handle it after the DARPA money is paid. It's not a done deal yet, but I've had a back-channel message from DARPA. They're going to approve the proposal and we'll be getting a considerable amount of up-front money from them. The contract will be for the people mover and the freight hauler, ten units each to start, and the contract is fat."

"What about the idea of vertical integration, keeping our device in-house?"

"I thought about that. I agree, it's something we need to do, but right now we can't afford it.

"We're not selling them the devices. We'll operate and maintain them ourselves, that's part of the contract since we're the only ones with trained people.

"There will be a contract manager and the rest of the employees will be classified as field engineers. Some of our employees have been complaining about the long hours, so I intend to offer them jobs on this contract if they're interested in switching.

"The target services will provide support troops for the user test, people to fill sandbags and such, but we won't be involved with that. Our only job is to provide machines and people to operate them and keep them maintained.

"Most of the testing will be done at White Sands, but the over-water tests might require us setting up a branch office in San Diego. When we're ready, the Marines will furnish troops from Camp Pendleton and the Navy will provide a ship from Naval Base San Diego. The idea is that we load marines on board the transporter, launch from inside the navy ship, and convey them ashore to a location on Camp Pendleton. The reservation has a lot of beaches, I'm told. But that won't start for about a year, not until the testing at White Sands is complete. The DARPA people tend to be thorough, and that takes time."

"It really doesn't matter, Frenchy. Government troops will provide security around the equipment, officers will be filing reports. The secret won't be a secret long."

"I decided it was worth taking the chance, Chuck. It's the only way we can put those refueling stations in orbit, and without those, the contract we're negotiating with the Japanese won't be doable. I think we have to try this."

"You're the majority stockholder, Frenchy. Considering that you also vote Will's shares and some of the other shareholders' holdings too, you've got roughly 60% of the stock."

"I've got more than that, Chuck. I bought out some of the other investors. They got nervous at spending all that money with no return, so I got their shares at a discount. I now own 42.3% of the stock outright. You and Will own the next biggest chunks, our original group of engineers own the rest. Will's given me his proxy, so yes, I do vote the majority of the shares. I hoped you'd support me in this."

"I don't think I'm willing to oppose you. Grandpa's idea was to get the invention developed first, make money from it second. I can't complain about providing lifters to DARPA. Still, I hope we're not doing the wrong thing."

"Dolph convinced me. No one will really be able to compete with us in space, at least no one who doesn't have the backing of a major national economy. China might be able to, Russia probably couldn't.

"Both are huge, but at the same time their economies are fragile. Russia's economy is based on selling commodities, not products, and they took a big hit when the price of oil tanked. Sorry about the pun, but you understand what I mean.

"As for China, they've got a huge economy, but it's weak. The interior is still poor and largely undeveloped, so their economy is really based on what happens in the coastal cities. They've also got a problem with housing, as well as a large financial bubble that could bust any time. They might *want* to move into space, but they won't be getting there first.

"Meantime, they've got a very antsy bunch of neighbors to deal with, people who claim some of the same territory that China does.

"Militarily, I don't see them trying to move in on us. If we build a dozen refueling stations, financed by contracts to move industrial waste off-planet, we'll *own* the near-space infrastructure.

"There's also this to consider; would South Korea or Japan prefer to do business with China or with us?"

"I hope you're right," said Chuck. "So the plan is to begin building adapted versions of the King for DARPA, one that's hollow in the middle and one that looks like a capital H?"

"Right, we build the frames, buy the computer control units off the shelf...it's the programming that's important, not what platform it runs on...and then do final assembly either here at the plant or down south at White Sands. I don't intend to install the impellers until everything is ready, including having our operation and maintenance team on hand ready to go.

"We still need to hire more people, so I've got ads running already. This gives me enough lead time to check out applicants. The first group will be operators, not mechanics, and we'll train them using the King. As soon as we get the initial payment for the DARPA contract, we start buying the materials for the refueling station.

"As for the DARPA contract, Joe tells me we've got enough aluminum on hand to build the first few frames. We used mostly titanium on the ship, so the scrap aluminum panels and frame members are in the shed, the one where the ranch hands stored hay for the dairy-cattle feeder operation."

"I didn't know that. I knew you were buying usable scrap, but as for storing it..."

"Morty knew. Matter of fact, it was his idea. He had guys culling the scrap, keeping some and shipping the rest to the refinery for recycling. The part they kept went into the hay shed. He figured we'd use it eventually."

"I guess he was right. So what does this have to do with me? Do I get involved in the building, or do I keep flying the ship? That thing needs a name, you know."

"Lina wanted to call it Enterprise, but I vetoed that. Space Truck doesn't work, although that's what it really is. You got any ideas?"

"Let me think about it. Newton, Galileo, Einstein, maybe something like that?"

"Some of those are already being used for spacecraft. If you named one Darwin, for example, that would probably fly, but Galileo and Newton won't, because they're unmanned craft. Our ship would be confused with theirs."

"That might be a good thing, Frenchy. But I'll think about it. Maybe call it Frenchy, or Morty."

"Maybe Morty, we could justify that, but not Frenchy. Get real."

***

Newly-promoted Colonel Kotcheff waited, more or less patiently, by the car. General Stroganoff was clearing customs and immigration, and he'd be along in due time.

"Why was there no one to meet me, colonel? I had to carry my own damned bags!"

"Sir, you told me to wait by the car."

"Are you the only agent in this miserable hole? Don't you have subordinates?"

"Well, yes. But when you told me to wait by the car, I believed that you did not want to attract attention by being met."

"You believed wrong, Colonel!" Stroganoff hissed. "Let that be your last mistake. Don't we have an office in New York? Take me there immediately!"

"Right away, sir. I'll get your bags, you have a seat while I put them in the trunk."

Mollified, the general sat down and looked around. The airport was busy, busier even than Domodedovo, but when combined with Vnukovo and Sheremetyevo, Moscow's airports served about as much traffic. Not to mention the several military or private airports that handled other flights. At least, this one was almost as clean and, honesty compelled him to admit it, better appointed. The Americans spent more money on nonessentials, that was certain.

The general had served in a number of units before getting this surprise assignment, moving around within the old Soviet Union at first, later on at various posts in the new Russian Federation. For some reason, he'd never been posted to the West before now.

Well, it was probably necessary preparation for his new command, the one he'd take over after he finished here. And really, there was only the one major operation to conduct; that shouldn't take long, and he'd soon be on his way back to Moscow. But first, get this clown with colonel's rank to do something more productive than scratch his arse!

Really, he couldn't manage to acquire *one simple secret*, not even a *government* secret at that! Disgraceful! Time was when the motherland's agents even penetrated the American Manhattan Project, the most secret operation they had! Seize the moment, *that* was the Russian way to do things!

Moving aggressively had first brought him to the attention of the party and he'd been doing it ever since. Not everyone could be approved to command a guards armored division, and very few had done so in a shorter time than he, Alexy Alexyevitch Stroganoff!

"I will require copies of everything you have discovered, Colonel. When I have studied the files, we will speak again. Is it too much to hope that there is an apartment for me in this place?"

"Sir, I leased an apartment in Washington," Colonel Kotcheff said uneasily. "It's where our main office is. This office is only a satellite, kept in case something of interest occurs at the United Nations. Our staff is limited; we have a lieutenant and four agents here in New York, but all of them are assigned to operations directed from Moscow. There are auxiliaries, but they're local hires, not field agents."

"I'll keep that in mind. Perhaps it would be better to engage a hotel room here and leave for Washington tomorrow. For now, I've had a long day and I feel the jet lag.

"I'll take the files with me to the hotel and read them tonight. That should be safe enough, you haven't even rented the room yet so no one will expect me to stay there."

"We do have a leased room, Sir; it's permitted, based on our instructions from Moscow," said Colonel Kotcheff.

"This car...it belongs to the agency? Is it secure? Have you swept if for listening devices? The Americans have come up with a number of very tiny bugs, I'll give them that. Are you certain the car is secure?"

"Yes, sir. We own it, and it's garaged each night after servicing. The garage is secure. There is a photographic record which is reviewed daily, and no one has approached the garage.

"Good tradecraft demands more! Have the car swept when you get back to your office, Colonel. We cannot be too careful; we are in the enemy's camp, they are literally everywhere. This room, is it suitable for me?"

"I'll see to the car, general. The room is kept as a safe house, not fancy but adequate. But I'm sure the car is secure enough for our conversation. Do you have new instructions for me?"

"Yes, but I wish to wait until I've read the files. I will want to know what went wrong on that last operation, the barge your people were too inept to steal."

Colonel Kotcheff winced. "General, it was only a barge and there was no tow unit to move it. There was an additional concern for our agents, some of the auxiliaries I mentioned, because the object appears to be very massive. I knew we could not offload it in the city, too many people would observe.

"I accept fault, I directed our agent to have men on shore and others to guard the boat that would tow the barge to a secure location. There was a crane waiting to remove the device and a warehouse to store it."

"So why did this not work? I read the summary report in Moscow, but I want you to tell me yourself what went wrong."

"It appears that the device was able to move the barge without need for a tow. It also made no sound, although one of my agents on shore suggested perhaps there was a humming noise that could have come from the barge.

"But police cars showed up before anyone could board it, and then somehow it sank before the tow-craft could reach it. There was one success, our people got away without being arrested, so no one can connect us with what happened.

"The Americans were careless before, they will be again. We must be ready when they make a mistake."

"That may not be soon enough, Colonel. We may have to make our *own* opportunity. Is this the place?"

"Yes, sir. We keep a room in this hotel year-round. It is safe, a bit austere, but comfortable, and tomorrow we can move you to Washington. I'll have the files delivered within the hour, General."

"See that you do! And get this car swept for bugs! Never underestimate the enemy!"

The colonel nodded.

There was nothing to say, really; the general had given him an order. Perhaps he would be in a better mood tomorrow.

Colonel Kotcheff carried the bags inside before conducting the general to his temporary lodging. If he complained too bitterly, the New York branch would simply have to lease another safe house. This one might end up compromised.

As soon as he was permitted to leave, Colonel Kotcheff telephoned the lieutenant in charge of the satellite station.

While technically correct, Colonel Kotcheff's comment about the agents being engaged in work for Moscow didn't keep them totally occupied. There would be time for them to carry out General Stroganoff's instructions, to deliver the case files to the hotel and sweep the car for bugs.

Unfortunately, the lieutenant reported that the sweep found a tiny listening bug. It was very difficult to detect, so there may have been more than one.

When could they have been installed? The garage was under constant surveillance, and a driver was with the car whenever it was used. How could they *possibly* have managed to bug the car?

And how much had they heard?

Colonel Kotcheff felt a chill on the back of his neck. He'd assured General Stroganoff that the car was clean; should he now confess his error?

Or say nothing, hoping that General Stroganoff would not ask him what results the sweep had revealed?

There was one other option, see whether the agent who'd made the sweep felt loyal to Kotcheff or to the motherland. He had, after all, been employed here for almost twenty years and he had an American wife. Would he want to be sent home to Moscow? Perhaps he might be encouraged not to report his findings?

"Martin, I have a question for you..."

Chapter Thirty-one

General Stroganoff was unhappy. How was he supposed to accomplish his mission when so little was known? He'd finally realized that Kotcheff was less of an imbecile than he'd thought. The man might actually have done as much as he could, considering the *other* imbecile he'd worked for!

Not that he would ever mention his new-found respect to Kotcheff! Better to keep him anxious, on his toes.

It was like punching a pillow. Nothing was known, other than that the damned Americans were flying *something*, perhaps an antigravity device. How *else* could the ship in the satellite photos float so close to the ground, no propeller, no jet, nothing?

Could it be...was someone at Army headquarters doing the same thing to *him*, to *General Stroganoff*? Was this a plot to ruin him, send him into a situation tailor-made for failure? That divisional command assignment he'd coveted, someone else might already have been mentioned! Someone with connections as good as his!

Damn them! Failure would ruin him, maybe see him shuttled off to a backwater posting somewhere in the Middle East!

But perhaps it was not too late? After all, he had assets here, including people and an expanded budget. But how to use them? What would his superiors accept?

Certainly not what he'd accomplished since arriving!

General Stroganoff wasn't panicking, not yet; after all, he was a veteran of Army infighting. There must be *something*!

"Kotcheff! Get in here!"

***

The ship finally had a name, *Farside*.

Will found Chuck helping install the second refueling probe, this one on the port wing. The probes, located at the very ends of the wings, were designed to connect to tanks on the not-yet-built orbital refueling station. New shipboard pumps, located near the probes, would transfer fuel and oxygen from the station to the *Farside's* tanks.

The ship's lines, originally sleek, now had lumpy external mounts that held the impellers and the fuel cells. There might be fairings over them at some point, but so far there had been no time. For now, the task was to finish moving the generating and propulsion systems, install redesigned plumbing, then find out if the arrangement worked.

The *Farside's* plumbing had been fairly ordinary in the beginning, but it had since evolved into an extremely complicated arrangement. Joe and his team were convinced it would work, but Chuck had doubts, enough that he wanted to make sure that no slight oversight would strand the ship in space. This was, after all, the only space-capable craft they had.

Not to mention that swapping a fuel tank for an oxygen tank had halved the Farside's hydrogen storage.

Chuck discussed this with Will. "I don't want to say anything to Joe, but I keep thinking that what started out as a simple craft now looks more like one of the ships that blew up before they ever got to space. Or came apart on the way down.

"The shuttle was second or maybe third generation, was always complicated and never really safe, and it showed. Four were built, thoroughly inspected and essentially rebuilt between missions, but even so, two of them blew up. Even a simple thing like a gasket can cause failure, and when it happens in space, it's catastrophic.

"The refueling system is necessary, I agree, but we've added a whole lot of extra connections and gaskets to what started out as a relatively simple ship."

"I've been thinking about that too, Chuck. That first flight to altitude, I know we'd tested the bird from tip to tail, but even so I was puckered until we got back.

"It's barely possible that we could fly the Twin into low orbit if we had to rescue people. Keep the batteries fully charged until the turbogenerators flame out, maybe even add an oxygen bleed system to increase the altitude where that happens. The only thing that kicks the generators offline is lack of oxygen from the air, so the idea is that we burn atmospheric oxygen until there's not enough, then supplement it from onboard tanks. Enriching the airflow might give us another twenty thousand feet, maybe more.

"No one's ever tried this, at least as far as I know. They didn't need to, they always lost lift before they ran out of air for the engines. Our wings or airfoils won't work either, but as long as we've got electric power we don't really need them; the impellers substitute just fine."

"No way you're going to pressurize that cabin, Will. It was never designed to be airtight and a redesign would add too much weight. Adding extra battery packs is out too; you're reaching the limit, where gains are offset by extra weight. You're up against the law of diminishing returns."

"I anticipated the problem with cabin pressure," said Will. "I'll reduce pressure to something the cabin *can* take, maybe a tenth of an atmosphere. The new door seals should tolerate that, and the maintenance crew has been over the cabin, plugging leaks. It's essentially a sealed capsule now, thin, but maybe good enough to keep us alive. Not all that different from the early Apollo capsules, but with wings and aerodynamic controls attached and no need to land without power.

"It won't be quite as bad as working in vacuum. If the pressure is high enough, the automatic systems won't even kick in and if the gee tubes don't inflate, we'll retain flexibility."

"Maybe. In an emergency, it might be worth a try. But we don't know, and conceivably we could end up with you stuck out there too."

"I plan to try it tomorrow, a limited trial, not with the oxygen bleed system but just take it to max altitude and see how it handles. I expect it to spin, but I think it's safe enough. Want to come along as copilot? There'll be a lot to do, and I could use the help."

"Sure, but my weight added to the plane's gross will affect your numbers."

"I won't get final numbers, but I'll know whether it's feasible.

I'll also get a better idea of how long it takes to discharge the batteries. I won't go below half charge, that's enough to get us down if I can't restart the turbogenerators after reentry."

"When do you want to go?"

"Tomorrow morning. Get a good night's sleep, I'll give you a wakeup call when I'm ready. And remember to wear your pressure suit. We may end up on internal suit pressure and heat until we get back to safe altitude. Low bulk meal tonight, no bathrooms available for maybe as much as four hours after we take off. Cleaning the suits afterward...nah. Better to be prepared."

"See you tomorrow morning, Will. This sounds like fun."

***

Chuck groaned and stretched. It seemed as if he'd only just gone to bed, but a glance at the digital clock mounted on the wall told him it was almost 8:00 am. Swinging out of bed, he walked into the bathroom.

Why hadn't Will called him? Had he *missed* the call, maybe Will found someone else to fly with him? He picked up the intercom phone and pushed the ring button.

He looked at the other bed, but it wasn't occupied. Where was Mel? He would normally finish work before morning and be sleeping now.

***

Chuck laid the phone down, shocked.

Will hadn't flown after all, and Mel wouldn't be sleeping in the bed again. He'd crashed during the night while flying the Bedstead.

Frenchy was waiting when Chuck walked in. "Grab a cup of coffee and we'll talk."

Subdued, Chuck nodded. He joined Will, and Lina at the table.

"What do we know?"

"Mel's instrument gyros locked up, the computers crashed, and as near as we can tell, the chute failed. The lines were twisted around each other when the riders reached the wreckage and Mel was still strapped in the seat.

"He was killed instantly. We think he came down from at least two hundred feet, maybe as much as a thousand, although he wasn't supposed to go that high. The body was pretty mangled, which is why I think he may have gone higher than intended."

"Damn. We talked about the high altitude tests, I intended to do them before I got tied up with the ship. *I* should have been flying the Bedstead!"

"Then *you'd* be dead, Chuck. This wasn't pilot error, it was a cascade of equipment failures."

"I asked Mel about using a personal chute," said Chuck, "but he said he didn't know anything about them. I don't have experience, but I know how the things are supposed to work!"

"Let it go, Chuck; we've got too much other stuff to do. The sheriff's office has been notified and they're sending an ambulance and an investigation team."

"Oh, shit! What are we going to tell them, Frenchy?"

"I don't know. I've called our legal team and they'll get here as soon as they can. They'll do most of the talking."

"Frenchy, it's going to be hard to keep this under wraps. We're going to have to tell them something," said Chuck.

"I don't have an answer yet. The lawyer I talked to said to say nothing, let them do the talking, but I'm not sure if the investigators will accept that."

"What about the Bedstead?" asked Chuck.

"Smashed. The frame is twisted, the forward impellers tore loose when it hit. It came down rear end first and the two rear impellers are half buried. It's in the bottom of an arroyo and the ground is mostly sand there. There apparently was some activity going on inside the impeller casings, but we can't be sure because they're smashed too.

"The investigators are going to want the wreckage, maybe not the sheriff's people, but there will be others. I don't see how we can keep them from taking the pieces."

"Can they reconstruct the impellers?" asked Chuck.

"I don't know. They might, given time.

"The computer was smashed too, but we've already picked up a couple of metal disks. They can reconstruct the computer, but they won't get anything off what's left of the hard drive.

"Pieces also came off the impellers after the crash, and we've managed to hide some of the debris. We can justify going in, because we had to see whether Mel survived, but they'll know something unusual was going on. So we're going to be under increasing pressure from now on."

"What if they grab our records? They'll soon learn about the Twin and they'll almost certainly shut it down if they realize it uses the same propulsion system. They might do the same to the *Tesla*."

"There are no *Tesla* records here, not anymore. Officially, we've set the divisions up as different companies, so I hope they won't realize *Tesla* is ours. Not right away, anyway.

"We may have to go public with the Twin. If we do, we immediately apply for FAA certification. We've got paperwork ready for the patent application when we need it. Until the FAA nit-picks through the wreckage, that's not going to happen, but no matter what we do now, there's a good chance that someone will figure out what we've already been doing. The Bedstead wreckage is still out where it went in, there's nothing we can do about that, and as soon as they see it they'll know we've been flying one or more aircraft that were never inspected for airworthiness.

"DARPA won't be happy. No question, the crash is going to slow us down, so we may not be able to meet the contract."

"What about the spacecraft?" asked Chuck.

"They don't know it *is* a spacecraft, and there's no reason for us to allow their investigators into the hangar or the assembly plant. As an extra precaution, our people have been moving parts for the power station, including PV panels, into the assembly building. They're stacking them right inside the rollup door.

I'll tell the investigators that I'm storing power station supplies in there if they ask, so I'm hoping they'll move on to other things. I'm also sending the rest of our people home, so with luck they won't be bothered by the sheriff's team."

"They'll know the Bedstead was flying before it came down. The parachute will tell them that much," said Chuck. "That means you'll eventually have to deal with the FAA and maybe the NTSB.

They'll be all over the crash."

"I know. But they won't be here right away, maybe for a day or two, so I'll cross that bridge when we come to it," said Frenchy.

"But what if someone decides this is a crime scene and locks it down? If that happens, all bets are off. We'd lose everything."

"You're right, I never thought of that. We don't have much time, but it's imperative that we get the King and the *Farside* out of here. Your place?" suggested Frenchy.

"I'll load the King inside the *Farside's* cargo bay, the stored impellers too.

"That leaves the Twin and maybe you should make yourself hard to find too. I suggest you and Will take the Twin and get the hell out of Dodge."

"The Twin doesn't look like it's anything unusual, and anyway it's got that experimental certification. Unless they connect the plane with the crashed Bedstead, which doesn't look like anything else that flies, we should be all right," said Frenchy.

"There's not much room at my ranch, not nearly the shop facilities we have here, but maybe we can still do something on the DARPA contract," said Chuck. "But even if we can't, we can hide stuff there. No one except you, Dolph, Will, and Lina knows about it, so it's best if you're not here to answer questions.

"The guys who worked on the PV plant know about it too, but they're still on vacation. I'll call them and tell them not to come back until I send for them."

"You and Lina take the King and the *Farside*, Chuck. Load everything and be ready to take off on short notice. That idea you had, prepping a bolt-hole to hide stuff, is turning out to be pure genius. Take Joe with you too.

"The investigators will go to the crash site, not here, and by the time they get back, I want you two long gone. It would be better to leave after dark, but if you don't have a choice, just take off through the roof hatch.

"Will and I will stay here, at least for now. We'll take the Twin if we have to, but I'm hoping it doesn't come to that. Running away will make us look guilty. They may not know *what*, but they'll figure we must be guilty of something.

"We may have to hide the Twin too, but if so, Will can fly it out of here.

"With the King gone, the *Farside* gone, and the impellers cleared out of the storeroom, there won't be much here for them to find. They can even bring the parts of the Bedstead back here if they want, spread them around the floor of the assembly building while they're doing their investigation."

"There's also the warehouse, Frenchy. It was never sold. You could stash things there, maybe even the Twin if you took the wings off; otherwise, it won't fit though the cargo door. There's already a guard on the building, unless you laid him off. It's not the best solution, but it might be necessary and that would be better than leaving it here."

"Maybe. I can send some of the gate guards with you if you think you need them. They know something's happened and that we're going to have a lot of unwanted visitors to deal with."

"I don't think so, Frenchy. People know we have guards at the gate, we don't want to make them think anything has changed. Anyway, we want to *hide* on my ranch, not make it obvious we're concealing something.

"I hope we're not forgetting anything," Chuck fretted. "The priority is to get the King, the extra impellers, and the *Farside* out of here before anyone sees them. If we run out of room in the *Farside*, I'll load the King's frame into the van and send *it* to the ranch. I'll have to take off the impellers anyway, it won't fit in the van otherwise, but that won't take long and we can add them in with the ones we're hauling in the *Farside*. We've got the crane for loading the frame, so the whole job won't take more than three or four hours. We'll have the van out of here while the investigators are still at the crash site, and meantime the shop crew can finish loading the *Farside*."

"I can't help but think we're not well organized, Chuck. All those people coming in, they'll be asking questions and we don't have answers. We're floundering around, just trying to decide what to do. And what about Mel? Did he have a family?"

“Panit’s handling it, Frenchy,” Will said. “He’s got the records. I don’t think Mel had a wife, he’s divorced, but maybe there were children. I don’t know if his parents are alive; he never mentioned them, brothers or sisters either. But the office people have the personnel records, so let them take care of it.

“Anyway, our job is to get through the day. About letting the lawyers do all the talking, it will look suspicious, but you can claim it’s corporate policy or something. I hope they get here quick, because we’re going to need them.”

Chapter Thirty-two

The phone call was not unexpected.

"Mister Fuqua? I represent the Department of Transportation. Will you be available later today? I can meet you at your business in New Mexico, but it will take time for me to get there. The Learjet is off on another errand, won't be back until later this morning. The pilot anticipates arrival in Roswell sometime around three this afternoon. I'll rent a car, so shall we say 4:30pm?"

"First, let's discuss your business with me. I haven't contacted the DOT."

"I understand that, but I'm afraid we're contacting *you* this time.

"If you're busy, then perhaps a subpoena would help? I'm sure one can be arranged, either judicial or perhaps Congressional. There are serious questions regarding the role you played in the death of your employee."

"Before you waste your time, I won't meet with you unless my own attorneys are present. I can't imagine they'll allow me to say much."

"I see. Then perhaps a subpoena will be necessary."

"You must do what you must do. 'Serious questions', the term you used, is meaningless. *What* questions? Why would you think I had something to do with the unfortunate accident that took the life of my friend and employee?

"This sounds very much like a fishing expedition, so any answers to your 'serious questions' will come only after our legal team approves."

"I hoped we could do this more informally, but if you insist, we can do it the hard way. You should expect to hear from us shortly."

Frenchy broke the connection.

The phone rang again. This time, the call came from the Federal

Aviation Administration. The gist was much the same as the first and Frenchy responded as he had before.

A third call, from Colonel Ponder, the Army representative who'd visited with the DARPA group, was different.

"Mister Fuqua, it looks from here like the buzzards are circling. Are you going to be able to build the prototypes we talked about?"

"Colonel, I just don't know. They're not looking for information, they intend to shut us down. We only have one factory and I've already been threatened with a subpoena, maybe Congressional."

"It will take them time to get one. Who's going to issue the subpoena? Which subcommittee?

"Regardless, we've got friends on Capitol Hill. The defense budget is huge and there are a lot of benefits for elected officials. While we can't directly oppose Congress, we *do* have influence. Even among committee members, some have more influence than others."

"Pork, you mean."

"I didn't say that, Mister Fuqua. Benefits is how I see it. Factories have to go somewhere, and the labor climate and other things can influence the choice. End-user tests can be viewed favorably or perhaps less favorably, with considerably more scrutiny of the product before acceptance. They understand how the game is played.

"It's a kind of dance on the Hill, and we understand the system. As I said, we have friends and I'll see that they understand that we need your project completed."

"I'll do my best, Colonel. But if they shut down the factory, I'm not sure what I can do."

"They'll have a much harder time if they have difficulty serving that subpoena. I can't advise you of what to do, of course, but..."

"I understand," said Frenchy. "My legal team will be arriving later today, so I'll put the matter in their hands."

"Of course. And about the cargo unit and the personnel transporter, I'm authorized to say that we would really like an opportunity to test those."

"I'll see what I can do, Colonel. There may be other options, even if the New Mexico plant is shut down temporarily."

"You have my personal phone number, and I can contact the rest of the team. The crash was very unfortunate; it may be that flying cargo or people over walls and buildings won't work."

"I don't anticipate a problem, Colonel. The crash may have been caused by the design of the craft, maybe because the Bedstead uses only four impellers. The King has eight and dual control systems, so it's safer as well as more flexible.

"It's temporarily unavailable, but I hope to have it ready within a few days and we'll repeat the series of tests Mel was working on.

"We expect considerable disruption in our operations, a memorial service, things like that to deal with. Mel was a personal friend as well as a valued employee."

"I understand. I won't keep you longer, Mister Fuqua. I'll keep you advised of happenings in Washington and I'd appreciate you notifying us here if there's going to be a significant holdup in production of the test units. Are you the only one authorized to contract with us?"

"No. I'll make sure that others are included on the list, Chuck Sneyd from the operations side, Panit Jindae from management, and my daughter Lina as my personal representative."

"That should be sufficient. Admiral Sessions asked me to inquire about the ship you're using, the cargo ship? He has a few ideas he'd like to talk about after you get through the next few days."

"Let's talk about it then, okay? That comes under swamp drainage, but first I've got to chase off the alligators."

Colonel Ponder chuckled. "I'll talk to you later, then."

***

General Stroganoff called Colonel Kotcheff into his office.

"What does this mean, Kotcheff? Why are we interested in what American agencies are doing?"

"They're going after the company that makes the device, General. I don't know why, but it's a complication. One good thing, we now know where they're located. It's a considerable distance from here in a place called New Mexico."

"Ah. I've read of this place, a wild west place with outlaws and gunfighters. Even kids carry guns out there, worse even than the Cossacks. Do we have anyone out there we can call on?"

"No, General. We have two people, deep cover, in Texas. I don't know the names or their assignments, just that they watch the operations at the Pantex plant. That's where the Americans build their nuclear weapons."

"Hm. I don't think our headquarters would look favorably on disrupting such an important assignment. How long will it take to establish others in this New Mexico place?"

"Not long, General. I can have a better answer later today, if that's acceptable. I'll need to make a few phone calls."

"If that's the best you can do, then go ahead. But I want to know what you find out, just as soon as possible. This might be the opportunity we're waiting for! Just think of it, Kotcheff, actual antigravity!"

"Uh, antigravity, General Stroganoff?"

"It's obvious to the trained eye, Kotcheff! You must pay closer attention! That's very disappointing, Colonel. But you have work to do, so get to it."

"Yes, General. Right away!"

***

"Sorry to disturb your weekend, gentlemen, but something has come up," said General Fuller.

He had called a meeting of the committee charged with investigating the impeller-powered craft. The others had departed, but Fuller had recalled them. Admiral Sessions glowered at him; the others accepted the recall with equanimity. Unlike flag officers, colonels and majors could expect recalls from time to time.

"What's up, Fuller?" asked Admiral Sessions.

"I've become aware of a development that may affect our project. I can't say anything about the source of my information, but it appears we're not the only ones interested in the impeller system. Our eastern friends are also stirring about, and they're interested in New Mexico."

"Goddamn it, Fuller, just *say* Russians! I don't have time for cuteness, I've got a sailing date, so let's cut to the chase! My boy is home from the academy and he's got a girl with him, first time that's happened. Might be serious, and settling down would do him good."

"I hadn't realized I was being cute, Admiral." General Fuller's tone was frosty. "But according to my source, this same group was behind that attempt to hijack the marine system. I would think you'd be interested in that."

"I am, Fuller, I definitely am. But let's get on with it. *Are* the Russians making another try?"

"That's what my source says, Admiral." General Fuller's tone was curt.

"You've got a source in the NSA, eh?"

"I didn't say that, admiral, and I'd prefer that none of you speculate on things you don't understand. Suffice it to say I have a source, and the intelligence is good."

"So what do we do about it, Fuller? Got a plan, or are we supposed to keep nattering?"

Damned fighter jocks, thought Fuller. *Just blast straight ahead, bomb the hell out of everything, let God sort out the victims*. But none of this showed in his tone.

"I don't have a firm plan, but I think we should prepare a couple of just-in-case options. My source thinks their factory is the Russians' target, so this is what I propose..."

***

Frenchy sighed and answered the phone. Would the thing *never* stop ringing?

This call was not expected, nor was it particularly welcome. But it was the result of a short conversation that had taken place during the DARPA visit.

He'd mentioned idly that applications from veterans were encouraged, so perhaps when the major retired he might consider coming to work for New Frontiers? There were several options, all well-paying jobs, and all competitive with salaries paid to retired military officers by defense contractors. Perhaps contract manager? But of course, no direct offer could be made before retirement, it was just something to keep in mind.

And to pass on to his associates, all of whom would be welcomed should they decide to apply after their military career ended. Chuck was a veteran, after all, a former Marine, and he was now a senior official with the company.

Frenchy had not expected the conversation to pay off this quickly. First the officious regulators, then the DARPA committee, now *Russians*? What could possibly go wrong next?

He shouldn't have asked.

***

"Frenchy, I can't fly *Farside* out of here," said Chuck. "I've got battery power, but the fuel cells aren't working. I'm thinking it's something we did when we moved the machinery outside the hull.

"Maybe it's the piping, I don't know, but I'm getting no output from one of the pumps. Joe and Lina are checking, but until we know what's wrong I can't fly. Not very far or very high, anyway."

"How far *could* you fly on battery? If you had to leave in an emergency, I mean? I don't know how long we've got before someone shows up to shut down the plant. Could you fly over to *my* ranch house? You could do the repair work there."

"Probably. But we can't reach space without the fuel cells and we don't have wing area enough to glide in for a landing. It would all have to be done on battery power. We've got enough lift to get off the cradle and out the door, but pushing *Farside* hard enough to get the airfoils to work is questionable. She's a brick until speed builds up."

"I understand, but I don't know how much time you've got."

"They'll be driving here, right, the people that are coming to shut down the plant?"

"I assume so. They could be in a plane, maybe a helicopter."

"Then we close the runway so they can't land. Park your Gator in the middle and if anyone has a car available, park that too. Use that trailer you've been hauling the PV panels in to block the factory's doors. If you can think of a way, block the front gate so they can't get through. If they ask why, tell them we've had a threat. That's real enough."

"I can't do that, not yet. I think the sheriff's people are still out at the crash site."

"Oh, shit. You said the Bedstead crashed in an arroyo?"

"That's what I was told, but I haven't been out there. Why, what difference does it make?"

"Frenchy, I had a spot of trouble a while back. It was just before Lina and I had that misunderstanding. I... ah, it could be a problem. I never expected anyone to be snooping out that way."

"Chuck, the investigators are technicians, they'll be interested in the crash debris. They've already removed Mel's body, they might even have finished by now.

"If they find something that creates a problem, it just makes it more important that you not be here. For that matter, unless there's some way to tie you specifically to... whatever they might find... they'll be looking for me as the property owner. I can honestly say I know nothing of whatever they might have questions about, but I also need to leave if possible before a subpoena can be served. He didn't say so, but that's what Colonel Ponder implied. If the busybodies can't find me, they'll be left spinning their wheels.

"On the other hand, if I suddenly disappear, that's going to look suspicious to the sheriff's people. Damn."

"Damn indeed, Frenchy. Okay, I'm not doing anything productive here and I might be able to help get *Farside's* problem fixed. That's where I'll be if you want me."

"I'll send one of the gate guards out to the highway. He can park there and let us know as soon as any strange cars start down our road."

"Good plan. See you later."

Chuck trotted away, heading for the assembly area, already thinking about the fuel problem. *The fuel cells worked before and nothing had changed except where they were mounted. More than likely, it had to do with the fuel flow. The hydrogen supply was essentially the same, except that the pipes now ran externally. But the oxygen system was different. New tanks in the wings, a new pump, new pipes...*

Joe was tracing one of the pipes when he arrived. Lina was in the cockpit, monitoring the gauges, ready to report if he succeeded in restarting the fuel cells.

"Joe, I had an idea. Look, we went from drawing in atmospheric oxygen for the fuel cells to piping in oxygen from the port wing tank. Could we open the oxygen lines and draw in ambient air?"

"Maybe. Disconnecting the oxygen line won't be a problem, but unless you're feeding oxygen under pressure you won't get enough to run the cells. Not for long, anyway. You *might* get something, reduced efficiency, maybe even enough to fly at low altitude. I'd rather we worked on fixing the pressurized oxygen system; anything else is redneck engineering."

"I may not have a choice. I may have to get *Farside* out of here quick, but if I do I'll fly it by myself. There's just too much chance of crashing. You and Lina can meet me after things quiet down. Fly into Andrews and I'll pick you up there."

"You're sure? Chuck, I don't like the idea of flying this thing without enough juice."

"I like the idea of being locked up in a New Mexico jail even less."

"I can understand that. All right, I'll do what I can," Joe agreed.

Thirty minutes later Chuck called Frenchy.

"That problem we talked about is still there, but I think I've got a workaround. If it comes to that, I'll be working alone. You take care of Lina, Joe too."

"Lina, yes. Joe, that's different. Chuck, he knows too much. If you think you can...ah, solve that transport issue with a little more time, I think you should take Joe with you."

"Shit. All right, Frenchy, I'll ask.

"He knows the risks. That workaround I mentioned, Joe's still looking at the problem but we've got about 40% efficiency at low altitude, up to maybe 5,000 feet. That's an estimate, and it's based on where we are right now with no electrical load on the system. Low and slow, that's all we've got."

"I understand. Do what you can, and tell Lina to give me a call later. Will and I are leaving; I just got a radio message, a convoy of cars is heading this way."

"Damn. Did you block the runway? How are you going to take

off?"

"Chuck, we don't need the runway. Will says he can get us in the air."

"Right, I must be more rattled than I thought. Be careful, I'll see you when I see you.

"What about you?"

"I'll talk to Joe, but I think we're out of here too."

Chapter Thirty-three

Chuck cocked his head. “That’s the Twin. Will just started the turbogenerators.”

“Want to watch, Chuck? We’re just about done here, as much as we can do until we’ve got time to tear down the oxygen system.”

“Yeah. Will says he’s got room enough, just, by using impeller trim assist during takeoff. Even so, he’s only got about ten degrees of up-angle to work with. It’s going to be tight.”

“Frenchy couldn’t wait?”

“No. If they subpoena him, he won’t have a choice. Even worse, someone might take it into their head to arrest him. Mel’s death was an accident, but that doesn’t mean someone won’t try to twist it around.”

The two watched from the rear personnel door. Moments later, the Twin clawed its way into the sky, leveled off to gain speed, then soared north.

“I thought he was going west.”

“He is, Joe. No use in giving whoever is out there more information than we have to; let them look for him in Albuquerque instead of Denver.

“Time for us to buckle in too; we won’t have much warning. Esteban is standing by the roof controls and Lina won’t tell him to open the hatches right away. The idea is to leave them open until we’re gone. Assuming this bird holds together.”

“Knock on wood, Chuck. No reason to giving fate a hint.”

“I hear you. We’ll turn on main power, the fuel cells can handle that with no problem using just ambient air, but leave the impellers powered down. Someone might hear the whine before Esteban gets the hatch open.”

“Hope we’ve got enough recharge power. You want to listen to the radios?”

“Yeah. Lina will have hers in voice-activate mode, so we’ll hear what she’s saying.”

***

“General, how soon can you activate Sudden Drop?”

“Less than an hour. Has something happened?”

“That Skycrane the Russians leased? It just took off from the Las Vegas airport.”

“Damn. If they’re heading for the factory, it’s going to be close. They’ve got a head start and the factory is roughly an hour's flight time from Vegas. Cannon Air Force Base is closer and the Ospreys are faster than a Skycrane, but it’s going to be tight.”

“Cannon’s got troops, right? Special Ops people? Are you sending troops along?”

“I will if they’ve got anyone available. The Special Ops wing is on alert this weekend. They’re tasked to participate in Desert Fury II and that kicked off two days ago. I’m not sure if they’re really all that involved, it’s mostly a ground exercise, but they might be there to pull the governor’s chain.”

“Governor?”

“Give me a minute, I’ll explain.” General Fuller dialed a number. “General, sorry to bother you. Request you activate Sudden Drop.”

“It’s happening, then? Wait one, I’ll get back to you.” The phone went dead. Moments later it rang. “General Fuller.”

“Stan, most of the wing is deployed. They had an Osprey in the shed for maintenance, checking part of the special ops package, but the rest of the systems are operational so it can fly. I ordered it sent your way immediately and Rich will divert a couple of others from the exercise. He says he can spare them, but it will take a while for them to reach the objective.

"You’ve got your Sudden Drop, but be careful. We don’t want a lot of bad publicity over this. Or, for that matter, we don’t want questions at all if we can help it. So far, we’ve just got an ongoing training exercise, meaning the extra flight is easy enough to explain.

Are you in position to personally oversee Sudden Drop?"

"No, sir, I'm in Washington; I got the word by phone. The Russians leased that Skycrane, you know about that, but they loaded people into the cargo pod before it took off.

"I might be overreacting, but if so it won't cause a problem. If we're overwatching the factory and nobody shows, no harm done. If the Russians see an Osprey orbiting overhead, I hope they'll be smart enough to head for home. No harm, no foul."

"What if they get there first?"

"That... might present a problem. We can't let them get that device. No matter what, we can't allow that to happen."

"I'll get on the phone. Where's the wing commander, Stan? Is he taking part in the exercise?"

"He's there. We're not really expecting a problem with the exercise, but you never know. Here's the thing, the Texas Air Guard is not part of the exercise but they're flying too. They're patrolling just across the border and so far, our guys are watching them while they watch us.

"I hope that governor was just trying to make points with his voting base. But I can't decide if that's what's going on or if their politicians are *really* crazy enough to open fire on federal forces."

"Jesus. And the Russians are sticking their noses into this?"

***

"Chuck, can you hear me?"

"Loud and clear, Lina. Are they here yet?"

"They're stopped outside the gate, but they might have gotten creative. There's a helicopter approaching, a big one that looks like a huge dragonfly. It just circled the area at first, but now they're heading back."

"That sounds like a Skycrane. It's a cargo lifter that's been around since the Vietnam War. Why would the FAA or DOT be using a heavy lift helicopter?"

"I don't know, but it's slowing down. The people that just got here are still outside the gate. They're pointing at it and some are on their phones. Maybe they're working together after all?"

"No idea, but watch your step. Tell you what, why don't you go over to the gate and stay with the guards? I'd feel better. That cargo chopper, it might be here intending to take the...ah, things in the truck, by force."

"Fat chance. They're gone, or about to be. Chuck, be careful. I don't like the looks of this."

"I haven't even seen it and I don't like it! Let me know when that chopper lands, okay? I don't want to open the roof hatch until they're on the ground."

"Will do. I'm heading for the gate now. I'm leaving a man on the door controls, he's got a radio too."

"Okay, when you get there, stay in the guard building. Where's the helicopter now? I can hear him, but I can't tell where he's coming from."

"He's coming from the west, and there are *two* of them now. The other one just came in sight, it's one of those funny ones with engines that pivot? It can take off or land like a helicopter, but it flies like a propeller plane?"

"The Marines use those, call them Ospreys or something. Okay, I don't have a choice. I'm going to have to chance it.

"Love you, Lina. If I make it, meet me you know where as soon as you can, but don't let anyone follow you."

"Love you too. Chuck, be careful!"

"I will. I'm going to be kind of busy now, so..."

Motors inside the assembly building burred and gears rumbled, opening the roof hatch. *Farside's* impellers added their high-pitched whirr.

Outside the fence, the Skycrane eased toward a landing. Perhaps the pilot had realized there was insufficient room inside for the huge rotor blades.

The engine spooled down as soon as it landed and the cargo box beneath the fuselage descended to the ground. The support cables slackened, but remained attached. The front hatch opened and six men, all carrying assault rifles, trotted toward the front gate.

The group that was already waiting there were using their phones, most making calls, but two appeared to be taking pictures.

"Inside, Miss Lina! I don't know who those people are, but I don’t like it.

“There’s another Osprey heading this way. I’ve seen them before, the Marines used them in the Sandbox, but they're not showing Marine insignia. That first one is already transitioning, the motors are turning upright. It's getting ready to land.

“Just stay inside and take cover below the walls. *Don’t* stick your head up, I know it’s tempting but you’ll get it shot off. Stay down until we find out what’s going on.”

“What about those men? They’ve got guns.”

“I know. I already pushed the alarm button, our people will get here as soon as possible, but it will take a couple of hours. This will be over long before then.”

“What...what will you do?”

“What I get paid to do, Miss Lina.”

The man’s face suddenly looked old. Funny...Lina had seen him dozens of times, but she’d never noticed those deep lines around his mouth.

Outside the gate, the group was breaking up. People were running for their cars and some had already entered.

The rearmost vehicle backed up, then swerved off the road. It hesitated for a moment as the wheels lost traction, then jerked forward, heading away. Others followed, leaving only Lina and the guards at the gate that was still blocked by a car.

“We couldn’t have stopped those people, but we can’t even shut the gate now. You stay inside, and keep down!”

The man racked back the charging handle on his M4, stripping a round from the magazine and loading it into the chamber. His thumb clicked something on the side of the weapon as he crouched by the building’s door. The other guard had already loaded his weapon; he crouched on the opposite side, preparing a crossfire.

If they ever got a chance to use it.

The newcomers spread out as they came around the corner of the fence, heading for the gate while holding their weapons at high port.

An Osprey roared in over the gate, hovered for a moment, then sank to the ground outside the fence. Dust puffed from beneath the spinning rotors as men dressed in camouflage clothing and protective vests raced out the open rear hatch and spread to either side of the plane. They carried short black rifles that now pointed toward the line of men approaching near the fence.

The dust was still settling when the *Farside,* impellers whining, rose through the open roof.

Still seated inside the helicopter, General Stroganoff froze, face going pale. Where had the airplane come from? And what was happening at the large building? That sound… was it from the antigravity device?

"General, they're getting away! That craft is what we came for and if we hurry we can still catch it! Pilot, take off *now* or I'll shoot you myself! Get over its top and force that thing down!" ordered Colonel Kotcheff.

The Skycrane revved its engines, huge rotors spinning up. The cargo box jerked upward, finally locking in place just as the big helicopter lifted off.

The *Farside* was already moving. It accelerated slowly, turning eastward, then sinking until it was barely twenty feet above the ground. The helicopter, now almost five miles behind, took up the chase, abandoning the men that had flown in the cargo box.

Flying eastward, the Skycrane accelerated after the fleeing *Farside.*

***

"What the hell was that?" The question had come from the pilot flying the formerly-deadlined Osprey.

"I don't know, Captain, but that big chopper is after it."

"You'd better call in for instructions. Nobody mentioned that thing, whatever it was. Did you see all those things hanging on the fuselage?"

"I saw something. You reckon it's one of those flying saucer things? I didn't see an engine exhaust or props," offered the copilot. "If it's some kind of extraterrestrial, those could be weapons pods. Maybe missiles, maybe even lasers or some kind of ray. I'll call in a sighting report."

The pilot nosed down, picking up speed. Whatever was going

on down on the deck at that factory, the other Osprey had it under control. This was more important. Could that helicopter *really* be chasing a UFO?

Maintaining altitude above the Skycrane and the UFO, the Osprey closed the distance. The UFO appeared to be gaining speed, leaving the clumsy Skycrane behind. The Texas state line was just ahead...

"Fuck! I've got a threat warning light!" yelled the pilot. "Hang on, I'm evading to port."

"What about the radar? Are we getting that UFO on radar?" asked the copilot.

"I can't tell, not enough separation between it and the chopper. I'm far enough now...okay, I've got two images. Better power up the Sidewinders, just in case."

"Roger, power up...shit, what happened?"

"Fuck, they *went off*. They both launched. I didn't do it, it just happened. Are they tracking?"

"I can't tell yet. Hang on, I've got something. The exhaust trail is bending, they look like they're tracking."

"Fuck, fuck, *fuck*, we're hosed. How the *fuck* did that happen? Goddamned hangar queen, this bitch just came out of the avionics shop. Look, you can see, I never even selected missile! They just went off!"

"Okay, okay, calm down and fly the bird," said the copilot. "I better call this in."

***

Across the Texas line, there was a different reaction.

The pilot of the F-16 was flying lazy circles, thinking about his upcoming date. She looked like a sure thing, and for sure, she was a stone fox.

Suddenly a high-pitched tone sounded, warbling slightly. Bitching Betty, a recorded female voice, added to the confusion.

"Shit, I've got *a missile launch*! The bastards lit me up! Colonel, I've got a threat warning, Bitching Betty is going off, I'm heading for the deck!"

"Negative, grab some air and join on us after you evade. I've got four Falcons at angels twenty. Was there a warning call?"

"No sir, nothing. But I've still got that threat warning."

"Do you have visual contact?"

"Negative visuals. I'm climbing. Bitching Betty just shut down."

"Don't panic, you know what to do. We'll orbit until you join up. What happened to your wingman?"

"Uh, sir, he didn't make it. I took off without him."

"You did *what*?"

"Sir, it's not the first time. We've had maintenance issues, not enough money in the budget to stock spare parts. This is not the first time we've been short when the order arrived. The governor himself ordered the sortie."

"Roger. Okay, what about the threat warning?"

"It's off. Let me check...okay, bulb checks good, no damage, no sign of a hostile track."

"Roger. Join up, we're pulling back. We'll orbit north of here, farther away from the border. If the governor wants a close patrol of the border, let *him* fly up here with us."

"Uh, Colonel, should you be saying that on the air?"

"Son, I've just decided this is a good year to retire. I've got my time in, there are a lot of bass in Lake Livingston I haven't caught yet. I'm getting too old for this stuff."

***

"The wing commander is *not* happy, Lieutenant. He wants to know what happened to the helicopter and the UFO."

"The helicopter is on the ground about a mile ahead. I can't tell, there might be damage. The UFO is gone, there's no sign of it. I lost it in the ground return. Let me check the radar...nope, no sign of it. It just vanished."

"Damn. Half of me hopes we hit it, the other half is scared shitless. Suppose we shot it down? What if they get pissed and show up like that Independence Day movie?"

Chapter Thirty-four

The caravan returned two days later, escorted by a sheriff's department SUV. The gate guard stepped through the gate and closed it behind him. Approaching the first car, he nodded at the driver.

"This facility is closed to the public, sir. May I ask your business?"

"I represent the Federal Aviation Agency. I have business with the owner."

"Do you have an appointment, sir?"

"No. I attempted to gain an appointment with a Mister Fuqua, who I'm given to believe is the owner of record."

"I'll need to check the log book, sir, but I don't believe Mister Fuqua is here."

While they were speaking, a second, then a third man had exited the cars and they now came forward to join the conversation. One of them asked, "Where is Mister Fuqua?"

"I don't have that information, sir. All I can tell you is that we keep a log of who is on site, and he is not here."

A uniformed deputy stood by, listening. His expression was bland. Perhaps his eyes twinkled behind the sunglasses; it was impossible to tell. Local police. as a rule, tend to dislike federal agents of any type.

This might have to do with the tendency of federal enforcement officials to respond with arrogance when dealing with those they view as hicks.

"I don't see anyone moving around. Are there other people inside? Is anyone working?"

"I'm not allowed to make statements about company affairs, sir.

I must ask you to leave; you do not have an appointment, and the person you're seeking is not here. I can't help you, gentlemen, and as I said, this facility is closed to the public."

"By God, I'll get an *injunction* and I'll be back! You people have a lot of explaining to do!"

"Yes, sir. I don't know what you're enjoining or why that might affect me, but I'm sure you'll tell my replacement when you return. I'm a contract employee, charged with maintaining security, so I have nothing to do with what happens inside. I'll also be going off duty soon, so I won't be here when you return."

The guard opened the gate, went inside, and locked the gate behind him. There was a folding chair by the building's door and he sat down to wait.

A short meeting took place outside.

"This is a *stall*, I've seen enough to know one when I see it!"

"Maybe, but there are no cars here and no sign that anyone is working. I can't hear anything, and if they're really manufacturing something inside that big building, we'd hear people working. I've never been to a factory that didn't sound like...well, like a factory. There are always motors running, banging noises, people talking and moving around. This place is as silent as a tomb. Maybe when those others were arrested they decided to shut down?"

"Maybe. Deputy, do you have those other men in custody? The ones from that helicopter?"

"No, sir. They're not in local or state custody. I have no information whether they're still being detained by someone else, or if they are, who might be doing it."

"I can't *believe* this. Armed men approaching this place and a standoff between them and military forces? And you don't know where they *are*?"

"No, sir. It wasn't mentioned during the morning briefing. I spend most of my time out in the field, so perhaps the sheriff can answer your questions."

Fuming, the men got back in their cars and left. The deputy waved casually at the guard, then turned his car and followed the federal vehicles.

He was smiling, despite the dust they'd stirred up.

***

The abortive raid of a week ago wasn't mentioned when Frenchy telephoned Colonel Ponder.

"Morning, Colonel. If you're still interested, I'm prepared to provide the lift units we discussed and personnel to operate them. I will require the initial payment on the contract before I ship the units to White Sands."

"I understand. Mister Fuqua, I mean no offense, but I'm told your plant is shut down."

"It is. I may reopen it at some point, once the legal matters are resolved, but your units won't be built there."

"I… see. Permit me to ask, are you building them in-house?"

"Not completely. I've subcontracted some of the work. The frames are being manufactured in Mexico; they have quite adequate facilities for such work. The passenger modules, which are really no more than racked seats, are also being made in Mexico. As a matter of fact, they can build those cheaper than I could have. Final assembly will be done at a satellite factory; I'm not at liberty to tell you where that is."

"I see. But you're handling the assembly, and in any case you're responsible for the quality of the units?"

"Of course. They'll be thoroughly checked out before shipment."

"Contract as discussed? No change in unit pricing?"

"No changes. Payment to our corporate account, as specified originally."

"I'll get right on it, Mister Fuqua. And the delivery date, you won't need a delay?"

"No delay. You do your part, I'll do mine."

"Nice talking to you, Mister Fuqua."

***

"Mister Goldman, Senator Byington's office is on the phone. Shall I put the call through?"

"Find out if it's Byington himself or one of his staff. I don't have time for them. Byington I'll talk to, but interrupt me in five minutes; I don't want to listen to him hit me up for more money."

"Yes, sir. I'll call you in five minutes."

"Sol, how are you?"

"Doing reasonably well, senator. What can I do for the government today? This is not about that committee subpoena, is it? I'm busy, I don't have time to spend days listening to your colleagues posture for the media. I've got a business to run."

"No, and I'll do what I can to make sure your visit is short and as pleasant as possible.

"I was calling about that question we discussed before. You were concerned with the possible economic effects that fellow Sneyd might cause. I don't know if you're aware of this, but Sneyd died a couple of months ago. No public mention was made, but there was a coroner's report. He's definitely gone."

"Too bad. What about the rest of the people involved?"

"Shut down, Sol. Their factory is locked and the employees have been laid off. Most of them, anyway. They filed for unemployment insurance payments through New Mexico, although the numbers don't add up. Some may have already found other jobs, as much as half of them I'm told. Anyway, I don't think you need worry about that little problem."

"Excellent, Senator. I'm very glad to hear that. Did this have anything to do with that dustup on the Texas border?"

"That's not clear. I can check on that if you'd like. It probably doesn't mean anything. I'd have heard if there was a connection."

"Probably. Thanks for calling, Senator. Was there something else?"

"Now that you mention it, Sol, there was one thing..."

***

The captain glanced over his copilot's uniform, found nothing that needed correcting, and led the way into the conference room.

"Be seated, gentlemen."

The speaker was an Air Force major general. He was flanked by four other officers, the lowest ranking one a lieutenant colonel. All wore pilot's insignia.

The general waited for the two men to be seated, then picked up a stack of papers that were on the table in front of him.

"I've decided to keep this informal. We're interested in facts; whether those facts warrant a full investigation is yet to be determined. Are you clear on this, Captain? Lieutenant?"

"We understand, General."

"I need to hear it from the lieutenant too. Do you understand, Lieutenant?"

"Yes, sir." The lieutenant had already decided to keep his mouth shut. The brass across the table were fellow pilots, but that didn't mean they were friends. Lieutenants were easily made into scapegoats and disposed of as readily as used office supplies.

"Let's begin by laying out the facts as I understand them. You correct me if you believe the report is in error. Is that understood? If there are no objections to the report's conclusions, I'll consider the facts to be as stated. I should mention that the officers on this panel supervised preparation of the reports, based on what was said during the engagement. Subsequent to the event, they inspected the avionics installed in the plane you were flying on the date in question.

"Do you understand that this is your last chance to challenge the facts in the report? Failure to do so will indicate that you agree with what's stated."

"Yes, sir," the captain replied. The lieutenant echoed his agreement.

"The aircraft in question had not been flown in the past two weeks, is that correct?"

"Sir, I can't attest to that. I believe that to be the case, but I can only say that the flight on the day in question was the first time I had flown that particular aircraft."

"Lieutenant?"

"No sir, first time for me too. I believe it was deadlined awaiting parts for the avionic system prior to our being assigned to fly the mission. The aircraft was considered airworthy, but not combat ready. I understand the delay was caused by not having the part immediately available due to funding constraints."

"We'll avoid mentioning the exact mission, I don't want classified information in this report. It's my understanding that a review of this sortie and other events that took place during the exercise are being looked at by the Department of Defense. Have you heard the aircraft referred to as the 'hangar queen', Captain?"

"Yes, sir. I've heard that."

"To your knowledge, was a test flight conducted before the aircraft was returned to operational status?"

"I believe such a flight was made. As to whether a full exercise of the avionics was conducted, I have no knowledge of that."

"So perhaps the pilot took the plane up, ran through a set of standard maneuvers, and returned it to service?"

"I have no knowledge beyond what I've stated, General."

"Tell me, Captain, are flight standards different in special operations units?"

"I don't know how to answer that, general. I'm not familiar with what other wings do."

"I see. Very well, let's move along. During the flight, had you armed any of the weapons systems prior to the time the accidental launches occurred?"

Thank Christ, they were calling it an accident, not pilot error!

"No, sir. It was a routine flight until we observed the helicopter pursuing the unidentified flying object."

"Strike that, I don't want any mention of a UFO in this report. You read me, Captain?"

"Yes, sir. I understand."

"But you had occasion to believe that your weapons system might be needed, perhaps in self-defense?"

"Yes, sir. I was made aware the possibility existed that units engaged in the maneuver might be fired upon by the Texas Air Guard. The governor of that state had made certain public statements to cause me, as aircraft commander, to be concerned."

The general covered his microphone with his hand and leaned back. After conferring briefly with the other officers on the panel, he spoke. "Leave that in the record. It's needed to explain why the crew armed their weapons.

"Now then, Captain, had you been engaged to that point?"

"No, sir. Arming the missiles was precautionary."

"And did you select missiles in preparation for firing?"

"No, sir. I also observed that my copilot had made no such selection."

"This report," the general picked up another paper, "indicates that subsequent testing of the fire control module by a depot inspection team found an intermittent fault, involving the ground return system. This was further isolated to the power plug. Are you aware of this?"

"No, sir. We made the usual checks before takeoff, but there was no indication of a fault."

"What do you conclude from this, Captain?"

"Sir, I believe that the missiles launched without a specific command from myself or my copilot. I believe it was an accident, sir."

"Are you aware of what happened subsequent to the unintended launch?"

Yesss! We're off the hook! "I believe that one of the missiles struck the helicopter. It suffered a hard landing and three persons, two of whom were later identified as Russian officers, were arrested. The pilot of the helicopter was also detained, but he was subsequently released. I don't know whether the second missile hit the... other aircraft."

"Strike that, it's hearsay, and anyway I don't want it part of this record. We're keeping this unclassified, other than For Official Use Only. Do you have anything more to add?"

"No, sir."

"Lieutenant? Any comments you wish entered into the record?"

"No, sir."

***

Chuck met Lina in Andrews, and they headed for the ranch.

"Any problems?"

"No real problems. There were people with guns heading toward the gate, but they gave up when that Osprey landed. One of the government people had already called the sheriff's department and when they showed up, the men were taken into custody for trespassing. I think the FBI claimed jurisdiction. They took the men and also two Russians from the helicopter that were on their watch list. Have you heard from my dad?"

"I talked to him this morning; he thinks things are under control, at least for now. Some of the engineering guys are here; they, and Joe, got the oxygen system fixed. Turned out it was a misconnected tube, so *Farside* is now operational. He's working on fairing over the stuff we moved outside the fuselage, but he doesn't need me for that. You either."

"Oh. Well, shouldn't we be doing something?"

"Actually, I think there is.

"We need to stay out of sight for a while, just in case. Your father is avoiding contact too. He's waiting to see whether there's going to be a subpoena, but for now the lawyers are dealing with things. The plant is shut down, I don't know if we'll ever be able to reopen it.

"Anyway, I've been expecting you. I've got something for you, and we'll be at the ranch house in a minute or so."

"Something for me, eh?" Her tone was flirtatious.

"Not that. Okay, that too. But something else."

Chuck parked the car, then escorted Lina into the house. "Hang on a second."

Moments later, he returned. "I had an idea. Let's start with this. It was my grandmother's, and I think she'd like the idea of my passing it on to you."

"Oh, Chuck. It's lovely. But it's small, I don't think it will fit."

"We can have it resized in Hawaii. I'm sure we'll have a *little* bit of spare time during the honeymoon."

The Series will continue in NFI: New Frontiers, Inc.

About the Author:

Jack Knapp grew up in Louisiana and joined the Army after graduating from high school. He served three tours in Germany and traveled throughout western Europe before retiring. His current circle of friends and acquaintances, many of them fellow members of Mensa, live on every continent except Antarctica. Jack graduated from the University of Texas at El Paso before beginning his second career, teaching science.

Always an avid reader, he took naturally to writing. He's experimented with ESP (The Wizards Series) and woodcraft/survivalism. The deep woods of Louisiana were his playground, the setting for his Darwin's World Series. He's a knight of the Society for Creative Anachronism, so combat scenes involving swords, spears, and bows and arrows are reality based.

Recent novels examine the challenges humanity will face when we begin to spread out into space. Beginning with a startup company building the first practical spacecraft (The Ship), to growing a business in space while overcoming Earth-based obstacles (NFI: New Frontiers, Inc), to humanity's first contact with a non-human species (NEO: Near Earth Objects and BEMs: Bug Eyed Monsters) the novels are largely based on current events. A fifth novel in the New Frontiers Series, MARS: the Martian Autonomous Republic of Sol, is due out early in 2017.

Jack's boundless imagination is evident in all his books.

How imaginative? You'll have to read his novels to find out!